Death in the Saddle

A.J. Harris, M.D.

Not a Western!

D1736874

Murder Mystery Press
Palm Desert, California

ISBN   978-0-9829361-9-1 (paperback)
          978-0-9847825-0-5 (ebook)

Published by Murder Mystery Press, www.murdermysterypress.com

Murder Mystery Press

Palm Desert, California

Author: A.J. Harris, M.D.
Marketing: Michael C. Green, M Carroll Communications
Book Shepherd: Mark E. Anderson, www.aquazebra.com
Editor: Michael C. Green, M Carroll Communications
Cover photo: Close Encounters, www.photoxpress.com
Author photo: Mark Davidson, www.markdavidsonphotography.com
Cover/interior design: Mark E. Anderson, www.aquazebra.com

Library of Congress Control Number: 2011942834

Printed in the United States of America

To—
Rita and Lee
with kindest regards

Al Harris

Dedicated to the memories of
Max, Mollie, Morris and Anna

Acknowledgments

The following people were exceedingly helpful in providing suggestions, information and technical data: David Weiel, Doctor Joyce Wade-Maltais, Jean Denning, Rita Lamb, Brad Oliver, Nina Markos, Sylvia Selfman, Pamela Farr-Collaro, Elia V. Gentry, Richard Vasquez, Lou Ann Henkens, Detective Sergeant Manny Lopez, Captain Selwyn House, Mark E. Anderson, Eve Weber and Michael C. Green.

1

"You know, Josh, I swear I'm going to kill that sonofa-bitch one day. I can't stand having him around. The very sight of him nauseates me." Mary Bruxton said abruptly as she adjusted her skirt after the examination in Dr. Josh Harrington's office.

Dr. Josh sat, taking notes, then looked up. "Mary, you're upset and your aching back isn't helping your disposition. I'll order physical therapy, and give you a few samples of muscle relaxants, as well as some mild pain medication. Hang on."

Dr. Josh got up, walked over to the cabinet, pulled open a drawer, and took out some sample packets. "Yes, these should work," he said, handing the packets to his patient. "And take this too." He added, handing her a note. "These are the dosages and instructions."

Her edginess subsided as she placed the samples and the note in her purse. She smiled. "Josh, you're sweet as ever to give me these freebies. But you know I can well afford to buy my own medication. It's not like it was twenty five years ago when we were all neighbors, without a pot between us."

Mary Bruxton, prominent socialite, the doyenne of charitable institutions in the Coachella Valley and wife of the lumber baron, Peter Bruxton, was recalling a time of profound penury. "Do you remember how the four of us—you and Sally, God rest her soul, Peter and I struggled so damned hard to eke out a living? And how we dreaded the bills that came due on the first of the month? Looking back, I think, what a wonderful time that was. We were in love, we struggled, we had great hopes for the future, we had our babies...." She stood up then, leaving the sentence unfinished as she drifted off with her memories.

Standing erect increased Mary's low back pain, and she gripped the edge of the examining table, then took two labored steps toward Josh and embraced him. "You're just as kind and considerate now as you were as a young doctor trying to make enough to keep your little family together." She released her grip and leaned against the table, shaking her head before continuing. "And look what's happened to Peter and me. Can you believe he's become the largest private owner of forested land in the country? Rich as Croesus, but it's changed his personality. He went from being a considerate loving husband and father to one rotten, depraved money-grubbing sonofabitch."

She put her hand up. "And for heaven's sake, don't try to defend him. You can't possibly know what it's like living with him. It's as though he made a pact with the devil and traded his soul and sanity for all that money. He treats me like dirt, or worse. He's become a womanizer; no one in a skirt is safe around him, that filthy lecher. I won't let him touch me. God only knows what he's been exposed to. I suppose my hands-off treatment has made him even more resentful, but hell, he brought it on himself. I'm sorry, but I just can't deal with that, anymore."

Josh listened, dismayed to hear Mary castigate his old friend. But he knew that what she said was most probably true. Although reluctant, he asked, "Has he been abusive?"

"Has he been abusive, you ask? Hah! Oh, yeah, big-time, physically and verbally. We got into it pretty good several weeks ago. He went absolutely berserk—started swearing and calling me his usual vile names. Smashed some of my precious antiques. He said I loved them more than I loved him. And you know what? The bastard was absolutely right. When I tried to stop him he grabbed me and twisted my arm till I thought it would break. Then he slapped me across the face. I broke away, called the police and ordered him to get the hell out. He knows I can get a restraining order, so he packed a bag and got a suite at the Springs Hotel. I'll allow him to come home when our daughter, Deena, comes in for a visit from U.S.C. In the meantime, he's on his own. And I can tell you this: if he ever lays a hand on me again, I'll kill that sonofabitch. I will. I swear it. I'm still pretty good with a pistol...got a few trophies to show for it."

"Now, now Mary. When your backache eases you may feel a bit more charitable. Who knows, Peter may even put all his philandering behind him one day, and come back home to his true love."

"Yeah, and I'm the virgin queen."

Josh knew immediately how empty his words sounded, but he didn't want Mary to leave without a word of hope or encouragement. "Does Deena know that you two have been at odds?"

"Of course. She enjoys a special relationship with her father, and I know she would like to see our feuding come to end." Mary breathed deeply and sighed. "Truthfully, Josh, the prospect of a divorce, with the problems of property division and the inevitable court battles are more than I dare think about. I'll try my best to tolerate the jackass— that is, at least until Deena finishes school or gets married."

Josh bent over and kissed Mary on her cheek. "Try to rest and take the medication. I'll notify PT to make arrangements to go to your home. Call me in a couple days and give me a progress report."

Mary gave Josh a melancholy smile and held both his hands. "Why couldn't I have married a sweet guy like you?" She took a small mirror from her purse to apply lipstick. She smacked her lips then ran her tongue around her lips before putting the mirror away. "When this back gets better I'm going to find me a virile dude for companionship." She looked at Josh and arched an eyebrow. "Say, do you still make house calls?"

2

At his ornate oversized desk, Peter Bruxton sat with a phone in one hand and a smoking panatela in the other. Looking up, he saw his new secretary at his door. Holding his hand over the mouthpiece of the phone, he said, "Come in, come in," then leaning back in his tall leather chair, he signaled for her to sit down. He put up his index finger, denoting a moment longer on the phone, then placed the phone closer to his mouth and shouted, "Bullshit! Call in those mortgage payments now. I'm not running a fucking credit bureau—that's right, if they can't pay, we're repossessing. They bought quick enough at sub-prime rates. No more extended payments." The phone was slammed onto the cradle as he looked at the young woman seated opposite his desk. He made a quick assessment of the exotic beauty. "Now, what do you want?" He flicked the cigar ash into a tray.

"Mr. Bruxton, Mr. Kurtz, your partner..."

"I know he's my partner. What does he want?"

"Yes sir, sorry sir, it's just that the mortgage department from the Continental Bank called a third time asking for payment on Mr. Kurtz's estate loan."

"Chrissakes! How much does he owe, d'ya know?"

"No sir."

"Tell Kurtz—no, get him on the phone. I'll talk to him.

The secretary punched in the call-waiting button and handed the phone to Bruxton. He grabbed the phone and ordered the secretary to wait.

"Kurtz? Bruxton here. Listen, I know you owe the bank a pot full of money and you're tapped out—don't interrupt. I know the real estate market is in the toilet and you're gonna be tossed out on your ass. Here's what I'll do for ya. Shut up and listen. I'll pay off the bank, you're gonna be free and clear. What d'ya mean, what's the catch? No catch. Haven't I always pulled your balls out of a vise? The house becomes mine, and you pay me rent. Think about it, Kurtz, before I develop buyer's remorse. The offer is good for forty-eight hours. No, I'm not joking. I'm doing it for the same damn reason I've done everything else for you and your buddy, Jake." Bruxton replaced the phone, leaned back in his chair, clenched the cigar with his teeth and stared at the seated young secretary who pulled her hem over her knees.

She attempted a tentative smile. "I beg your pardon, sir, did you want me for anything else?"

"How long ya been working here, Miss...?"

"Ouvray, Bonnie Ouvray—just three days sir."

"Like your job?"

"Yes sir."

He pointed to his side. "Come over here. Stand here, next to me. Let me get a good look at you." Bruxton eyed the flawless café au lait complexion and the trim figure of the tall beauty. Cascading jet-black hair framed the large almond-shaped eyes with long lashes and full sensuous lips. She smiled nervously, revealing perfect glistening teeth. At age twenty-four, the young woman stood with the confidence borne of beauty and aplomb.

"Come closer—I won't bite you," Bruxton reached out to hold her arm. Instinctively, she withdrew as the office door opened. A woman with coarse platinum hair, and a face made youthful by plastic surgery strutted into the long office. A St. John knit only partially concealed her early matronly mid-section and the fullness of her bust. She waved her hand quickly and repeatedly in front of her face and frowned. "Phew! This place stinks of cigar smoke." She walked to the window and threw it open, then turned and glared first at her husband, and then at the young woman. "Am I interrupting a tête-à-tête?"

"I was just welcoming Ms. Ouvray here, to the staff."

Fifty-two year old Mary Bruxton, bedecked with diamond stud earrings, a gold necklace and matching bracelets, surveyed the young woman, then nodded toward the door. "Would you mind giving us a few minutes alone?"

Bonnie Ouvray left the room hurriedly, and closed the door behind her quietly.

Standing with hands on hips and bent slightly forward, Mary Bruxton stared at her husband. "Listen, you jerk, what did you mean when you said you were welcoming that little cookie to the staff? You make damned sure you're not welcoming her to your private staff. Must I remind you of your paternity suit with that last chippie who worked for you? Why can't you keep your pecker in your pants?"

Then, before Peter Bruxton could respond, she scowled and continued, "When I actually still wanted to have sex with you, you acted like you'd forgotten what the hell that thing was used for. Now it seems like it's all you can think about. Not that I care. I don't want any part of it now."

"For chrissakes, Mary. Let's not have another shitty scene. Why'n hell did you come here, anyway?"

Mary raised her chin defiantly. "I've every right to be here, and besides, there are a few things I need to discuss with you."

Bruxton looked at his watch and shook his head. "I can't spare the time."

Mary looked at her watch. "Take the time! Have lunch with me. I detest eating alone, and my mahjong girls are busy today. There are things we need to discuss and I'm just NOT taking no for an answer, so come on."

"Okay, but no nagging or arguing. I don't want to aggravate my ulcers."

The chauffeur opened the door and Mary Bruxton slid into the rear of the Bentley. Primping before a vanity mirror, she bared her teeth and wiped them with Kleenex. The chauffeur walked to the other side to open the door for Peter Bruxton. "Jim, take us to that overpriced French hash joint in Rancho Mirage, and don't take the scenic route."

Mary closed her eyes, shook her head and sighed, "Why must you be so boorish?"

"You inspire me, I guess," Bruxton replied. He pushed himself back into the plush leather seat, pulled down the armrest dividing their seating and withdrew a silver cigar canister from his jacket pocket.

"Put that damn thing away! Don't you dare smoke in here!"

"I paid three hundred and twenty five thousand clams for this fuckin' hearse, and you're telling me I can't smoke in it?"

Mary pointed her finger at him. "That's right and you better not use it for fucking your floozies, either."

"C'mon, Mary, don't talk like that. You'll give Jim here, the wrong impression."

"Oh, really?" Mary responded coldly. "Would you like me to ask him how many times he's seen you in this back seat with a whore?"

Her husband returned the cold stare, then looked out the window. Both of them remained silent the rest of the way to the restaurant. When they pulled in, Peter Bruxton opened his own door and abruptly exited the car. His wife waited for the chauffeur. "Thank you Jim," she said as she got out of the car. "At least someone's a gentleman!"

The valet held the tall door as the Bruxtons walked in.

The maître d' smiled and bowed slightly at the familiar patrons. Mr. Bruxton not-too subtly put folding money in his hand, and the maître d' ushered them quickly to a corner booth. Bruxton eyed two young women with halter dresses seated at a nearby table and nodded his approval. Mary ignored his flirtations and walked briskly to distance herself from him.

Seated at the table, Bruxton stretched his arms to either side of the back of the booth and looked up at the exposed rough-hewn beams of the ceiling and walls of the recreated auberge. He nodded and said, "This is *real* class, this is what the customer pays for—the atmosphere, the pizzazz and the hokey props. That's what I'll give our clientele at the Sunburst Club in Montana. Yes sir, we'll snow 'em with class." With his unlit cigar he pointed to the décor.

"Put that damn thing away, for heaven's sake!"

"I wasn't gonna smoke it."

She stared at him. "Don't you dare stick that napkin in your collar, and take your elbows off the table. You are the epitome of vulgarity."

"Is that a compliment, Mary? No? I didn't think so." Bruxton gazed upward and moved his lips as though communicating with a compassionate spirit, then cast a baleful eye at Mary. "Thanks for not naggin'." Bruxton took the tall padded menu offered by the waiter, gave it a perfunctory glance and said, "Give us two dry martinis and be damn sure they're dry." As the waiter left, he continued, "Okay, let's have it, what's on your mind that'll aggravate my ulcers?"

Mary sighed, "We have an ongoing problem with your daughter, Deena."

"What d' ya mean, *my* daughter? She happens to be *our* daughter. What does she want now, besides that gorilla stud at U.S.C. who can't put two sentences together?"

Mary leaned into the table and spoke softly. "I don't want her involved in that family. That kid's old man, Oscar

Brazilowicz, is a union boss; that means trouble—goons, guns, payoffs—all that crap."

Bruxton nodded. "Listen, I don't want her involved with that yokel either, and she knows it."

The conversation stopped as the waiter returned and set the martinis down.

"Bring two more," Bruxton said.

Mary plucked an olive out of her glass, chewed it and said, "And he knows how you feel. He's becoming extremely resentful."

"Too damn bad about him, he's not gonna get my consent for marriage. He'll have to kill me first."

"He might be thinking just that."

"Screw him." Bruxton studied the menu. "Can you believe a cup of onion soup is eight-fifty? They've got a hell of a nerve. What is it—boiled water, sliced onions, pieces of stale bread and cheese?"

Mary ignored his comments. "What do you intend to do about Deena's dating?"

"I'll talk to her and that ape boyfriend and lay down the law. I'll tell em I don't want em to get married, simple as that."

"Yeah, that ought to stop nothing." Mary took a carrot stick from the relish plate and crunched down on it. "There's another matter—I got a call this morning from Lucy Kurtz. Your partner's wife."

Impatiently, he shouted. "I know who the hell she is, what did that prima donna want?" People at a nearby table turned to look.

"Hold your voice down. She was crying. She told me they were about to lose their home. They can't meet the bank's demands for payment, and they're facing foreclosure."

"Yeah, I know. I talked with Larry this morning. I made him an offer to pay off his mortgage."

Mary's eyes widened. "You did what? You offered to

pay off his mortgage? Why? Still trying to salve a guilty conscience?"

Bruxton put his drink down. "Jesus, don't bring that thing up with Lucy again. You're never gonna let me forget, are you? You know damn well it was consensual."

A waiter returned with two more martinis. He was joined by another waiter who presented them with a half loaf of warm crisp pre-cut French bread on a wooden server with a porcelain tub of whipped herb butter.

Bruxton glared at the second waiter. "What took you so long, Buddy, I'm starving here and you're moving like a goddamned slug." Bruxton reached for an end piece and slathered it with butter. "I could make a meal out of this and a bowl of onion soup."

Mary rolled her eyes. "Now tell me about this new secretary. How did you find her? What experience has she had? What's her background? Is she single?"

"Hold it. I already forgot your first three questions. Oh yeah. Well, she's had two years at the local college. Majored in Business and Communications or something like that. She's got good computer skills and handles the phone well. That's all I need."

"You be damn sure that's *all* you need."

With his mouth full, he grumbled, "What the hell's that supposed to mean? She's probably got a boyfriend anyway."

Mary placed the last of a buttered slice of bread into her mouth, then licked her index finger and thumb. "That never stopped you before."

"What the hell do you want from me? Are we going to eat in peace, or are you just going to nibble away at my ass? You've already spoiled my appetite." He rubbed his mouth with his napkin, then replaced his unlit cigar in the corner of his mouth and sat back in obvious frustration.

"Eat what you can, because if you think your appetite is spoiled now, you're absolutely going to puke when I tell you this...."

3

Before Bruxton could respond, the waiter returned, made a half bow, then smiled and asked if he could take their entrée orders. They both ordered, then Bruxton shoved his empty martini glass at him. "Hit me again." With elbows on the table, he leaned forward, his beady eyes penetrating Mary's. "All right, what other sorry ass news do you have?"

Reaching into her shoulder bag she handed him a thick brown envelope. "A courier came to the house this morning and had me sign for this. I opened it, thinking it was an urgent matter."

Bruxton grabbed the envelope, looked at the return address and shook his head. "This can't be anything good, it's from Farquaahr, that fat ass commie lawyer, that loud-mouthed socialist. What the hell does he want?" He snapped open the folded pages and put them on the table. He reached for his glasses and scanned the first of several pages. "Listen to this bullshit...."

"Don't bother, I've already looked at it."

Bruxton ignored her, "...as part of the Civil Rights Act of 1968, the Fair Housing Act prohibits discrimination in the sale of houses...." Bruxton looked up as though to scold Mary who was chewing her second piece of celery. "Goddammit, I can sell to anyone I choose. No one's gonna force me to sell to any niggers, Jews, Muslims, chinks, fruitcakes or other undesirables. My property is for sale only to successful Anglos. Guys like me who enjoy golf, poker, and a quick trip to Vegas, that sort of thing. And I don't want any fly-by-night four-flushers, either. I want solid citizens...."

"Like yourself?"

"Yeah, that's right—hey, you bein' sarcastic?"

Mary arched her brows. "Oh, no, you're such an upstanding member of polite society...."

"Listen, I give plenty to charities, and I'm a member of all the important committees to raise funds for the needy. I'm on a first-name basis with every other big giver in this valley. And what's more, I can buy and sell most of them. I'm in the Fortune 400, and I intend to stay there—maybe climb up a notch or two every year."

Mary pointed to the papers he held. "Getting back to this law suit...."

"Forget it, I know enough about the law. I'm not interfering with the goddamn civil rights of anyone, and I'm not engaged in interstate commerce. That's where the Feds can get you. Hell, I'm smarter than that."

Two waiters arrived with entrées covered by domed lids. They were placed before the Bruxtons, and the domes were removed simultaneously. Mary thanked the waiters; Bruxton ignored them.

"As a matter of fact, you *are* engaged in interstate commerce—you sell Washington and Oregon lumber to a number of companies outside those states."

"For your edi-fi-cation," he syllabified the word for emphasis, "the last holdings of our lumber corporation are being sold to Georgia-Pacific. We won't own any more lumber mills, log loaders, warehouses, trucks or logging equipment. We're going to be out of it, done, fini, caput."

"Thanks for keeping me informed." Mary leaned back and folded her arms across her chest. "What about the assets? My name appears on those papers."

"The deal isn't finalized. We're transferring the lumber holdings to finance our resort. You'll get all the details from the lawyers in a week or two. It's a complicated deal that only those goddamned overpaid Beverly Hills shysters can finagle. Don't worry, you're not going to lose one goddamn red cent—in fact, you'll be the richest broad on the hill, next to Melinda Gates." He appeared pleased with his explanation and expected no objections from his wife. He got none.

Sampling his filet of sole, Bruxton smacked his lips. "Jesus, these Frog cooks use a lot of butter. It's no damn good for my gall bladder, but what the hell, I'll take bicarb after."

Without looking up from her plate, Mary asked, "Why did the suing party hire Farquaahr? And what infraction of the law was committed by those geniuses in our housing sales department? I'd think anyone who can buy a home for two to five million would be welcomed with open arms."

Bruxton held up his knife and fork on either side of his plate. "No. We can't allow just anyone to buy into our country club, and don't make me go through all the reasons why. As for the money, hell, we got more multi-millionaires wanting to get in than we can accommodate."

"Are you looking to establish an outpost for wealthy members of the Aryan Nation?"

Bruxton stammered and sprayed food in his excited reply. "Mary, don't get on my fuckin' back with your smart-ass wisecracks. You do this all the time, and then you wonder why the hell we can't have a civil meal together. Jesus H. Christ, lay off, will you?"

Mary dabbed her lips with the corner of her napkin, then paused before speaking, "Bruxton, did it ever occur to you that life with you these past few years has been one big pain in my ass?"

Bruxton jerked his head back, set his utensils down and growled, "Is that so? Seems to me you accept your monthly allowance without complaining. Listen, any time you

decide this marriage is too much for you, just let me know."
He pointed his fork at her. "But, if you think you're gonna
get half of what I fought for all my life, well, you're sadly
mistaken. Let's be clear about that."

Mary pushed her plate away from her, stood, then
threw her napkin on the table. Her eyes flashed as she
leaned forward with her hands on the table. "Listen, you—
you poor excuse for a human being. Who helped support
you twenty-five years ago when you were licking the boots
of that straw boss at Crown Zellerbach? Who got up night
after night to walk the floor with that colicky baby? Who
did the laundry and cleaned that miserable, stinking one
room apartment?" Before the beleaguered Bruxton could
reply, she continued, "Now you're a big shot, a celebrity,
an honorary elder in that fancy Episcopal Church. Do you
think the church members know you're a womanizer? That
you scam the government to avoid paying taxes? That you
make deals with shady politicians?" Her face turned fiery
as she grabbed her purse, got up from the table, and walked
toward the restaurant exit. "Don't bother to get up. Jim will
drive me. You can take a cab."

The maître d' hurried toward Mary and asked if there was
something he could do. She waved him off. Several patrons
watched, listening with interest to the heated diatribe.

"Wait a goddamn minute, don't do anything stupid!"
Bruxton shouted as he stood and walked toward her. In an
attempt to defuse her anger, he said in a softer voice, "We
can talk about all of this at home. Baby, you know we need
each other."

Looking over her shoulder as she pushed through
the door, she countered, "You couldn't be more mistaken,
you sonofabitch."

***

At the end of the office day, Maggie removed her
nurse's uniform, and placed it on a hanger in the closet
she shared with Josh in his consultation room. She stood

there in her half-slip and bra, rotating her head and neck to relieve muscle tension. Josh walked up behind her, placed his arms around her waist and kissed her neck lightly, then slipped his hands upward to cup the fullness of her breasts. Maggie brought her head back, closed her eyes and made purring sounds. "Don't stop now, lover. If you think this is adequate payment, you're mistaken, I'm asking for a raise." Maggie turned around, placed her arms around Josh's neck and gave him a breathy open-mouthed kiss.

Josh pulled her in tightly. Maggie feigned limpness and total surrender. "Whew! Hold on sailor, let me catch my breath." She pushed him away playfully. "You're incorrigible. Do you know what that does to me? You make me feel like a lovesick teenager."

"Happy to accommodate. You stoke my furnace too."

"Moments like this make me grateful we are who we are. Unfortunately, life isn't nearly as sweet for two of our patients traveling in the fast lane."

Josh turned and looked at her. "Meaning?"

"I'm referring to the Bruxtons. The gossips already have them divorced and battling in court. We may be seeing a lot more of Mary if she develops any more psychosomatic complaints from all her grief."

Josh nodded. "She might, but before she's through, she'll have Bruxton developing a few pains of his own."

4

Jim Keyes, chauffeuring the Bruxton's Bentley north on Monterey Avenue, looked in the rear view mirror to watch Peter Bruxton reviewing the pages of questions prepared for him. This was the morning Bruxton's public relations agency had scheduled a TV appearance at the studio in Desert Hot Springs, and his boss was clearly nervous. The sedan pulled into the parking lot one hour before scheduled airtime, and Bruxton rushed out before the chauffeur could open his door.

Alice Green, who would ask questions to his rehearsed answers, greeted Bruxton in the studio where several cameras were mounted, and heavy cables lay on the floor.

Green, a petite woman with a dazzling smile, reached up and kissed Bruxton, then embraced him with the easy familiarity that is known among socialites. The TV interview, which was being billed as another newsworthy community program, was, in reality, a ploy to advertise Bruxton's properties.

Seated at a small table, Alice Green and Bruxton faced each other. A crew of three technicians were adjusting the lights and positioning mike pickups on the two participants. Bruxton, with a jovial smile that was entirely uncharacteristic, and large horn-rimmed glasses that gave him an owlish look, wore a sport jacket with an open-collared shirt. He struck a casual pose as he crossed his legs at the ankles, then folded his arms and glanced briefly at the camera and the monitor behind the interviewer. One of the techs behind the camera facing Alice Green, held up his finger and counted: three, two, one, then pointed to her and mouthed, "Now."

Miss Green referred to her notebook. "Mr. Bruxton, you're one of a rare breed of highly successful entrepreneurs who started out almost, if not completely, penniless, and built an empire that boggles my mind, an empire consisting of magnificent homes with recreational facilities here in the Coachella Valley and in Montana. These places have eighteen hole golf courses, Olympic-sized pools and spas. In Montana you have ski runs that rival those in Norway. I've seen pictures of some of those luxury homes and condos, and I can't possibly begin to describe their beauty in settings that are absolutely breathtaking.

"Let's allow our viewers to see some of these fabulous places." Several digitally enhanced color photos were projected on a screen, as well as an artist's rendering of a clubhouse that resembled a colossal Swiss chalet. "These pictures are simply marvelous," she gushed.

Bruxton acknowledged the exaggerated praise with a modest smile.

"I'm told that the first phase of homes in the Sunburst Village in Montana has been sold out even though construction is not complete."

Bruxton knew that this was sheer hype promoted by his PR agent, but he wasn't going to contradict her. He nodded with false modesty "That's true."

"You've created a kind of winter wonderland for the rich and famous. Tell us how you accomplished this. How did it all begin? Start with your days as a youngster."

Bruxton removed his glasses, placed them in his jacket pocket, folded his arms across his chest and cleared his throat. "Well, Alice, it wasn't easy." He leaned back in his chair enjoying the self-serving narration. "Can you believe that at one time our family had to accept welfare handouts? My father was a post-World War II immigrant from Sweden, a woodsman, who came to Washington State where he had relatives working in the lumber mills. He got a job as a logger for a wildcat outfit. You probably know, logging is one of the most dangerous jobs in the world. My dad worked for about two and a half years when unfortunately, he was killed in a logging accident. I never really knew him; I was too young, of course. There was no insurance and our savings were meager. My mother tried to keep her young family together by taking in laundry, baking breads and cakes for sale to neighbors and family. Like I said, it wasn't easy. In fact, life was just damned hard."

"How many children were there?"

"Two of us. My brother is a year younger."

"Is he also a developer like you?"

"No, he took a different path. Unfortunately, we're not close." Out of camera range, Bruxton signaled Alice with a thumb down sign meaning he did want not to pursue that line of questioning.

"Tell us how you became so successful? I'm sure our viewers would like to know."

"Even as a kid of about twelve I worked every day, even weekends. I delivered groceries and newspapers, swept and shoveled sawdust at the lumber mills and cleaned toilets in taverns after closing hours. I worked all night and went to school during the day. I often got scolded by my teachers for falling asleep in class, but by the time I got to high school, I probably made more money than the principal."

"Did you go on to college?"

"I sat in on some classes at the community college for about three months, only half-listening to lectures on psychology, sociology, physiology—courses like that. I said to myself, what good are all those things for me? I got to get out and make money. I wanted some things so bad, things I never had, a decent home for my mother and me, a car and three squares a day. As it turned out, Uncle Sam didn't give me much time to think about all that since I was drafted for 'Nam."

"You were in the military?"

"Yeah, two and a half rough years."

Alice Green continued the interview without referring to notes. "Before you left, did you leave any pretty girl behind?"

"Yes, I did. I met her at a church picnic in Spokane one summer—she was sweet sixteen, and I was eighteen, and I knew she was the girl for me. She was a beauty with long dark hair, big brown eyes, pearly teeth and a knockout figure."

"My she sounds engaging, and did you marry her?"

"Let me tell you what happened. One day after a twelve-hour patrol slogging in the Mekong Delta, I went to mail call and received one of those 'dear John' letters. My sweetheart told me she found someone else. Naturally, I was dejected for awhile but not for long. I always recover and come back stronger. I measure life's meaning in terms of achievement. That's my driving force, my credo. A guy can't stop and feel sorry for himself. No, sir, he's got to go forward. Hard work finds its own rewards. I met the girl I married after my discharge."

"That would be Mary?"

Bruxton nodded but said nothing more, indicating he wanted no further discussion of the matter.

"Earlier you mentioned a church picnic. Are you a religious man?"

Bruxton began to fidget. *Why is she asking me that? I don't remember seeing that question on her list. I'll just skirt this as well as I can.* "Not as much as I should be, I suppose, but I try to live by the golden rule. I support my church, and my accountant encourages it." Both of them laughed. "Have you ever experienced business reversals?"

Bruxton pushed back in his chair, straightened his shoulders, and thought, *this question is more like it.* "You're looking at an expert on the subject. Alice, I'd been a million-aire and a pauper three times over before I had my thirty-fifth birthday. I know what hard knocks are. I know what it's like to go hat in hand to the loan officer and have him tell you he thinks you're a damn poor risk. I know what it's like not to be able to pay utility bills or feed my family and have doors shut in my face. Oh, yeah, I've had financial reversals, all right. But let me tell you, I've become a lot more savvy, and no one is going to sucker me again."

"You said you were in Viet Nam, and I know you were decorated for heroism. Can you tell us about that?"

She's going to get short shrift on this one, too. "The whole unit received a commendation." Bruxton cast his eyes downward, the tempo of his response slowed as he spoke softly. "Frankly, it's an experience I'd just as soon forget, too many got killed—it was ugly."

Alice Green looked at her notes. "Is it true that you went before Congress some years ago to plead your case for switching some of your Montana land for some government-owned land?" She looked at her notes again. "At that time, wasn't the National Environmental Protection Agency about to confiscate your land?"

Bruxton uncrossed his legs and cleared his throat again. *Dammit, I didn't want to discuss this.* "Yes, well, that's quite a long story, and I know most of our viewers wouldn't sit still for the dull details. Suffice it to say, both me and the government came out all right." The interview was going astray and causing Bruxton some uneasiness, but he continued to parry questions by saying that the answers were too complicated to explain adequately in the limited time they had.

"Initially you and your partner, Mr. Kurtz, owned the Montana land; now as I understand, you are the sole owner. Did you buy your partner's share of the holdings?" Bruxton hesitated just long enough to create a gaffe. "Does that question cause too much personal disclosure? If so, we can go to another topic."

"No, no. I just wanted to get the sequence of events in order, and I had to think. My partner, Larry Kurtz," he hesitated then added, "we go back a long way. We fought in 'Nam together and became close buddies. After our discharge, we pooled our small savings and bought a few acres of timberland in Washington. We sold our trees and borrowed money to buy larger tracts of forested land. Buying and selling like that, we came to own large tracts in Washington, Oregon and Montana. Eventually, we owned several thousand acres in Montana near Yellowstone National Park. Larry was always strapped for cash, and I frequently bailed him out. His ownership got watered down to much less than half. He sold his smaller portion designated as timberland for immediate cash. I invested in land which was designated for development."

"What does that mean?"

"The government agency approved my share of the land for residential development and associated leisure activities, such as a golf course and ski runs—a lodge with facilities for snowboarding, sledding, ice skating—that sort of thing."

Alice Green looked at Bruxton. "I would think that ultimately your selection of acreage for developmental purposes was much more profitable than your partner's." Bruxton closed his eyes and nodded slowly. After ten minutes of questions and guarded answers interspersed with intervals of advertising, Alice Green ended the interview. "So I can look forward to visiting your magnificent developments here in Rancho Mirage and in Bozeman, Montana, one day soon?"

"Yes, of course. I would be happy to escort you around. If you win the state lottery, we'll offer you an estate package." The ensuing laughter was constrained. A red light flashed denoting the ending time for the interview. Bruxton reached across the table to clasp Ms. Green's hand.

He thanked her for the opportunity to chat with her, while inwardly, he wondered whether the several thousand-dollar tab he'd paid for the interview was worth it.

5

While seated in the limo parked at the TV studio lot, Jim, the chauffeur, had watched the TV program on the screen mounted from the headliner in the passenger compartment. When it was over, he shut the set off and moved to the driver's seat, anticipating Bruxton's arrival. He knew Bruxton was going to ask him his opinion of the program and more specifically, what he thought of Bruxton's performance. Already, he was thinking of ways to answer the questions, but keep the conversation to a minimum.

Since shortly after he began working for the Bruxtons years ago, Jim had learned to avoid rendering comments unless pressed to do so. Most of the time this strategy worked, despite Bruxton's constant need for affirmation. Bruxton's chameleon-like personality, appeared congenial, ingratiating and encompassing when in the company of influential people or those he wished to impress. But among subordinates, he tended to be impatient, demanding and often insulting. He almost never asked staff for their opinion—on anything! Jim was the rare exception, and it was a mostly unwelcome honor. Seeing Bruxton emerge from the TV recording studio, Jim hurried to open the rear door of the limo.

"Well, what d'jah think of the telecast?" Bruxton took his cigar canister out of his pocket and tossed his jacket onto the rear seat.

Jim answered perfunctorily, "It was fine, yeah, just fine."

"That bitch threw me a curve when she asked about acquiring the resort and then asked about my partner's role in all that. It was none of her goddamned business and it was definitely not part of the plan." He lit the cigar, took several puffs, then looked at the lighted end. "But what the hell, I guess I finessed it okay. The public's never gonna know what it took to get that prime land or how many so-called charities I contributed to. Did I say charities? Isn't that a fuckin' laugh. Political pay-off is what it was, pure and simple." Bruxton extended his left wrist to look at his watch. "10:45; Jim swing by the office, I want to pick up something before we head to the Springs Hotel for that afternoon meeting."

Jim parked the Bentley in a "no parking" zone on El Paseo while Bruxton hurried into his office with his brief case. He got out of the car, removed his visored hat and wiped the leather sweatband with a handkerchief. He hand brushed his graying hair and replaced his hat. In addition to the hat, Mrs. Bruxton demanded that he wear a black suit, white shirt, black tie and black patent leather oxfords. It was not the best uniform to have to wear in the desert climate, but appearances were important to Mrs. Bruxton, and he enjoyed pleasing her.

Jim walked to the curb, reached into his inner jacket pocket and removed one cigarette without taking out the whole pack. After lighting it, he inhaled deeply for several seconds, retained the smoke, then exhaled with a cough that produced mucous. He looked around before spitting on the curb. Smoking inside the limo was prohibited. Mrs. Bruxton objected to it vehemently. Even the faintest odor of tobacco evoked a tirade from her. He kept a small deodorizer in the glove compartment and sprayed his jacket after each smoke, then would pop a Lifesaver into his mouth from one of several rolls he kept in the compartment under the folding armrest.

Seeing Bruxton emerge from the building, Jim dropped the cigarette on the pavement and ground it under his shoe until the paper was torn to bits and the shredded tobacco dispersed. Following closely behind Bruxton, and carrying his brief case, was a tall attractive young woman. Jim hurried to open the rear door of the limo. He glanced at the woman and nodded with a slight smile.

"Jim, this is my new secretary, Miss...."

"Ouvray," she added quickly.

"That's right, Miss Ouvray. She's going to assist me at the hotel meeting. We'll probably be busy for an hour or two. I'll call you when we're ready to return to the office. If Mrs. Bruxton calls, and asks you to drive her somewhere, tell her I've given you strict orders not to leave the hotel parking area. Understand? Good. And for God's sake, whatever you do, don't tell her I'm with my secretary." Now let's go!

Jim swung the Bentley into the drive of the Springs Hotel, and pulled to a stop at the valet stand. A young valet immediately came over and opened the door. Bruxton, with his secretary at his side, got out and walked briskly into the hotel and across the expansive hotel lobby to the long reception area. Bonnie Ouvray followed quickly behind him, gawking at the sheer opulence of the surroundings; the marble columns, the capacious easy chairs, sofas and love seats. Two perched, uncaged cockatoos, part of the tropical décor, ignored the staring passersby with haughty indifference. Bonnie watched in awe as a gondola traveled in a serpentine waterway in the recessed area of the lobby, carrying tourists from restaurants to specialty shops on the main floor.

As he approached the reception clerk, a young woman smiling cheerfully greeted Bruxton. "Good afternoon, Mr. Bruxton, good to see you again, sir." She handed him a card key. "Your suite is ready for you. Would you like help with luggage or packages? Would you care to have anything sent to the suite—a snack or perhaps luncheon?"

"No, no, my secretary and I are going to be in the bar for a cocktail before we go upstairs." Bonnie, confused by the conversation, was seized by a premonition of betrayal.

"Mr. Bruxton—I don't understand: aren't we attending a board meeting?"

"Yes, of course." He looked at his watch, "We're a little early. I thought we'd have a bracer at the bar—something to fortify ourselves before confronting those tedious old goats."

"But, I don't drink."

Bruxton took her hand. "Don't concern yourself about it. I'll have Sam, the bartender, fix you a refreshing cooler. Trust me, you'll like it." They walked into a dimly lit room with Art Deco furnishings, booths and small round tables. Piped in music of the 40s and 50s added to the romantic ambience. Bruxton guided the cautious young secretary to a secluded corner booth. A cocktail waitress followed them.

"Have Sam fix his special Cuban drink for the lady and a double martini for me." He placed a ten-dollar bill into the pocket of the abbreviated lacy apron the cocktail waitress wore over her black mini skirt. His hand brushed against her inner thigh, but the cocktail waitress made no complaint. He turned to Bonnie. "Relax, Dear—you don't mind me calling you Dear, do you?"

"No sir."

"These meetings are just too damned dull for sober people. The drinks will help us relax and make the afternoon more tolerable. Now sit. Relax."

Minutes later, the drinks arrived. Bonnie's came in a

tall frosted glass with a creamy white froth and a maraschino cherry. She unwrapped the plastic from the long straw to take the first sip. It surprised and pleased her. "Oh, this is lovely." There was none of the strong alcoholic taste she anticipated and dreaded. A warm comforting sensation was engulfing her; she pushed herself back into the leather upholstery, smiled and closed her eyes.

Bruxton offered her the olive in his drink, but she refused. He insisted that she take it until she relented. The olive tasted sour and bitter, but she was fearful about complaining. He reached across the table and held her hand. Although wary, she was reluctant but did not withdraw her hand. Bruxton was forceful and accustomed to having his way; she could see that. He looked into her dark eyes. "You're a beautiful young lady, do you know that?"

"Thank you, sir."

"I knew the moment I saw you that you were something special." He leaned back and appraised her like a work of art to be acquired. Unconcerned or oblivious to her possible embarrassment, he continued, "I see a wonderful future for you in our organization—providing you play your cards right." He looked at the empty glasses and signaled the waitress to bring another round.

Bonnie said, "Oh, no, please, I shouldn't...." She shook her head and held up her hand.

"Nonsense, drink up, Dear, you'll feel more relaxed, besides, there's hardly any liquor in it."

"Mr. Bruxton, I'm rather confused...."

"Call me Peter." While holding her hand he squeezed it but gently. "Now, tell me why you're confused?"

"Aside from the fact that my head is beginning to spin, I must confess: I saw you much differently in the office. I thought you were abrupt and at times a bit well, vulgar, but now you seem friendly and even kind of sweet." She tilted her head coquettishly and smiled. "I like you this way better—Peter."

"Good!" Bruxton leaned back and assumed a tutorial air. "Now let me tell you something about my business so you can understand me better. I'll admit my language gets crusty when things don't go just right. In public, I make an effort to sound polite; I don't always succeed. At times I'm forced to make decisions at the expense of others, and that doesn't always endear me to them. I'm in the game of land development; often I use other people's money, but I guarantee nothing. If my investment judgments pay off, I have a group of happy investors who think I'm great. If the investments fail, as they do on occasion, I become a target for abuse. But everything is spelled out legally before any deals are made. Naturally, I've made a few enemies along the way."

Bruxton continued to talk, and Bonnie continued to sip her cocktail. She was well into her second drink when she began to feel excessively warm. She unbuttoned the top two buttons of her blouse. "Mr. Bruxton, uh, Peter, I'm feeling a bit warm, and a bit woozy. I think I need to lie down."

"No worries." Bruxton replied. "I'll take you to my suite where you can rest until you're feeling better."

6

"Mrs. Bruxton, there's a call for you on line three." Melinda, Mary Bruxton's personal secretary spoke on the intercom as Mary, in the upstairs dressing room, adjusted her bra. She thought how her bosom over the past several years had become fuller and required a larger cup size.

"Who is it Melinda? If it's my daughter, Deena, tell her I'll call back as soon as I get myself tucked into this damned harness." Having succeeded with the bra, she was almost breathless, pulling up the elasticized girdle to conceal a roll of belly fat.

The intercom interrupted again, "It's a Mr. Frank Parma calling from the Screen Actors' and Writers' Guild. He says he wants to thank you and give you some kind of award."

"Who? Oh, who cares. Take his number, and tell him I'll call back later." She lurched to one side, then the other, and continued to pull upward trying to get the garment symmetrical. She looked in the mirror sideways and mumbled, "How in the hell did I get so round?" She sucked in her abdomen and thought: well at least my butt hasn't drooped as yet. But hell, Peter isn't interested in what I look like, anyway. How many months had it been since their last attempt at intercourse when he complained about maintaining an erection? Hah! I'll bet he has no trouble with those bitches at the office, Mary thought bitterly.

The intercom crackled again, "Mrs. Bruxton this guy says he's shooting on location in the desert and would like to deliver whatever he's got for you, in person. He says he'll take only a minute of your time."

"Melinda, I don't know who in the hell he is, and right now, I don't care to entertain any strangers. Get rid of him."

"Okay, but I think you should know he's that hunk who's on daily TV soap re-runs in a show called, *Lovers' Lives*. He's tall, dark and kinda looks like an Italian George Clooney. And you know, there's nothing wrong with Italian salamis." Melinda's unsolicited opinion was followed by the sound of her giggling on the intercom.

Mary straightened a crease in a flower-patterned sheath and smiled. "Melinda, you've got a big filthy mouth. Where's this guy now?"

"Fifteen minutes from here at the Indian casino in Rancho Mirage."

Mary looked at her watch. 12:30. "I've got a hair appointment at 1:30. If he gets here by 1:00, I'll give him fifteen minutes. If he says he can make it, fine; if not, sorry Charlie."

Minutes later, the maid called up to let Melinda know that Mrs. Bruxton's guest had arrived. Melinda came out into the foyer and found a six-foot Adonis standing in the doorway of the Bruxton estate. He had thick black, curly moist-looking hair; a face tanned and dimpled, a cleft in his chin, and teeth too white and even to be God-given. His V-necked sweater sans shirt revealed black and silver chest hairs, and his broad chest tapered to a narrow flat waist. He was holding a gift-wrapped package that looked like a two-pound box of candy. "Mrs. Bruxton?" He presented his card.

"No, no, I'm her secretary. Mrs. Bruxton will be down shortly. Please, follow me. You can wait here." Melinda led him into the spacious living room. He moved about, studying the many objets d'art; the kind he had seen in other well-appointed homes furnished by interior decorators. An eclectic arrangement of oil paintings adorned the walls. He scrutinized the paintings and leaned forward to read the artists' signatures. He was about to touch the textured surface of a Monet Giverny garden scene, wondering if it was an original or a copy, when Mary Bruxton approached from behind and cleared her throat.

He spun around, "Oh, I beg your pardon—Mrs. Bruxton?"

"Ye-es." Her eyes danced and explored the manly visage. She stood fascinated by this virile creature, oozing sexuality.

"Mrs. Bruxton, I'm at a loss for words. I wasn't expecting anyone as young or as beautiful. I'm completely charmed." Mary's face was aglow as she continued to stare at the handsome figure. "Permit me to introduce myself, I'm Frank Parma, and I'm here to deliver a small gift, a token of appreciation from the Actors' and Writers' Guild of America. Your generous contribution in support of our art is greatly appreciated and hereby acknowledged." He smiled. "I spent five minutes rehearsing that line. I certainly hope it came out right." She chuckled and the air of formality was broken. He handed her the box, then put his hands behind his back.

"May I?" she said, removing the ribbon.

"Of course." The actor's sonorous baritone thrilled her and made her skin prickle.

"What a lovely gift," she said while removing the tissue from a Lalique crystalline plaque on which were etched her name and a tribute to her generosity in support of Theatre Arts. "How nice of you to take the time and trouble to bring this to me. Where did you say you were working?"

"We're shooting desert scenes in the Yucca Valley for the next few weeks. It's a Western—well, a sort of modern-day oater with a new twist and dark overtones. Not an old time shoot'em-up with horse-chasing scenes. This has to do with a mineral discovery and a boss' wife lusting after the hero, who just happens to be me. It's a hokey old story line, but we're hoping it'll work. Some of the actors have been kidding me, saying that with me in the picture it's a bona fide spaghetti western."

"My, how clever of them. Where's Yucca Valley and why are you filming there?"

"It's a high valley about forty minutes west and north of here. About sixty years ago, some Hollywood cowboys like Gene Autry and his cronies bought some desert property up there to shoot their own westerns. The area is about ten miles northwest of the town center of Yucca and is called Pioneer Town. It's named for Autry's old singing group, Sons of the Pioneers. There's not much up there except a recreated frontier post office, community hall, saloon, general store and old wagon parts."

"Are you able to live there?"

"The film company's taken over a small motel on the premises. Not exactly the Ritz, but it'll do. Frankly, the arrangements are primitive and the chuck wagon grub is kinda tiresome."

Mary Bruxton continued her assessment of the stranger before saying, "I hope you don't think me forward, but if you don't mind driving in, I can offer you our casita. The accommodations, I'm sure, are better and the food is pretty good, at least our cook thinks so. On her day off, you can have kitchen privileges. I might even help you from time to time."

Parma's eyes widened. "Mrs. Bruxton, that's more than generous...."

"Call me Mary. What do your friends call you?"

"Frank or Frankie or Diego or just Hey You!"

Mary chuckled. "I think I'll call you Frankie."

"Mrs. Bruxton, er, ah, Mary, are you quite sure you want to make this offer? Mr. Bruxton won't mind?"

"Having you here might put some life into this

mausoleum. As far as Mr. Bruxton is concerned, well, he probably won't even notice anything different."

"I don't know how I'll ever be able to repay you."

"Don't force me into a clichéd answer." He bent forward, and kissed the back of her hand.

"My, how gallant! Are you always so gracious?"

"Only with charming and beautiful women." He took a step backward and bowed with a flourish.

7

The elevator stopped at the twelfth floor and Bonnie Ouvray held on to Bruxton's arm for support. Her legs were unsteady and the floor seemed to move in a sine-wave pattern. "Just a few more steps, and we'll be home safe," Bruxton assured her as he maintained a delicate balance, propping her up and reaching for the room card key. When the bedroom came into view, Bonnie lurched forward to fall face down across the bed. She turned over and lay spread eagle, her glassy eyes unable to focus.

Bruxton rushed to remove his shoes and unzip his trousers; he jumped on the bed and straddled her. He reached over to unbutton her blouse and unfasten her bra when she sat up suddenly; her head collided with his, causing a brilliant burst of pain for both. She had a retching spasm and projected an arc of vomit that splashed Bruxton's shirt and the bedding. Dazed, she moaned, "I'm so sorry," as she brought the back of her hand across her slobbering lips. Bruxton arched backward, jumped off the bed and with an ugly grimace, stared at his foul-smelling shirt and the wet vomit around him.

"Jeezus, just look at this fuckin' mess!"

In a quivery, distant voice she repeated, "Oh, I'm so sorry. What should we do?"

"Shit! The first thing we're gonna do is get out of these

shitty clothes and take a shower! Then I'll call the clothing shops downstairs and have some clothes sent up." He tossed a towel at the disheveled, embarrassed Bonnie and shook his head as though he alone suffered humiliation. Turning his back to her, he said, "You owe me big time for this, girlie."

Lucy Kurtz emerged from the pool climbing the vertical stairs and pulling on the chrome rails. She rubbed her eyes, then wrung the excess water from her hair. As she reached for a beach towel on the chaise lounge, she stopped. "Larry is that you? I'm at the pool side." At forty-two, Lucy Kurtz retained her youthful figure—the result of total and constant self-absorption and reverence to holistic medical programming: dietary restrictions and almost endless physical-fitness. She indulged in weekly massages and the slathering of emollients on exposed as well as concealed body parts. At five feet eight inches, slender and willowy, she moved with cat-like grace. She lay in the semi-recumbent position, chin up, facing the sun, then reached for sunglasses on a small table beside her. Hiking one shoulder, she slipped the bathing suit strap off and did the same on the other side. Then she pulled the top of her suit down to expose her chest with its well-formed surgically enhanced breasts, like two grapefruit halves topped with crimson cherries and separated by a wide valley.

Larry Kurtz in a three button gray suit walked onto the decking and stopped to look at his wife on the other side of the pool. He hurried to her side hurling invectives as he ran. "Chrissakes, Lucy, cover-up! What the hell's wrong with you? This is no freakin' nudist colony. The neighbors will report you for indecent exposure. Are you trying to get us arrested?" He reached for her beach towel and threw it at her.

"Oh, for God's sake, relax Larry; no one can see me over these walls and the hibiscus. They'd have to climb an eight-foot ladder to see me. If they take the trouble to do that they should be rewarded." She looked down at her breasts. "You spent twenty-thousand dollars to have these boobs shaped. Someone ought to enjoy them. God knows, you don't seem to know what to do with them."

"If you weren't such a goddamned exhibitionist...."

Lucy anticipated Larry's comments. It took very little to get him started on one of his favorite themes. "Now don't bring that up again! That happened three years ago." She sat holding the towel against her chest, pushed her glasses to the top of her head and scowled. "It was *your* partner who got me drunk or slipped me a mickey that night. And I still don't know where-in-the-hell you were while that was going on. For all I know, you were diddlin' that fat cow, Mary Bruxton."

"That's ridiculous."

An awkward silence followed until Lucy said, "Besides, if Bruxton didn't feel some remorse, he might not have saved this house by paying off the mortgage."

Larry removed his jacket and loosened his tie. "I'm not convinced he did us any favors. Now we have no equity, and I'm paying *him* monthly installments instead of the mortgage bank."

Lucy started for the house then stopped to look at her husband. "No responsible person advised you to sink a million dollars into that stupid invention. How could you— even in your usual unconscious state—figure that a device could make a car go by feeding it water—plain old water?" She shook her head and walked into the house, Larry followed.

He protested. "It was just plain water. I saw a demonstration...."

"Spare me the details, Einstein, you were scammed to the tune of one million dollars. If we had that money today, Bruxton wouldn't own our mortgage." Before entering the bedroom, Lucy stepped out of her swimsuit, leaving her shapely backside and sensuous movements to her husband's appreciative gaze. Again he was gripped by the thought of Bruxton, that gross pig, having had his body next to hers and forcing her to screw him. This recurrent thought always caused hyper-somatic responses in which his heart raced, his temple pounded and his hands shook with fine tremors. He mumbled, "That sonofabitch oughta be killed."

9

Oblivious to the other students around them, Deena Bruxton and Johnny Brasilowicz swung their arms slowly as they strolled hand in hand along the tree-lined campus walkway.

Johnny's hand completely engulfed Deena's. "I don't know why we can't have an official engagement, and I don't know why your ol' man is against us gettin' married." The burly football player in his USC lettered-sweater towered over the petite Deena Bruxton at 5'2" who wore another of Johnny's sweaters that fit her like a graceless sack.

"Jeez-uz, Deena, every time I touch you, I—in fact, I don't even have to touch you—I just have to think about you, and I get the biggest goddamndest hard-on in the world and practically cum in my shorts. Sometimes my balls really ache."

"Sh-sh, Johnny you mustn't say those things—someone might hear you, and well—that's really not nice."

His eyes widened. "But, it's the truth, so help me God, it is." He put his arm around her shoulders and let his hand migrate to the side of her breast. "What's your ol' man afraid of? Maybe he thinks I won't make a living for ya? I got a job waitin' for me as soon as I graduate—if I ever graduate. I can work for my dad's union. He said I could start out at fifty grand as an enforcer."

"What's an enforcer?" Deena's inquiring eyes looked up at him.

"It's just someone who reminds guys when their union dues are delinquent."

"How do you do that?"

"A little friendly persuasion—that's all. After I do that for a while I move up the ladder to makin' business decisions. It's a damn good future."

"Johnny, supposing my daddy won't give permission for us to marry? What then?"

"I thought about that. We could run away—ya know?—elope."

"I'd never do that Johnny. I just couldn't do that."

"Wouldja marry me if your old man wasn't around? I mean supposing he had an accident or something...."

"That's a horrible thought, Johnny." She pulled away and glared at him reproachfully.

"Yeah, but wouldja? Huh, wouldja?"

"I don't even want to think about that. Shame on you Johnny."

He stopped, looked down at the annoyed Deena, and said, "I'm sorry. It isn't like I was thinking of killing him or anything like that." Then he picked her up with one arm and with the other hand held her face against his and kissed her repeatedly. With both her feet dangling off the ground, she held his big bold face and reciprocated.

10

At 1:45 p.m. Bruxton and Bonnie emerged from the Springs Hotel wearing clothes sent from the boutique shop; Bruxton in a Hawaiian shirt emblazoned with wild tropical flowers that hung over knee-length shorts of shocking pink. By contrast, Bonnie wore a flattering simple strapless black and white sun dress.

They stood in the porte-cochere next to two shopping bags of foul-smelling clothes.

Bruxton looked impatiently at his watch. "Dammit! Where the hell's that chauffeur?"

Bonnie's state of intoxication had improved, although she repeatedly opened her eyes wide and closed them tightly in an effort to focus better. She held Bruxton's arm firmly trying to maintain her balance.

Jim approached hurriedly from the side and reached for the shopping bags.

"Where the hell ya been?" Bruxton asked.

"Sorry, I'd been watching the entrance, but I guess I didn't recognize you two in different clothes."

"Huh?" Bruxton looked at his clothes then at Bonnie's. "Yeah, well, we had an accident—a waiter spilled soup or something on us. We needed a change." He gave no further explanation and continued, "Put these bags in the trunk and run them over to the cleaners later. And for chrissakes, don't mention any of this to Mrs. Bruxton. It's none of her damn business." The chauffeur glanced at Bonnie and gave her an abbreviated nod. She turned her head to avoid eye contact.

At the end of the filming day, Scooter, still in his cowboy costume, walked into Parma's motel room. "Where ya goin', Diego? Got a date with one of them local squaws or hot tamales?" He watched Parma using a straight razor on his lathered face. "Wanna be careful ya don't become a daddy to a *breed*. If ya knock-up one of them ya better be prepared to marry her, or ya could find yourself with an arrow up yer ass and yer mis'rable carcass strung to a fence post. Folks 'round here don't take kindly to fly-by-night Johnnies who leave their daughters or sisters in a family way. No sir! That's jes a little friendly advice from a guy who's been 'round the horn a few times."

Parma feeling his smoothly shaven face and looking in the mirror said, "Scooter, you old shit-kicker, you might know a lot about trick horse-riding, stand-in pratfalls and taking phony bullets, but you don't know squat about the folkways of these people. Your concept of western lifestyle is about a hundred years old, and furthermore, your hero, John Wayne, was probably no better informed."

"Careful how ya use the Duke's name. Him and me got along just fine." Scooter, the oldest bewhiskered movie stunt man in the industry no longer performed dangerous tricks but appeared as the loveable but wretched cowhand, the foil to the handsome star. He smiled a toothless grin and did not argue. Just to hold conversation and get animated responses from the leading man, Frank Parma, pleased him.

In the dingy, low-ceiling room of the motel, Parma had packed a valise and was preparing to leave. "I've been invited to share the hospitality of a wealthy, wonderful and beautiful lady who lives forty minutes from here in a virtual palace. Yes, sir, tonight I get to sleep on a magnificent bed...."

"Alone?" Scooter scratched the back of his head and tilted his cowboy hat forward.

"She's a married woman. I've met her only once, just briefly...."

"Knowing you, Frankie, I'd say you'll be in her britches in no time. D'ya meet her ol' man yet?"

"No, not yet...."

Scooter removed his soiled, greasy, misshapen cowboy hat and slapped it against his chaps. "Hot dog! I'd give the rest of ma teeth to be there when ya meet him. Maybe 'bout the time you're ready to slip the log into the furnace, the ol' man'll come in—heh, heh, heh." Scooter shook his head and danced a little jig.

Parma picked up his overnight bag and headed toward the door. "Okay, that's enough, you withered old cock. I'll see you on the set at six tomorrow."

At 6:15 p.m. the door chimes sounded and Mary Bruxton, in a shimmering burgundy cocktail dress, touched her hair gently, sucked in her abdomen and pulled at her dress before opening the door. "Welcome, Mr. Cowboy. My, you're looking mighty fresh after a long day of prospecting. Find any treasures in those Yucca Valley sand dunes?"

Parma's eyes explored his radiant hostess. "I believe there are more treasures here, and if you don't mind my saying so, I think I'm looking at one. You, Madame, look absolutely stunning. I have a confession: I thought about you all day, causing me to muff some of my lines."

Mary reached out to touch his arm and smiled. "How sweet of you to have told me."

Wearing a dark blue silk shirt, white linen sport jacket

and light blue slacks, Frank smiled as he handed Mary a wine bottle in a satin bag. "Thought we might enjoy this tonight."

"My, my, aren't we getting fancy. Should I be wary of Greeks bearing gifts?"

"In this case, it's an Italian, and no, you have nothing to fear."

"Nothing to fear? Well, I hope that doesn't mean you're flat-out passive." She laughed.

He bent forward and sniffed. "Mm-mm, you smell wonderful."

"Good, I'd hoped that French perfume had more drawing power than a sprinkle of talcum." She took the bottle of wine out of the bag, looked at the label and said, "1958 Lafitte Rothschild Bordeaux. I like a man who has impeccable taste."

"In wine and women." He bowed, then leaned forward to kiss her lightly on the lips.

"Careful cowboy! You're riding into Dodge at a mighty fast clip, and you don't know what the territory's like or if the pilgrims are even friendly."

"I'm a pretty good judge of people, and I think this lady pilgrim is friendly, or I'd like to think so." He looked deeply into Mary's eyes and pulled her gently toward him. Right at that moment the Bruxton's cook appeared "Pardon me, Mrs. Bruxton, should I set the soufflé in the oven now?"

Mary pulled away and looked at her watch. "No, wait another half hour; take this bottle of wine and decant it. Mr. Parma and I will have an aperitif in the great room before dinner." She looked at Parma. "Would you like a little something now? A cocktail? Bourbon? Scotch?"

"Scotch on the rocks will be fine, thank you."

"I have some twenty-five year old Ambassador. I think you'll enjoy that."

"I'd enjoy sharing anything with you."

Mary looked over her shoulder coyly.

"Is Mr. Bruxton joining us?"

"No, he's gone for the week, thank God, supervising his favorite project in Big Sky country." Mary, with Frank behind her, walked into an adjoining room with a splendid, long, nineteenth century restored saloon bar in black polished walnut. A floor-to-ceiling mirror behind it and an enormous array of liquor bottles and crystal stemware glittered, jewel-like from overhead lights. "Please help yourself: there's an ice bucket on the bar. I'll make a gin and tonic for myself."

"Let me make that for you," he said. "I made a living doing that sort of thing. Tending bar was one of my many jobs along the way. Here. How is it?"

"Nice. My. You're quite talented. What else have you done?" Before he responded, she said, "Oh, wait. Let's bring our drinks into the great room and you can tell me all about yourself." Mary led the way into another room, then sat down on a settee. She patted the cushion next to her for Frank.

Before sitting, he proposed a brief toast; one he had delivered many times. "To a new and exciting friendship—one that I hope to cherish for as long as I shall live."

"I like that," she said as their glasses clinked. "Now tell me all about yourself, and start from the beginning."

He sat next to her and looked into his drink. "If you're thinking I had an altogether wholesome life, you'll be disappointed."

"I can assure you that wholesome is not my primary interest."

Parma settled back into the settee. "I played football in a Catholic high school in Brooklyn where I was captain and quarterback. I took the team to an unbeaten season; that was in 1975. We were state champions. A scout from Notre Dame spotted me and apparently liked what he saw. They gave me an athletic scholarship, and I played on the varsity team in my sophomore year. That was quite an achievement. But I developed knee and ankle injuries, and that put the kibosh on my playing." He hesitated. "Truth is, the injuries did hurt, but I also found girls, and they found me. Football and studies interfered with my social life. After I left the football team, I caroused and had a good time. My grades, of course, went south. Nothing helped. I dropped out before graduation.

"Following that, I went back to New York, got a job as a bouncer in a night club. There was some gambling and prostitution going on at the club. I roughed up a few guys and took a few punches myself, but that's another story. Anyway, some guy at the nightclub saw me and told me my face was photogenic. He asked me if I could act, and I said 'Sure.' I'd never acted a day in my life, but I figures, 'How hard could this be.' Plus, I figured the guy was handing me a line. But sure enough, I got a call a week later to report to the Goodwin Theatre to read a part from an Arthur Miller play.

Mary's eyes glistened with excitement as she listened. "And? What happened?"

"They threw me off the stage five minutes after I started reading. Boy, I really stank!" He swirled the ice cubes in his tumbler then took a long gulp. "After that, I saw an ad for male escorts—good pay and benefits, it said. I figured anything had to be better than working as a bouncer, and after all, there are worse things in life than providing plea-sure to lovely ladies. So I checked it out."

Mary moved closer, crossed her well-contoured legs as the slit in her dress opened to reveal more of her thigh. "Really?"

"Yep. And they put me to work, just like that." He snapped his fingers. "I never knew there were so many rich and lonely women out there—married, divorced, single, young, old...."

"Did you make love to all of them?"

"If you mean: did I have sex with them?" He leaned back with his drink and smiled, hesitating to answer immediately. In drama classes he learned the value of an extended pause. "About half. Some just wanted company—a little dancing—a shared meal—conversation. Yeah, some were sexually starved and tore right into it—no inhibitions."

"Sounds intriguing. What was the down side to all of that?"

"After awhile, it started to become depressing. I should have quit, but the money was good—damn good. And, of course, that was about the time I was introduced to some so-called mood-elevating drugs—marijuana, bennies, 'ludes. They made the intimacies more tolerable, but then I got into coke, and that led to shooting heavy stuff. I became terribly dependent. I hit the skids and sank as low as a vagrant. The cops picked me up, and I wound up in the loony bin at Bellevue for three months. One day after counseling, a light went on in my head, and I said 'What in the hell am I doing with my life?'"

He took another sip of Scotch. "I really shouldn't be giving you all these rotten details of my misspent youth, and I apologize if I'm boring you."

"Oh, no, please don't stop. I'm completely fascinated."

"The rest of the story has to do with my salvation, but...."

The cook made a meek entrance into the great room. "Pardon me, Mrs. Bruxton, dinner is ready."

"In a moment, Esmeralda."

"No, really." Frank interjected. "The timing's perfect."

Frank stood, then extended his hand to help Mary up. He placed the empty Scotch tumbler on the cocktail table and put his arm around her waist as he escorted her to the dining room. She looked up at him and whispered, "I feel so secure having you next to me."

"That's nice to know; maybe I can earn my keep."

"I sure hope so."

The entire second floor of the only office building in the heart of the exclusive El Paseo shopping district in Palm Desert was located one block West of Saks Fifth Avenue and was occupied solely by Peter Bruxton Enterprises of North America.

After a long and busy week in Montana, Bruxton had returned to the desert to find even more work waiting for him. He was impatiently going through contracts at his century old ornate mahogany desk, when his secretary's voice came over the intercom. "Mr. Bruxton, there's a Mr. John Smith here to see you." In a muffled voice she added, "He seems awfully agitated."

Bruxton looked at the intercom and said, "I don't know who he is, and I don't see his name on my appointment list."

"He says...."

The door flew open. A hulking, bald, red-faced man stood ape-like; his mouth contorted, his fiery eyes glared at the bewildered Bruxton.

"Who—who the hell are you and what do you want?" Bruxton stood and backed slowly away from his desk.

In a voice like thunder, the stranger bellowed, "Listen, you illegitimate son of Lucifer. I hear you're the one responsible for my daughter's pregnancy, and I'm here to see that you repent and pay!" He whipped out a forty-four magnum from his jacket and held it with both hands. "Get on your knees sinner; pray to God Almighty to save your worthless carcass from eternal damnation!"

"Now just hold your horses, Mister. There's no need to pull a gun." Bruxton said as he lowered himself to his knees. "Who in the hell's your daughter?"

"Missy Ellie Bissell. She was your secretary until two weeks ago. I'm her father, the Reverend Ezekiel Jacob Bissell. Figured you wouldn't see me if you heard my real name. I'm a Southern Baptist minister. I had to leave my flock in Enid, Oklahoma just to come here. Now, let's you and me talk about your repentance and salvation."

"Mind if I get off my knees?"

"Not just yet, Brother. That position might be better for prayin'."

Just then, the office door flew open, and three uniformed police rushed in with guns drawn and shouted at the overwhelmed minister, "Don't move! Put that gun down! Now! Slowly! That's right. Now walk backward towards us—slowly. Hands in the air!"

The Reverend Bissell complied, although he was clearly not pleased with the turn of events. One of the officers came up to him, turned him around, and said, "Hands behind your back." He cuffed the man, while one of the other officers bent to get the gun.

"Sinner, you'll pay, yes you will, by God Almighty." The handcuffed minister said.

Bruxton got off his knees and crawled into his chair where he collapsed. "That crazy bastard was going to kill me—I swear it." "You want me to come to the station to file a report?"

"Yes," said one of the officers. "We can take your statement, but we'd prefer it if you could come on in with us to file the report."

"Okay, just let me catch my breath.". Bruxton's pallor was slow to disappear, his thumping heart slowed, and a sensation of utter exhaustion followed a shivering cold sweat.

11

In a clinging black silk dress that enhanced every sensuous curve in her body, Lucy Kurtz, stood before the full length bedroom mirror, preening and thinking she resembled the late Audrey Hepburn—or was it Jackie Kennedy? She placed her hands on her hips, turned to look at her left side, then turned to look at her right side. Hell, she looked better than either one of them. They were dead and she was quite alive, thank you. She reached into her jewelry chest for a double strand of pearls and placed them around her neck but had difficulty fastening the clasp. "Larry, can you help me here?"

Her husband stopped what he was doing and came over to help her. He fumbled with the locking mechanism but was unable to fasten the clasp.

She pushed his hands aside. "Never mind, I'll do it myself."

"Sorry about that."

"Story of my life—if I want something done, I've got to do it myself." She turned to look at her beleaguered husband. "Aren't you dressed yet? The Bruxtons are expecting us at six thirty, and I don't want to be late. It's already six ten; I don't want to miss what those investment bankers have to say, and I don't want the Bruxtons to be angry."

"Bruxton will be happy to see you any time you get there."

With hands on hips she assumed an aggressive tone.

"What's that supposed to mean?"

Larry buttoning his collar stretched his neck upwards. "You figure that out."

"Listen: you can thank me that you're still a partner. All right, a minor one, but at least you're getting an income. You just don't know how lucky you are to have me." She brought her face close to the mirror, licked her middle finger and ran it over her eyebrows. "If I could get a job in that office, I'd make sure you'd become an equal partner." She snapped her fingers. "Just like that. In fact, I may approach him yet and ask for a job."

"You'll do nothing of the kind. I don't want you to pursue that possibility," he said. "Besides, you know Bruxton won't permit family members to work in the company. He's still pissed over those two Johanssen brothers who squeezed him out of one of his sawmills. He called it goddamned thieving nepotism. I wouldn't buck him on that issue. And I wouldn't trust him with you in the same room. If I thought he ever intended to do again what he did three years ago, I'd kill him. I swear it! I'd kill the sonofabitch."

"Relax my brave hero." Lucy walked away with a swagger. "If he ever tries something like that again, you won't have to kill him—I'll do it myself!"

"Come in, please," the maid greeted the Kurtzes and whispered, "The gentlemen from the bank are already here. They're with Mr. Bruxton in the den. Mrs. Bruxton is in the great room having a drink with Mr. Parma."

Larry Kurtz left his wife and joined Bruxton and the bankers in the den.

Lucy asked the maid. "Who's Mr. Parma?"

"Oh, he's a famous TV and movie star."

"Really? So famous that I've never heard of him?" Lucy asked with a dismissive sneer. She walked past the maid and headed toward the great room. "This I must see." She reached the room and stopped suddenly at the entry. "Oh! Excuse me. Didn't mean to intrude, but I thought I could find a drink around here." She put her hand to her swan-like neck. "I'm absolutely parched."

Parma left Mary's side on the settee and stood.

Mary set her drink down and assessed Lucy rather coolly. "Lucy Kurtz, this is Mr. Frank Parma, star of Light House Productions. Frank is starring in a movie that's being made in Yucca Valley. You know of him, I'm sure."

"Why, yes of course." She smiled broadly and drank in the handsome figure from his curly black hair to his dress boots and still didn't have a clue as to who he was. She extended her hand. Frank kissed it as he bowed.

"My, how courtly." Lucy's eyes glommed onto him then looked at Mary. "I love him already."

"Mind your manners; he's my guest, and I'll brook no competition."

"My dear, no one can possibly compete with you."

"Just remember that," Mary said without a trace of humor.

In the dinner seating arrangements, Mary had placed herself between Frank Parma and one of the bank officers. On the opposite side of the table, Lucy Kurtz was seated between her husband, Larry, and the other banker. Peter Bruxton sat at the head of the table. Jim, the chauffeur, acted as a butler; a chore he had performed many times before. With white gloves, he presented a bottle of wine to Bruxton for his approval. Bruxton gave the label a cursory glance and waved it off. "Yeah, that's fine—just pour."

Once everyone had been served, Bruxton stood and raised his glass. "Ladies and gentlemen, here's a toast to your good health and good fortune—wait now, don't drink just yet—he nodded to the bank officers, right and left—here's to our bank friends. We hope you loosen your purse strings for our new recreational project in Montana." He smiled broadly. "And don't worry boys, you'll make your profits, but good!" His laughter was followed by their polite but limited chuckles.

Mary recoiled, stared into her plate and thought: why must he be so damned boorish and offensive? Frank, sensing her embarrassment, placed his hand on hers as they rested in her lap. She looked at him, thanking him with her eyes.

Lucy thought as she watched Mary: I know exactly what you're feeling: you're ashamed because Bruxton's a coarse pig. You'd like to be rid of him and run away with that handsome thing next to you. He's probably already made you feel like a real woman again. I know the feeling because I'm saddled with a guy who's also a class A jerk. The difference is: your husband has money to go along with his monumental ego and repulsiveness while mine is a hopeless clod.

After dinner, Bruxton, concluding his role as major domo, gulped the last of his brandy, then banged the snifter on the table. He wiped his mouth and tossed the napkin on his plate. He looked at one banker, then the other. "Well, fellas, have we got a deal or not? Three hundred million semoleons at 6.3%. The first payment of twenty million, payable at the completion of the first phase of the new building program in approximately one hundred twenty days. The accountants can wrestle with the details. Final approval will be made after *I* give the okay."

The bankers looked at each other across the table; one raised his eyebrows, the other lowered his head to conceal a smile. Both knew that Bruxton had pleaded for the loan.

Larry Kurtz engaged the bankers in conversation as he walked them to the door. Mary remained at the table with Frank while Bruxton followed Lucy as she entered the great room. She turned and was startled to see Bruxton behind her.

"Lucy, you're more gorgeous than ever—couldn't take my eyes off you all evening. I've thought about you many times."

"Bruxton, stop! You disgust me!"

"Oh, yeah? You didn't seem to mind at the time."

"You must have drugged me. I'd never consent to...."

"Don't give me that bullshit! You were damned hot to trot. Listen, if Larry can't satisfy you...."

"Shut up! You're nothing but a filthy degenerate...."

"Are we intruding on a romantic interlude?" Mary asked as she walked into the great room with Frank at her side.

Bruxton showed no emotion. "I'm going upstairs to look over some papers before I go back to the hotel."

Larry, having said goodnight to the bankers, joined Mary, Frank and Lucy in the great room. Lucy, still angered over Bruxton's comments, walked over to Larry. "Time for us to leave, Dear. I have a splitting headache." She gave Mary a perfunctory peck on the cheek and thanked her for a lovely evening. She turned to look at Frank, and asked, "Are you returning to Yucca Valley tonight?"

"No." He explained with aplomb that the Bruxtons had made their casita available to him while he was on location.

"Really?" Lucy's voice escalated an octave as she sang out, "How very convenient. How very convenient, indeed." She walked slowly toward the door and looked over her shoulder. "Mary, dear, we must get together again soon."

Mary closed the door behind them. "Whew! Thank God she's gone."

Frank reached for Mary and embraced her with a passion that squeezed the breath out of her; then he planted a long open-mouth kiss on her. She closed her eyes and held his face in both her hands, then pushed him away gently, looking at her watch. "It's 10:15, darling; you have to get up at 4:30 to be on the set...."

"Will you come to the casita and turn down the bedding for me?"

"Not while that ogre is upstairs. His presence anywhere

around here turns me off. Completely off."

Frank glanced at the stairs then returned his gaze to Mary. "We've got to talk about our future."

"I'd like that. I've rehearsed my lines a thousand times, you know. I'm anxious to tell that loud-mouthed egomaniac that I want out."

Frank cast another glance at the stairs. "I've got to know: is he physically abusive? Has he laid a hand on you?"

"Don't concern yourself with such matters. It'll be my choice when this marriage ends." She turned and ascended the stairs as Frank looked after her.

12

At a booth next to a window, a waitress approached Frank. "Mornin', Mr. Parma. Black coffee and cinnamon toast? Gotcha. Comin' right up." The waitress at John's Place, a popular restaurant in the Yucca Valley Town Center, shouted the order to the cook behind the counter.

"Frankie, ol' buddy, mind if I join you?" Scooter, almost unrecognizable in his open-collared button-down shirt, tailored narrow-legged Levis and polished Italian snake-skinned boots, slid in opposite Frank on the long seat. He looked at his watch. "Should be ready for make-up in about an hour. We'll be shootin' action scenes again. Same ol' roof jumpin', fallin' off horses and pretendin' to get *kilt—ya* know the drill. Acourse, you won't have to be on the set fer a while—your stunt man is probably there already. They ain't gonna risk having their star bust his ass."

Scooter motioned to the waitress, "Honey, bring me a cuppa joe an a piece a apple pie, and shoo the flies off'n it. Get it? Shoo fly pie? Heh-heh-heh."

The waitress rolled her eyes, "That's cute and so-oo original."

Scooter leaned forward. "Tell me about the rich gal in the lower valley. Ya gonna make any perminint arrange-ments fer squirin' her? Is she a pretty filly—kinda soft and cuddly?" He put up his hand in anticipation of Frank's objection. "I know, ya told me she's hitched, but heck that don't pervent ya from getten a little on the side, does it? I done it a few times. Yessir, it's a mite more excitin' knowin' you're knoodlin' some married gal. Besides they're better, they got experience."

"I think I've really fallen for her, Scooter."

"Yer soundin' kinda sappy, like a young un jes discoverin' what his pecker's fer. C'mon, Frankie; how many times ya been hitched?"

Frank put up two fingers. "Twice—two disastrous encounters—five years the first time and six months the second. But this time it's real. I knew she was the one the minute I saw her." He became reflective as he sipped the coffee and absently tore a piece of toast.

Scooter watched him. "Aside from your new doll, what bothers ya, Frankie?"

"I've been thinking: how old are you Scooter?"

"Sixty-four, why?"

"Got any money set aside?"

"A few thou. If ya need cash, I c'n scrape some up..."

"No, no, thanks. I've been thinking; here you are at the end of your career in this goddamn business that caters to young pissers—you never know when the next gig is coming or whether you've had your last, and you're being turned out to pasture, like a worn out hay-burner...."

"Hold on pardner! I've got me a nice little home in Studio City, all paid fer, seventy years ol' but the plumbin's good and the lectricity's workin'. I got me a sweet little divorcee, works as a waitress, keeps my bed warm on cold nights. Next year, I'm on Social Security. Git residuals that don't amount to much, but they help. If I need long term care, I've got the retirement home fer actors in Woodland Hills. Hell, I'm all set...."

"With all due respect, Scooter, I don't want that for me. I'm pushing fifty-seven and aside from this oater and a few TV cameo appearances on the Sopranos and the CSI series,

I'm not sure what the hell the next year or two will bring. Not every senior actor gets a starring role like Harrison Ford who's still playing that old fart, Indiana Jones. Frankly, I'm concerned about my future."

Scooter raised his brow and leaned across the table. "Ya thinkin' ya oughta settle down with that rich gal who could let ya play house and give ya a few toys?" He pushed back and said, "That'd be nice work, Frankie, if ya can get it. How d'ya propose to git rid a her ol' man? If he's got any gumption he's not gonna let some fancy Dan diddle his wife while he's pickin' up the tab. No, sir! You and your sweet patootie gotta shake him off, but first, she's gotta come away with a lotta loot. Yes sir, a lotta loot." Scooter held the fork with his fist and placed a large morsel into his mouth. "He's gonna claim infidel—whatever the heck one calls it when a missus is cheatin'."

"That's no longer a point of legal contention."

"Zat so? What the heck ever happened to the sank-titty of marriage?"

Frank shrugged. "I'm certain she's going to start divorce proceedings soon."

Scooter continued, "This bein' a community property state and the old man richer'n Rockefeller with money tied up in developments and such—hoo whee! Frankie, she's gonna have a real mess on her hands."

13

Bruxton tilted back in his chair, propped his feet on top of an open desk drawer and grunted into the intercom, "Ms. Ouvray, come in here."

Entering tentatively, with a steno pad held like a shield of armor, Bonnie Ouvray, hesitated at the door. "Don't stand over there. Come in." Bruxton pointed to a chair on the other side of his desk. "After we finish here, I'd like you to accompany me to another meeting at the Springs Hotel this afternoon."

Bonnie sat upright and held her pad more defensively. "Mr. Bruxton, I'm happy to accompany you, but I simply cannot join you for a drink again. I...."

"Of course not, sweetie. I don't want you to do anything you don't wanna do."

He became uncharacteristically solicitous. "And just to show you how sorry I am, I bought you a little gift, a token of my appreciation for your understanding and forbearance." He smiled. "Forbearance, isn't that a classy word?" He reached into a lower desk drawer and handed her a narrow gift-wrapped box with a lacy ribbon.

Nonplussed, she stood, placed her steno pad on the chair then looked at Bruxton. "Should I open it?"

"That's what you gotta do to find out what's inside."

She untied the ribbon carefully and removed the

wrapping slowly, then opened the hinged lid. "Oh!" She placed a hand over her mouth and stared wide-eyed. "I don't know what to say! This is so exquisite." Her long, tapered fingers gently lifted a double strand of brilliant pearls. In a breathless but troubled whisper, she said, "Mr. Bruxton, it's so beautiful."

"Here, let me help you put them on," He grabbed the pearls out of her hand, stood behind her, placed them around her neck, then fastened the clasp. He held her hips and turned her around. "That looks great. It'll look better with some cleavage showing—just my opinion, of course."

She caressed the necklace and looked into his eyes. "How will I explain this to my dad?"

"Tell him they're from an admirer. If you're worried, stash 'em somewhere for a while. Hell, do whatever you want with them. Look, baby, I'm crazy about you. That little gift is just the beginning. After I divorce that bitch of a wife of mine, I want to marry you. Then you'll be getting all kinds of gifts from me."

He put up his hand to stop her from commenting. "You don't have to say anything now—just think about it. As a matter of fact, while we're at it, I have another little present for you." Again he reached into his desk drawer, removed a large brown envelope and handed it to her. "Don't open it now. I'll tell you about this while we're at the hotel."

She appeared confused. "I—I don't know what to say...."

"Don't say anything. Just remember that I've got enough dough to buy you anything you'll ever want...."

A staccato knock at the office door preceded the appearance of a young man who walked briskly toward Bruxton and stopped abruptly in front of him. "Mr. Bruxton?"

"Yeah—who the hell are you?"

The young man handed Bruxton a folded blue form. "Sir, you've been served."

Bruxton grabbed the form and opened it. "A subpoena?" He growled and made a menacing move toward the messenger. "Goddamit, get the hell outta here!" The young man left hurriedly. Bruxton read the print naming him in a divorce proceeding initiated by one Mary Elizabeth Bruxton. His eyes scanned the three sheets, and he frowned. The legal jargon initiated a penetrating ulcer-type pain, the kind he experienced after eating spicy Mexican or deep-fried foods. He slammed the form on his desk and grumbled as he reached into his desk drawer for two antacid tablets. "Shit. My attorneys can handle that bitch's shysters. She wants a fight? She'll get one."

Bonnie, cowed by Bruxton's burst of anger, sat primly, her brows furrowed, her eyes fearful. She fingered her new pearls nervously.

Pressing his lower chest in the midline with his fist, Bruxton emitted a long, low, rumbling belch that went unexcused. "Sweetie, let's forget about this crap and make plans for the evening." He picked up the phone and punched in a number. "Jim, I want you to pick up my bags at the estate, then meet us here at the office. Call the hotel and tell them to have my reefer stocked with liquor and good wine—not the crap with the hotel label. Then have the concierge make arrangements for two at that fancy French joint at seven. He listened a moment, then barked, "What do you mean that might present a problem? I don't give a shit what she wants! She's got her own cars: a Mercedes and a Jaguar. She can cram her fat ass into either one and drive herself—she doesn't need a chauffeur. Listen, I'm still your boss, and I'm paying the bills. Yeah, you can tell her I said so. You just follow my orders. What's that? No, for chrissake. Don't tell her I'm having dinner with—tell her a business associate. That's right, a business associate. It's none of her goddamn concern."

He slammed the phone down and looked at Bonnie, who returned his gaze with a timid, concerned smile—a smile that only served to arouse him further. He pushed his chair back, stood, then walked toward Bonnie, who sprang to her feet and moved to the back of her chair. "Don't run from me, Baby, I'm not going to hurt you. I just want to be close to you. Especially at a time like this."

He extended his wrist and looked at his watch. "Oh hell! It's five o'clock, closing time for us, but the stores are open late tonight. Go downstairs to one of those fancy-shmancy dress shops and buy yourself an outfit for tonight. Then you won't have to go home to change, and we'll have more time to enjoy the evening. Here's some money." He reached for his wallet in his back pocket and peeled off ten one hundred dollar bills.

Bonnie started to shake her head, but Bruxton grabbed her wrist and forced the money into her palm.

"Look, this is a legitimate business expense. I'll dictate some letters to you while we're in the hotel. Afterwards, we'll go to dinner and you can wear your new duds and pearls. We'll talk some personal stuff, then we'll talk about some business matters. That'll make it all kosher. Later, I'll take you home."

Bonnie backed away. Bruxton put up his hand to quell her concerns. "Call your folks and tell them you'll be detained, or if you prefer, I'll call...."

She interrupted. "No, no, I'll call."

14

Mary Bruxton held a cell phone to her ear and stopped in front of the dressing room mirror. She released the tie to her sheer robe, studied her partially nude form, and pouted. "It's seven o'clock. Are you still on the movie set? Yes, Darling, he's been served and he's out of the house except for a few remaining items that his chauffeur collects and brings to him. Oh sure, there'll be a court battle—you can count on that. The attorneys' fees will be staggering—can't be helped—he's as stubborn as he is conniving. My attorneys will plead incompatibility, spousal abuse, and rape—that's right, rape. More than once he's forced himself on me when I was ill and emotionally non-receptive—that and a lot of other charges I can't even begin to recall. The lawyers are convinced my case is gold-bonded.

"As far as our relationship—yours and mine—strictly platonic. You're a guest in our casita here. You go your way and vice versa. I'm sure you've been discreet. Nobody needs to know—not that it really matters. As far as the help here, they know nothing about our close relationship. My secretary and maid have been sworn to secrecy and threatened with eternal damnation. Anyway, enough talk. Get over here, and I mean pronto. I need you here desperately."

Less than an hour later, the doorbell to the Bruxton estate rang. Mary Bruxton, already downstairs, shouted "Never mind, Melinda. I'll get the door," Mary walked toward the entryway wearing a dark plum-colored, strapless gown. She paused at the mirror in the foyer to glance at her side view; she took a deep breath and sucked in her abdomen before opening the door. "Welcome, Cowboy." She curtsied. "Mi casa es su casa. Impressed? I learned that from Melinda twenty minutes ago."

"Señora, you look absolutely ravishing." Parma handed her a bouquet of roses.

"Gracias, mi amore." She tilted her head to look at his right hip then his left. "Did you bring your six shooters?"

"No, but I've got a loaded Howitzer ready to fire."

"Oh, you are bad, and I love it."

He stepped into the foyer, embraced her firmly and nuzzled her neck. She extended her head back and giggled while he dropped one hand and gently squeezed her buttocks.

"Naughty boy!" With mock objection, she slapped his hand. "Come, we'll have a drink and you can tell me all about your day in cowboy and Indian town. Did you do the scene where you make love to the unfaithful wife yet?"

"I'm saving all those good feelings for the one I really love." Frank spun her around then bent her backward as in an adagio movement and kissed her lips. She closed her eyes, then reached for his face to prolong the tender moment.

"Oh, that was delicious," she said. "Make any wish and it shall be granted."

"Love me tonight."

"That's just what I had in mind." She walked to the sofa, then motioned for him to sit beside her.

"Funny that you should have mentioned six-shooters a moment ago. My gun coach showed me how to fire a revolver and twirl it into a holster. He was impressed with my target practice too. Actually, I'm pretty good with my piece."

She raised one brow. "I can vouch for that."

Frank smiled, and headed for the bar where he mixed her vodka gimlet with the ease of a professional bartender, then poured his aged Scotch on the rocks into a tumbler. They toasted to everlasting love and devotion. After that, Frank sat quietly and stared into his glass.

Mary placed her drink on the cocktail table. "Frankie, why so quiet? What's troubling you?"

"I'll be through shooting the desert scenes next week."

Mary reached for his hand, her mien turned serious. "What will you do?" Before he could answer, she said, "Frank, you know I just can't bear the thought of you being away from me. I don't want you returning to Hollywood. You're a part of my life now."

He gave her a side-glance, a crooked smile, a cinematic ploy emblematic of old screen lovers who combined the look of wanting and pathos. "Mary, what am I going to do here? There aren't any more movies scheduled for the desert. Even this one was sort of a fluke."

"Stay here. Be my partner,. Be my manager. Help me with my charities. There are a thousand things we can do together."

"No, no. I love being with you, Baby, but I've got to do something on my own. I want to stay in the movie business—do some acting, directing, producing. Nothing gives me a rush like working on the set, unless of course it's being with you."

"Why don't *you* make a movie with a Palm Springs setting? You could direct, act, produce...."

"Mary, whoa! Are you aware of all the money involved in that?"

"Answer one question. Can you do it?"

"Well, yes, but...."

"Then start making plans."

15

The chauffeur, walking behind Bruxton and Bonnie, carried a lap top computer and a clothes bag into the hotel lobby. A bellhop hurried to relieve him.

Bruxton looked at his watch. "6:15. Jim, be ready to pick us up at 8:00. I'll phone you when we're ready. Park the car and grab a bite in the coffee shop." Bruxton, escorting Bonnie through the spacious lobby, was openly possessive. With his arm around her waist, he strutted for all to see. She was his trophy—a youthful beauty, arrayed in a couturier's black silk skirt and white ruffled silk blouse made more striking by the contrasting tone of her café-au-lait skin.

Although pleased with the attention of turning heads, Bonnie felt a certain bit of unease—a wave of insecurity; not knowing precisely what was expected of her. She was hoping that this second out-of-office meeting would not presage another dreadful event. She began to soliloquize in her head: Was he sincere when he said he would divorce his wife, then marry me? Do I really even want that? He's old enough to be my father! He's not particularly good-looking, and certainly not well mannered, but he's dreadfully wealthy. But I wonder...will I be able to live with myself if I....

Bruxton dropped his hand down to caress Bonnie's well-rounded buttocks, oblivious to the scene he was causing in the lobby. Bonnie allowed it, despite her continued inner struggles with herself. Maybe I should resist him until he gives me an engagement ring, she thought. Dad says that if I marry him, I'll be one of the wealthiest women in the country. That would please him. But, I must be honest; Bruxton is vulgar and shamefully coarse at times. I've seen the way he treats his wife. Would he ever treat me respectfully? Could I enter his complicated world of business, or would he shut me out? In the express elevator to the suite, Bruxton again placed his hand on Bonnie's rounded derrière. This time, without expression, she removed his hand and placed it at his side. The door to the suite was already open, and the bellhop was inside putting things away. The computer was on the desk, and the clothes bag was hung in the hall closet.

"Will there be anything else, sir?" The bellhop asked.

Bruxton shook his head and reached into his pocket. He handed the bellhop a ten-dollar bill. Bruxton walked away, then glanced back in time to see the bellhop smile at Bonnie. He gave her a thumbs-up sign.

Bruxton reddened. "Who the hell're you smiling at, buster? Huh? And what was that hand signal? Get your ass out of here, right now! Buddy, you just lost your job. I'll see to that."

Obsequious and apologetic, the bellhop walked backwards toward the door. "Sorry, Sir, I meant no disrespect."

"Get the hell out of here!" The bellhop exited the room, and Bruxton slammed the door after him. "The nerve of that punk, giving you the eye. I should've punched his face."

"I'm sure he meant no harm," Bonnie said. Bruxton's mercurial temper once again caused her concern, but his fiery outburst collapsed like his chameleon-like temperament, and he became immediately mellow again.

She sat at the desk and opened the computer. Bruxton approached from behind and placed his hands on her arms. She turned around and asked insouciantly, "Did you want to give me some dictation?"

"Yeah, yeah, sure. Well not at this very minute. Why don't we put the business aside for a while? I'll get us a couple drinks from the bar. What'll you have? A martini, a screw driver, a glass of wine?"

"Some sparkling water or a Coke would be fine."

"Well, I'm gonna have some bourbon and water, then I'm gonna shower." With a smarmy smile, he asked, "Want to join me?"

"Mr. Bruxton, really!"

"Suit yourself," he said, before heading in the direction of the bathroom.

That's it, she thought to herself. Enough of this going back and forth. She decided, finally, that she was simply not going to respond to his sexual entreaties. He made her feel cheap—as though she were only good for his bed and nothing else. Sure, the gifts were fine, but the sweet and tender romances she had known with some young men were missing. Bruxton was callous, and physically repulsive. Besides, it was that time of the month and she couldn't stand the embarrassment of being indelicate. If he forces himself on me, I'll just make him take me home, she thought to herself.

Humming, Bruxton emerged from the shower, toweled himself off, and reached for a terry cloth robe. He stopped at the mini bar to refill his tumbler with bourbon and water, stirred it with his finger, then, once again approached Bonnie, who was still seated at the desk. "Come on, Baby, let's enjoy a little smooch before we do any work." Bruxton took her by the hands and brought her to a standing position, then pulled her toward him.

He forcefully embraced her, letting his robe fall open, and then he kissed her, pushing his tongue into her mouth. It was all to no avail, though. His brusqueness, the rigidity of his erection, the smell of liquor, and the cigar on his breath, simply served to strengthen her newfound resolve. The man repulsed her. She forcefully pushed him away.

"You need to stop, Mr. Bruxton."

"Come on girlie. I already told you I wanna marry you. You can be a rich woman."

Mr. Bruxton, I can't...."

"Oh, you want to play rough? Okay, I like that game too." He grabbed her arms and threw her onto the bed, lifted the hem of her skirt and started to pull down her panties. His bull-like strength and clawing terrified her. She beat on his chest and attempted to knee his groin.

"I said stop, you animal!" she shouted.

Bruxton's red-faced smile turned to a seething leer. "Who the hell you calling 'animal'? I just spent five grand on that necklace, paid for your damn clothes, and you haven't even had a chance to see the big surprise that's waiting in that envelope I gave you. Now come on. I'm gonna get some sweet payment."

"Mr. Bruxton, You can take your damn gifts back as far as I'm concerned. Now get the hell off me!"

"Not until I get some pussy, girlie!"

"But I'm menstruating."

"That's okay, Baby, you can still satisfy me."

Get off!" She screamed and scratched his face. He grabbed her arms and straddled her. His anger mounted, his eyes reddened and bulged, his nostrils flared. He held her face and neck in a vise-like grip and forced her to take his erection into her mouth. She responded by biting down, then gagged. He yelled, "Jeezuz Christ! You bitch! He pulled backward reflexively, then leaned forward to slap her face, first with his palm, and then with the back of his hand.

Still not satisfied, Bruxton grabbed her swan-like neck and squeezed. Unable to breathe, she pleaded desperately. Terror filled her eyes, but he pressed even harder. Her complexion turned blue and her body fell limp.

Two muffled shots rang out! Bruxton's head jerked forward, then backwards. His hands fell to his sides. His upper body tilted forward and with increasing momentum his head struck the headboard with a thud. Bonnie's eyelids fluttered, she coughed in spasms then took a raspy breath. The lifeless, dead weight of Bruxton's body impaired her breathing. Mustering all her strength, she took a deep breath and heaved him off to the side. He tumbled to the floor. She lay motionless then, in shock, and in an incomprehensible fog. Touching her neck gingerly, she winced, reached down to pull up her panties and straighten her skirt. Rolling to the edge of the bed she opened and closed her eyes repeatedly until she could focus. Bruxton lay dead on the floor. His open eyes stared out of a stony-white face marred by two red scratches on his left cheek; his head lay in an expanding pool of blood, forming a crimson corona.

With heart thumping, she moved unsteadily off the bed, her rubbery legs barely supported her. She reached out for the phone on the dresser. The operator asked, "How may I help you? Hello? Hello?"

To add to her mounting fear and panic, Bonnie discovered she had no voice except for a guttural grunt, making her feel terribly isolated. She replaced the phone on the cradle quietly, then walked toward Bruxton's lifeless body and bent over it to cover his groin with his robe. The dreadful reality of what had just occurred was becoming clearer. She looked around the room wondering who had fired the shots? She entered into an emotional yin-yang. Whoever it was had probably saved her life, and for that she was grateful, but was the murderer still there? Was Bruxton the only target or was she next? Stealthily, she crept from room to room hoping not to find anyone, but obeying a fierce compulsion to look for the intruder. The last place to look for the shooter was the hall closet. She held her breath and cautiously opened the closet door, her skin prickled with fear and dreadful anticipation. She hoped to God no one was there. To her relief, only darkness and the hanging clothes bag faced her. With relief she shut the door quickly. There simply was no one else in the suite. Whoever killed

Bruxton had fled and closed the hall door behind them.

Glancing in the washroom mirror, Bonnie looked at her harried reflection—the disheveled hair, the smeared lipstick and the red irritation around her face and neck. Looking more closely, she discovered a spattering of blood on her left collar. She inverted the collar to conceal the spotting, and the altered appearance of the blouse seemed acceptable. She splashed water on her face and removed her smeared lipstick with a tissue and flushed it down the toilet. A grooming set consisting of a hairbrush, comb, and nail file placed on a hand towel was aligned next to the basin. She picked up the brush, ran it through her hair, then reapplied lipstick. Her thinking remained unsettled. Should she call the police and tell them what happened? No, she didn't even have a voice. Besides, they would link her to the murder and there would be too many questions. It was all too frightening and confusing. Maybe she should just leave. Yes, that would be the best solution. She'd leave and go home. Her dad would know what to do.

With a moistened washcloth, Bonnie ran to wipe the computer keyboard; next she reached for her drinking glass and wiped that as well. Then came the doorknobs. Did she touch anything else? She surveyed the bedroom and washroom, then jammed the damp washcloth in her purse.

Bonnie walked to the entry door, opened it, got the washcloth out again, and wiped the inside doorknob. Stepping into the hallway, she looked in both directions then wiped the outer doorknob as well, before depositing the washcloth back into her purse. Walking briskly to the elevator, she pushed the button, waited for the door to open, and stepped inside. She was grateful that the elevator was unoccupied. She breathed a bit more slowly, then looked down. A glance at her shoes, revealed a spot of blood on the right shoe tip. Quickly, she pulled the washcloth from her purse and wiped it. As she was about to put the cloth back in her purse, the elevator stopped; the door opened onto the lobby, and two people entered. She exited with the washcloth still in her hand. Hurrying to the hotel entrance, she stuffed the washcloth back into her purse, approached the valet and whispered hoarsely into his ear, "Cab."

16

The radio blared "Code 187—Springs Hotel, room 1226."
Detective Brad Oliver picked up the handset and
said "We're on our way...be there in ten minutes." In the
passenger seat, Detective Sergeant Mannheim reflexively
felt for his holster, then looked at his watch. "9:16. Sort of
early for our amigos to be wasting each other." Detective
Oliver ignored the comment.

Mannheim exhaled noisily, "Don't tell me I offended
you, Mr. Civil Rights Man-of-the-Year. In case you've
forgotten, at least seventy-five percent of the homicides in
this valley involve Hispanics."

Detective Brad Oliver shook his head. "Mannheim,
it's my opinion that you never quite got the gist of those
community sensitivity lectures for social awareness. You
remember, the ones on understanding cultural differences
among ethnic groups."

Mannheim, took another deep breath and sighed.
"Save the goddamned preachy, charm-school crap for your
rookie buddies. I've got no prejudices when it comes to
homicidal maniacs. I don't give a shit about their race, religion, gender preference or origin. They're all a bunch of
turds, and I don't have to apologize to you or anyone else
for my opinions. You got that, Buddy Boy?"

Detective Oliver, recently assigned to be Mannheim's

assistant on the Riverside County Homicide Division drove the Crown Victoria. He felt an urge to rebut Mannheim's acerbic comments but knew the effort would only aggravate the cynical detective. Even so, he couldn't resist one more verbal joust. "You want odds on the ethnicity of the murderer? You think this is just another killing between two hot-blooded peons?"

Mannheim turned slowly to look at his junior partner. "I didn't say that, buster. This is not *just* another killing. To me, murder is the shittiest crime, the lousiest insult to humanity, no matter who commits it. Don't ever speak of it flippantly." Oliver didn't respond to the obvious put-down.

The car stopped at the outer edge of the porte-cochere at the Springs Hotel. Both detectives walked past the valet who acknowledged their presence and backed away. Mannheim, his gaunt figure and head carried forward like a preying vulture, looked to either side and pointed to two parked Rancho Mirage squad cars in the shadows. "The boys beat us to it."

The hotel manager, a portly, balding man, standing near the reception desk, approached the detectives with quick short steps. "Can I assist you gentlemen? Are you looking for...?"

Mannheim interrupted. "Room 1226."

Walking briskly ahead of them, the manager led them to the express elevator for the hotel suites. "Mind if I come with you?"

Mannheim looked down at the two-eager-to-please man. "Thanks, anyway, but I'd prefer you didn't. There're probably too many people up there mucking up the crime scene already. Tell you what you can do. Get me the names of all the hotel personnel who came in contact with the victim tonight."

Yellow tape had been placed across the door, and a uniformed officer standing guard acknowledged them. "Evening, Sgt. Mannheim." He nodded toward Oliver then looked at his watch. "We arrived about five minutes ago. CSU should be on their way."

"Who called in the murder?" Oliver asked.

"The evening maid reported it to the manager—she's the one who turns down the beds and leaves chocolate mints." The officer followed the detectives inside.

Mannheim put on a pair of latex gloves, stood in the entry, then tried to open the locked door to the left. The officer said, "It's just the door to an adjoining suite."

"Find out if anyone occupied it." Mannheim opened the closet door to his right and inspected the hanging clothes. He patted the pockets of several pairs of pants and jackets. He walked further into the suite and confronted two officers. Upon seeing him, they abruptly stopped their conversation. They regarded the chief homicide detective deferentially: a humorless hard-ass with no tolerance for small talk or fucking-up. Mannheim acknowledged their presence with an off-hand two finger salute, then surveyed the room like an animal of prey, sniffing the air, listening to sounds and studying the surroundings. His eyes moved methodically from the floor, then over his right shoulder to the wall, up to the ceiling, then over his left shoulder until he scanned the entire room. Wrinkling his nose, he sniffed again. "Anyone here smoke?"

One of the officers said, "Yeah, I do. But not in here."

"Cigarette and gunpowder stink is still in this room." He walked toward the older of the two officers. "Do we have an ID on this guy?"

"We sure do. Went through his wallet—name's Peter Bruxton, *the* Peter Bruxton of Rancho Mirage, multi-millionaire and general pain in the ass."

Mannheim, leaning forward, hands in his back pockets looked from under his bushy brows. "What d'ya mean pain in the ass?"

"Well, we've gotten several domestic violence calls from his missus over the past two months—nothing of a serious nature, but he's been a major asshole every time we've been called out there."

Mannheim looked at the corpse and asked, "What the hell was he doing here, and who was he doing it with?"

"The manager said the suite was reserved for him. We don't know who was with him—yet. The bellhop who carried the laptop and a clothes bag gave a description of a gal—gorgeous with light tan skin, dark hair, white blouse, dark skirt, killer smile, about twenty to twenty-four years of age. Said he never saw her before."

"What's her name?" The officer shrugged.

"Front desk ought to have that information," Oliver said.

"As a matter of fact, they don't. The suite was in Bruxton's name. He could bring any guest to his room," the senior officer said.

Mannheim moved toward the rumpled bedding. He bent over the bedspread and used a pen to point to an irregular area of discoloration. "This guy either missed his mark or had a premature ejaculation." He kneeled next to the corpse and peeled back the terry cloth robe to look at the corpse's dependent side. "Lividity has set in." He studied the face. "Fresh scratches on his left cheek. Somebody put up a battle." Examining the genital area, he said, "There's blood on the tip of his pecker, several possibilities there." He asked Oliver to examine the laptop. "See if you can get anything from it."

Walking into the washroom, Mannheim sniffed then mumbled, "Expensive perfume or cologne. Maybe both." He looked at the shower stall, touched the toweling, then noted the sink top with the hairbrush, comb and nail file. He called out to no one in particular, "Here's some long, fine dark, hair strands on the brush, definitely not the victim's—probably a gal's."

A brilliant flash of light reflecting off the mirror startled him. He spun around. "Jee-zuz! Don't go sneaking up like that!" Two members of CSU had arrived and were taking photos. Mannheim ordered, "Take this hair brush and examine the strands. Get a Lumalite on that bedspread and check for blood and semen. Better yet, take the whole damn spread. Look around for spent cartridges."

"Mannheim, don't tell us what to do, for chrissake."

Annoyed by the CSU agent's lack of respect, Mannheim became more demanding. "Be sure to dust for prints and take the drinking glasses."

"Mannheim, you're a real pain in the ass."

"I've been called worse by really important people." He walked out of the washroom to look at the corpse again, his deep-set eyes staring, and his tongue poking his inner cheeks rhythmically.

"What're you thinking?" Oliver asked.

"I think someone got Bruxton while he was in the saddle." He rubbed the stubble on his narrow chin. He turned Bruxton's head to the side and pointed to the back of his head. "That, my friend, is damn good shooting. How exacting and professional can one get?"

"The work of a hired assassin?" Oliver asked.

Mannheim shrugged and nodded. "Could be. But why the hell in a hotel room?" He turned toward the senior officer. "What did you find in his pockets?"

"Some keys, credit cards, two hundred and fifty bucks in a wallet, room entry card...."

"Automobile keys?" Mannheim asked.

The officer thought for a second. "Come to think of it, I don't remember seeing any. Maybe he took a cab, or maybe the other party drove."

"Or the other party took Bruxton's car." Mannheim watched as the man and woman from the coroner's office entered the room with a gurney and prepared to remove the body. "Just a minute. Hand me the robe." Mannheim reached for the garment. The back of the collar had been blood-soaked. From the right front pocket of the robe he removed a brown plastic medicine container with an unmarked label. Several capsules rattled as he shook it. "What the hell is this?" He gave the container to the CSU officer who opened it, sniffed the contents then held one of the capsules to the light.

"Can't say for sure, but I believe it's Ecstasy. Happy hallucinations and fornications. This guy was a real sweetheart."

Glancing around the room once again, Mannheim asked, "Did we miss anything? Any shells lying around?"

Oliver shook his head. "I want to talk to the bell hop, then I'll stop at the front desk and see if they've got a license number on Bruxton's car. If his car is missing we'll put out an APB." Alone in the room, Mannheim walked slowly backward, canvassing the walls and the floor. Examining the carpeting, he bent over and picked up several glistening particles and put them in a small plastic bag. He retreated into the hallway and was startled when he bumped into a man wearing dark clothes and a cap with a visor. "Who the hell are you and what are you doing here?"

"I'm Mr. Bruxton's driver. He said he'd call about 8:00." He looked at his watch. "It's 9:15. Since I didn't hear from him, I got worried and came up to see what the delay was. What's going on?"

Mannheim studied the stranger, then became more conciliatory. "Sorry, your boss was shot."

"What? He's going to be all right, isn't he?"

" 'Fraid not. His wounds were fatal."

The driver backed away, dread and questioning filled his face. "You mean he's dead? What happened? Who did it?"

"He was shot. That's all we know."

"Jeezus, does Mrs. Bruxton know?"

"We're on our way to see her now. What time did you bring Bruxton here? Was anyone with him?"

"A young woman was with him. The three of us got here about 6:30."

Mannheim took notes. "Do you know anything about her, her name?"

"No." The chauffeur shook his head.

"Had you seen her before tonight?"

"Just once."

"Could you identify her?"

"Maybe. I'm not sure."

Mannheim got into his face. "Listen, Mr. Sphynx, I don't like one word answers that tell me nothing. Now again, who's the girl who came here with Bruxton?"

The chauffeur backed away. "I—I don't know. She was new. I think she worked for Mr. Bruxton. A secretary, maybe."

Mannheim hiked his shoulders. "You're not planning to leave town are you?"

"No—I mean, no, I'm not."

"Good, 'cause we might have a few questions for you. Now tell me how to get to the Bruxton place—in more than one syllable."

Oliver, behind the wheel, notified the dispatcher where they were headed.

"What did you learn from the bell hop?" Mannheim asked.

"Not much, except that Bruxton was a loud-mouthed, demanding SOB, who was disliked by just about everyone here at the hotel. He took women to the room on a regular basis and even propositioned some of the staff."

"Why doesn't that surprise me? That sonofabitch had too goddamned much money and thought his pecker needed constant entertainment. Well, his pecker was entertained for the last time tonight."

He looked through the windshield with a dour expression and grumbled, "Let's visit the new widow and give her the good news. This is the worst part of the job. You get to do the next one without me."

The serpentine road in the foothills off Highway 111 was outlined with Malibu-type lamps at fifty-foot intervals. The natural desert flora changed to organized plantings with base-lighted palms rising high like elegant sentinels. The massive estate perched on a hilltop was lit up like the Alhambra with multiple Moorish arches bordering a perimeter walkway. Mannheim came forward in his seat. "Christ, would you look at that spread? It's bigger than city hall and a helluva lot more impressive. What the hell do they do in those ritzy surroundings? Do you think the fucking is any better?"

Oliver shrugged and smiled tolerantly.

17

Mannheim flipped open his leather-encased badge when Mary Bruxton, in a white terry cloth robe with matching turban and slippers, appeared at the door. "Mrs. Bruxton? I'm Detective Sergeant Mannheim, and this is Detective Oliver. Sorry to disturb you at this hour. Mind if we come in?"

Mary clutched the top of her robe and stood apprehensive in the doorway. "What's the trouble Officer?"

Standing behind her with his hands on her shoulders and also wearing a robe, Frank Parma asked, "Just what seems to be the trouble here, Officer?" The stilted dialogue was right out of a class B, forties' film noir. Mannheim made no response. He took a step forward until Mary stepped back and was compelled to say, "Come in." She directed the detectives into the large room then pointed to two club chairs opposite a sofa where she and Parma sat. She sat on the edge of the seat, tugged at the lapels of her robe and studied Mannheim's impassive expression. She became aware of what she and Parma were wearing, and said hurriedly, "Excuse our appearance. We just finished a swim. Is this about Deena? Did anything happen to her?" Mary's eyes begged for a merciful response.

"This is regarding your husband, Ma'am." Mannheim hesitated, then cleared his throat. Uttering these words after so many years still made him uncomfortable. "He's been murdered."

Mary gasped and put her hands to her mouth, then cried, "Oh, no!" Frank slid closer and placed an arm around her shoulders.

"Where did this happen? How did it happen?" Frank's questions sounded flat.

Mannheim gave a brief description of the murder scene, with Oliver adding details.

Mary's head was bowed; her face held in her hands.

"Would you know anything about the woman he was with?" Mannheim asked.

Mary shook her head, then turned away. Her initial shock turned to resentment. "No. We were separated. I recently filed for divorce. As for women, my husband was always finding someone to...." She broke off her statement.

Mannheim studied her face. "You're about to say?"

Mary raised her head. "Perhaps it was his new secretary, that Moluccan girl. Have you talked with her?"

"Not yet, but we will. Mrs. Bruxton, do you know why anyone would want to kill your husband?"

Mary squared her shoulders then looked into her lap as she twisted a Kleenex. "Detective, that man was my husband for twenty-five years. I can tell you that he was liked by a few, but utterly detested by many more. I'm sorry to say that, but there are plenty of people who would probably celebrate at his funeral."

Mannheim took a spiral notebook from the inner pocket of his jacket. "Can you name a few of those people?"

Parma sat up. "Is all this necessary now, Detective? You can see Mrs. Bruxton is overwrought. Can't this wait until morning?"

Mary patted the back of Frank's hand. "I'm all right now, dear." She appeared composed and spoke confidently. "I can't possibly know everyone who disliked him, he managed to offend so many, but I do know a few who harbored particularly bitter feelings. I'm not sure how valid my list would be."

"Let *us* make that decision, ma'am."

Mary hesitated. "I don't want to incriminate anyone unjustly...."

"Don't concern yourself with that. We have to check out all suspects."

She took a deep breath before continuing. "There's Larry Kurtz, his partner. And Larry's wife, Lucy. Both have had festering grievances over the years. Then there's Oscar Brazilowicz, a union boss. He resented my husband's opposition to his son marrying our daughter."

"Would you spell that name please?"

"That's Brazil as in Brazil nuts, and the rest you'll have to fill in. Then there's that Southern Baptist Minister, Reverend Bissell, I think. He's the father of my husband's former secretary. She accused my husband of fathering her child. Her father, the Reverend Bissell, pulled a gun on my husband. I think he's still in custody." She touched her fourth finger. "Then there's Amon Eagle Feather, an American Indian, who believes his tribe was swindled out of forest land by my husband." She looked at the ceiling and heaved a sigh. "There's Susan Bird Song, my husband's sister-in-law, who's never forgiven him for mistreating her husband, Sven. Sven's Peter's younger brother. And I'm sure there are others."

Oliver looked at his watch, 11:15. He stifled a yawn. "Mrs. Bruxton it's late, and we've taken more of your time than we intended. If you don't mind, we'll come back in a day or so." He stood and motioned with his head for Mannheim to follow. Mannheim cast a baleful eye at his partner, but joined him in walking to the door. He paused to look at the wall-mounted photos in the foyer.

"Where is he? Can I see him?" Mary asked as she followed the detectives to the door.

"At the coroner's. They'll want you to make a positive

ID in the morning," Mannheim said; he turned and headed back down the walkway to the car. Oliver followed.

In the car, Oliver glanced at Mannheim's pouty expression. "Okay, Boss Man, what's eating you now?"

"Listen, Mr. Congeniality, if you hadn't been so damned quick about letting them off the hook...."

Oliver interrupted, "Mannheim, you may be able to function on four hours of sleep, I can't. I'm barely able to drag my ass around."

Mannheim uncharacteristically did not argue; he slumped in his seat and remained silent for a moment, then croaked, "Did you notice that studio promo still in the foyer? The one showing a cowboy with a bulge in his crotch, padded shoulders and hands resting on two holstered revolvers?"

"I saw it, but didn't pay much attention. Why?"

"Oh, ye who look but see not.... And what about the photo of the dame with the shotgun, Miss Skeet Shooting Champion of 2010?"

Oliver rolled his eyes upward. "Okay Monsieur Poirot, what's your point?"

"That was the widow Bruxton and her tinsel-town cowboy."

"So what?"

"So either one of them might be able to shoot well enough to put two rounds into the back of a skull at twenty feet. Kinda like pickin' off a melon settin' on a fence post."

"Wait a minute. You're not thinking Mrs. Bruxton and Parma are suspects, are you? How would either one of them get into the hotel room? And what about the time factor?"

"Okay, Junior, let's start with the time factor. The murder took place some time between six-thirty and eight-thirty. That would have given either one of them plenty of time to whack Bruxton and get back to the big house. As for motive, Mary Bruxton admitted that she'd recently filed for divorce. How convenient for her if the guy is wasted. Do you know how long that case could have been hung up in the courts? Years. With Bruxton out of the way she gets her money ASAP. As for gaining access to the hotel suite—a piece of cake. Cleaning and maintenance crews have keys. A little persuasion with a sawbuck or two and bingo! Any other questions?"

Oliver shook his head. "Uh, uh. You make it sound too easy. Forgive me, if I don't buy that. A bribe brings in a third unpredictable player." He looked at Mannheim who gave no response. "What did you think about the widow's reaction when you told her about the murder?"

Mannheim, his arms folded across his chest and his eyes closed, said, "Her first response showed surprise, but there was no great outpouring of grief. Frankly, I think she was just relieved to know the news didn't concern her daughter. Let's face it. Bruxton's death probably answered her prayers as well as those of a few other folks."

"What did you think about her friend's reaction?" Oliver turned to look at Mannheim whose eyes remained closed.

"That cowboy? His response showed about as much excitement as a eunuch's limp dick. With Bruxton out of the way, he can be sure of *mucho dinero* from the cash cow widow."

"So you think one or both of them could be in on the murder?"

Mannheim mumbled, "Why not? They had cause, and there was plenty of opportunity."

At Sunrise the following morning, Mary punched in Deena's phone number. Even as she held the phone, she anticipated her daughter's response when she learned of Bruxton's murder. The phone rang twice, then Deena picked up.

"Deena, dear, are you sitting down? Good." Mary's voice became soft and delayed. "I have some sorry news, dear, and there's just no easy way to tell you this. Deena, your father was murdered last night." Mary jerked the phone from her ear as Deena's shrill cry pierced through the earpiece. "Are you all right?" Mary waited until the loud sobbing subsided.

"No, Darling, the killer has not been identified. It will be just a matter of time.... It happened in his hotel suite.... Deena, I can't be more explicit than that...I simply don't know.... Your father was, well, you know he's had a few dalliances. Yes, Dear, I forgive him. I'm going to the morgue to identify...no, Dear, there's hardly a chance of mistaken identity.... Yes, of course, there'll be a memorial service.... He loved you dearly. I'm sure the minister will be discreet. When he finishes the eulogy, we'll all be proud of your father."

Mary replaced the phone on its cradle then looked upward and declared to her spirit, "Forgive me for I lie without shame and with malice."

18

The recorded sounds of Sinatra provided the background music for the leisurely breakfast Josh and Maggie were enjoying Saturday morning. At the station break, the announcer said, "We are saddened to report the loss of one of the Valley's most prominent citizens and a benefactor to this broadcast station. Mr. Peter Bruxton of Rancho Mirage was murdered last night at the Springs Hotel. Details of the killing have not been released...."

Maggie dropped her toast and gaped at the radio. "Josh, did you hear that?"

"Oh, Christ! I'll call Mary. She may need help." He grabbed his cell phone and punched in Mary's number.

"Mrs. Bruxton, please. This is Dr. Harrington. Yes, I'll wait."

While he waited, Josh reflected on those early years when Peter and Mary had been happily married, and the four of them were friends who found so much to laugh over.

"Mary, we just heard. We're in shock. Are you all right? Is there anything I can do?" He looked at his watch. "Yes certainly, I'll pick you up at nine-thirty."

Mary, in a black pants suit, met Josh at the estate entryway. Her eyes were ringed with dark circles and she held tissue in her hand. Without makeup, and with little sleep, she appeared haggard and suddenly older. Josh reached his arms out, and Mary embraced him. She smiled wistfully and held onto his embrace, firmly resting her head on his shoulder. "Thank you for coming, you dear man. I would not have troubled you, but Frank and I were up most of the night. He had to be at the movie lot at six, and I insisted that he go. As luck would have it, Jim Keyes, the chauffeur, left this morning. He said he had to attend his mother's funeral in L.A. Said she'd died suddenly just two days ago. He left word at the police department that he would be gone several days. I could have taken Melinda and driven myself to the coroner's, but I'm so grateful to have your shoulder to lean on."

Josh hurried to open the passenger door of the SUV. She patted his cheek. "If ever you get tired of doctoring, I'll be happy to hire you as my personal chauffeur."

"That might be more work than what I'm doing now."

Mary reached over and placed her hand on his. "Don't believe that for a minute. Although I'm quite fond of Jim Keyes, and his services are quite convenient, I can tell you that he has a great deal of free time around here."

"Why do you keep him around?"

"Oh, originally, Peter kept him on the job for reasons I never fully understood. When I asked Peter why he kept him on the payroll, he said he needed Jim—simple as that. Once when I insisted on a more reasonable answer, Peter threw a fit. From that time on I made no further mention of it, and over time, I actually developed quite a fondness for Jim."

The small waiting room at the coroner's building in Indio was empty when Mary and Josh entered. The secretary recognized Mary from her photographs in the local newspapers, and especially from the article in the morning edition, which featured archival photos of the Bruxtons taken at various social and charitable functions. "I'm terribly sorry, Mrs. Bruxton," she said softly. Josh handed her his card and told her that they had come to identify the body. After several minutes, the coroner, Dr. James Schmitz, weary and unsmiling, emerged in a white lab coat. He made some perfunctory comments to Mary about her loss, then led them to the morgue.

Mary's dreaded anticipation of seeing the corpse grew as they passed into the stark whiteness of the morgue with its strong smell of disinfectant. The cold stainless steel dissection tables made her shiver and hold onto Josh's arm firmly. To add to her angst, she glanced at one autopsy table where the naked corpse of an emaciated woman lay. The corpse's sallow face, sunken abdomen, and the stick-thin extremities covered by skin that hung like crepe made Mary turn away.

Dr. Schmitz hurriedly draped the corpse, then walked briskly toward a bank of steel lockers with vault-like doors. He read the name on one door, then asked Mary and Josh to stand to either side as he turned and pulled the handle. The door to the dark chamber opened, emitting a slight odor of decomposing tissue. He tugged at the sliding carriage until the corpse covered with a gray cloth slid slowly forward.

Mary's heart hammered; her eyes widened as Dr. Schmitz uncovered the head and torso. Looking down, Mary shook her head in disbelief. The corpse's facial features had been distorted by swelling and blue discoloration. The head had been shaved, and the baldness made more striking by coarse black sutures that closed a circumferential incision like a crown of thorns. The bloated face combined with the odor of early tissue putrefaction and disinfectant made Mary's legs tremble. Josh placed his arm around her waist to steady her. She leaned against him, nodded and whispered hoarsely, "Oh, God, that's him."

Dr. Schmitz covered the corpse and slid it back into

place. Mary, with Josh's support, followed the coroner to his office just beyond the morgue. There she signed papers verifying the identity of her husband's corpse. The coroner offered her a glass of water. She refused.

Mary sat and stared blankly ahead. Dr. Schmitz said he'd like a word with Dr. Harrington and asked Mary to excuse them. They walked out of the office and returned to the morgue. Dr. Schmitz asked his diener to place the Bruxton skull x-rays on the viewing screen.

"I came in early this morning at the request of *hizzoner*, the governor, to conduct this autopsy. As you know, the governor and Bruxton were buddies, and the governor wanted this done so that funeral services could be held before his scheduled trip to Europe. As a courtesy to the family, the governor was going to deliver the eulogy since Bruxton had been a major contributor to his campaign. I had to examine the brain and assess the damage. The tissue was badly assaulted. Hemorrhage and destruction caused instant death, no mystery there. What I found of enormous interest, was a berry aneurysm in the circle of Willis, and even more remarkable, was the fact that it had ruptured. That, in itself, as you know, would have caused immediate death."

Josh shook his head. "I'll be damned."

"There's something else of interest which I didn't want to mention in front of Mrs. Bruxton."

Just at that moment, the conversation was interrupted as Mary Bruxton walked into the morgue, and, with a pained expression, said "Josh, would you take me home? My back is killing me."

"Sure Mary. Excuse us Dr. Schmitz. I need to take Mrs. Bruxton home."

"Certainly." Replied the Coroner.

As Josh and Mary were about to leave the building through the waiting room, they saw Detectives Mannheim and Oliver chatting with the secretary.

Seeing Josh and Mary, Mannheim said, "Mrs. Bruxton, please accept my condolences again. You're here to identify your husband's body?"

Mary nodded and turned away, not wanting to make conversation. She walked toward the door.

"Well, well, we meet again Doc." Mannheim smiled sardonically at Josh. "Doing a little forensic research?

Mannheim held Josh's arm to keep him from leaving and whispered in his ear, "You'll be sure to let me know when you solve this murder, won't you?"

In the SUV, Mary looked at Josh. "May I ask what you and Dr. Schmitz discussed?"

Josh thought there was no reason for her not to know. "Aside from the bullet wounds that caused Peter's death, there was an aneurysm in the brain that had ruptured. That, too, would have caused instant death."

Mary bit her lower lip.

Josh looked at her as the color drained from her face. "Are you all right Mary?"

She whispered, "Yes. I'm all right."

During the drive back to Mary's estate on the winding, switch-back road, Mary asked Josh to slow down on the curves as the rolling motion was aggravating her low back pain.

"I'm climbing into bed as soon as I get back. Do you have an injection you could give me? Something stronger than those anti-inflammatory pills to relieve this damn pain?"

"I have something in my medical bag that should give you relief. I'll see you in your bedroom."

"That's the best offer I've had today." Mary smiled, then grimaced with pain as she exited the vehicle. With Josh's support, she walked slowly into the house and was greeted by her personal assistant, Melinda. Josh returned to his SUV to get his bag, then stopped briefly to call his office.

When he finished, he came up to the door and knocked. The Bruxton's maid answered.

"She's up in her room, Dr. Harrington. You go on up."

"Thank you." He turned to the staircase and made his way up to Mary Bruxton's bedroom.

Inside, Mary Bruxton lay on her four-poster bed. Her lacy, see-through nightgown left little to the imagination, but Mary seemed quite unconcerned with modesty. Her assistant, Melinda, stood nearby. Josh reached into his medical bag. "Okay, Mary. Sunny side up, please."

Melinda turned to leave, but Josh reached out and held her forearm. "Please stay; I'll need your help."

Truth is, he didn't need her help, but he also didn't want to run the risk of creating gossip among the domestics. Melinda helped the complaining Mary turn on her abdomen and lifted her gown to expose a well-contoured buttocks. After putting on sterile gloves, Josh felt for a tender spot over the left sacroiliac joint. He painted the area with an antiseptic solution and injected a local anesthetic followed by a steroid solution. He patted her derriere, and said, "That ought to give you some relief. Have Melinda place warm, moist compresses on your back every three hours and continue with the muscle-relaxant and anti-inflammatory drugs. I'll call you, and if you're no better in three days, we'll hospitalize you in that fancy suite that bears your name."

19

The detectives were escorted into the autopsy room by the coroner's diener, although Mannheim didn't need his guidance. He had been there many times and was on a first-name basis with the coroner, Dr. Jim Schmitz. They approached the coroner, who was wearing a white rubberized apron flecked with blood, as he was performing an autopsy on a female corpse. Schmitz looked up and saw the detectives. The stump of an unlit cigar distorted the side of his mouth, making his speech sound like a growl, "You guys here to help or kibbitz? If you'd been here twenty minutes earlier when Mrs. Bruxton and Dr. Harrington were here, you'd have saved me time." Having voiced his annoyance, he continued, "All right, tell me what you know about the murder, and I'll tell you what I know."

Mannheim and Oliver alternately gave their impressions of what had occurred in the hotel room. Their descriptions of the circumstances made little noticeable impression on the coroner who was continuing his autopsy; at the moment, examining the thoracic contents of the corpse. As the detectives watched, he reached into the chest cavity and elevated the lower part of the fist-sized heart with his left hand. With his right hand, he started to sever its attachments to the aorta, vena cava, and pulmonary vessels. He called out the names of the structures as though lecturing to a class of medical students, although in reality he was dictating his findings to an overhead mike.

"No gross evidence of recent or old coronary artery disease, no ischemic involvement, cardiac muscle tissue is grossly normal in appearance and consistency...." He cut into the left auricle when Mannheim raised his right index finger.

"Jim, excuse me, but could you take a moment to tell us about the Bruxton case? You know, the bullets in the head case?"

Dr. Schmitz placed the heart on a scale and turned to the detectives. "And here I thought you guys came in to learn post-mortem anatomy."

"Some time when we have an extra hour, you can teach us, but right now we've got a murder to solve."

Dr. Schmitz put his dissecting instruments down and said, "Okay, I'll put his skull x-rays on the view box." On the wall mounted x-ray screen, he snapped four x-rays into place. Schmitz with an elongated probe pointed to two bullets lodged near the front of the skull. "The bullets pierced the occipital area back here and carried small fragments of bone into the interior of the brain. The bullets disrupted tissue in the occipital lobe, corpus callosum and ..."

"Hold it, Doc." Mannheim said. "I don't know what you're talking about. Do you have the actual bullets? We need them."

The coroner continued his lecture. "Upon opening the skull, I divided the cerebral hemispheres to locate two foreign objects, bullets, which came close to the inner diplöe of the skull, that is, the inner layer of bone next to the forehead." He nodded in the direction of the instrument table. "The bullets are over there."

"Can we have them, Doc?"

"Take them, but sign the forms." He returned to the autopsy table and continued his dissecting without looking up and said, "I'm not a ballistics expert, but you can see the bullets are .22 caliber. From the trajectory in the brain, the missiles were fired on a parallel course. In other words, the gun was held at about the same level as the victim's head."

"Meaning?" Oliver asked.

"The killer was not crouching and shooting upwards. He may have been ten to fifteen feet behind the victim, but he was directly behind, not to the right and not to the left." Schmitz put the scalpel down and asked, "What was the victim doing just before he was shot?"

"I'm pretty sure he was straddling some broad on the bed," Mannheim said.

The coroner stopped his dissection and walked to the stainless steel vault, opened it, and pulled the sliding drawer containing the Bruxton corpse forward. He uncovered the body to a level below the scrotum, lifted the head of the flaccid penis and pulled it upward to expose the entire shaft. "Come closer. Look at the skin behind the head." He released the organ and walked to a side table where he picked up a magnifying glass and gave it to Mannheim. He reached for a floor lamp, directing the rays to the stretched penile shaft. "What d'ya see Hawkshaw?"

Mannheim stared through the glass, adjusted the focal point, then looked up at the coroner. "Teeth marks?"

"Bingo!" the coroner declared.

"But this didn't kill him." Mannheim said. "The bullets did. Right?"

The coroner, biting on his cigar stump, waited a moment before answering. "Maybe."

Both detectives stared at him. Mannheim asked, "What the hell is that supposed to mean?"

"There's a matter of a ruptured brain aneurysm that may have been just as lethal."

"Oh, shit, Jim. Don't fuck up these muddy waters any more than they already are," Mannheim said.

"I just report what I find and try to come to an intelligent conclusion."

Mannheim put his face close to Schmitz. "The cause of

death resulted from the gunshot wounds. Right?"

When Schmitz didn't answer immediately and walked away, Mannheim persisted. "Yes or no?"

Without looking at either detective, Schmitz said, "Most probably."

20

At home, Maggie and Josh were discussing the details of his trip with Mary to the coroner. "Did the coroner show you the bullets in the brain? There couldn't have been any question about the cause of death."

"This may be academic or coincidental or whatever you want to call it, but Bruxton had a ruptured brain aneurysm which of itself would have been fatal."

"Oh my God, so what killed him?"

"Take your choice. But, I'm sure the prosecution will say, if they ever find the suspect, that the gunshots would have been fatal. There was the undeniable intent to commit murder."

"Does Mary know all this?"

"Yes, I told her."

"How did she react?"

"Actually, she fell silent after I told her. I really don't know what she was feeling or thinking. At the morgue she developed back pain, which became severe. When we returned to her home, I gave her an injection which should have given her relief."

"Considering her animosity toward Bruxton, I wonder if Mary felt a sense of relief after his death?"

"Maybe. Maybe not. It's been my experience that when a spouse dies, even when there's been a contentious relationship, the loss evokes an outpouring of grief. That may not make sense on the surface, but it's often the case. Whether it's guilt or loss of companionship, or both, it's hard to say. Occasionally, the bereaved may develop physical symptoms, a type of conversion hysteria."

"Do you think Mary's low back symptoms will be aggravated by this?"

"I don't know. When I examined her, I didn't find anything suggesting actual nerve root involvement, that is sciatica; however, one of the sacroiliac joints was tender."

"So what does she have?"

"Have you ever heard of *low back honeymoon syndrome?*"

Maggie looked askance and put her hands on her hips. "Really! In all my years of nursing, I never heard of *that* diagnosis. Are you sure you didn't just create that term?"

"No, I swear it. That diagnosis probably can't be found in any textbook, either. Years ago, shortly after Sally and I married, when I was an intern, I reported to the outpatient clinic with low back pain. An orthopedic surgeon with a number of students at his side, examined me, asked a few questions then told me to let up on the frequency and intensity."

"The frequency and intensity of what?"

"Maggie, you can't be that naïve. I made the mistake of asking the doctor for a diagnosis. He said, 'Son, you're suffering from *low back honeymoon syndrome.*' Those were his exact words, I swear, and the students roared."

Maggie looked at Josh suspiciously and asked, "We never suffered those symptoms, did we? At least I didn't."

"I never complained to you, but shortly after our marriage, I treated my own aching back."

21

Oliver walked into Mannheim's office with a cup of coffee and a copy of the *Daily Desert Times*. "Did you see this morning's paper?"

"I try to avoid that rag. What do those wanna-be reporters in Palm Springs have to say?" He cleared enough clutter on his desk for Oliver to spread the front page. The headline blared, *Prominent Rancho Mirage Millionaire Murdered*. The story in the right hand column read: *Attractive Mystery Woman to be Questioned In Clandestine Affair at Local Hotel*.

Mannheim looked at Oliver. "Who the hell's going to question her? Are you?"

"Hell, no. With four hours of sleep and driving you around all day and night, listening to your endless carping, I don't have time for that."

"Don't go bitching to me, Buddy Boy. You volunteered for this job, remember?" Mannheim flicked his hand contemptuously at the newspaper. "You can't believe the garbage they write. What those bastards don't know, they make up."

"How'd they get news about the woman?" Oliver asked.

"Probably some bird at the hotel kept singing while a snooping reporter peeled off a few Andy Jacksons. Fact and fiction get blurred during those transactions. The more the money is flashed, the more the bullshit is piled on."

The phone rang. "Mannheim here." In a deliberate monotone, he said, "Well, well, if it isn't my friendly enemy, the legal adviser to those falsely accused, and the upholder of habeas corpus. What guilty slob are you defending that's gonna aggravate my hemorrhoids?" While listening, he looked with resignation at Oliver. "Jeez-uz, she didn't waste any time finding you, did she? Tell me counselor, and don't give me any bullshit, is she implicated in this murder?" Mannheim listened, nodded slowly, then closed his eyes. "Of course she's not. I don't know why I even bothered to ask." He extended his wrist and looked at his watch. "Yeah, bring her in now, and we'll go over a few things."

Mannheim replaced the phone on its cradle. "That was Farquaahr; he's bringing in his new client—Bonnie Ouvray."

The rotund attorney barged into Mannheim's office like a fawning, pre-election politician extending a glad hand that Mannheim accepted reluctantly. Facing each other, there could not have been another two who better exemplified the extremes of adult male morphology. Mannheim, the essential ectomorph, over six feet tall, lean, lanky and loose-jointed, exhibited all the sartorial splendor of a weathered scarecrow.

Farquaahr, at about five feet six, the classic endomorph, had belly fat spilling over his belt line. Like Mannheim, he too, had ill-fitting clothing that concealed a seriously out of condition body. A dated seersucker jacket remained unbuttoned over his bay window, and his thick, foreshortened neck and multiple chins did not permit the buttoning of his shirt collar. A narrow tie, reminiscent of a bygone style, rested on a shirt straining at each button.

"Mannheim, you hawk-faced son of an ugly harlot, we meet once again in these illustrious surroundings magnanimously sponsored by the charitable citizens of Riverside

County. Yes, the charitable, but obviously undemanding citizens of Riverside County."

Mannheim sneered at the obese Farquaahr. "What scheming bullshit are you peddling? If your client is guilty of murder, or was complicit, and you're concealing evidence, we'll fry your fat ass, just so that you know where our sentiments are."

"My, my. And since when have you been granted prosecutorial privileges, my rancorous friend?"

"We just want to ask your client a few questions. Don't see any reason why you had to accompany her if she's innocent." Mannheim already seated, pointed to a chair on the other side of his desk for Farquaahr.

"Before she comes in," Farquaahr said, leaning on the desk, "I want you to know she's a fragile, sensitive young woman who might become quite emotional. Just being here, in police headquarters, frightens her. Frankly, I believe she's terribly naïve, and this dreadful event has caused great psychological trauma, yes, great psychological trauma. What is more, I can state without fear of contradiction, that she had no inkling as to the evil intent of that man Bruxton. He simply lured her into that hotel room and proceeded to try to have his way with her." Farquaahr pushed back in his chair, apparently pleased with his brief analysis of events. "Getting murdered while molesting an innocent girl—well, there's an element of social justice there. Wouldn't you say?"

"Farquaahr, give it a rest. Stop bullshitting me with your preemptive gobble-de-gook. We have a few questions to ask. Do me a favor and don't interfere."

"Mannheim, you are by any conceivable accounting, the most disrespectful person I've ever had the displeasure of knowing. You are the epitome of...."

"Okay, okay." Mannheim stood and waved his hand. "Just let us do our job." He pushed the intercom button. "Detective Oliver, bring in Ms. Ouvray."

Both men turned toward the door as Bonnie Ouvray walked in haltingly. She surveyed the dismal quarters, then searched Mannheim's eyes, hoping for a sign of understanding. Walking behind her, Detective Oliver nudged her elbow gently forward.

Surprised by the elegant appearance of the attractive, well-dressed young woman, Mannheim directed her to sit next to Farquaahr on the opposite side of his desk. His eyes encompassed her exotic face, her comely figure, her bust line, the roundness of her buttocks and her shapely long legs. "No need to be frightened, Miss. We're just going to ask a few questions." He looked at his note pad briefly, then fixed his sights on her again. "Can you tell me why you went with Mr. Bruxton to the Springs Hotel the day he was murdered?"

She adjusted to the straight-back wooden chair, then pulled the hem of her charcoal gray skirt over her knees and folded her hands in her lap. She began tentatively. "He, that is, Mr. Bruxton, asked me to accompany him to a board meeting."

Mannheim raised his brow and tilted his head. "Really? A board meeting in his hotel suite?"

"No, sir. He said he needed a change of clothes and had to have a drink before the meeting."

"I see, but why was it necessary for *you* to accompany him to his suite?" Mannheim could hardly conceal his cynicism.

"He said he needed me to get information from the computer before he went to the meeting."

He glanced at his notes. "Did Bruxton ever ask you to his hotel suite before?"

Farquaahr interrupted and pointed excitedly at Mannheim. "What has any of this to do with my client's involvement in the murder?"

Mannheim cast a stony gaze at Farquaahr, then shifted it to the young woman. "Please answer the question."

She hesitated. "No, he never asked me to his suite before."

Mannheim made another notation. "How long had you worked for Mr. Bruxton?"

"Less than one month."

"Where did you work before?"

"I had a number of part-time jobs: sales and cashiering at Macy's, I was a waitress at I Hop, and of course, I attended business college three nights a week."

"Do you have a boyfriend?"

"I beg your pardon?"

"One who might have been jealous about you being with Bruxton?"

She shook her head. "No, sir." She looked at Farquaahr, who nodded approval.

"Was there anyone other than you and Bruxton in that room?"

"Not that I knew of. Certainly not when we arrived."

Mannheim laced his fingers behind his head and leaned back. "Do you own a gun?"

Bonnie looked at Farquaahr again for advice. He nodded, and said, "Answer him truthfully, my dear."

"I have a .38 caliber Smith and Wesson that my daddy gave me on my sixteenth birthday."

"Did you have it with you at the time of the murder?"

"No, sir."

"Bring it in to us tomorrow." He made another notation. "I'm going to ask a few more questions, and I want you to tell us everything, just as it happened. Did Bruxton rape you?"

She lowered her head and spoke softly, "He tried."

"Did he succeed?"

"No."

"Tell us what happened just before his murder. Don't omit any details. It's all very important."

Bonnie swallowed, cleared her throat and coughed nervously. "I was sitting at the computer posting figures when Mr. Bruxton came out of the shower. He walked up behind me wearing a terry cloth robe."

"What were you wearing?"

"I was fully clothed. I wore a white satin blouse and a black silk skirt."

"Go on."

Tears welled; she bit her lower lip and hesitated before responding. "He leaned over and put his hands on me."

"Put his hands where?"

"On my breasts. That frightened me terribly. I jumped up and faced him. He had a kind of crazy smile, and his robe was open."

"You mean he was exposed?" Mannheim asked.

"Yes, and he had an...."

"An erection?"

"Yes. He grabbed my hand and forced me to touch it." She hesitated again.

"Please, go on."

"When I pushed him away, he said, 'So, you want to play?' He threw me on the bed and tore at my blouse and started to lift my skirt. He straddled me. I begged him to leave me alone. I cried and told him I was menstruating, but that didn't stop him. He said there were other ways to satisfy him." She hesitated then started to sob openly.

Mannheim reached into a Kleenex box on his desk and handed her a tissue. "You're doing fine. Please go on."

She swallowed and sniffed. "He grabbed my face and my neck until I could hardly breathe. He tried to put his— thing in my mouth."

"So he forced oral sex?"

Farquaahr jumped up. "Where are you going with this questioning? I don't think it is at all germane. No, not at all germane. Can't you be more circumspect; show a little more propriety?"

Mannheim ignored the attorney's pique. "Please answer the question Ms. Ouvray. Did you have oral sex?"

She continued to stare into her lap. "No. After I resisted him, he seemed to go crazy; he slapped me across the face." She became more animated as she attempted to recall the details. "He started to strangle me. I couldn't breathe. I thought for sure I was going to die. I prayed for my life. Then I heard two soft pops. Suddenly everything was quiet. I felt this awful heavy weight fall on me. I coughed and gasped for air." She placed a hand on her neck; tears welled again, and she dabbed at her eyes. "I shouldn't say this, but I was grateful that he stopped—not that I wished him dead. I took a deep breath and with every ounce of my strength I pushed him off. He rolled and fell onto the floor. I got up on one elbow and turned to look at him. Blood was pouring out of the back of his head, and his awful eyes were staring up at me. I was terrified and turned away."

Mannheim leaned forward. "And you saw no one else in the room? Heard no other sounds? Take your time and think about that."

She shook her head. After a short pause, she continued, "I can't be sure, maybe I'm just imagining this, but I thought I saw a figure run out of the room."

Mannheim perked up at this disclosure, walked to her side and bent over to place his face close to hers. "What did he look like? Young? Old? Tall? Short? What was he wearing?"

Bonnie shook her head rapidly. "I don't know. I don't know if I even saw.... I was so confused and frightened."

Mannheim backed off. "Okay. Tell us exactly what happened after you got off the bed."

Bonnie's recall was not as spontaneous as Mannheim might have hoped. She became hesitant, while trying to reconstruct events.

"I felt dizzy, kind of light-headed. I rolled off to the other side of the bed to avoid the body on the floor. Somehow I managed to get to the washroom. I gagged, then gargled and washed my face. I ran a brush through my hair, then found safety pins to close my torn blouse."

"Why didn't you phone the operator or the police?" Detective Oliver asked.

"I tried, but I had no voice. The strangling left me hoarse."

"You could have stopped at the front desk and given the clerk a written note." Mannheim said.

Bonnie's eyes shifted from Mannheim to Farquaahr then back to Mannheim. "I wasn't thinking clearly. I was too frightened and wanted desperately to get away. I know now that was wrong. I felt so ashamed for my dad and for Mrs. Bruxton."

Mannheim stood and started to walk slowly around the small office, keeping his eyes on the floor while Bonnie watched him closely.

"Ms. Ouvray, how did you leave the hotel?"

Her voice was tremulous. "I took a cab."

"Your voice came back?"

"I whispered into the cabbie's ear."

Mannheim continued to pace slowly. "Did you talk to anyone in the hotel lobby? Did you see the chauffeur?"

"No."

"Tell me about the episode with the bell hop."

She sat upright with a quizzical expression. "I beg your pardon?"

"We talked with the bell hop who brought bags to Bruxton's suite. He said your boss made threatening comments to him. Why was that?"

Bonnie's eyes looked away from Mannheim's and focused on her hands, twisting a Kleenex in her lap.

"I don't recall."

Mannheim arched his brows. "Are you sure?"

Farquaahr bolted from his chair. "All right, Mannheim. Enough of this fishing trip. My client is innocent of this murder, and you are well advised of that. She's answered your blithering questions, and you have no valid reason for detaining her further. We're through here. Unless you are charging her with murder, we'll leave these premises. I sincerely hope you find your murderer without inflicting further stress on this innocent young lady." Farquaahr took Bonnie Ouvray's arm and escorted her to the door.

Mannheim called out, "Be sure your client is available for further questioning." After they left, he turned to Oliver. "Why the hell do I think she knows more than she's telling us?"

"Because you're a suspicious old fart whose already concocting excuses for seeing her again."

"What the hell makes you such an expert on reading minds?"

"Just being around you has honed my cynicism and made me super suspicious."

Mannheim smiled. "I knew you had some redeeming qualities."

22

Detective Mannheim came through the rear door of Dr. Harrington's office through the parking lot, and walked into the unoccupied consultation room. He sat opposite the doctor's desk, crossed his lanky legs and studied the wall before him where a display of framed diplomas, certificates and commendations all attested to the doctor's expertise. He was about to get up to examine the fine print on some of the certificates when Carmenita, the head office girl, approaching the room with a patient's chart, was startled to see the detective.

"Oh, I beg your pardon. Is the doctor expecting you?"

Mannheim made a quick study of Carmenita as she stood in the doorway. "What's your name, Miss?"

"Carmenita."

"Lovely name. Would you tell the good doctor that Detective Mannheim would like a word with him?" He handed her his card and looked after her as she left. Minutes later, Josh entered the consultation room, looked at the detective, then glanced at his watch. "Mannheim, you've caught me during the busiest time of the day." He looked around. "Where's your side kick, Detective Oliver?"

"He's back at the station doing some paperwork. He's good for that, and I hate it. Hey Doc, I need to ask you about some terms that appear on Bruxton's autopsy report."

"I'll help if I can, but why don't you ask the guy who dictated the report, the coroner, Dr. Schmitz?"

"Why do you think? You know him. He takes his sweet time returning my calls, and when he finally gets around to it, he sounds as though he's got a hot tamale in his mouth, or he's chewing on a goddamn cigar. Then he uses Latin or medical terms, and I don't know what the hell he's mumbling about." Mannheim removed a folded report from his jacket pocket. A report with inked circles around some words. "Look at this Doc, and tell me what the hell these words mean."

Josh took the report and explained the term *berry aneurysm* at the circle of Willis in the brain, and explained once again its role in causing immediate death upon rupture. He looked at the other terms that had been encircled and explained their meanings also.

Mannheim thanked him and replaced the report in his jacket. However, he showed no inclination to leave even though he knew Josh was eager to get back to his patients. "Something bothers me about the crime scene, Doc, and you being an amateur sleuth, I thought I'd run this by you." Josh was flattered and immediately lost his sense of urgency.

Mannheim continued, "Bonnie, that is Ms. Ouvray, the gal who was attacked by Bruxton, said she might have seen someone, probably the shooter, leave the hotel suite. From her position on the bed, at the time, how could she...." His voice trailed off.

Josh anticipated Mannheim's thinking. "You want to recreate the scene?"

"Yeah, Doc, That's exactly what I'm thinking."

"All right, but find your own female."

"Do you think your office girl would volunteer?" He wasn't completely successful in suppressing a tight smile.

"Mannheim, you're a dirty old man. And to answer your question, no, she wouldn't volunteer. Nor would I ask her or permit you to ask her. However, for the price of a

Coke, I could be persuaded to go to the hotel with you and try to reenact the probable sequence of events."

"Doc, you're just aching to do some sleuthing, aren't you? If the chief ever finds out that I've allowed a maverick, a would-be Sherlock Holmes, to muck around a murder scene, he'll have my ass in a sling."

"How about tonight? I'll be done here at about 5:00 p.m. Maggie's teaching First Aid to a class at the senior citizens' center."

Mannheim, pleased with Josh's response, threw him a two- finger salute. "I'll meet you in the hotel lobby at seven-thirty. Don't wear your deerstalker hat, or smoke your cala-bash pipe. They might not appreciate looney-tunes there."

The penthouse suite, still regarded as a crime scene, had been off limits to everyone, including the house staff, under orders of the State's Attorney General. Mannheim opened the door and felt for the wall switch. To the right of the entry way was a sizeable hall closet where Bruxton's clothes and luggage had been stored. Beyond the closet, to the left, was a washroom for guests. To the right of that, on the other side of the hallway, were French doors leading to the sleeping area with its king-sized bed, walk-in closet and adjoining master washroom. Atop a desk, facing a window, was the computer and telephone. In the expansive sitting room, two sofas and four oversized chairs were directed toward a sixty-inch TV. To the left was a wet bar, complete with a refrigerated wine cellar and a stock of aged Scotches and Bourbons.

Using a handkerchief, Josh closed the French doors, then he and Mannheim stood facing the bedroom.

"With these doors closed, and the curtains drawn, the view of the sleeping area is obscured. We know the doors had to be open for the shooter," Josh said. He turned and opened the French doors.

"The shooter could have been hiding in the hall closet," Mannheim said, pointing behind him, "and probably would have waited until they settled in bed before he came out." Mannheim stood at the open French doors, took out his pistol, and aimed it at the imaginary victim. "Okay, Doc, let's simulate the action. Lie down on the bed and let me straddle you in a position where my wang would be close to your face."

"Mannheim, don't get any funny ideas, and don't even think of unzipping your fly."

"You're safe, Doc. The last time I got into this position with someone, I was stinking drunk and the dame beneath me turned out to be a circus hermaphrodite. I puked all over him or her and stumbled the hell out of there. I'm more discriminating now, and anyway, you're not my type."

Josh lay on the bed, his head resting on a pillow, and his eyes facing the French doors. When Mannheim straddled him, his view of the doors was completely obscured.

"Well, what can you see?"

"I can't see a damned thing but your urine-stained crotch. Now get the hell off me. It would have been impossible for the Ouvray gal to have described anyone as the shooter. I can't even imagine that she could have seen anyone." Josh said.

Mannheim moved to the edge of the bed, then paused to take out his pad and make some notes. "My crotch isn't really urine-stained, is it?"

Josh ignored the question, got up off the bed, then walked into the hallway to open the closet door. He flipped the light switch on and opened the hanging clothes bags to feel the pockets of the pants and jackets.

"We looked at all the clothes, Doc. Even turned the pockets inside out."

Josh got on his hands and knees and picked up several tiny metallic particles from the carpeting. He rubbed them between his thumb and index finger.

Mannheim got up and came over to the closet, and, hovering over Josh, said, "Hey, Doc, you're horning in on my territory now. I'll take those." He held out a plastic bag, let Josh drop the particles into it, then sealed it and walked away muttering, "I know my crotch wasn't stained with urine."

23

With the North wind howling and the humidity rising, the wintry evening in the desert was uncomfortably cold, with the temperature hovering in the low-forties. The crackling and sparking of pine logs burning in the baronial-sized fireplace interrupted the stillness in the darkened great room. Frank stood behind Mary as they watched the dancing flames. His hands rested on the shawl covering her shoulders. She reached back with one hand and held one of his. The fire cast a flickering mosaic on the lovers' faces. "I don't know how I could have survived these last few days without you, sweetheart." Frank said nothing, but bent forward to kiss the top of her head.

She stared into the fireplace. "God knows, I lost whatever love I felt for Peter these past few years, but I never wished him dead." After a quiet moment, she continued, "And this place is so big and so empty whenever you leave, even for a short while. I count the hours, and the minutes until you return. Promise you'll never leave me, Darling."

He whispered, "I promise."

She gathered the shawl more snugly around her shoulders. "I feel a kind of ambivalence, or maybe it's just plain guilt, about his death. I suppose I could have been more loving, and yet, it was difficult for me to be with him. He was consumed with making money, and that occupied all of his time and energy. That is, at least, when he wasn't whoring around. In spite of that, I suppose I should hold some kind of memorial service and invite those who liked him, or made a pretense of liking him."

"There had to be some who were genuinely fond of him."

Mary grew pensive. "Maybe—but not many."

"There's your daughter, Deena, for one."

"You're right. She could convince him to do anything for her, except allow that Brazilowicz kid to marry her." Mary led Frank to the love seat facing the fireplace.

"What about your early relationship with him? You must have loved him, and he must have loved you."

"We were quite young, and as I look back, I think we might have mistaken infatuation and physical desire for a meaningful relationship. After awhile, the so-called flames of passion burned out, and he became more restless and uncaring, at least where I was concerned. I suspect that's when he started looking elsewhere. I even thought having a family would improve our failing relationship."

Frank took Mary's hands in his. "I think you're about to make a confession."

Mary snuggled against him, then peered into his eyes, demanding complete attention.

"As God is my witness, Frank, what I'm about to tell you, I've never told anyone. You're so much a part of me now, I feel I can divulge this most secret secret."

She took her hands out of his and started to twist the fringe on her shawl. "Maybe I shouldn't even mention this. What was done, was done long ago, and perhaps there is no point in bringing it up. No, just forget it."

"Now, Mary, I'm too curious to allow you to stop. Come on. Tell me this deep, dark secret of yours."

She hesitated. "This must never go beyond us."

Frank held her firmly and listened intently.

"After three years of being unable to conceive, I

thought about adoption, and approached Peter with the idea. I could have predicted his response. He blew up and started to scream. He absolutely would have none of it. Any child he raised, he argued, had to be his—no one else's. That was typical for that egomaniacal bastard. I had gone through the usual fertility procedures. The gynecologist assured me I was perfectly healthy and saw no reason why I couldn't conceive. After that I even thought about taking on a lover. God knows I enjoyed intercourse, and early in our marriage, Peter's demands were frequent, if sometimes unromantic. He expected me to do outlandish things in bed and didn't care whether I enjoyed them. But I digress." She paused. "I really cannot believe I'm telling you all these sordid secrets."

"But Mary, we're soul mates. After all, I've shared all my darkest secrets with you...."

"You're right, Frank. Anyway, Peter initially resisted the doctor's suggestion to be tested for his sperm count and viability, but after my coaxing he finally consented. Following the test, the doctor, a personal friend, and a man who understood Peter, confided that the problem was Peter's, not mine. I was relieved, but that didn't solve my problem. His semen specimen revealed almost no sperm, and the very few present showed little or no motility. Before his test, Peter had decided that the problem was mine, of course, and all of that was so predictable. I asked the doctor not to say anything to him about his infertility. At that time, I worried that if he learned that he couldn't father a child, it would probably make him crazier than he already was."

"So, how did you become pregnant?"

Mary glanced around the room as though an eavesdropper might be listening; she lowered her voice, "Without Peter's knowledge, I started on a program of donor sperm insemination at the university hospital, and insisted on having specimens supplied by handsome, intelligent students. I went through the procedure six times before becoming pregnant. I can't begin to tell you the utter disappointment I felt after each failed implantation. The day I learned I was pregnant was one of the happiest days of my life."

"So Bruxton thought he was Deena's biological father?"

"That's right. He still does—well, did—and you're the only person I have ever confided in." She smiled as she poked her finger into Frank's chest. "If you tell anyone my secret, you're a dead man."

"You're too sweet to commit murder," he said.

"Don't bet on it." She tugged at his arm as she stood. "But I can be sweet. Come to bed, and I'll show you how sweet I can be."

24

At 6:30 p.m. the two detectives found themselves seated in a booth at the I Hop off Highway 111 in Rancho Mirage, sipping refills of coffee.

"Who are the beneficiaries in Bruxton's will?" Mannheim asked Oliver.

"According to a ten-year old copy of the will released from his attorney's office, the main thrust of Bruxton's holdings goes to his wife. The will was not updated. Bruxton was evidently still on pretty good terms with her at that time. He's probably cursing in his grave at the thought of his wife inheriting all his money and enjoying it with that gigolo of hers."

"Nothing was left to the daughter?" Mannheim asked.

"Disbursements were left to the discretion of the survivor, that is, the wife. The daughter would get whatever her mother decided to give her."

Mannheim placed a toothpick in his mouth and began a slow excursion of it from side to side. "Suppose Bruxton and his wife were killed simultaneously? Who would have inherited that fortune when the daughter was still a minor? Did the will cover that situation?" Mannheim asked as they walked toward the exit.

"The attorney gave me all kinds of information, more than I needed to know or can remember. Apparently there was no family executor named, if that's what you're getting at."

"No one? Didn't Bruxton have any living relatives?"

"We ran a profile on his family. There is a brother living in Desert Hot Springs. He should be on our list of persons to interview. Maybe we ought to get in touch with him."

Mannheim's deep-set eyes bored into Oliver's. "Maybe? What d'ya mean, maybe? Do you know any reason why *you* shouldn't get in touch with him, pronto?"

Oliver sounded defensive. "Since he wasn't going to inherit Bruxton's money, there didn't seem to be any urgency in...."

"Money isn't always the reason for murder, Junior. Call the guy and let him know we want to talk to him."

Oliver looked at his watch. "Mannheim, I'll drive you back to the station; then I'm going home to watch TV and hit the sack. I can't put in the number of hours you're putting in on this case. What plans do *you* have for the rest of the evening?"

"I was thinking about talking to that Ouvray gal again."

"Are you out of your mind? You're courtin' harassment charges. If you go over and start questioning that girl without a really good reason, and Farquaahr finds out, which he surely will, he'll report you to the chief, and he'll burn your ass. It's after seven—go home for godssake."

Mannheim said nothing. Oliver turned slowly to study him. "Hey, wait a damn minute, you've not got a thing for that chick, have you?"

Mannheim climbed into the passenger side of the car, opened the window and tossed out his toothpick. "Don't be ridiculous. I'm old enough to be her father."

"Yeah, sure. So was Bruxton."

Mannheim made no comment.

Oliver continued, "Listen, Methuselah, before you decide to try to get your rocks off on this dame, you might want to think twice. Better yet, take a cold shower, or go to a whorehouse and satisfy old Willie." Oliver started the vehicle and slipped into the stream of traffic on Highway 111 heading west.

"I have no intention of screwing around with that broad."

"Just remember that. I know it's none of my damned business, but do you date at all? Have you ever thought about marriage?"

"You're right. It's none of your damned business, but to answer your first question, I do date, and to answer your second, whenever I think about marriage, I dismiss the idea immediately."

"Why?"

"Is this some kind of psychiatric evaluation?"

"I'm just curious."

"My hours are too irregular. I couldn't be a good companion."

"That sounds like a cop-out, if I ever heard one."

"Maybe it is. But I've been a loner so damned long, I don't have the slightest desire to be harnessed to anyone's apron strings again. When I want to follow a lead or chase a perp, I don't want anyone telling me to take out the garbage or pick up some Tampax. If I want to get laid, I'll pay the tab on a dinner at a decent restaurant, take the lead on a dance floor, and afterward, if I'm damned lucky, I might get to enjoy a respectable fuck with some nice lady."

Oliver nodded. "Elegantly stated. For you. Okay, I'll accept that. Now, for the next subject. Why are you being so damned compulsive about this case? I mean, I know you're compulsive, but this seems extreme. Why can't you turn it off after eight hours?"

"You know damned well that good police work doesn't stop with a time clock."

Oliver raised his brows and nodded again. There could be no rebuttal to that.

Mannheim continued, "More than that, I suppose it's my up-bringing, my background."

"Meaning?"

"You can guess from my kraut name, Mannheim, that my father was German—born outside Berlin. He was a stickler, obsessive-compulsive; it was in his DNA, I suppose. Had unquestioned loyalty to the Fatherland before the war, with all the virtues of the stereotypical German round-head." He paused.

Oliver looked at him. "Don't stop now. Where are you going with this magillah?"

Mannheim took a deep breath and exhaled slowly. "Before the outbreak of World War II, my old man went to the University of Heidelberg.... A philosophy major— about as useful to the war effort as tits on a boar. Anyway, he wrote his thesis on the writings of Heinrich Heine, the critic of German institutions and customs. Heine's writings were banned by the Nazis and my old man came under suspicion as a subversive."

Oliver parked the car at the police station but did not open his door. "What's the rest of this saga? Was he forced to join the party?"

"The Nazis? Christ, no! His whole being screamed against those goose-stepping morons."

"What happened to him?"

"He was thrown into Buchenwald. He told me, many years later, that he weighed ninety-six pounds, down from one hundred seventy-five, when the Allied Liberation Forces rescued him. Friends nursed him back to health. Two years later, he made his way to California where relatives invited him to make a new life for himself. His entire German family had been sent to the gas chambers. He resumed his studies at U.C.L.A., got a doctorate, and eventually a teaching post there."

Oliver turned and studied Mannheim closely. "How did you get the names Timothy and Aloysius? They sure as hell don't sound German to me."

"I thought you were eager to get home to your TV. Besides, I didn't intend to spend the evening giving you my family history."

"This is better than TV re-runs."

Mannheim slumped in his seat and looked up at the car's headliner. In spite of his initial reluctance to talk about his family, he was quite willing to relate this story. "My mother named me after a couple of her favorite priests. I was told my old man objected at first, but gave in."

"Sounds like your parents were an interesting couple."

"You got that right. My mother was a student in my father's Philosophy 101 class. She fell for the old man's intellect, and he charmed her with his courtly manners. I suppose he was flattered by her attention. Anyway, she fell in love with him. Theirs was a sort of scandalous student/teacher love affair—a typical May/December romance between two very different people: she was twenty, and he was forty something. She was loving and patient; he was aloof and impatient. When I was a kid, I thought she was beautiful. Truth is, later I realized she wasn't particularly attractive. In fact, her pictures actually reminded me of Eleanor Roosevelt, but she had a pleasant smile and a loving disposition. Not at all serious like the old man.

My mother was a fourth generation American—a devout Roman Catholic from a large Irish family. Dad was fond of her, I suppose, in his own way, but he never could understand her blind devotion to the church. He was a confirmed atheist and regarded organized religion as a poison for the ignorant, superstitious, and anti-intellectual. Those incidentally, were his words. He refused to recognize the existence of the Almighty. He would say if there was a God, he must have been sitting on his ass while mankind was on a never-ending mission of self-destruction. Mother would roll her eyes and cross herself repeatedly during his ranting."

Mannheim lowered the car window and placed his hand on the sill. "Naming me after her two favorite priests in the hope that their religious fervor would somehow rub off on me, never happened. She lived in hope but died in despair on that account." He turned slowly to look at Oliver. "Well, Buster, now you know it all. I got my wacky name from my mother, and my tendency to be a compulsive misanthrope from the old man.

"Yep, the old man was a character. He never forgave those sonsobitches, you know. I mean for the atrocities of World War II and his own near-death. He believed criminals of every ilk, including politicians on the take, all murderers, and child molesters should be banished from society. For a guy who taught Philosophy he had some pretty damn narrow and radical ideas. I had to listen to his diatribes when he read the morning paper. He told me that he hoped I would study the law and become a prosecuting attorney."

"Did you ever think about becoming a lawyer?"

"Yeah, as a matter of fact, I went to law school for a year. Longest goddamned year of my life. I couldn't hack the boring lectures and regurgitating notes for exams. I hated that. Besides, I was as poor as a goddammed beggar. I'd reached the point where I wanted the feel of folding money, at least enough to buy a decent meal once in a while, and enough to take a dame on a date now and then. My mother wasn't working except for her charity volunteering, and the old man didn't make a hell of a lot as an assistant professor. I felt like shit every time I accepted money from him, but he insisted I take it.

"The clincher for my decision to quit law school came when he died of a massive heart attack about the time I started my second year. I felt obligated to support my mother, but I couldn't do it while I went to school. Then I read a notice in the LA Times about the police academy accepting candidates for the next class starting in two weeks. I went to the recruiting office, inquired about the salary, which seemed huge to me at the time, and like they say, the rest is history. Best of all, I felt good about police work; it was real, not that phony or hypothetical shit. You get a call, you respond, you size up a situation and you resolve it, one way or another."

"Do you really consider yourself a misanthrope? Have

you ever loved a woman? I mean *really* loved a woman? You ever been married?"

"Who the hell appointed you chief psychologist? Yeah, I've been married—she was the sweetest, most wonderful girl in the world." He cleared his throat and his Adam's apple bobbed. "She died in childbirth, twenty-years ago. The baby, a girl, was stillborn." He hesitated, then took a deep breath. "Right after that I lost it—drifted into a funk for months. I swore I'd never let a situation like that happen again. Besides, I like things just the way they are. I can dip the wick now and then without legal hassles. In two years, I'll have twenty-five years of service and a comfortable pension." He opened the car door and turned toward Oliver. "See you tomorrow after you've talked with Bruxton's brother, and after I pay a visit to the Ouvray gal."

25

At 8:25 p.m. Mannheim checked the address on a slip of paper in his hand. He opened the door of the Ford Taurus and walked toward the single family dwelling on Mountain Shadow Drive. The well-established neighborhood in Palm Desert was undergoing an upward transition. Following the influx of GIs after WW II, this area of the Coachella Valley had burgeoned with single-family homes. In the 1950s, lots were modestly priced and building codes were less stringent. However, in recent years, these homes located in a desirable area, had undergone costly renovations, additions and imaginative landscaping; this house fit those criteria. Mannheim walked up two steps and knocked gently on the door recently lacquered a forest green.

"Yes, who is it?"

He recognized Bonnie Ouvray's voice. "It's Detective Mannheim. May I come in?"

"Just a moment." The voice projecting from a distance hinted anxiety.

While waiting, Mannheim surveyed the exterior of the house, the fresh paint around the windowpanes and sills, the faux travertine fascia, and the new lawn sod. The mailbox at the berm had been recently installed, and the welcome mat on which he stood was new and spongy. After the clinking release of a security chain, the door opened slowly. In a lounging robe, with reading glasses in one hand, her dark hair piled neatly on top of her head, Bonnie Ouvrey's look was questioning but not unwelcoming.

"Detective Mannheim, this is a surprise. What are you doing here at this hour?"

"Is this an inconvenient time?"

She hesitated. "No, it's just that this is so unexpected. This place is hardly ready for visitors. I don't even have window treatments or any furniture, to speak of, yet."

Mannheim put up his hand to dismiss her concerns. He stepped in, looked about the living room, and noted the recently sanded and waxed flooring, and the modest ceiling chandelier.

"So how can I help you?"

Mannheim attempted to put her at ease. "I'd like to compliment you on your home. Is it a rental or have you purchased it?" He smiled, a rare effort for him.

Bonnie became more cordial. "I guess it's hardly a secret that Mr. Bruxton, was fond of me. He gave me several gifts." She pulled her robe more snuggly around her. "Please have a seat." She sat on the sofa and asked him to join her. "As you can see this is the only piece of furniture in here." They sat at opposite ends; Mannheim's gangly arms extended along the top of the sofa backside; Bonnie's hands were pushed deeply into the pockets of her robe. She continued, "Just before we left the office to go to his hotel suite, that awful evening, Mr. Bruxton presented me with a lovely double strand of pearls." Mannheim's deep-set eyes studied her as he nodded.

"He gave me something else that evening as well, although I didn't know it until after he'd been murdered."

"Really? Do I dare ask what?"

"The deed to this house."

Mannheim's brows arched.

"Mr. Bruxton explained that he was divorcing his wife, and he didn't want her to know about this property.

Something about joint tenancy. Of course, the property is really his, or was, or would have been. It's all very confusing, really. I guess he planned to put it back in his estate after the divorce. I asked my attorney, Mr. Farquaahr, about my right to ownership, given the circumstances, and he said it was all quite legally mine."

Mannheim reached for a spiral notebook in his inner jacket pocket, moistened his index finger on his lip, then flipped a few pages. "Do you recall telling me the other day that you had never been to Bruxton's hotel suite prior to the night he was killed?"

Bonnie's eye movements quickened. "I—I really don't remember."

"Well, you did. We questioned a bellhop who had been reprimanded by Bruxton earlier that evening. He said he remembered seeing you in the lobby, and entering the elevator with Bruxton, about three days before the murder."

Bonnie shook her head. "He could have been mistaken."

"Yeah, I suppose he could have." Mannheim stood and turned toward her. "Look, I'm not sure how important it is that you were with Bruxton in the hotel three days before he was murdered. But what is important is that you may be lying. That means everything you tell me becomes suspect. If you lie under oath, the penalty for perjury could be severe. Prison time. Besides, we could verify the bellhop's story by reviewing the security tapes."

Bonnie put her hand to her mouth, then lowered her head.

Mannheim continued, "You said that Bruxton forced himself on you and attempted oral sex, but you fended him off. Is that right?"

Bonnie, seated, looked up at Mannheim standing in front of her. She cleared her throat and said softly, "Yes, that's right."

"Then how would you explain the fact that the coroner found teeth marks on the shaft of Bruxton's penis?"

Bonnie put her face in her hands, braced her elbows on

her knees, and began to sob softly.

"Look, Ms. Ouvray, frankly, I don't care what you did as a consenting adult. Of course, if Bruxton raped you.... All I want is truthful answers. Do you understand?"

With her hands still covering her face, Bonnie nodded.

"Good. Now tell me exactly what happened that night. Take your time and give me details."

Bonnie wiped her eyes with a tissue she had taken from her robe. She spoke haltingly. "He tried to force me to perform oral sex on him. I resisted. He forced his penis into my mouth. My jaws must have clamped down. After that, he became violent and tried to choke me. That's when the two shots rang out. He fell forward and the rest is exactly like I already told you."

"I see. Then what happened?"

"I pushed him off me. He rolled over and fell to the floor."

"Did you see who fired the shots? Don't shake your head. You've already said you thought you saw someone leaving the suite." Mannheim became less patient. "Now think about it, and tell me the truth."

Bonnie's eyes pleaded for understanding. "I—I thought I saw the side and back of a man rushing away, but I could have been mistaken."

"You certainly could have been. Truth is, with Bruxton on top of you, cutting off your vision, you didn't see anything. Isn't that right? Don't give me any false clues or lies. Like I said, perjury is a serious offense."

Bonnie shook her head. "I'm confused, I just don't know. I just don't know." She began sobbing again.

Mannheim stood in front of her and placed one hand gently on her shoulder. "All right, let's calm down."

At that precise moment. a deafening explosion shattered the large living room window. A second blast followed immediately. Shards of glass flew everywhere. Bonnie's scream pierced the empty room. Mannheim pulled her off the sofa, and on to the floor, then threw himself on top of her. He reached for his gun and motioned for her to lie still as he placed his hand over her mouth. After several seconds, he rolled off her and crawled on his belly to the edge of the window, slowly edged his way up, and peered out into the night. The light from a nearby lamppost revealed no street activity.

Bonnie, in a breathless whisper, said, "My God, what happened?"

Without taking his eyes off the outdoors, Mannheim tilted his head back toward her and whispered, "Stay down. And stay away from the window."

"Did someone try to kill us?"

"Yeah, that's a distinct possibility. Just try to stay calm. I'll call the station and get some men up here."

As soon as he heard the sirens stop outside, Mannheim turned on the lights and opened the door. Four police officers got out of the police cars with guns drawn. Two of them went to search the perimeter, and the other two came into the house. The senior officer asked, "What the hell's going on Sarge?" Placing his revolver back in his holster, Mannheim briefed him while the other officer looked through the debris for clues.

"Hey, look at these babies!"

The officer used a pocketknife to dig out two .45 caliber shells from the wall opposite the window and dropped them into a plastic bag. "These could have done a lot of damage if they found their mark. You both lucked out."

Mannheim took the bag holding the bullets and held them up to the light. "Take these to the lab. After a few minutes, the officers who had been outside came in and reported that there had been no sign of anyone outside the house or in the surrounding area. The other officers took statements from both Miss Ouvray and Detective Mannheim, then all the officers prepared to leave.

"Miss, are you going to be okay here tonight?"

Before she could answer, Mannheim said, "I'll give Miss Ouvray a hand cleaning the place up, then see if we can either get someone to stay with her, or find somewhere else for her to stay. I'd like you boys to cruise the area."

"That's S.O.P., Sarge. Do you want us to stick around for awhile?"

"No need," Mannheim replied. "I doubt that whoever did this is coming back tonight."

After the other officers left, Mannheim asked Bonnie for a bed sheet to cover the broken window and a broom to sweep the glass. She brought a portable toolbox and handed it to him, then began picking up some of the larger shards of glass. Mannheim stood on a card table chair and secured the sheet from above the window with tacks. "Barring a wind or rain storm that ought to at least provide some privacy until you can get this fixed tomorrow. Sorry there's not more I can do tonight, but short of covering the window with a sheet of plywood, there's really no way to secure it."

He stepped off the chair, and took a step back to survey the temporary curtain. "Well, that's it." Looking at his watch, he continued, "11:45. It'll be the witching hour soon. Why not stay with your parents or some friends tonight? I can drive you or follow you while you drive."

Bonnie turned away. "I can't."

"Why not?"

"My kitchen appliances are coming at eight in the morning, and I can't just leave all my things here. I'll have to get someone to board up this window."

"Sounds as though you're finding excuses not to leave."

Anxious and distressed, she said, "You don't understand. I have things here that I cherish: things like family pictures, trophies, certificates. They're all in those cardboard boxes. I don't want to risk losing them to a break-in. Mannheim shook his head. "Well can you at least call someone to come over and stay with you? I'd feel better if you weren't here alone. Whoever's out there is not likely to come back tonight, but there's no guarantee. They may just be crazy enough to come back."

"There's really no one to call. I'm not sure what to do at this point, but I know I'm not leaving."

Mannheim's disapproval was obvious. "Then I'll wait in my car outside and keep an eye peeled for any suspicious activity. You stay in here and try to get some sleep."

She tilted her head and in a kind of little girl's voice, she asked, "You'd do that for me?"

"Yeah, no trouble." He hiked his belt up.

Bonnie smiled and approached him, then stopped before embracing him. "It's going to be chilly and uncomfortable out there in the early morning hours. Why don't you stay inside?"

He shook his head. "No, no, I...."

"At least you'll be warmer, and I won't worry about you being out there."

"Thanks anyway, but I...."

"Look, there's nothing improper about staying, and it will make me feel much safer with you inside." She turned toward the sofa to fluff the pillows. His initial response was to head for the door and not allow himself to even debate the idea. It was just not proper. She was part of a murder investigation. Not a suspect, but certainly a person of interest. Somehow, all that didn't seem to matter at the moment. Bonnie's pleading eyes begged him to stay, and finally he succumbed. A fleeting notion of guilt continued to gnaw at him, but he rationalized that she was vulnerable, needed protection, and he could provide it. He sat down on the sofa and stretched his long legs.

Bonnie returned with a blanket. She handed it to him, rechecked the lock on the door, then turned off the lights and came over to where he lay on the sofa. She whispered, "I can't begin to tell you how grateful I am to have you here." She bent and kissed him lightly on the forehead;

her eyelashes brushed his brow, then she disappeared into her bedroom.

Mannheim, in the meantime, felt as if he'd just been set on fire. Her feathery kiss and the delicate aroma of her perfume was intoxicating. Maybe this hadn't been such a good idea after all. The sweet, feminine softness of a young and beautiful woman had kindled sensations he thought were long gone. Unable to sleep, and thinking about what had just happened, he listened for alien sounds with the awareness of expectant prey. His heart thumped, and a sudden rise in body heat became almost unbearable. He threw off the blanket, removed his tie and unbuttoned his collar. His eyes accommodated to the darkness, partially penetrated by the light of the street lamp. Finally he drifted off, only to be awakened by a muffled sound coming from the direction of the bedroom. Reaching for his gun on the floor; Mannheim sat on the edge of the sofa and held the gun with both hands. He stood and walked slowly toward the bedroom. Listening for further sounds, he turned the knob and opened the door quietly.

A dim light from the adjoining washroom revealed Bonnie in a semi-recumbent position. She held the top of the blanket against her; her eyes wide as she whispered, "Detective Mannheim, is that you?"

"Yes," he said. He walked into the room and stood at her side. "I thought I heard a sound. Are you all right?"

She smiled and lowered the top of the blanket. The low cut nightie revealed the fullness of her breasts. Her pearly smile was almost iridescent against her café au lait skin. "How sweet of you to be so protective. "She sat upright and moved to make room for him. "Come sit here next to me."

Mannheim looked for a chair, but there was none.

"No, no, come sit here next to me on the bed."

Mannheim became confused. His impression of her as a rather shy person did not fit at all with the comely, seductive woman next to him. Was this a kind of game she was playing on an old yearning cock, or was she truly just grateful? And even if she did have a genuine fondness for him, he had no business responding. He could be risking his career and everything important to him by being intimate with someone involved in a murder case he was investigating. He struggled. Again, she wasn't a suspect. Only a person of interest. A victim, really, and technically he wasn't on duty. Hell, he knew he was rationalizing, but....

26

Desert Hot Springs, an unincorporated community established well before WWII, had once ascended the heights of glamour with the Hollywood luminaries who adorned its spas and nightclubs. But its meteoric rise flamed out after the war when it was abandoned by the movie crowd and further deteriorated until it became notorious for its indigence and high crime rate.

Brad Oliver drove the unmarked Crown Victoria defensively, avoiding potholes, uneven pavement, and broken glass. The global navigational system guided him toward a house on a street called El Camino Paradiso. Desert sand had drifted onto the curb-less properties, partially covering the weedy lawns strewn with discarded tires, beer cans, and fast-food debris. Several of the houses had boarded windows, sun-bleached sidings with peeling paint, and graffiti.

By contrast, the home indicated by his navigation system, had more than a semblance of orderliness. The green, grass-covered lawn, free of trash, was bordered by a six-foot high Cyclone fence. The gate was closed, but unlocked, clearly in anticipation of his arrival. The front door smelled of recently applied varnish and the brass hardware had been polished to a high luster. Oliver rang the doorbell and looked at his watch, 8:50.

Seconds later, the door opened. Standing before him was a short, trim swarthy woman with shiny, jet black hair pulled into braids on either side. She wore a loose-fitting white blouse over a knee length dark skirt, and had a welcoming smile. Her neat appearance and friendliness were reassuring.

"Please come in." she said.

She extended her hand, and Oliver shook it, then handed her his card.

"I'm Susan. Sven Bruxton's wife."

The woman led Oliver into the living room, severe in its simplicity, but clearly furnished with love. Colorful accents were provided by Navajo-type blankets that had been draped over the backs of a sofa and two club chairs. A coffee table, two floor lamps and a wall cabinet completed the furnishings.

"Please sit down," the woman said. "Sven is on his way. He moves a bit slowly."

As if to prove her statement, a rhythmic pounding from the back of the house began, then grew louder and louder, until at last, an unsmiling, one-legged man on crutches appeared, and stopped at the entrance to the room. Wearing khaki shorts and a T-shirt with a faded NRA logo, the thin man had a right, above-knee amputation with extensive scarring and deformity on the left leg. He hunched over the armpit supports of his crutches to extend his right hand to Oliver. "I'm Sven Bruxton; my friends call me 'Swede.' I see you've met Susan. She's the smarter and nicer member of this team. What can we do fer ya?" With his crutch, he motioned for Oliver to sit on one of the club chairs.

"I want to extend my condolences on the death of your brother," Oliver said.

"Huh?" Swede groused. "Save your breath, Detective. Peter and I had no use for each other. For thirty-five years he didn't say a goddamn word to me." Pointing to his amputation, he said, "He's the one responsible for this—a plain, dumb accident that coulda been avoided. It never shoulda happened and wouldn't a, if he weren't so goddamned greedy." Swede Bruxton, in ten seconds had spilled his bile. Scowling, he turned his head and muttered a curse. Oliver thought the scene probably played out a thousand times. Swede lowered himself on the other club chair and placed his crutches on the floor beside him.

Sitting on the edge of the chair, Oliver took out his spiral notebook. "Would I be opening some festering wounds to have you tell me more about it?"

Susan interrupted to quell an anticipated firestorm. "We're not being very cordial to our guest, Swede." She looked at Oliver. "I baked a coffee cake, and I'll put the coffee pot on...."

"Please don't bother. I...."

"It's no bother at all. You gents can entertain yourselves. I'll be but a few minutes."

Oliver sat across from Swede who remained sullen. "You get along pretty well on those crutches?"

Swede mumbled, shrugged and scowled.

"Were you ever fitted with an artificial leg?"

Swede showed a glimmer of interest. "Yeah, I got a prosthesis, but I don't use it unless I have to."

"When would that be?"

"When Susan wants me to look like a whole man wearing a pair of pants."

"I'm curious. Why wouldn't you wear a prosthetic leg all the time?"

"Talk to a hundred guys with artificial legs, and ninety will tell you they're a pain in the ass. They cause blisters and irritations on the stubs that get infected."

"So you drive a car without crutches..."

"Hell, I can drive a car with or without an automatic transmission."

Susan returned with a tray of sliced cake, three mugs of coffee and napkins imprinted with the *Springs Hotel* logo.

Seeing Oliver looking at the napkins, Susan smiled and said, "That's just a discard from the hotel. We get stuff like that after its been replaced. Management does that now and then."

"You work at the Springs Hotel?" Oliver asked.

"Going on eleven years. I'm in charge of laundry and washroom supplies."

Oliver studied her face. "You're aware, of course, that Peter Bruxton was killed there?"

Swede interrupted impatiently, "Of course, she knows that. There's no secret to that. It's been on TV and all the newspapers; still is as far as I know."

"Didn't anyone at the hotel ask questions? Your name's the same as the victim's, and it's an unusual one at that," Oliver said.

She shook her head. "My name isn't Bruxton, if that's what you're getting at. It's Bird Song. I'm what some would call a half-breed. I was born in Neah Bay, Washington. In my Makah family, the elders would say I was the daughter of a wild white woman and a gentle human being, but that's an inside tribal joke." While serving the cake and coffee she continued, "I didn't know Swede's brother very well. He wouldn't have much to do with us since I am what I am, and Swede and me have a common-law marriage." She watched Oliver make notes. "Now, Mary Bruxton was different. I knew that the moment I met her. What was it Swede, about eight years ago at that Bruxton family funeral I went to, that I met Mary? I think that's right, anyway. Have to be around that long ago."

Bruxton's brother grunted what must have been a reply. Oliver couldn't tell, but it was enough to spur Susan Bird Song on with her story.

"Funny thing is, neither Swede or Peter attended. Mary and me paid our respects to the old gent who was an uncle to our husbands. We talked, and found out we shared a common interest in skeet shooting. She'd invite me to the skeet-shooting club in Riverside on occasion. She was a right smart shooter, too."

Without coaxing, Swede interrupted Susan's story, and started a diatribe on Peter Bruxton again. "I come to hate him for a lot of reasons, you know. It wasn't just the legs."

Oliver waited for him to elaborate.

"Thirty-five years ago, me, Pete and one of his Viet Nam buddies were harvesting trees in the Olympic Forest, on a government auction sale. We stood to make a pretty good chunk of cash. I was setting chokers; putting chains around fallen trees. Pete was the hotshot busheler cutting down a tree—a seventy-foot cedar. Damned fool was less than one tree length behind me. Hell, he knew I was out there, and he knew goddamn well he shoulda been at least two tree lengths behind, but he was too goddamn greedy. He wanted those logs bucked and yarded before sundown, so that he could get his grubby hands on a few more dollars. Money was a goddamn passion with him. The only thing that really mattered was money, money, money. That's all he knew."

"What happened?" Oliver asked.

"You ask, what happened?" Swede's face reddened, and he began to speak rapidly. "I'll tell ya, this goddamned thing happened." Swede pointed to his right amputation site, then the deformed left leg. "The whistle blasted, and I heard this mother coming down. It's a noise every logger knows. I ran like hell, but one of the branches whacked the shit out of my right leg and caught some of my left leg too. I was pretty close to death from shock and loss of blood, and the goddamn pain I couldn't even begin to describe. Once they got my leg freed up, or what was left of it, they took me by whirly-bird to Harbor General in Seattle. No way that leg coulda been saved. It was mangled something fierce. As far as the left leg goes, they patched it up with plates, screws and wires from the knee to the ankle. It works pretty good, but the knee still gives me fits at times."

"Were you angry enough to want to kill your brother?" Oliver asked.

"Are you kidding? Not a day goes by, I don't think about it."

Susan reached for Swede's arm. "Dear, you're overreacting," Susan glanced at Detective Oliver, then shut her eyes and shook her head.

"What d'ya mean, overreacting?" He folded his arms across his chest and scowled. "Pete promised as soon as he made a few bucks, he'd share his profits with me." Swede looked around at an imaginary audience. "Hah! That was thirty-five years ago. Have you seen a red cent from him? Well, I haven't either, and he became one of the richest, goddamdest lumber thieves in all of America." Swede shook his head and spoke more slowly, "Hell, I didn't want his money. All I wanted was a little understandin', maybe an apology. Instead, he just turned his back on me like I was some freakin' cur. Hell, he turned out to be the cur, if you're asking me."

"Swede, give me a simple yes or no answer, did you kill Peter Bruxton?" Oliver asked.

"Now how in the hell could I do that?" He sneered. "Man, look at me. I've got one damn leg. How am I supposed to hold a gun, aim it, then shoot the damned thing and escape unnoticed? I'll tell ya this, though: I ain't angry with the one who did do it. Pete probably fucked somebody else like he did me and he finally got what was comin' to him."

"You told me you had a prosthesis you could use. Wouldn't that allow you to use two hands to shoot?"

"Mister, you talk like a guy with a paper asshole."

Oliver closed his spiral notebook, stood and thanked the couple for their cooperation. He glanced at the wall cabinet and stopped to look at several trophies and plaques in it. "I see you're handy with small firearms, Swede. You must shoot pretty well."

"About as well as I can dance a jig." On his crutches he

walked to the cabinet. "If you look close, you'll see Susan's name on all those awards. She's the sharpshooter in this house. She can fire two rounds into the same four inch target at twenty feet."

"Oh, Swede, don't go braggin' on me."

Oliver looked at Susan. "That's quite impressive. Just for the record, may I ask where you were at about six-thirty on the night Peter Bruxton was killed?"

"Probably on my way home. I work from ten in the morning till six. I heard about the murder on the evening news."

"Is there anyone who can vouch for your whereabouts at that time?"

Susan said, "Oh, Detective Oliver, surely you don't think...."

Swede interrupted. "Detective, all of us got better things to do than speculate on such ridiculous nonsense."

Susan looked at her watch. "It's well after nine. Gents, you'll have to excuse me, I gotta run. I'll be late as is." She turned and picked up her purse, then walked to the front door. "Pleased to have met you Detective Oliver."

Oliver walked toward the door after Susan left. He stopped, then turned around. "We'll want to talk to you and the Mrs. again. If you make plans to leave the area, notify our office first." Oliver opened the door, stepped outside then turned to face Swede.. "Does your wife own a .22 caliber gun?"

Swede's eyes narrowed and his face darkened. "I don't know, and what's more, I don't give a shit."

"Mind if I come back and look around?"

"Unless you got a search warrant, you can just say goodbye."

"Goodbye, then. For now...."

Swede slammed the door shut and bolted it.

In the quieter back room of Coco's restaurant off the I-10 in Palm Desert, Mannheim glanced at the breakfast menu, then set it down and looked at his partner, Oliver, who was seated across from him. "So you're saying Swede Bruxton's a bitter guy who hated his brother with a passion, and you're thinking his wife, the sharp-shooter, could have iced Bruxton?"

Oliver shrugged. "She had opportunity, being in charge of linens and such at the hotel. We know she's a crack shot, but what would be her motive? It's been thirty-five years since Swede lost his leg. That's a long time to resolve a vendetta. There has to have been plenty of other times in the past thirty-five years that would have been easier and drawn less attention if she really wanted to kill him."

"Ummm." Mannheim grunted and nodded.

Just at that moment. The waitress came up, refilled their coffees, took their orders and left again. Mannheim's eyes followed her firm buttocks until he lost sight of her. Oliver continued, "I got information from the Weapons Registry in Sacramento. Several weapons were listed for Susan Bird Song." He reached for a folded paper in his wallet. "Here's one that might be of interest: a .22 caliber Ruger Standard automatic. Same bullet size they found in Bruxton's head."

Mannheim raised his head partially and looked up

from under his bushy brows. "Have her bring that weapon in. If you get any flak, tell 'em we'll bring a warrant and rip their goddamned hovel apart looking for it."

"Here's breakfast," said the waitress. "Can I get you boys anything else?" She placed two heaping plates of food in front of them.

"Why don't you pull up a chair and keep us company?" Oliver asked.

"Uh-uh, no thanks Darling, you'll be too busy feeding your faces, and besides you guys are much too serious for me." She left with exaggerated hip movements knowing they were watching and most probably enjoying the view.

Oliver put the sheet of paper back in his pocket and said, "You haven't briefed me on your late night meeting with the Ouvray gal. What did she say?"

Mannheim put down his fork, took a sip of his coffee and avoided eye contact with Oliver. "The meeting went well enough."

Oliver stared at him. "Don't give me any of your cryptic messages and expect me to sit still. What d'ya mean, 'well enough'? Someone attempted to murder either you or that dame, half the police force is on the alert, the whole damn town's talking, and you say 'well enough'? The only way it could have gone well enough is if you found out who killed Peter Bruxton and/or who attempted to snuff you or the Ouvray gal last night."

Oliver watched Mannheim's facial expression and hoped he'd start to talk, but Mannheim remained expressionless. Oliver continued, "Of course, everything might have 'gone well enough' if you forgot about police work and got laid, but I don't suppose that was likely."

Mannheim still made no response, but his jaw tightened. Without speaking, he placed a dollar tip on the table, pushed his chair back, then stood and walked toward the cashier. Oliver abandoned his own breakfast, dropped another dollar on the table, and followed him. "Listen,

Zipper Mouth, tell me, what's going on with that Ouvray gal? What in the hell happened last night? Exactly what did she tell you?"

Mannheim looked over his shoulder at Oliver. "She said she thought she saw the backside of a guy running away after Bruxton was shot."

"Really? A guy, eh? Would that eliminate Susan Bird Song as a suspect?"

"Not necessarily." Mannheim took a toothpick and, with his tongue, guided it around his mouth. Walking toward the exit door, he slowed down to study the faces of the people seated in the waiting area.

"Are you expecting someone special?" Oliver asked.

Mannheim tilted his head toward Oliver. "See that skinny kid in the corner—the one who jumped up, then sat down when we came into the room?" Without taking his eyes off the kid, Mannheim said, "Now, look in the parking lot. See that blue Chevy in the disability space? The driver's got his eyes peeled on this door. Go out there and see what he's up to. I'll talk to Kid Twitchy here."

Oliver walked outside and headed toward the idling Chevy; the driver, a young male wearing a baseball cap backwards watched nervously as Oliver approached. Just before Oliver got to the car, the driver gunned the vehicle, causing a high-pitched screeching of tires, skid marks, and a cloud of blue exhaust that hung in the air. Oliver reached reflexively for his holstered gun, then stopped and, instead, pulled out his cell to call the station.

Meanwhile, Mannheim walked toward the nervous kid in the waiting area. The kid bolted to a standing position; his face paled and his eyes widened. Mannheim grabbed his forearm, twisted and held it behind him, then pushed the kid out the door. Oliver hurried toward them.

Mannheim swung the kid against the building and ordered him to spread his arms up and out and to spread his legs. Oliver patted him down while Mannheim covered him with a gun.

"Well, what have we here?" Oliver said as he pulled a .38 pistol from the kid's trouser pocket, while a group of onlookers gathered. At about the same time three police cars, sirens blaring, pulled into the parking lot. Mannheim cuffed the kid, then turned him over to the uniformed officers.

Inside their vehicle, Oliver turned toward Mannheim. "Okay, Ace, would you mind telling me how in the hell you figured all that out?"

"Buddy Boy, you don't have to be a hot shot to identify a perp who practically announces his intentions. Let me take you through the thought process. It's called deductive reasoning." Oliver rolled his eyes and shook his head in resignation. Mannheim ignored him. "This is a week-day morning, right? Most of the patrons are senior citizens, so a young kid waiting for a table is kinda unusual. If eating was what he really wanted, he'd go to a fast food joint or a place with counter service." Mannheim waited for Oliver's response.

Oliver nodded. "Yeah, I suppose, but that still doesn't explain..."

"Hold on. The kid was as nervous as a novitiate in a whorehouse. He was waiting for the line to clear at the cash register for his heist. In the meantime, he sat with his right hand on the gun in his bulging pocket. That is, until he saw us. When he saw us, he just about shit in his britches."

"What do you mean? How did he know we were cops?"

"Are you kidding? These snots can spot a dick a mile away."

"And you're saying you got all that just by looking at him for ten seconds?"

Mannheim pursed his lips and moved the toothpick from one side to the other. "That, and the fact that there was a string of restaurant robberies within a five mile radius in the past three weeks. Incidentally, the kid's picture was posted on the suspect-wanted list."

""Oh." Oliver said.

"Oh yeah. And there's one other thing. If you ever

get close to one of those nervous nellies, you can detect a smell—a body stink that goes with their hyped-up sweating and pulse rate; maybe it's related to methamphetamine. I don't know, but I can smell 'em across the room."

"I don't remember learning that at the academy."

"You know damn well most of what you learned, you learned on the street after you left the academy. Besides, how much information could they give you in a seven-month course?"

Oliver had taken more than enough of Mannheim's patronizing attitude and found an opening to reclaim some dignity. "If you suspected that the kid had a gun, why in the hell did you take him on without me? You know that's dumb, just plain dumb. In fact, you acted like some grandstanding, vigilante cowboy with a burr up his keester. If that kid got hold of his gun before we did, you could have kissed your bony butt goodbye."

Mannheim nodded. "You're right. Now before you continue chewing my skinny ass, let's get the hell away from this crowd."

28

"Deena, baby, I'm gonna' be leavin' the campus at the end of the semester. The coach said he can't pull any more strings to keep me on the team, or for that matter, in school. I'm failin' all my classes except Phys Ed." Johnny Brazilowicz, with a hangdog expression, pushed his hands deep into his pockets and kicked a few pebbles on the University Park Plaza walkway. He looked at the diminutive Deena at his side.

She placed an arm as far as it would reach around his waist and, with soulful eyes, returned his gaze. "Johnny, you know I'd help you study, if you'd let me. But the last time we tried to study at the Doheny Library...."

"I know, Baby, I couldn't help myself. Every time I'm with you, this pecker of mine blows up, and all I can think about is...."

"Johnny, you mustn't think of that—well, not constantly."

"Why can't we get married? Dammit, your old man, sorry, I mean your father, is gone now. He was the only one who didn't want us to get married."

Deena pouted. "Mother isn't exactly all ga-ga about it either. She's still hoping I'll marry someone with, well, you know, a fancier social background."

"Your ma's got it all wrong. Don't you think she could learn to like someone with power over 12,000 dues-paying union members in three states? My old man says if we combined our families' fortunes, we could practically run the union on the west coast and control operations like garbage management and sewer maintenance and other good stuff like that. He wants us to marry so bad, he said he'd do anything to make it happen. Of course, that was before your father was murdered."

29

In his sparsely furnished apartment, Mannheim slumped uncomfortably in a Lazy Boy recliner; his long legs extended and crossed at the ankles. He was half watching a Turner Classic Movie; some lame crime drama with Edward G. Robinson playing an overly aggressive detective. On either side of his chair, lay a clutter of magazines: *Sports Illustrated*, *Field* and *Track* and *True Crime*. A slight smile broke the craggy lines of his dour expression as he thought about his evening two nights ago with Bonnie Ouvray. She had managed to make him forget every rule there was about not getting involved with the people in a case under investigation, simply by rekindling the magnificent sensation of shared passion.

Twenty years had passed since he had known that kind of intimacy, and it felt good—damn good. He played the scene over and over in his mind: her soulful eyes, her warm smile, and her yielding body arousing sensations he thought he might never know again. Oh, he had been with a number of women; some were decent, but most were callused and indifferent—buy them a drink, slip them a C-note, and hope to hell you didn't catch the clap or something worse. This was different.

The fact that this beautiful creature had given herself to him was more than he could have ever imagined. And he wanted nothing more than to simply relish it. But he couldn't. His elation was tempered with a kind of gnawing in his gut. Spoiled by the fact that he knew he had compromised his objectivity in this case. Was he truly that old? Truly that needy? It wasn't like him at all, and yet here he sat, torn between his job and this woman.

He tried to rationalize the whole thing. She was a good girl. That bastard Bruxton raped her. She needed protection. What had happened between them was...well, there was what he wished it was, and what it probably was in reality. How the hell did he permit himself to get into this mess? This could fuck up his entire career. His entire life, for that matter. If the captain learned of his indiscretion, several things might happen: he could be demoted, asked to take an early retirement, or worse, thrown off the force. And yet, knowing all that, and knowing it might have been just an accident of fate, he still knew one thing for sure: he was going to see her again. He had to.

The penetrating chill of the northerly winds sweeping down from Alaska caused high-pitched creaking sounds in the Bruxton mansion perched high and unprotected in the San Jacinto Mountains. Despite massive timbers used to stabilize the structure and provide a Southwestern/ Moorish appearance, eerie sounds *occurred* as the foundation continued to settle. Mary glanced at her watch, eager to have Frank home since the domestics were off for the weekend, and the moaning wind had taken on what she imagined to be the sounds of agitated ghosts.

She might have enjoyed the coziness of burning logs in the huge fireplace, but starting a fire and feeding it was a man's job. Peter, earlier that year, had put in several cords of coniferous logs. They were stored in a bin adjacent to the fireplace. Now it was Frank who tended the fire and shared the warmth of a drink and conversation before the hearth. She glanced at the stately gothic grandfather clock in the dark corner. As if on cue, it mournfully bonged eight o'clock. Where in the hell was Frank? He said he'd be home by seven-thirty, at the latest.

To ward off the chill, Mary walked to the bar and poured bourbon over ice, took two gulps, then sat on the sofa with her legs under her. She took the afghan off the back of the sofa, and shuddered as she wrapped it around her shoulders. She picked up an issue of Vanity Fair, thumbed through it, but could not concentrate on reading. With the constant howling of wind and the flickering lights, she felt more than a twinge of apprehension; almost like a premonition of something sinister. The sudden banging of the front door startled her. She jumped and spilled her drink. A blast of cold air whipped though the great room.

"Frank, is that you?"

The wind responded in a wavering low-pitched, sustained whistle.

"Frank?"

Besieged with terror now, Mary stood, walked to the fireplace and reached for the iron poker. She walked warily toward the entrance. To her horror, the door was wide open. She pulled the afghan tightly around her shoulders and held the poker over her head as she stepped beyond the threshold; the wind forced her eyes shut. She stepped back quickly into the foyer—just as the lights went out.

Engulfed by panic, she slammed the door shut, locked it, then gasped when she thought something had brushed her side. She whirled around but saw only the profound darkness. She dropped the poker and stretched her arms to either side hoping for some familiar tactile sensation. Edging toward the right, she felt the firmness of the wall. Her fingers advanced along the wall, and she walked slowly until her eyes accommodated slightly to the darkness and the indistinct outlines of the furniture in the great room.

Locating the sofa, she sat on its edge and continued to search the darkness hoping to see nothing move. The unrelenting, mocking, howling winds caused a clattering of the shed door outside, and the foliage whipped relentlessly against the windows. Shivering, she huddled into the corner of the sofa, pulled her legs up under her, and wrapped the afghan snuggly about her.

Suddenly the front door opened again, and the room was bathed in light. Something cool touched the base of Mary's neck. She let out a piercing scream, jumped up and flailed her arms; then whirled around to find Frank holding the poker.

"Whoa! Whoa! Sweetheart, it's only me" Frank was utterly apologetic. "Sorry, I didn't mean to frighten you. I came in and almost tripped over this thing." He held the grip of the poker with both hands.

Mary hadn't quite caught her breath; her heart pounded and she felt faint. Frank dropped the poker, rushed around to the front of the sofa, sat beside her and embraced her. Trembling through sobbing gasps, she related her frightful experience.

"It's all right, baby, I'm here now. Nothing's going to happen." He kissed her on the forehead and wiped her tears with his handkerchief. "Has the power ever gone off before?"

In a sobbing staccato she said, "Yes, when the winds are fierce the trees fall against the power lines. I should be used to that, but I've never been here alone before, and I don't know where things are in this damn barn. Thank God they came back on. I hate it when the lights go out." Mary started to whimper again. "And, besides, you promised you'd be home almost an hour ago."

Frank held her more closely and stroked her hair lightly, "I'm sorry sweetheart, I should have called, but I got to arguing with the agents from the film production company, and time slipped away." Mary sobbed, her shoulders heaved. He continued, "Now, let me make you comfortable." He kissed the tip of her nose and brushed a few strands of hair away from her eyes. "I'll pour a couple drinks, then start a fire. We'll talk, and I'll tell you how much I love you."

"Don't tell me. Show me." The tension eased.

An hour later, the room suffused with warmth from the glowing embers, and with the winds becalmed, Mary stretched out on the sofa; her head rested on Frank's lap. He caressed her face as she looked up and asked, "What are you thinking, sweetheart?"

Frank hesitated. "I'm almost reluctant to ask you. Fact is, I hoped it wouldn't be necessary."

"Oh, oh, this sounds serious. What's wrong?."

Frank got up, walked toward the fireplace, put his drink on the mantel, then held his chin in his hand. "They miscalculated. The production company wants more seed money. The New York bankers will put up only half the projected costs of the movie, and we're talking several millions. We've got to get more investors."

Mary pursed her lips. "I've already committed two million to the project. I can go further, but my attorneys will want some guarantees. Is that a problem?"

"Mary, darling, your attorneys sound naïve. Investing in a movie or a Broadway play is a crapshoot. There are no guarantees. That's the nature of the business." He hesitated before continuing. "Another concern I have—if something should happen to you, heaven forbid...."

She bolted upright. "What do you mean, Frank? I'm not going anywhere. I'm healthy, and I feel young, especially when I'm with you."

Frank threw his head back and laughed, a theatrical gesture he had mastered well.

"Oh, I understand. All right, Darling, don't you worry. I'll ask my lawyers and accountants to create a separate account for your filming costs. That way you can draw from it without having to come to me every time. You're a man, after all, and a man shouldn't have to ask his lover for money all the time."

Frank, smiling, placed his arms around her and gave her a lingering kiss. He slid one hand around her breast, caressing it gently.

"Thank you for understanding, Mary."

She moved her hand up his thigh and messaged his tumescence.

"Good. Now let's go upstairs, and you can show me some real appreciation."

The next morning, while sitting across the breakfast table from Frank, whose face was buried in the pages of *Variety*, Mary cleared her throat and spoke loudly, hoping to get his attention. "Isn't it the damndest thing, Frank? I talked with Betty Rogers, the mayor's wife, this morning, our closest neighbors. I mentioned the power outage last night. She said they didn't experience any, although the lights flickered a couple times. Isn't that strange, Frank?" Mary tapped the side of her cup twice with her spoon. "Frank, your star performance last night doesn't excuse you from holding a conversation with me."

"Huh? Oh, sorry, Sweetheart." He folded the paper and set it at his side. "What were you saying?"

"Oh, never mind. I'll have the electrician check the wiring, though. After all, we have a generator; I don't know why the damned thing didn't kick in when the power went out. I don't ever want to be caught in the dark like that again without you."

"Don't worry sweetheart. I'll always be there to take care of you."

"Just hearing you say that makes me feel better, Frank. I

guess I should go in and check some emails. Care to join me?"

"Sure."

Mary took Frank's hand and guided him into the combination office/library. The room, located just off the kitchen, was a lush affair with hardwood bookshelves on all four walls, a built-in desk unit, and a mahogany leather sofa and chairs. It looked very much like the old English studies depicted in so many movies from the fifties, except that it also contained a large electronics console with two large screen computers, a home theatre and sound system, a fax, and a security system with a bank of TV screens showing views of the front entrance and lawn, the rear exit and garden, and both sides of the house. Mary, of course didn't know how most of it worked, but she could operate the computers well enough to check and send emails.

Approaching one of the computers, she turned it on and bent toward the monitor. "Let's see, who made requests for donations?"

Frank, meanwhile, explored the room. He'd seen it once before, and that was only briefly. Now he took his time. He walked along the bookshelves, taking note of the volumes of leather-bound literary classics, reference books, and novels he knew he would never read. On another wall, the shelves contained a collection of professional photographs and amateur snapshots depicting Mary's family, as well as Mary, at various stages of her life: a swaddling child, a teenaged majorette, a high school graduate and a bride. Pictures of Peter growing into manhood adorned the same wall. Later photographs showed him as a GI in dress uniform and in combat fatigues with a group of buddies somewhere near or on a field of battle.

Seated in front of the computer, Mary went down a list of e-mail messages. She pointed to one and called out, "Here's a note from Deena." Her smile became a frown. "Oh, for crying out loud. She'd like to bring her Johnny here with his father, Oscar Brazilowicz, who would like to pay his respects and offer condolences." Her shoulders sagged, and she sighed. "I really don't want to see those men. I just don't want Deena getting more deeply involved. Why couldn't she find a guy whose father is a banker, or a broker or even a politician?"

"Oscar Brazilowicz may be all of the above," Frank said.

30

Oliver perceived a change in Mannheim's appearance—not a striking change, but a change nevertheless. "Got your suit pressed, I see. Is that a new tie?"

He sniffed. "Old Spice after shave?" Then he glanced at Mannheim's hair. "A little axle grease to shine the pate too? Man, you're a complete makeover. Who's the lucky gal who gets this newly dandified dick?"

As usual, Mannheim sat in the passenger seat of the unmarked sedan as it sped along highway 111, and totally ignored the comment. At the next intersection, Mannheim said "Pull into Walgreens here. I need to pick up something."

Oliver's wry smile preceded his next unappreciated question. "You don't trust those twenty-year old Trojans in your wallet?"

From the side of his mouth, Mannheim muttered, "Wise ass, I'm getting something for my old maid aunt."

"Righ-ht."

Oliver nodded as he pulled into the Walgreens parking lot.

Mannheim got out of the car and walked briskly into the drug store. Minutes later, he came back out of the drug store carrying a flat bagged package under his arm. He opened the door of the vehicle and placed the package on the console between them.

"So, what d'ya get your old maid aunt?"

Before Mannheim could answer, Oliver reached for the package and pulled out a pound box of candy. "Well, aren't you the sport. *Whitman Samplers,* hot dog. That ought to make your aunt real happy. Tell her to watch her dentures when she bites into those nougats."

Mannheim jerked the box out of Oliver's hand and replaced it in the bag.

"Before we check in tonight, Mannheim, I'd like to remind you that the chief is catching hell from the State's Attorney General. He wants answers in the Bruxton murder, or at least some suspects hauled in for questioning within the next forty-eight hours. The press is pushing hard for answers on this one."

"I know all about that." Mannheim turned to look out the side window. "Does he want us to pull in some tattooed pool hall slobs that have nothing to do with the case, just to show people we're working?"

Oliver continued, "The governor threatened to send down his black-suited crime busters from Sacramento to snatch this case from us. Don't forget that."

Mannheim lowered his window, snorted and spat a mucous wad onto the street. He turned to look at Oliver. "They can all kiss my ass. I haven't seen one of those sonsabitches contribute a goddamned thing to solving any one of our hard cases. They come in like envoys from the Vatican, demand all our goddamned records, spread 'em around, make believe they've studied 'em, then ask a lot of stupid questions to prove they haven't read or understood a goddamned thing."

Oliver drove into the police parking area at the station. Mannheim unbuckled his shoulder harness, opened, then slammed the car door. He clenched and alternately released his jaw muscles while walking into the station reception area. He acknowledged the smiling face of Officer Alana Garcia behind the desk with a return grin. Seeing Garcia had a way of defusing his anger; he enjoyed her big black dancing eyes, her full moist magenta tinted lips, and her magnificent bust, that reminded him of nothing less than a couple of pomelo grapefruits topped with nipples of succulent black cherries. The fact that she was a single mother of two did not diminish his interest. He would have enjoyed a little flirtatious talk right then, but was propelled by his compulsiveness to get to the business at hand. He motioned for Oliver to follow him to his office. "Before those pricks come down from Sacramento, let's plan a new strategy."

Mary Bruxton came out of the house and approached the slow moving elderly man who was carrying a metal tool box to the panel truck parked on the garage entry way. He saw her, stopped, pulled down the visor of his baseball hat to shield his eyes from the sun, and said, "Mrs. Bruxton, I checked the wiring, the circuit panel, and the voltage—"

"Yes, yes, what did you find?" Mary interrupted the slow-speaking electrician.

"Ain't found nothin', ma'am."

"Nothing? Then why was there a power outage here the other night when my neighbors had no trouble?"

"Well-ll, for one thing the circuit panel cover was opened, which it shouldn'ta been, and there was fresh marks in the dust around it."

The electrician had Mary's full attention. She stared at him. "Meaning what?"

"Near as I can figure, someone most likely pulled the main circuit breaker off for awhile, that's all."

Mary put her hand to her mouth; her eyes moved from side to side. She hesitated, then spoke softly, "I see."

"Did anyone have any reason for shutting down the power?"

"What's that?" Mary said, mulling over the electrician's question. She had turned to walk back to the front entrance then stopped, and turned around to look at him. "No, no, not that I recall."

31

Maggie brought a copy of *The Desert Times* to the breakfast table. Josh reached for the sports section while she took the business section.

"Here's an interesting by-line, 'Sun sinks below horizon as light disappears from soaring housing market. Sudden loss of mortgage money forces potential buyers to turn tail.' What do you think of that?"

"The journalistic style smacks of sophomoric metaphors."

"No silly. I'm talking about the news, not the style. There'll be no money to buy those multi-million dollar homes Mary Bruxton is peddling in Montana."

Josh shrugged. "I thought those millionaire buyers were immune to the inconveniences of us poor shnooks."

"I'd hate to be saddled with the costs of development if the banks are going to withhold loans. It'll be interesting to see how Mary handles all that in a declining financial market."

Maggie folded the paper and placed it on the table, then looked at Josh curiously. "Didn't you tell me you invested money with Bruxton some years ago? About five thousand dollars?"

"You've a good memory. It was penny ante stuff for him. Within weeks, it tumbled to less than half my purchase price, and I sold it, thinking it would go lower. Sure enough, it did...right down until it dropped completely off the board. Before I sold, I talked with Peter about the stock; he took little interest in my petty losses and blew me off by saying I could do whatever I thought best. I realized then how far our friendship had drifted, and I vowed never to talk with him again about business, or, for that matter, much of anything. Small potato investors like me didn't interest him.

"You know, I knew his relationship with Mary had been facing rough weather even then; there were rumors about his womanizing and abusive behavior. Mary was the one with whom I remained friendly. To be quite candid, I was never fond of Peter. I felt that he was sort of slick—always conniving—always waiting to consummate the next big deal, forcing someone into bankruptcy or engaging in some illicit transaction."

"Josh, I didn't realize how much you disliked him."

"He wasn't always despicable. But, over the years his increasing wealth and political clout caused a change in his personality. He could put on the charm and be gracious in the presence of those who could help him, but he turned his back on lesser people, and along the way, he made some serious enemies."

32

The dark green Ford Taurus stopped in front of the house on Shadow Mountain Drive. Mannheim checked his watch, 6:30. Looking at his image in the rear view mirror, he patted a few strands of erstwhile blond hair turned gray. He adjusted his tie and observed his crooked smile with yellowed, irregular teeth. The smile seemed unfamiliar, even to him. To hell with it, he wouldn't smile; he'd try to look pleasant anyway. He sauntered up the walkway and noticed the window had been replaced and dressed with drapes.

Twenty years had passed since he courted a gal, and he felt a gnawing insecurity. Maybe he was just out of practice, despite having spent a gloriously intimate evening with Bonnie four days ago and having phoned her every evening since. He thought about their age difference: twenty-four years, but she seemed older than she was, more worldly, and heaven help her, she was in love with him. Best of all, he felt young being with her. He remembered the difference in ages between his parents and felt reassured as he buzzed the doorbell.

Framed in the doorway, Bonnie appeared statuesque, like a model posing with one hand on her hip and with a slight forward and provocative pelvic tilt. A black satin sequined halter over a black velvet mini-skirt enhanced an hourglass figure that melded onto magnificently contoured legs. Her shiny dark hair cascaded over rounded shoulders, and an inviting smile with full lips set off perfect glistening teeth. "My, doesn't the chief detective look handsome tonight. Come in, dear sir." She made a brief curtsy.

Mannheim set the box of candy on the vestibule table, made a half turn and placed his arms around her, smothering her with a prolonged kiss. She pushed him gently and said, "Whew, time out while I come up for air." Taking a step back she tilted her head, smiled and said, "Let's save some of that ardor for later. Right now, I'm starved."

He smiled and rubbed his hands. "You certainly jacked-up my appetite. We have reservations for 7:00 at The Homestead. I asked them to seat us in the garden area." He relished her hip and derrière movements when she turned to get her shawl. She was aware of his interest.

As the maître 'd escorted Mannhem and Bonnie Ouvray to a table in the relatively secluded garden area, heads turned to follow the tall, striking beauty.

Mannheim reached across the table to hold her hands. His deep-set eyes drank in her joyous youth, made even lovelier by the subdued light of the candle glow.

"I love being with you; you make me feel secure and wanted," she said.

"We can make more permanent arrangements any time you say."

Bonnie withdrew her hands as the sommelier approached and asked for their wine preference. She deferred to Mannheim who ordered the house red wine. "You've got to excuse my ignorance about wines. My uneducated palate goes to light and dark beers."

When the waiter left, she asked, "So, any developments on the shootings: Mr. Bruxton's murder, or the shots fired into my home?"

"Nah, the lab is making microscopic and chemical analyses on some fibers found around the door of the hotel room. Maybe they belong to the shooter and maybe not. We need the fibers from the shooter's clothes for comparison. Some finger prints were sent to the FBI." Mannheim shrugged. "I don't hold much hope for those findings, but we'll keep plugging away. Someone's going to get careless and give us a few answers." He pushed himself back into his chair studied Bonnie with all the excitement and anticipation of a youthful lover. Her exotic beauty, the delicate mocha coloration of her skin, her perfect teeth and the symmetry and voluptuous curves of her body and extremities were, to him, perfect beyond belief. "Tell me about yourself. Who's responsible for that beautiful face and body?"

"You make me blush. As for my family history, I'm one part Moluccan, one part Dutch and a variety of other things. My maternal grandmother was Moluccan."

"You'll have to forgive me; I know nothing about Moluccans."

"Most people don't. Moluccans are natives of the Dutch East Indies, a Netherlands colony for several hundred years—the old Spice Islands. They fought with the Allies in World War II against the Japanese. After the war several thousand Moluccan soldiers and their families considered themselves Dutch citizens. When the island wars broke out, they migrated to Holland. When they arrived, they weren't exactly welcomed with open arms by the Dutch. They took whatever work they could find. Often that meant menial labor. Anyway, my grandfather, a colonel in the Dutch army, inherited a large estate and hired a beautiful Moluccan girl as a domestic. He fell in love with her, and my mother was born out of that relationship. She remained in that household until she was in her teens. After that, her father, my grandfather, sent her to live with his relatives in Los Angeles. She met my father there, and that's where I was born."

"Did your grandfather marry your grandmother?"

"Heavens no. He already had a Dutch wife and children, but he never denied his paternity. He took care of her until she died, and he provided for my mother right up until she married my dad."

"Are your parents living?"

"Father is. Mother passed on when I was quite young."

"Did you ever see your maternal grandfather?"

"Once. After his wife passed away, he visited us in California. I remember him quite well. He was a tall, distinguished man, with kind and loving eyes. I was thirteen, and fell in love with him completely." She smiled and toyed with her wine glass. "I guess I'm partial to older men."

"I'm grateful for that."

Sipping the last of her wine, she asked Mannheim about his past. "Were you ever married?"

Swirling the remaining ounces of wine in his glass, Mannheim spoke with little inhibition. He related the loss of his young wife and unborn child in a botched delivery, twenty years ago. Bonnie reached for his hands and looked into his melancholy eyes.

They continued to speak of their families and backgrounds long after the last espressos had been served. He gazed at her longingly, completely unaware of the time until Bonnie said, "The waiters are looking at us, I think they'd like us to leave." She leaned forward and spoke softly. "You can take me home, and put me to bed."

He pushed his chair back, stood and walked behind her to pull her chair back for her. He leaned over, kissed her gently on the neck, and whispered, "Putting you to bed—there's nothing I'd like more." They exited the restaurant and headed back to her place. Once there, Mannheim pulled into the driveway and they got out, then walked up the walkway. She got out her keys to open the door.

"Here. Let me."

Taking the house key from Bonnie, Mannheim moved

in front of her to open the door. The lights had been turned on in the living room before they left. He stood beyond the doorway surveying the room, then motioned for her to follow him.

"Mannheim, you *are* cautious."

He took her hand and led her into the living room. She put her arms around his waist, and whispered, "Thank you for caring." She reached for his hand and pulled him toward the sofa and sat beside him. "I think I know you well enough to call you by some name other than 'Mannheim.' Don't you have a nickname? What do friends call you?"

"Besides Mannheim? Nothing particularly nice."

Her eyes were playful.

"If you don't tell me, I'll make up my own name for you. I'll call you *Poopsie.*"

"I've been called worse."

"Such as?"

"Most of them are unflattering. How do you like, *Scarecrow, Grumpy* and *Man Hammer?* I've also been called *Big Dick,* and don't ask me to explain that."

Bonnie turned aside and giggled, but made no comment.

"The moniker, *Mannheim,* seems to fit best. Hell, I never did look like my given name, *Tim,* and even less like *Timmie,* the name my mother called me all her life."

Mannheim leaned toward her, and covered her face with kisses. He stood, pulled her up and held her tightly. She became limp as he cradled her in his arms and carried her to the dimly-lit bedroom scented with a delicate lavender fragrance. Mannheim lowered her gently onto the bed. With heavy-lidded eyes, she pursed her lips in anticipation. He sat on the bedside and responded with a light kiss, then caressed her cheeks. She slipped the sequined halter over her head to expose her full and exquisite bosom. Mannheim cupped the youthful breasts with perky nipples arising from dark, broad areolar bases; he bent forward and suckled them while she made small, rapturous sounds and ran her fingers through his hair.

Eagerly but gently, he pulled her skirt down, exposing lacy, sheer panties that revealed a dark triangular escutcheon overlying the rounded Venus mound. She brought his face toward hers for an open-mouth kiss. Mannheim hastily removed his clothes and dropped them to the floor. His tumescence was complete. When he reached into his wallet for latex protection, she touched his hand and murmured, "Darling, let me help you with that."

33

Oliver walked into Mannheim's office with a mug of coffee and approached his superior, who was uncharacteristically whistling while studying some reports.

"Things must have gone well last night," Oliver said. "Did you get anything out of that Ouvray gal besides a thank-you for that box of candy? Oh, excuse me, I forgot, that was for your old maid aunt."

Mannheim did not look up; he ignored the remark. "I learned things about her family but nothing that'll solve the murder."

"She still kind of stand-offish?"

Mannheim did not respond for a moment, then said, "Yeah, more or less." He remained nonchalant and changed the subject. "I think we should visit the merry widow, Mary Bruxton and her tinsel-town cowboy-lover again. What's his name?"

"Parma, Frank Parma. Want me to bring them in?"

"No, no. We don't want to antagonize them unnecessarily. These people are accustomed to respect and decorum."

"I think a more proper term is *deference*."

"Whatever. Let's make an unannounced visit. Like I said, don't give'm a chance to rehearse their fuckin' lies or consult their shyster mouthpieces."

The unmarked police car drove up the switchback road toward the sprawling estate perched on a hillside summit.

Oliver whistled. "Get a load of this place in the daylight. It's bigger than the college I attended."

Pointing his finger, he counted, "One, two, three.... twelve arches on one side. Can you believe the sheer wealth and ostentation of these people?"

Mannheim showed no reaction. "Pull up behind that Mercedes convertible. That's it, closer, closer still, good." He stepped out of the sedan and walked toward the open convertible painted a customized persimmon color that bordered on the gaudy. He bent over, looked at the instrument panel, observed a few objects on the seat, then walked to the rear and bent over to touch one of the dual exhaust pipes.

He motioned with his head for Oliver to follow him, and they both approached the double door front entrance. Mannheim pushed the doorbell and looked around the spacious enclosed entryway. The door opened; a maid stood looking at the two.

"Yes? Can I help you gentlemen?"

"We'd like to talk with Mrs. Bruxton." Oliver flashed his badge.

"Uh, she's not in." The maid started to close the door.

Mannheim pushed against it. "Are you expecting her soon?"

"I—I don't know when she'll return."

Mannheim and Oliver stepped into the foyer, forcing the maid to step aside. "You won't mind if we wait, will you?"

She stood and stared at them. "Well, no, but—"

Mannheim said, "Why don't you go about your business; we'll sit on these chairs. Maybe we'll get lucky, and she'll return soon."

The maid left hesitantly and looked over her shoulder as she walked away. Oliver leaned toward Mannheim and spoke softly. "Are you crazy? We could be sitting here all day."

Mannheim looked at his watch. "Nine twenty-five. She'll be here within five minutes—ten at the most."

"How in the hell can you be so sure?"

"Lady Macbeth left her open purse on the Mercedes seat. She had a card for a dental appointment at ten-fifteen. With our car parked against the back of hers and the front of her car just inches from the garage door, she can't go anywhere. Incidentally, her key was in the ignition and the tail pipe was warm. The way I figure it, she backed the car out of the garage, forgot something, and went back into the house."

"Aren't you clever? Mannheim, sometimes your reasoning ability astounds me."

Mannheim nudged Oliver with his elbow as they heard a determined stride coming from the back of the house. Mary Bruxton's stern expression preceded her curt question, "What can I do for you fellas?"

"Thank you for seeing us, Mrs. Bruxton," Oliver said as the detectives stood.

She looked at her watch. "I don't have much time. I have a dental appointment in a half hour."

"Just a few questions, Mrs. Bruxton. I know we've asked you before, but now that you've had time to think about it, do you know anyone in particular who wanted your husband dead?" Oliver asked.

Mary shook her head impatiently. "I thought we went over all of this the other night."

Oliver followed his question quickly with another. "Have you received any strange or threatening calls? Has anything unusual occurred around here?"

With the last question, Mary's demeanor changed; she became less patronizing and spoke more deliberately. "Now that you ask, something strange did happen. Do you recall that windstorm three nights ago? It caused a power failure, the lights went out, and the front door blew open. But the door shouldn't have blown open, because I know I shut and locked it. And the power should not have gone off, but if it had, our generator should have kicked in, which it didn't. Then, when I went into the foyer to close the door,

I had the strangest sensation that something touched me. I suppose I could have imagined it, and yet...." she trailed off.

"Yet, what, Mrs. Bruxton?" Mannheim asked.

"The following day, the electrician said the circuit breaker box was open, and there were fresh marks in the dust around it. He thought the main breaker might have been pushed off, then pulled on again."

"Where is the circuit box?" Mannheim asked.

"In the garage." Mary looked at her watch again.

"Who would have access to the garage?" Oliver asked.

"The kitchen door leads to the garage, so the entire house staff. And the chauffeur, of course."

"Mind if we look around?" Mannheim asked.

"Help yourself, but I'm leaving. Melinda, my secretary, can see you out, or you can see yourselves out." Mary Bruxton walked briskly through the kitchen, her high heels clicking on the tiled floor. She entered the five-car garage with the detectives close behind her, and pointed to a vertical, gray metal panel mounted on a wall near the far end of the garage. "There's the circuit box," she said, and immediately pushed one of the garage door remote control buttons mounted on the wall. When the articulated door opened she saw her Mercedes hemmed in by the police car. With hands on hips, she said, "Would one of you move your vehicle, so I can leave?"

Oliver said, "Yes, certainly." He pulled the police car out of her way, and she wasted no time leaving. The tires squealed as she sped off. Oliver yelled for her to buckle up, but she was out of hearing range, and probably really didn't care. Mannheim walked toward the circuit breaker box and scrutinized the area around it. The garage floor had been finished with a polished granite epoxy, giving it a showroom appearance. The entire garage was tidy and the two remaining vehicles had mirror-like finishes.

The stately black Bentley limousine towered over a ruby red Maserati sport coupe with a license plate that read: *MB* followed by a heart, then *FP*. Mannheim walked slowly around each vehicle before returning to the circuit breaker panel. He squatted to study the floor closely. Almost completely camouflaged by the speckled coloring of the floor were small brownish particles. He picked them up, rubbed them between his fingers and sniffed.

Oliver came in while Mannheim was still squatting. He extended one arm to keep Oliver away from his investigative site. "Cigarette tobacco," Mannheim said. "Can't believe anybody'd be stupid enough to smoke in a garage." He stood, pursed his lips, wrinkled his nose and sniffed. "Can't smell any stale or trapped cigarette odors. Too many other smells around here."

"Maybe the tobacco was carried in on the bottom of someone's shoes. Should be easy enough to find out if anyone smokes around here."

Mannheim nodded and looked at the Bentley again. "What the hell does the chauffeur do when he's not driving or cleaning that gas guzzler?"

"Want to question him?"

"Not yet."

Both detectives walked toward a workbench at the other end of the garage. A four-foot high red-tiered tool chest on casters stood in a corner next to an air compressor. On the wall, there was an assortment of cleaned and oiled saws, files and rasps, all mounted according to size. "We got some fussy, spit and polish guy working here," he said.

He walked beyond the workbench to a closed door with a sign that read, *J. James Keyes*. Mannheim tried the doorknob, but the door was locked. He looked at Oliver. "Okay, Houdini, open this up with one of your magic keys." Oliver took out his ring of keys: he tried several unsuccessfully.

Taking the keys from him, Mannheim selected one, examined it closely and inserted it; the tumblers engaged.

"I'll be damned. Either you're using black magic or you've just got dumb luck."

"Neither, I've just been at this longer than you have."
He took a step into the room. Oliver remained behind.

"Aren't we trespassing here?"

"Listen, Junior, we're investigating a murder. That gives us legal and moral rights. Besides, who the hell's going to know?"

"Well, I for one—"

"Forget your Boy Scout pledge."

Mannheim felt for a wall switch. A single flush-mounted ceiling light lit a room the size of a one-car garage. Without visible ventilation, the sparsely furnished room smelled musty. An electric outlet-mounted deodorizer may have once made some difference, but it had long ago lost its ability to cover up odors. Mannheim sniffed. "This place stinks of stale tobacco and marijuana." A small light-stained oak desk and chair occupied the middle of the room, and a matching upright clothes rack in the corner held a black jacket. A single gray-green file cabinet stood against the back wall. On a side wall, several framed old black and white photos undergoing sepia-like aging discoloration showed GIs in platoon and company formations.

Among the photos was a framed certificate verifying that Corporal Jacobius James Keyes received an honorable discharge from the United States Army at Fort Lewis, Washington. A list of commendations was noted under the document. Oliver pointed to it. "Can you believe his first name is Jacobius? No wonder the guy calls himself Jim."

On the desk, there was a dated glossy magazine photo of Mary Bruxton in an evening gown. It had been placed in an inexpensive frame. Oliver picked up the photo. "Hey, look at this. Whoever stood next to her has been scissored out."

A stack of unpaid bills were impaled on a spindle. Oliver took them off and proceeded to study them. Suddenly, Mannheim touched Oliver's sleeve, then put his finger to his lips and tilted his head toward the door. Both men froze. They placed their hands on their holsters.

The chauffeur appeared in the doorway holding a

monkey wrench like a weapon above his head. "What the hell are you two doing here?"

Mannheim attempted a casual response. "The door was open, so we came in to look around, that's all."

"That door is *never* open unless I'm here." The chauffeur, agitated, stepped into the room.

"Hey, calm down, Old Buddy, and put the hardware away." Mannheim assumed the offensive. "What's the big deal? You concealing a murder weapon? Or maybe it's a stash of pot or coke?"

The chauffeur, now more belligerent, said, "A murder weapon? I don't know what the hell you're talking about." He hurried to the desk, placed the wrench on it, and began gathering the papers Oliver had been perusing.

"Tell me, Mr. Chauffeur, you smoke?" Mannheim asked.

"Yeah. So what? That's no secret. Mrs. Bruxton knows." He continued to replace the papers on the spindle, then walked to the door and stood beside it, waiting for the detectives to leave. Neither moved.

"You own any guns?" Oliver asked.

"Yeah, a service revolver, a couple pistols and an automatic rifle, all registered and legal."

"You got that junior arsenal somewhere around here?" Mannheim asked.

The chauffeur went into a coughing spasm. "No. They're at my house."

"Bring them to the police station first thing tomorrow morning." Mannheim walked slowly past Keyes, and gave him a surly look. Oliver followed, but avoided looking at him.

Behind the steering wheel, Oliver glanced at Mannheim. "What do you make of that guy? I thought he was anxious as hell to get us out of his bailiwick. And what about the tobacco particles on the floor around the circuit box?" Before Mannheim responded, Oliver added, "And he's another one who can handle a gun well."

"Almost everyone we talked to handles a gun well. At least well enough to have put a couple slugs into Bruxton's head at a distance of twenty feet."

He looked out the side window of the sedan as it descended the winding road. "He might have had something in his office he didn't want us to see. As for the cigarette tobacco on the floor, I suppose anybody could have brought it in."

"Sure, but I'm not talking possibilities; I'm talking probabilities. Hey, look at that!"

In the hairpin turns, Oliver glimpsed a speeding sport coupe coming up the mountain road. The vehicle was alternately hidden by the hills until suddenly it seemed to be on top of them, crossing the double yellow line. Oliver yanked the steering wheel to the right and stomped on the brakes. The car skidded, and lurched. Dust and dirt spewed in a cloud when the car hit the shoulder and rammed the broad metal guard rail with squealing, crunching and flying sparks. Oliver fought to keep the car upright until it stopped. Pushing back in his seat, he blew out a long breath. "Where the hell was that moron going? If it weren't for that rail, we'd have dropped over the mountain, and that would have been all she wrote."

Bracing himself on the dashboard, Mannheim yelled, "Turn this goddamned crate around and get that sonofabitch."

Oliver put the car in gear, shoved the accelerator to the floor and made a careening U-turn. The car shimmied, and the smell of burning rubber filled the interior. They opened the windows.

"Let's call Chips and let them handle this. We're on a county road; this is their bailiwick and this crate sounds like it might not make it."

"No, goddamn it! That sonofabitch could have killed us."

"Okay, hold on to your jock strap. We're going to be

flying low." At eighty-five miles per hour on hairpin turns, the tires squealed and the car leaned from side to side. Both looked for the speeding vehicle after every acute turn. Suddenly, a slow moving sedan loomed in front of them. "Shit!" Oliver slammed on the brakes. A vehicle traveling in the opposite direction kept him from passing. He sounded the siren and flashed his lights. The startled driver pulled over to the right. "Move over you old fart," Mannheim screamed as the police car roared past. "Goddamit, we'll never find him now. Where is that sonofabitch? I don't see anyone in front of us. Could you identify that car?"

Without taking his eyes off the road, Oliver, exasperated, responded, " "It was light gray with a split grill, maybe a BMW, maybe a Jag, or a Pontiac, and don't ask me the license number."

Mannheim sat forward. "At ninety to a hundred miles an hour, that sonofabitch is probably DUI or nursing a hard-on he wants to lube before it shrivels. He'll have plenty time to jerk-off in the slammer—if we find him." After they sped another two miles up the mountain without seeing another vehicle, Mannheim croaked, "Hell with it, that right front wheel might come off if we're not careful, and the stink of rubber is getting worse. Turn this wreck around and let's go back down, slowly. I want to check out some of these driveways." About a half mile down, Mannheim jerked his head to the right then backward. "Hold it! Back up. There's a gray sedan in that driveway." Oliver put the vehicle in reverse and backed up slowly. The name on the mailbox read, "L. Kurtz.

34

"Mother, I'd like you to meet Mr. Oscar Brazilowicz, Johnny's daddy." Deena, petite at five feet two inches, stood between two goliaths who seemed to dominate the large living room of the Bruxton mansion.

Johnny at six feet two inches, two hundred ninety seven pounds wore a USC maroon-lettered sweater and faded Levis; his father at six feet, and well-over three hundred fifty pounds wore a shimmering silk-blend, custom-tailored suit. His open-collared shirt revealed several gold chains hanging loosely around his thick short neck. French cuffs were fastened by cuff links of large rubies with gold bezels. Gaudy gemstone and diamond rings adorned his puffy, manicured middle, ring and little fingers. He extended his beefy hand, which engulfed Mary Bruxton's. His voice, made gravelly by years of yelling, smoking and hard liquor, announced, "Pleased t'meetcha, ma'am." The jowly leviathan pushed back a few strands of hair rising from a gray corona around his ears and the back of his head.

He looked around the room and nodded. "Got yourself a nice little place here, ma'am. Set you back a few pesos, I bet. Heh, heh."

His comments embarrassed Johnny. "Dad, this is no time—"

"You gotta excuse my enthusiasm, Mrs. Buxbaum. When I see something classy like this, I gotta express myself. I called on you mainly to offer my condoloments on your husband's unsuspected and quickie demise."

Mary, stunned into momentary silence, both by the size of the man and by his conversation, finally found her voice. "Thank you. Won't you sit down? May I offer some coffee, tea, a glass of wine?"

Oscar Brazilowicz sat on the edge of the sofa; his patulous abdomen hung over his belt line. "A cuppa java would be just dandy."

Mary reached for the remote to summon the maid.

"Mrs. Buxbaum—"

"That's Bruxton."

"Sorry, ma'am. I don't always pronounce good. Like I started to say, now that your husband ain't among the living—if you'll pardon the expression—there can't be no more objection to our kids getting married." He turned to look at Johnny and Deena, who were holding hands on the love seat.

"You can see they're nuts about each other. I'd like for them to tie the knot. But I don't mind saying, I'd like a concession or two from the bride-to-be's family."

Mary's brow arched as she looked at him in utter disbelief. "I beg your pardon."

He continued, "After all, she'll be coming into an important family. It so happens that I'm the union boss of nearly fifteen thousand waste management workers. Johnny'll fit right in, and will come out smelling like a rose, if you catch my drift."

Mary's polite constraints vanished. She took a deep breath, raised her head and crossed her arms over her chest. "Mr. Brazilowicz, did it ever occur to you...." The maid stopped to offer coffee to Mary, who dismissed her impatiently, pointing her toward Brazilowicz. When the maid proceeded to the others, Mary resumed her conversation, "Please understand. I have no intention of giving my consent for my only child to marry your son, whose future in garbage collection I find quite frankly distasteful, to say the very least. I had hoped Deena would find a companion who was in the professions, and if not, at least someone with a college degree. Obviously, Deena's a grown woman and she can make her own choices, but that's how I feel."

Oscar Brasilowicz pulled his head back, his jaw dropped, and his eyes saddened as though he had been grossly insulted without cause.

Mary's jaw tightened; she squared her shoulders. "Your son may be a nice young man, but I don't know what those two would talk about, once the glamour and excitement of the honeymoon ended. Furthermore, your implied promise of financial security hardly impresses me. One day, Deena, will inherit a great deal of money. She will not be at the mercy of anyone's monetary assistance."

Oscar Brazilowicz listened, and sipped his coffee with his fat pinky extended in the manner of those in polite society. He placed the cup and saucer on the cocktail table before him. "Mrs. Brookstone, I did not wish for you to be offended, but God forbid, if something was to happen to you, and your little girl inherits a ton of money, she's gonna need help managing and investing it. Our union offers that kind of service, and I personally would see to it...."

"Mr. Brazilowicz...."

"Call me Oz; all my friends do."

Mary sighed. "Mr. Brazilowicz, in the event of my death, there is a team of lawyers, bankers and accountants to assist Deena in handling her inheritance. If your union is looking for investments, I can suggest a motion picture property, of which I am the executive producer."

Brazilowicz again patted the few hairs on his head. "Mrs. Bridgestone, the union does not invest in enterprises of a, errr., speculatorial nature. Now, if you was my son's mother-in-law, that would be a horse of a different color...."

Mary looked at her watch.

"You'll have to excuse me, Mr. Brazilowicz. I have a

meeting with the Wayward Angels of the Desert. Thank you for your condolences." She stood and looked at her daughter. "Deena, dear, why don't you show your guests around the estate? Perhaps they'd like to play croquet or badminton."

35

"Pull into this driveway behind the Beemer," Mannheim said. "You remember Kurtz. He was the business partner of the late, great, Peter Bruxton." Mannheim had difficulty opening his door; it jammed when it struck the guardrail. He turned in his seat, placed his long, flexed legs against the door and kicked it several times before it opened with a reluctant screech. He surveyed the damage. "Jeez-uz, the whole goddamned side is caved in." He walked to the front end. "The right fender is rubbing against the tire. That's what caused that burning rubber stink." He snorted and ejected a mucous glob onto the lawn. "When we bring this wreck in, we'll get a lecture on the cost of repairs, and you can bet your sorry ass, no one will say they're glad we're alive."

Oliver glanced at the damage and nodded.

Both men walked to the front entrance of the sand-colored two-story house with architectural features reminiscent of an eighteenth century Mexican church. The door chimes played the first few bars of "The Mexican Hat Dance."

"Good afternoon. Mrs. Kurtz? I'm Detective Mannheim. This is Detective Oliver. Is your husband in?"

The leggy brunette appeared in an open terrycloth robe revealing a deeply scalloped swimsuit that barely concealed her top and bottom. She pushed up her sunglasses to reveal a red puffiness around her left eye, the obvious precursor to a shiner that would be in full bloom shortly. "Yes, my husband is here, but he had nothing to do with this." She pointed to her eye.

Larry Kurtz came running to the door.

Lucy turned toward him. "Dear, these men are the police."

"How did you fellas hear about this? I didn't know anyone called the police."

Lucy wrapped the robe snuggly around her, tied the belt and led the detectives into the living room furnished in a Southwestern ranch motif. She pointed to a sofa for the detectives, while she and her husband sat opposite them.

With long shapely legs crossed and the folds of her robe opened casually to either side, she began an unsolicited recitation. "I was lounging on a deck chair catching a few rays when our pool maintenance man started to leer at me and make uncouth comments. Imagine the nerve of him! I tried to ignore him, but he became aggressive and started to sexually assault me. I kicked him in the groin and threw a few good punches, but he caught me good in the left eye. God, that hurt! Anyway, with the kicks I gave him between his legs, he won't be threatening anyone with rape for a while. He limped out of here bent over and holding his crotch."

"Did you call the police?" Oliver asked.

Lucy sat back and raised her chin. "No."

"Why not?"

"When I've called them for things like this in the past, they've questioned the hell out of me and then not done a damned thing. Frankly, I thought they didn't believe me. They made me feel dirty and cheap—as though I were the aggressor! The gall of them."

"This sort of thing has happened before?" Oliver started.

"Well, of course it has," Lucy replied. "Anyway, since no rape took place this time, I figured they probably wouldn't do anything again. Instead, I called my husband, and I'm grateful that he came as quickly as he did." She stood, removed her robe, and slung it over her shoulder, carefully watching the expressions on the two detectives' faces out of the corner of her eye. Walking toward the stairs, she looked over her shoulder. "If you fellas will excuse me, I'm going upstairs to change and put something on this eye. Larry can fill you in on any questions you may have." She continued her slow ascent up the stairs with exaggerated hip shifting movements.

"How did you fellas get here?" Larry Kurtz asked. "If Lucy didn't call, and I didn't call...."

Oliver looked at Kurtz. "Is that why you sped home?"

"Sure. What else could I do?"

"Why didn't *you* call the police?" Mannheim asked.

Kurtz stood up, dug his hands into his pockets, and shook his head. "It's a long, complicated story."

"Try us. We've got time."

"Lucy's had trouble before. She'll lie on the chaise lounge and think nothing of being naked from the waist up while men are working around her. The old guy next door spies on her every chance he gets. She's had psychiatric treatment, but she never responded. Hell, even the psychiatrist made a play for her." Kurtz drew in a long breath, then sighed. "She's just really in love. With herself, I mean—a real narcissist. She attracts males wherever she is." Kurtz stopped abruptly. "As I said, though, how did you fellas know about what happened just now?"

Mannheim cleared his throat. "Actually, we didn't. We were coming from the Bruxton mansion up on top of Kilimanjaro, there, when you came at us like a goddamned maniac, forcing us into the guardrail. You almost killed us, and you practically totaled our vehicle. Sorry to tell you this, buddy, but you're going to be charged with reckless endangerment with a lethal weapon, and leaving the scene of an accident. These, my friend, are serious charges."

"Fellas, I swear I was unaware.... "

Mannheim projected his lower lip, closed his eyes and nodded slowly. "I think you'll have trouble convincing a judge, unless we intervene, and you cooperate. It so happens, we wanted to talk to you about your late partner's murder."

A few beads of perspiration collected on Kurtz's forehead. "You can be damn sure I'll cooperate." Kurtz looked at the staircase. "Let me check on Lucy first, though. I'll be right down."

After Kurtz left, Oliver whispered to Mannheim, "You certainly twisted a fact or two."

"That, my friend, is the artistry of influencing a witness for the prosecution."

"You better Mirandize him if you're going to arrest him."

"Who the hell said anything about arresting him? This guy is so damned worried, he's ready to squeal like a stuck pig. Don't worry, Junior, it'll all be legal and documented."

Kurtz, still apprehensive, descended the stairs and walked toward the detectives. "Are you going to cuff me and take me down to the station?"

Oliver was reassuring. "I don't think you're a flight risk, but a conversation at the station might be more prudent."

In the drab gray interrogation room, the three men sat at a wooden table; Kurtz on one side and the two detectives on the other.

"We're going to record our conversation, so just speak normally and don't get nervous." Mannheim offered Kurtz a cup of coffee, which he refused.

Kurtz loosened his tie and unbuttoned his collar, then rubbed his sweaty hands on his pants. "I'm not going to need a lawyer, am I?"

"If you're not guilty of any serious charges, you won't need one." Mannheim had used that rejoinder many times on the naïve and unsuspecting. "Tell us about your personal and business relationships with Peter Bruxton."

"Where do I start?"

"At the beginning."

"Well, we were partners, in a manner of speaking; he owned ninety-two percent of the company, so I was a minor partner. Our latest business was the recreation enterprise— the ski and golf lodge in Montana. All that developed over the years out of profits from our lumber business, which we started as young fellas after our army discharge."

"So you got along well?" Oliver asked.

"I got along as well as anyone *could* get along with him."

"Meaning?" Mannheim asked.

"Pete had a short fuse, which got shorter as he got richer. Everything had to be done his way. He'd find ways to screw the competition: he'd over-bid on trees at auction and under-cut on sales. He had a lousy reputation; people in the industry hated him. The rumor was that he bribed some Feds who were on the take. Inside the company, he'd chew up the help and spit `em out, and every good-looking gal that worked for him either ended up putting out or losing her job. You want more?"

Mannheim looked up from under his bushy brows. "Sounds like a real charmer. Has your own position in the company changed since his death?" Before Kurtz could answer, Mannheim continued, "Do you come in for a greater share of the profits?"

"My percentage stays the same. Only my workload has increased. So far, there are no real profits to speak of. All the revenue gets pumped back into the building and developing of that lodge. I still collect a decent salary. Mary Bruxton, of course, is the big winner."

"Were you indebted to Bruxton for big bucks?" Mannheim asked.

Kurtz looked at Mannheim, then at Oliver, and hesitated. He placed his hands on the table and clasped his fingers firmly. "Pete held the papers on my home; I paid him monthly."

"Did you owe him other debts?" Oliver asked.

Kurtz looked around the room and then upward as though seeking divine intervention before answering. "I like to play the ponies, and I'm a regular at the casinos. I lose just enough to have favored status at Vegas—you know—free room, board, drinks. Occasionally, I'd run short, and Pete would peel off a few Ks for me. He never pressed me for payment."

That statement took both detectives aback. They looked at one another, then waited for him to elaborate.

"Long ago, we made a pact to help each other, and he'd been good about holding up his end."

"Tell me about the pact," Mannheim said.

"Well, we swore never to divulge this to outsiders, but since Pete's dead, I see no reason not to tell you. However, I'd be grateful if nothing were said about this to anyone else. Sort of 'Off the Record.' Can you turn the recording device off?"

Mannheim nodded and pressed a button mounted on the side of the table. "Okay, go ahead."

"Pete and me signed up for the army together. After basic training, we shipped out to 'Nam. We were assigned to the 1st Corps of the 39th Division, the one farthest north facing the Viet Cong. This was April, 1972. There were four of us who were close buddies: buck-ass privates who were alternately scared shitless on patrol. After a patrol like that, we'd celebrate like drunken fools back at the base. You probably remember what a fucked-up war that was. It was bad all the way down the line, starting with the Army Chief of Staff, General Billy-Boy Westmoreland, the poorest excuse for a commander with his goddamned mania for body bag counts. Most of the time, it seemed as though no one knew what the hell was going on, and Charley was knocking us off with booby traps and AK 47s. We were like sitting ducks half the time wondering if we were going to be Charley's next target.

"And our own supposed allies, the South Vietnamese, were aiding and abetting the enemy. Hell, you couldn't tell one gook from another. There were spies working as cooks, maids, laborers, even kids...."

Mannheim asked, "Where're you going with this magilla, Kurtz?"

"You won't believe what I have to tell you." If Kurtz expected an unusual reaction from either detective, he didn't get it.

"Anyway, the four of us, Pete, Jake, Slim and me, were on patrol late one afternoon, going toward the northern perimeter, when a Claymore mine exploded in front of Slim. BANG! The bomb ripped off his face and part of his skull. Jeezuz, that was the worst thing I ever saw." Kurtz hesitated. He cleared his throat and his eyes became teary. He wiped them with a handkerchief. Trying to regain his composure, he spoke again haltingly. "Slim's face disappeared. I mean it was blown off. Blood squirted up like a geyser and his brains were hanging out of his skull. His arms and legs were shaking like a chicken with its head lopped off. The three of us got up after eating dirt. Pete looked at the hole in Slim's head and started to convulse. He bent over, puked and gasped for air. Off to the right at about twenty yards some gooks stood in front of a hut and started laughing. Pete sees them and goes bananas, absolutely crazy. He picks up his M-16—yelling and cursing, running like a goddamned crazy man, and opens fire just outside the hooch. He gunned every one of them down in cold blood" Kurtz's voice reached a crescendo. "Seven in all, including two kids!"

"I ran after him and jumped on his back, but it was too late. I threw my canteen water in his face and slapped him a few times hoping to bring him back to himself. Finally, something must have clicked, because he dropped the M-16, looked at what he'd done, and fell to his knees. Jake and I grabbed him and dragged him away. He was staring wild-eyed and then looked at us like we were strangers. A Medavac Hughey was flying nearby. We waved it down. The chopper landed, and the medics could see Pete was acting like a fucking psycho, so they grabbed him and put him on board. They bagged Slim's remains and hauled them off too." Kurtz had begun sweating profusely and asked for a drink. Mannheim noticed Kurtz's slight tremor as he handed him a plastic cup of water. He took the cup, and held it with both hands, sipped, then set it down and ran his hands through his hair.

"A stink was raised about the gooks' deaths. An investigation was launched; one that wouldn't quit. Everyone in the company was queried for hours. C.I.D. came down, but the three of us dummied up and denied everything. If Pete had been found out, he would have faced a general court martial and could have spent the rest of his life in the can."

"So there was a conspiracy of silence," Oliver said.

Kurtz turned to look at him, then looked away. "Call it whatever you want. It was our pact. I hope you *never* know the hell of a war like...."

Mannheim interjected, 'Okay, let me connect the dots here. The three of you decided to keep your mouths shut to save your buddy's ass, and he owed you big time. Right?"

Kurtz turned slowly to look at Mannheim. "Yeah, something like that."

Mannheim began pacing the room, his eyes fixed on the floor. "After your discharge, Bruxton convinced you to join him in investing in forested land, and you became partners." Kurtz said nothing and stared at Mannheim who became irritated. "Come on, Buddy, fill me in. I can't guess it all. Tell me how he wound up with the lion's share of the partnership?"

Kurtz continued, "Like I told you, I gambled a lot and made some stupid investments. I lost money faster than I made it, even though I made a hell of a lot. I owed Pete a bundle, and he always bailed me out. Every time he gave me cash, he knocked off a percentage point or two of my partnership share. He was smart about numbers, like a goddamned actuary, and I owed him too much to ever square things."

"You said Bruxton was a womanizer?" Mannheim continued his slow pace around Kurtz. "Did that affect your relationship with him?"

"What're you getting at?" Kurtz asked.

"Think back about three and a half years ago. The police responded to a call someone made from your home at about 2:00 a.m."

Kurtz stiffened. "How would you know that?"

"All police calls are computerized and dated. Want to hear more about calls involving your place?"

Kurtz rubbed his chin nervously, then said, "Look, I came down here willingly, but if you're going to ask me a lot of questions that have nothing to do with...."

"Relax. Let's get back to your war experience. Who was the third guy in your trio from *The Silence of the Lamb?*" Mannheim asked.

At that moment, the door to the room burst open, and Farquaahr stormed in, wagging his finger at Mannheim. "See here, Mannheim. You are not to intimidate or harass my client."

"Who in the hell let you in?" Mannheim asked.

"Mrs. Kurtz was fearful that you might be taking advantage of her overwrought husband, and, of course, she was quite correct in thinking so. Now, unless you are charging my client with some dreadfully felonious crime, I shall escort him from your unwelcoming quarters. Come on Larry. Let's leave these detectives to entertain themselves."

"But..." Kurtz began.

"Unless they want to read you your Miranda Rights and book you, they have no right to keep you here." He turned, and with Kurtz following, they left the room.

With Farquaahr and Kurtz gone, the room fell silent. Oliver looked at Mannheim. "Kurtz told us a hell of a lot until that loud-mouth pulled him away. Too bad we didn't have it recorded."

"Don't be so damned naïve." In his flat monotone, Mannheim explained, "Every syllable can be replayed. I never shut off that recorder."

"Yeah, but even so, we'd never be able to use it."

"True. But we've still got it on tape if Kurtz ever tries to deny it."

"Right, Mannheim. Try telling that to a judge. Hey, what was that business with the three and a half year old complaint you were talking about?" Oliver asked.

"That's an actual fact. I remembered some of the boys talking about it, and then I reviewed the disc. There was background screaming and a CD or TV blasting in the background. But the conversation was recorded accurately. The complaint came in from a Mrs. Lucille Kurtz who sounded more blotto than pissed. She said she had been raped by one of the guests at a party they were having at their home."

"Oh really? By whom?"

"Who else? Who used his cock as a diving rod to find pussy?"

"Bruxton?"

"That's right, Peter Bruxton. When he was questioned, he denied everything, and the really strange part is that Lucille Kurtz didn't pursue the charges, despite having called in the original complaint."

"Why not?"

"From a cynic's point of view, which I just happen to have, I'd say Bruxton made some kind of payoff to the Kurtz coffers. Despite that, I would guess that incident only fueled Kurtz's hatred of Bruxton for two reasons: number one, Bruxton had figuratively screwed him out of a partnership in a firm that became lucrative. Secondly, and probably more importantly, Bruxton literally fucked his wife, and even though it might have been consensual, Kurtz could never forgive him."

"C'mon, Mannheim, that's only speculation; you don't know that for sure. Are you assuming those were sufficient grounds for Kurtz to commit murder?"

Mannheim looked at Oliver sideways. "Murders have been committed for a hell of a lot less, and you damn well know it."

"Yeah, I suppose so. Is it possible that Bruxton felt obligated to have Kurtz on the payroll all those years just as a sort of pay-off for keeping his mouth shut about the 'Nam murders?"

Mannheim said without hesitation, "You're beginning to think like a smart cop now."

"Yeah, that's what worries me."

36

The fierce Northerly winds roiled across the desert floor, blowing sand on the Pioneer Town movie lot, almost obliterating the site of the saloon, and the barn less than fifty yards away from where Frank Parma and Scooter stood in the protective doorway of the canteen. Leaning into the wind, extras held onto their broad brimmed western hats and wore kerchiefs over their noses and mouths.

"This here blasted wind must be clockin' sixty miles an hour, Frankie Boy. They ain't gonna be shootin' on the prairie this morning. That big city sissy director won't be able to stop shakin' with the cold, and nobody'll hear his squeaky voice above the howlin' wind, anyway. I just talked with his assistant; he said they're gonna wait till the wind settles down." Scooter looked at his pocket watch. "Let's step into the canteen here and grab a cuppa java. We'll wait until they call us. We've got only two scenes to shoot before they put this here epic oater in the can, then we can blow this Garden of Eden. Hell's fire, I'd rather be workin' in one of those North Hollywood or Culver City studios, anyway. Ya know the ones with the purty man-made sceneries."

Scooter took a sip of coffee and brought the back of his hand across his mouth to stop the drippings. "Frankie, you ain't said more'n two words. You look kinda serious. Anything bad happen between you and your rich lady friend? Course, it ain't none of my business, but tell me anyway. Has the pep gone out of the puppy? Cause if that's the trouble, I got Uncle Zeb's formula that'll make him stand right up and crave action till the lady begs for mercy. Yessir, it'll do just that."

Frank pushed his coffee mug aside, took a deep breath and sighed. "No, Scooter, I'm not sure what it is. Lately, she seems sort of distant, like she wants space between us."

"She ain't said nothin'?"

"She's made excuses. It all started about a week ago when a power failure hit the estate. The lights were out when I arrived. I opened the door and just about tripped over a fireplace poker in the entryway. I picked it up and felt my way into the living room where the lights came on. She was curled up on the sofa, scared out of her wits, and there I was, standing behind her with that damn poker. I don't know what she thought—maybe that I was about to bludgeon her. Since then she's found every excuse not to spend time with me.

"The damn Montana property takes a lot of her time too," Frank continued, "She flies up there every other week and doesn't want me along. Tells me I'd be too distracting."

"She got any real reason to be feared of you, Frankie?"

"Of course not." Frank looked absently out the window. "Unless she thinks I was responsible for turning off the lights in order to whack her." He shook his head. "But that doesn't make sense. The lights went on while I was standing behind her with that damn poker. I couldn't have turned them on. She knows that."

Scooter closed his eyes and nodded slowly. "Frankie, who woulda benefited the most from Peter Bruxton's death?"

Frank turned sharply toward him. "What the hell are you getting at? Are you suggesting Mary had him whacked?"

"Easy Sonny, I'm just askin'." Scooter sipped his coffee, but did not take his eyes off Frank. "I meant no harm."

"You know damn well Mary inherited all his money.

If you think she wasted him, you're dead wrong. Scooter, you're a suspicious old derelict, with a crazy mind."

"I wouldn't deny that, Sonny Boy, but I c'n tell you, I been right with my hunches more times 'n I been wrong."

The unmarked police sedan was conspicuous among the high-end vehicles as it ascended the two lane driveway to the Springs Hotel. A row of tall Royal Palms asserted their dominance over an assortment of geraniums, petunias, snapdragons and poppies that provided bold colors to the median on their left. A park-like undulating lawn surrounded the mundane, boxy, white multi-storied hotel, made up of squared-off cubicles with miniscule patios. Stretching beyond the lawn were immaculate fairways dotted by the occasional golf cart.

"What was that kid's name? The bellboy who helped Bruxton with his bags that night?" Mannheim asked Oliver as they emerged from their sedan.

"I don't remember; we'll get it from the bell captain."

The two men walked across the expansive lobby to the bell captain's stand. Oliver flashed his badge and questioned the captain about the bellhop on duty the day Bruxton was murdered.

Referring to a work log, the captain ran his finger down a list. "There were eight bellhops on duty that day." He handed the list to Mannheim. "Any names look familiar to you?"

Mannheim looked at the list. "Yeah, here it is, Jack Locke. Is he around?"

"No, sir. Jack quit shortly after the Bruxton murder. Can't tell you why or where he went. Sorry."

"Do me a favor and ring the manager's office. We want to reexamine the suite if no one else is occupying it."

"No one's in it. As I understand, that suite was rented

on a yearly basis to Mr. Bruxton, and the hotel hasn't settled with the estate yet."

For the third time, Mannheim was examining the crime scene: the first time was the initial homicide investigation, the second time was for the reenactment of the murder with Dr. Harrington, and now with Detective Oliver. He wasn't quite sure why he was re-examining it, but something had been gnawing at him. Intuitively, he knew he had failed to see just that critical certain something the two times before.

With Oliver close behind, he flipped the wall switch in the anteroom of the fifteen hundred square foot suite. They walked slowly into the living room, with its floor-to-ceiling windows lavishly adorned with swagged sheer drapes, deep-pile carpeting and flocked wallpaper. Mannheim's spidery fingers touched the embossed wall covering as though to absorb some message, some clue. Ornately framed prints: one of Monet's *The Artist's Garden at Giverny*, and one of Toulouse-Lautrec's untitled 'tired ladies of the bordello,' adorned two walls. A decorative walnut cabinet with a sixty-inch TV, a refrigerator and bar occupied another wall. In the center of the living room, Mannheim looked over his right shoulder into the bedroom area, which was separated from the living room by open French doors. Then he and Oliver both moved into the bedroom and surveyed the king-sized bed with its white, tufted head-board, floral-patterned bedcover, and oversized pillows. In the corner of the room, a French provincial desk had a '30s style European phone, a computer and a fax machine.

A reproduction of Goya's *Reclining Nude Maja* above the headboard held Mannheim's attention. With his hands in his back pockets, he leaned forward for a critical study and wondered if the painting was supposed to stimulate Bruxton and excite his companion. It kind of piqued his own erotic interest.

Oliver watched Mannheim's deadpan expression as he studied the painting. "I was hoping to hear your comments—a pearl from the noted art connoisseur."

"What the hell, why not?" Mannheim couldn't resist an opinion. He glanced at the nude again and muttered, "She's a little too zaftig in the belly and her tits and nipples are kinda small." He stepped two feet back but maintained his concentration. "Her face ain't particularly pretty, and the hair around her pussy is sparse, but her skin has good tone and texture, and her legs are well- shaped."

"Your overall appraisal?" Oliver asked.

"Wouldn't throw her out of bed." A faint smile transformed his dour expression. "All right, enough bullshit. Let's track the killer's moves." He walked back toward the entry in an attempt to retrace the murderer's steps. "I think he might have preceded Bruxton and the secretary into the suite—actually lying-in-wait for them."

"What makes you think so?"

"Just a hunch. He could have slipped into the closet here near the entryway and hid behind some hanging clothes to wait until Bruxton and Bonnie, err, Miss Ouvray came into the suite. When they got onto the bed, he left the closet and hugged the wall along the living room until he got to the side of the bedroom door. Then he saw Bruxton mounted on Miss Ouvray who was attempting to fight him off; he took aim and got two rounds off into the back of Bruxton's head. Then he high-tailed it."

"Probably used a noise suppressor?"

Mannheim didn't answer immediately. "Huh? Yeah, probably. No one reported hearing gun shots."

He looked fondly at the naked Maja again. "I spent a helluva weekend with a broad who looked like that. She was a great lay." He looked away, preoccupied. "How about Bruxton's sister-in-law, the little squaw from Desert Hot Springs? Isn't she in charge of housekeeping here? She'd have access to the suite, and you said she can fire a weapon pretty good. What's her name again?"

"Susan, Susan Bird Song. Want to question her

while we're here?"

"Yeah, if she's on duty, I'd like to talk with her, eyeball to eyeball, if you know what I mean."

Mannheim knocked peremptorily, then opened the second floor office door marked *Housekeeping.* "Miss Bird Song?" The petite, dark-haired woman behind the desk stood abruptly. She wore a dark blue skirt and a white blouse set off by a necklace of exquisite turquoise stones and hand-carved silver beading. Mannheim introduced himself, then made a half turn toward Oliver. "You've already met Detective Oliver at your home."

She smiled, acknowledging Oliver, although the unannounced visit clearly caused some trepidation and annoyance.

"How can I help you gentlemen? Are you still investigating the murder of Swede's brother, Peter Bruxton? Do you have any leads?"

Mannheim's eyes darted around the spartan room. "As a matter of fact, we were hoping we might be able to pick up some additional information from you."

"I'll be happy to help any way I can, but I really don't see how...." She fingered her beads, and her brow arched.

"How well did you know your brother-in-law?" Mannheim asked.

"As I told Detective Oliver, I didn't know him well at all. I wasn't the sort of person he would ever have socialized with. I knew his wife, Mary, quite well." Her cell phone rang. "Excuse me please." She listened for a moment, then snapped the lid shut. "Would you gentlemen excuse me? There's a problem in the laundry room." She looked at her watch. "I shouldn't be gone more than ten or fifteen minutes at the very most." She left her office but kept the door open.

Mannheim watched her disappear down the hall, then walked to the door, shut it and turned the dead bolt. He turned to Oliver. "Start looking through those steel file cabinets against the far wall and put some speed into it."

"What're we looking for?"

"Anything. I'll go through her desk drawers." He pulled open the wide, shallow drawer beneath the desktop and pushed aside pencils and sundries. "Nothing here," he muttered and slammed it shut. He went to the larger upper drawer on the right side and scanned the alphabetized folders of suppliers.

"These cabinet files are marked personnel. Anyone in particular you want to know about?"

"No. Come here and try your skeleton key on this bottom drawer."

"Mannheim, why must we continually break privacy laws? This is an illegal search and seizure." Oliver was irritated.

"Just an illegal search. We're not taking anything yet, and stop being so goddamned righteous. We're trying to solve a murder, remember? If this bothers you, turn around and don't look. Just give me the damn keys." Mannheim grabbed Oliver's key ring, selected a small key, wiped it on his pants, and inserted it in the lock. "Bingo!" He slid the drawer out. A black leather bag occupied most of the space. He picked it up and handed it to Oliver, who took it reluctantly and held the handle with his thumb and index finger.

Mannheim looked at him disdainfully. "Jeez-uz, the goddamn thing isn't gonna give you A.I.D.S. Dump the contents on the desk." He looked at his watch. "We've been at this for seven minutes. Watch the time."

Mannheim pulled the bottom drawer out further and ran his hand toward the back. "Well, I'll be goddamned." He took a handkerchief from his back pocket to pull out a handgun. He squinted at the handle. "It's a Glock automatic 22. Ain't that interesting?"

Mannheim copied the serial number and placed the weapon back in the drawer. He hurried to Oliver's side to examine the spilled bag contents on the desk. Picking up a Bank of America checkbook, he glanced at the register and ran his index finger along the deposits column. "Look at the deposits for the last two months. Weekly deposits of five hundred dollars."

"Is that her salary?" Oliver asked.

"No, look at the register closely." Mannheim ran his finger along the nameless entries from left to right. "She's paid every two weeks, fifteen hundred dollars. The deposits of five hundred are over and above. Copy those deposit dates and her account number. We'll find out where that money comes from."

"And if it was cash?"

"We still ought to know."

The sound of light footsteps approaching the door preceded a rattling of the doorknob, which was followed by several sharp raps. Both men froze. "Jeez-uz," Mannheim whispered. "Get all this crap back in the bag. Hurry!"

Oliver scrambled to put the contents back. Mannheim grabbed the bag, threw it in the open drawer and pushed it shut but did not lock it. A lipstick rolled to the side of the desk. Oliver grabbed it and put it in his pocket.

"Just a moment," Oliver called out. He rushed to unlock the door.

Susan Bird Song looked at him suspiciously. "Why was the door locked?"

Oliver had difficulty explaining. Mannheim intervened. "We had to make some calls to the station, and we didn't want anyone eavesdropping."

She looked at Mannheim sideways, then at Oliver. "I see." She walked around them and sat at her desk, straightened her shoulders and pushed back in her chair. Her earlier affable temperament was gone. "Just *what is it* that you men want?"

Mannheim assumed a patronizing expression. "We'd like some answers to a few questions."

Susan stood, walked to the door and locked it. Her eyes darted again from Mannheim to Oliver, then she looked at her watch. "Please make this short. I've given you too much time already."

"We just need a few more minutes. Please sit down." Mannheim parked half his behind on the edge of her desk and placed a pocket-sized, battery-operated recorder in front of her.

"What is this? I'm not going to talk to a recorder."

"We use this just to get the facts in order. There's no need to be fearful." He clicked the on button and spoke into the device, giving the time, place and name of the participants.

She shook her head. "I'm not going to talk into that thing."

Mannheim folded his arms across his chest. "I'd suggest that you answer our questions here and now, or we'll cuff you and walk you through the hotel lobby, then haul you down to the station for questioning."

"You'll do what?"

"You heard me." Mannheim was uncompromising.

Susan bristled, her nostrils flared and her eyes threw daggers at both men. "What do you want of me?"

"Why do you keep a loaded firearm in your office?"

Her eyes widened. "How do you know that?"

"We looked."

"You had no right...."

"We have every right. We're investigating a murder; that gives us lots of rights. I suggest you speak slowly and clearly." Mannheim pushed the recorder closer to her. Her anger mounted until she saw Mannheim place handcuffs on the desk.

She folded her arms and remained silent for several seconds, then she leaned forward and spoke with bitterness. "About a year ago, my brother-in-law, Peter Bruxton, barged into this office. I figured he was liquored-up. He flashed a wad of hundred dollar bills, peeled off five and stuck them in my blouse. I pulled the bills out, threw them on the floor and spit in his face. That got him crazy mad, and he raised his hand. I thought he was going to smack me across the room. He told me to pick up the money and use it to pay Swede's medical bills."

"Why did he offer you money?"

Susan started to hyperventilate; she paused, folded her hands tightly and lowered her head again. With a Kleenex she dabbed her teary eyes and runny nose, then resumed her recall. "Bruxton said over and over that the money was for Swede's medical bills. That was really unusual because he never showed any concern for Swede before. I was terribly confused. I didn't want his money. I didn't want to have anything to do with that man. But I couldn't argue about Swede's need for it, and he knew it. Then the real reason for his visit came out. He said he had a proposition that could be mutually beneficial."

Mannheim leaned in toward her. "Tell me about that."

"Bruxton wanted party girls whenever he came to the hotel. He told me his relationship with Mary had soured to the point where they no longer shared the same bed, and had not for many months. Actually, I found out later Mary had demanded that he find a place to live elsewhere. That's when he took that fancy suite here. He complained that when he brought a girl to his room she might charge a thousand dollars for an all-nighter. It wasn't as though he couldn't afford that, but he didn't want to deal with any escort service that had his name on a list, a list that might be discovered by the law or used by someone to blackmail him. The arithmetic was simple: he would pay me five hundred dollars a week, cash, if I could manage to get good-looking girls who didn't work for prostitution rings, and could keep their mouths shut. He would pay them separately, depending on their talent. With the kind of money he was offering me, I could pay for Swede's mounting medical bills."

She hesitated. "I knew it wasn't right, but I fought with my conscience, thinking that was the least I could do for Swede. I wouldn't touch that filthy money for myself, but

Swede deserved it after everything his brother had done to him. Bruxton threatened to kill me if I ever exposed his sexual rendezvous. When I think about it, he was a real Jekyll and Hyde. After he threatened to kill me, I started to bring my gun to work."

Mannheim's cold eyes locked onto Susan's. "Did you kill Peter Bruxton?"

She pushed back in her chair, exasperated. "That's ridiculous. Of course not." She hesitated, then looked Mannheim right in the eyes and said flatly, "But if I had, I wouldn't regret it."

"Do you have the names of the girls you referred to Bruxton?"

Defiant, she folded her arms across her chest. "No!"

"Really? Now why do I find that hard to believe?"

"I kept their names in my head."

Mannheim stood and walked next to her chair, his hands in his back pockets, his head and neck flexed forward. "I'd advise you to start reciting their names and phone numbers then."

Susan followed his movements and shook her head. "I couldn't do that. I'd be betraying a confidence. These are innocent girls who...."

Mannheim interrupted. "Hold on! Innocent? The word takes on a whole new meaning here, don't you think? I doubt that you understand the gravity of your situation. We can call you in for pandering; for the procurement of prostitutes. That's good for hefty jail time, you know."

"These girls are not prostitutes. They're professional entertainers; they help our guests spend leisure time." Her explanation had a hollow ring, even to her, as her voice trailed off and she gauged Mannheim's cynical expression.

She began showing signs of stress. Her eyes shifted rapidly from one detective to the other. She rubbed her turquoise beads nervously, and a thin line of perspiration appeared above her upper lip. "I'd rather not continue this conversation without speaking to my lawyer. In fact, I'll call him now; his phone number is in my bag."

Mannheim and Oliver stood and moved closer to her as she bent over to open the desk drawer. The detectives' sudden proximity and heightened alertness made her back away. "No, I've changed my mind; I don't need to talk to my lawyer. I have nothing to hide. I can answer all your questions right here." She fidgeted with her necklace again.

Mannheim asked, "Tell me, did Bruxton request different gals, or did he prefer a particular one?"

"He had his favorites. Sometimes more than one at a time."

"Did you also provide recreational drugs, a little pot?"

"Never. This is a smoke-free environment."

"How gauche of me to have asked."

Susan looked into Mannheim's eyes hoping for a glimmer of understanding. "Like I said, I needed the money to pay for Swede's hospital and doctor bills, his pain medication and antibiotics. My medical insurance doesn't cover pre-existing conditions and he's continued to deteriorate as he's gotten older. On my salary, I just couldn't afford all those bills."

Mannheim became less caustic but continued relentlessly. "Is management aware of what you're doing?"

"Of course not." She shook her head. "If my boss knew, she'd fire me on the spot."

Mannheim pointed with the toe of his shoe to the left lower desk drawer. "I'll ask you again. Why do you keep a gun there?"

She folded her arms across her chest. "I told you. To protect myself."

Her jaw muscles tightened; she raised her head defiantly. "And I think we're done here. I won't say another word without my attorney's advice."

Mannheim sighed. "Have it your way. But be prepared to tell your mouthpiece that you'll be facing prostitution procurement charges. For that matter, you can tell your boss that you'll be leaving. He or she, sure as hell, isn't going to be sitting in your corner when this crap hits the front page of *The Desert Times*."

Her burnished copper complexion had drained to a pasty hue. She sank into her chair and seemed to shrink into gnome-like proportions. With pleading eyes she looked at Mannheim. "Will you protect me if I tell you what you want to know?"

Mannheim was not about to lose his advantage, nor was he about to give any assurances that he was not going to hold her accountable. "I can talk with the prosecutor and tell her you've been cooperative. You were put into an untenable position, and you did what you thought you had to do. In a very real sense, Bruxton forced you into it."

Susan interrupted eagerly. "Yes, that's it. I was forced to...."

Mannheim put up his hand to stop conversation. He shut the recorder and placed it in his pocket. Then, motioning for Susan to slide her chair back, he put on latex gloves and reached into her desk drawer to remove the Glock. He placed it in a plastic bag.

The office air turned stifling for Susan, who felt emotionally whipped under the detectives' relentless questioning. She had carried the burden of procuring call girls for Bruxton too long. Prior to this confrontation, only her co-conspirator, the bellhop, Jack Locke, was in on the scheme, and she was in constant fear that one day he might spill everything to the cops. She was well aware that he had disappeared after Bruxton's murder and was being sought for questioning.

Her confession, however painful, had opened the pressure cooker valve of anxiety. She had anticipated the loss of her job and even possible incarceration, but rationalized her need to make money for Swede. If Mannheim could provide a measure of immunity from prosecution, or at least cushion the fall, she was sure she could find a job elsewhere.

"All right, so you engaged in the business of getting

girls for Bruxton, and you split the kick-back of two thousand dollars a month with your partner, the bell hop. Am I right so far?" Susan nodded without looking at her interrogator. "Good. Give me the names of the girls who entertained him. Don't shake your head. That's part of the deal if I'm going to plead your case before the prosecutor."

"I can't divulge their names. Bruxton warned me if any of those girls talked or word got out about his parties, he would hold me responsible."

"But he's dead now! Why are you still afraid?" Mannheim asked.

"He warned me if I ever double-crossed him by exposing him to the news media, he would have his friends take care of me."

"That's stupid talk. The man's dead. Now, tell me, where did the girls come from, and how were they selected?"

"Jack, the bell hop, interviewed them. They came from an escort service—Madame Tatiana's Escort Service." She fingered her turquoise beads nervously.

Mannheim's eyes locked onto hers. "If you had a gun when Bruxton threatened you, would you have killed him?"

She cast her eyes downward. "Probably not. Truth is, I hated him enough to do it, but I needed him alive for the added income."

Mannheim's initial eagerness to throw the book at her had diminished. He was facing a dilemma: upholding the letter of the law, which nagged at the very core of his being, or finding a way to lessen the charges against her.

He changed the subject.

"How would someone gain entry into Bruxton's suite if the door was locked?" He resumed his position on the corner of her desk, his arms folded.

"They could have used a master key. Every hotel has them."

"How many people carry that key?" Oliver asked.

"Everyone who needs to get into the room: maids,

maintenance, refrigerator stockers....all sorts of people."

Mannheim asked, "What are your feelings toward Mary Bruxton?"

Relieved by the sudden change in questioning, Susan said, "Mary's a nice lady; not at all like that animal she was married to. We've been friends for a long time. We practiced target shooting at the indoor range in Riverside for a number of years. Now that you mention her name, she sent me an invitation to attend a memorial service for her husband at the Sunburst Lodge in Montana. I'll go, not to honor Bruxton's memory, but out of respect for Mary. Besides, she offered to fly me in one of her jets, and Swede insisted that I ought to get away. She said we could do target practicing, and I could use my own gun. I'd like that."

Outside the office, Oliver said, "Now what? If ballistics can't match the murder bullets to her gun, what are you planning to do? Are you letting her off the hook, or are you going to press charges of prostitution involvement?"

Mannheim looked down his nose at Oliver. "Is prostitution illegal?"

"Of course. You know damn well it is."

In his loping gait, Mannheim made no response, but walked toward the exit stairway to the floor below, which was the lobby.

Oliver hurrying behind him said, "Well, what do you propose to do, Mr. Law and Order? And what about her cohort, the bell hop?"

"All in due time, all in due time."

Mannheim stopped just before opening the door to the lobby; he turned to look at Oliver. "Some anonymous source is going to advise management that a prostitution ring is operating in the hotel."

"Huh? So that's how you're going to cop out?"

"Not me, Junior. You're the one who's going to make that call. Not only that, but you're going to locate that bell hop, Jack Locke...."

"Fine. What're you contributing to this effort?"

"I've assigned myself the job of interrogating the prostitutes."

"Oh, brother, I should have known."

The detectives started walking across the lobby, when Mannheim glanced at the reception desk. He stopped, and without turning, reached behind to stop Oliver. Over his shoulder, with his mouth skewed, Mannheim whispered, "Look at the guy talking to the clerk. Isn't that, what's his name, Larry Kurtz, Bruxton's former partner?"

Oliver stopped to study the man's back and profile. "Sure as hell looks like him. Should we approach?"

Mannheim moved behind a marble pillar and pulled Oliver behind him. "I don't see any overnight bag or luggage, do you?"

Kurtz left the reception desk and walked toward the elevators. Both detectives hurried to the clerk behind the desk. Mannheim flashed his badge and asked to see the registration form completed by Kurtz.

The clerk, a young East Indian, stared dumbly at the detective, clearly immobilized by the officious request.

Mannheim leaned forward, and, with an escalating tone, said, "I said, let's see the information on the form that guy just filled out."

"Y—yes, sir." The clerk scrambled to find the paper. "Here it is, sir."

Both detectives studied the form. "Lawrence Short. Who the hell is Lawrence Short?" Oliver asked.

"What's his home address?" Mannheim looked at the form and scratched the back of his head. "I'll be goddamned. There's no street number; it's listed only as Rancho Mirage, California. No telephone or email."

Oliver ran his finger across each line. Make of

auto—Jaguar. Method of payment—prepaid. Room assignment, 1230.

Mannheim, in a characteristic scowl, faced the clerk. "Was he alone? Any miss or missus?"

The clerk retrieved the form and turned it towards him. "He didn't list anyone, sir."

The clerk's failure to react swiftly, or to get specific information, annoyed the detective. "Did you take the trouble to look at his driver's license for a positive ID?"

"Yes sir, his picture matched."

Mannheim brought his face close to the clerk's. "Did you bother to look at the name on the license, or ask for his address?"

"No sir, I didn't. The suite was prepaid by his corporation."

"What corporation?"

The clerk looked at the registration form. "Sorry, sir, it doesn't say. It just indicates that it has been prepaid. There's a corporate rate code, but I don't know the name of the company it's tied to."

Mannheim and Oliver had walked several feet away, when Mannheim turned back toward the clerk. The clerk took a defensive step backward.

"Has that room been rented to that guy, Short, before?"

"I—I don't know, sir, I would have to refer that question to our accounting department. He looked at his watch. "They're off duty now. I can have them call you tomorrow at 8:00 a.m."

"You be sure to do that." Mannheim handed the clerk his business card. "My number's on there."

37

Oliver got behind the wheel of the Crown Vic parked at the side of the hotel entrance. "What're you thinking Mannheim?"

"Going over the list I wheedled out of Bird Song, I found the names of three broads who frequented Bruxton's suite...."

Oliver interrupted. "Among a cast of thousands...."

Mannheim, confused, looked at him.

"Just an old slogan from the Hollywood promotions scene—not important."

"Thank you for your edification. What I started to say before I was interrupted, was that there are three names that come up frequently on Bruxton's visitor list. According to Bird Song, he was a guy who didn't want his name appearing on any escort lists. Now, that's a laugh."

"Meaning?"

"He's probably the highest paying john at the valley's premier prostitution palace for home delivery service, and his name is probably known to every cat house operator in Riverside and San Bernardino Counties. Those three mattress queens were from Madame Tatiana's exclusive emporium of exotic entertainers."

"Are you into alliteration or what?"

Mannheim ignored the question and asked Oliver if he would like to go with him to interrogate the women.

"Do you think for a minute I'd say no? That might be the

best part of this job. Are you going to call for an appointment?"

"Sure, like the fox calls the hen house to say he's dropping by."

"What's this Madame like, and what kind of place does she run?"

Slumped in his seat, Mannheim spoke slowly, "We go back a long way, the Madame and me. Twenty years ago I lost my wife and child in a botched home delivery. My world fell apart. I never experienced such goddamned anguish. Hell, I thought about quitting the force and running away— just running anywhere, but I didn't. Instead I buried my ass in my apartment—didn't answer the phone, didn't shave, didn't do anything. I just lay around in my pajamas and didn't give a shit about anything. After about a month, the chief came by and found me stinking and sour smelling.

"He tried to pound some sense into my noggin, and used what he must have thought was clever motivational psychology. He said I needed a serious change in outlook.... maybe a little pleasure to help me forget. With his hand on my shoulder, he said something like, 'Tim, I want you to come back to your post, you're too good a man to be lost to self-pity.' At about that time, I was getting pretty used to my self-pity and didn't know if I wanted a change. But the Chief wouldn't take no for an answer. He waited while I showered, and watched me while I shaved. On my unmade bed, he laid out clean underwear, a shirt and pants. When I finished dressing, he asked if I had any condoms. I told him I didn't. So what does the guy do? He reaches into his wallet and gives me two *Trojans*." Mannheim closed his eyes and nodded. "Damn, that guy was a real mensch."

"Mannheim, some time ago I asked you about this Madame Tatiana. Did I miss something?"

"Shore up your nuts, Buddy Boy, I'm coming to that. The chief, God rest his soul, was old-fashioned, Antediluvian, I think they called it. You know, there was a time when mavens thought a good lay could clear up a depressed and confused mind. Like all the negative spirits could be released through a good ejaculation. Well, let me tell you, a good lay certainly didn't hurt, but I'm getting ahead of my story.

"The chief made a call, and set up an appointment with this Madame Tatiana. He told her about me, then used a few Russian expressions I couldn't understand, and laughed like hell. I could hear laughing at the other end.... two conspirators who planned to exorcise my melancholia."

Oliver turned toward him. "You're sounding quite literary."

"You want to hear the rest of this? Don't interrupt."

"Sorry."

"The chief took me to this establishment perched on an elevated corner lot. It looked like a hodgepodge, with Russian style church onion spires and southwestern Indian pueblos—goddamndest thing I ever saw. I went up to the door, pushed the doorbell and the Volga Boatman tune played. About the time I'm having second thoughts about going in, the heavy wooden door with an inlaid Orthodox cross carved into the middle of it, opens up. Standing before me was this tall exotic beauty, like an apparition, with pale Tatar features and a see-through garment. With one hand resting on the door edge and the other on her hip, she looked at me as though I were a hayseed in my Sears polyester suit. She reached out and pulled me in, adding to my anxiety. Then I got a really good look at her mammoth-sized tits. Jeezus, they were like those personal sized watermelons."

Mannheim slumped in his seat, his eyes closed and a smile crossed his lips; he remained quiet with his reverie.

Oliver did a double take. "Hey! Gimme the rest of this story. Don't fade out on me now."

Mannheim sat up and continued, "So anyway, she locked the door and led me into a room with a four-poster bed that could accommodate four, spread eagle. A hint of lavender masked the stink of cigarette smoke on my clothes. The lighting was soft, and some Viennese waltz was supposed to create a sensuous atmosphere, I guess. Hell, I didn't need any help feeling jazzed up. The Madame turned some dials on the wall next to the bed, the lights got dimmer yet, and the music softer. In a move that I swear I never saw, she whipped off her clothes and was standing before me with those gigantic boobs and a tiny thong covering her crotch. Well, let me tell you I've seen plenty of naked broads in my time, but none that got me as excited as this one."

Oliver glanced over at his partner as the vehicle traveling North on Monterey approached Clancy Lane. "I hope to hell you finish this story before we get there."

"Maybe I ought to hold off until after we finish the interrogations."

"Oh, no you don't. I listened to you drag this story line to a fare-thee-well. Now tell me the rest, and hurry."

Mannheim, unfazed by Oliver's command, squared his shoulders, opened the window, snorted, leaned out and ejected a wad of mucous. He sat back and continued, "I was standing like a rube when the Madame sashayed toward me and started to unbutton my shirt. In the meantime, willie is already standing at attention and pointing north."

"For the next hour or so I lay with this sex goddess, who knew every trick, and invented a few of her own." He hesitated, then added, "Now twenty years later, I can still remember the feeling of putting it between those billowy bazooms, then suckling those maraschino cherries bouncing on top."

"You make it all sound so edible."

"When you get right down to it, it was."

"Did that one treatment cure your depression, or did you require subsequent visits?"

"She finished me off with an around-the-world job that blew me away—cured me of my testicular constipation and allowed me to return to active duty."

"Surprises me that you succumbed to prostitution."

Mannheim sat up, shook his head impatiently, folded his arms across his chest and said, "Did I say anything about prostitution? Did I say anything about paying for services? That's right. You can bet your tight ass, I didn't. That lady extended therapy to a law enforcement officer in need of rehabilitation—that's all."

"Well, ex-cu-use me. Seems to me there's a bit of tacit approval of whore houses among the police in this community."

"Listen, Buster, some things defy labeling. In fact, they don't even exist on any protocol. These gals operate under the generous purview of the law. Both they, and the department derive mutual benefits. And don't ask what they are."

"Mannheim, with your narrow view of right and wrong, you must face a serious dilemma here."

Mannheim, uncharacteristically, did not rebut.

"I'm eager to see how well you interrogate those charming working girls in this 'pleasure palace' while preserving their civil rights."

Mannheim threw him a caustic glance. "Don't be such a smart ass."

The building was everything Mannheim had described. Oliver pulled into the driveway and both detectives got out of the car. They climbed the steps to the massive wooden door and rang the bell. An attractive, diminutive gal in a revealing French maid's uniform welcomed the officers to Madame Tatiana's Escort Service. Her skimpy, black uniform was cut low to reveal the pearly skin of her breasts, and disclosed a well-demarcated cleavage. A small white lacy apron completed the uniform. She held a feather duster under her left arm and curtsied. In a little girl voice, she asked, "May I help you gentlemen?"

Handing her his professional card, Mannheim's solemn voice commanded, "Tell Madame Tatiana we want to talk to her."

She looked at the card and formed an "O" with her lips. Turning around, she revealed a completely bare backside, exposing a well-rounded derriere sporting a tattoo on the left cheek showing puckered lips with the words, "Kiss Me." In what appeared to be an afterthought, she placed the feather duster across the buttocks' great divide and walked toward one of the rooms. Oliver, entranced at the shifting movements of her behind, looked at Mannheim for comment.

"Put your eyeballs back into your head, Jocko. This is only act one."

"She's not really a maid," Oliver declared with a show of sophistication.

"Brilliant observation. That duster's probably a prop for tickling some guy's gazonkis and his tingling balls. She may be exactly what that French economist was hoping for at that New York hotel."

Madame Tatiana emerged from a room appearing somewhat frazzled; she adjusted strands of hair fallen over her forehead and was pushing up her sagging bosom. Mannheim studied the aging queen as she approached and noted her tired eyes with crow's feet and fine periorbital lines. Her once curvaceous figure had succumbed to the unrelenting gravitational pull of maturity.

Upon seeing Mannheim, she extended her arms to embrace him, and sang out in her distinctive dialect, "Dear Boy, I miss you. Vhy you don't come to see Tatiana more often? I see other police dicks, but not you."

"I'm sure you do."

She gave Oliver a hasty assessment, then turned to Mannheim. "Who is your handsome young friend here? You are inviting him to taste the delicacies what Madame Tatiana serves?" She laughed and elbowed the uneasy Oliver.

"Let's go where we can talk," Mannheim said.

"I have appointment...." She looked at her watch.... "in twenty minutes with judge from superior court."

"Is he here on official business or monkey business?"

Tatiana threw her head back and laughed. "Monkey, with a long tail business."

"That figures. If you tell us what we want to know, it will take less than five minutes. If it takes longer, I'll talk to the judge and ask him to hang onto his cajones for a few minutes more."

38

With the two detectives following behind her, Tatiana walked slowly across the lavishly furnished parlor that served as a showcase of nineteenth century opulence, and as a waiting room for johns who had appointments. Oliver, slack-jawed and wide-eyed, looked in amazement as he studied the baroque and rococo furnishings and wall hangings. Everywhere, there were over-sized framed photos of scantily clad escorts in sexy provoking poses. He looked at two johns seated in over-stuffed chairs. The men were clearly trying to conceal their identities. One held an open newspaper in front of him; the other buried his head in a girlie magazine.

Pausing before a glass covered alcove in the wall that housed a ubiquitous, expressionless haloed Christ's Icon, Mannheim tilted his head toward *Him* and asked Tatiana if she thought *He* might object to the activities of her establishment.

"Oh, no, He say is good to enjoy all pleasures in life; not to make war or killing. Besides, we make big contribution to church and get special blessings."

Mannheim doubted the accuracy of Tatiana's understanding of the teaching of Jesus, but accepted her account of largess to the church.

Tatiana continued, "I learn important lesson early in life: to make much money you must do good fucking."

Mannheim poked Oliver. "There you have the solution to all of mankind's problems reduced to the lowest common denominator."

In a small utilitarian room quite unlike the grandly furnished room they had just walked through, Tatiana sat at an unadorned desk with one wooden chair. The arrangement discouraged others from lingering in the establishment business center. With her elbows on the desk and her chin cradled on the back of her hands, she looked up at the detectives. "What brings your flat feet to my office?"

"We came to hear you murder some idiomatic expressions."

She looked askance.

Mannheim took a small spiral notebook out of his shirt pocket, licked his index finger and flipped several pages. "Tatiana, three of your employees...."

She interrupted. "Please, Mr. Policeman, these girls are not *my* employees. They are free agents—social escorts who entertain gentlemen in their own quarters, and pay to me rent...."

"Save the palaver. I know you run a first class establishment that caters to a select clientele who pays through the nose for the kind of screwing their own wives have either forgotten how to give, or never knew how to give in the first place. I also know you come in for half the girls' take...." He put up his hand. "Don't argue the point. Look, we came to talk with those three gals. They participated more frequently with Peter Bruxton in his suite than any of the others."

Tatiana listened but said nothing.

"Their names are: Tootsie Flambé, René Flaming and Pussy Galoire." Replacing the notebook, Mannheim stared at Tatiana. "I want those girls to report to the sheriff's office on Gerald Ford tomorrow at 9:00 a.m. with their appointment books."

Tatiana shook her head. "But that is not possible."

"I'm not asking," Mannheim raised his voice. "I'm telling you. Tomorrow at 9:00...."

Still shaking her head, Tatiana said, "You don't let me finish. Those girls are gone. Poof."

"What? Where the hell are they? Where did you send their last pay checks?"

Pushing herself back into her chair, Tatiana said, "You do not understand what I am saying. These girls don't work for me. They are free agents. They only rent space here. After Bruxton was murdered they disappear."

Mannheim grabbed the edge of the desk and leaned toward her. In a deliberate and harsh monotone, he said, "Tatiana, you're not talking to a raw recruit here who believes any bullshit that's thrown at him. Don't try to tell me the girls working here are free agents who pay you rent. I know your modus operandi. You collect all revenue from every gal based on her performance, combined with quarter hourly rates. Now don't tell me different. Furthermore, you keep books on all receipts, you accept major credit cards, you have instant credit checks, and all checks are accepted or rejected by you. Answer us honestly, or we'll subpoena all your books."

Tatiana started to fidget. "So what you want I should do?"

"Tell me what arrangements were made between those women and Bruxton?"

"You want I should tell you what kind of tricks they make for him?"

Mannheim straightened up and took a long breath. "No, dammit, I want to know what payoffs were made, and to whom, and I want to know if Bruxton ever reneged on a payment, or if he ever threatened or harmed any of those girls. That's why we wanted to interview them."

"You must believe me when I tell you; I do not know where they are. They never tell me that he hurt them. They don't say anything about their time with him, except that sometimes they laugh."

"What was so damned funny?"

She paused.

"They laugh and say he was too small. They call him junior size. But they don't tell him. They make good show for him by making sounds like pleasure."

Turning his head aside, Oliver attempted to remain serious by contorting his mouth then putting his hand over it.

"Who kept the records on the girls' time with Bruxton, and who collected the monies?" Mannheim asked.

Annoyance and resentment exacerbated Tatiana's weariness, and she stood, uttering a sigh. "You ask too many questions, and you have no right to know." She looked at her watch. "Besides, I have next client to meet, and I must have time to freshen up."

Mannheim blocked the exit, folded his arms across his chest and raised his chin. "Answer my question: did Bruxton pay the girls directly?"

"Yes."

"And who did they turn their earnings over to?"

"A bell hop."

"Jack Locke?"

"Yes."

"What was your take?"

"The escort service took twenty-five percent." Tatiana pushed Mannheim aside, opened the door and walked away.

Mannheim called after her, "We'll be back."

As they walked to the vehicle, Oliver asked Mannheim, "What the hell did we learn there?"

"Nothing much, except that it's a pretty good bet none of the call girls or Tatiana or the bell hop wanted him dead. They all made a pretty good living off that fucking jack rabbit."

Mannheim looked at Oliver. "Now, what the hell are you laughing at?"

"Tatiana said the girls described Bruxton's cock as small—junior size."

"Small cock, big ego, too goddamn much money—must be a syndrome to cover all that. I'll ask Doc Harrington to name it. Docs always have names for everything. They can always name a condition, even if they can't cure it."

Oliver looked at Mannheim, who grew quiet, and asked, "What're you thinking?"

"Kurtz at the hotel this evening...."

"Yeah, what about him?"

"Let's go back there. Something about that whole scene bothers me."

At the hotel entrance, the detectives were about to emerge from their sedan when Mannheim elbowed Oliver. "Look at the dame getting out of the cab. Isn't that Mary Bruxton's secretary? What's her name?"

Oliver turned in his seat to catch a glimpse of the woman. "You mean Melinda?"

"Yeah, isn't that her?"

"Could be. You supposing there's any connection between Kurtz and her?" Oliver asked.

Mannheim shrugged. "It's a big hotel, lots of affairs...."

Once inside the hotel, both detectives walked slowly, maintaining a distance of ten to fifteen feet behind Melinda. They stopped as she walked to a bank of elevators and stepped into a waiting one. The door closed, and although the detectives approached it, they hadn't a clue as to the level the passenger had gone.

"Let's find out if she's registered in the hotel," Mannheim said.

"Do you know her last name?"

"No, but...."

Oliver looked at his watch. "We've been farting around all night, swiping at cobwebs. It's nine o'clock. Let's get the hell out of here. We can get her name tomorrow, and you can chase her up a flagpole if you want to. I've got to turn in...."

"Okay, okay. I just don't want to lose perspective."

39

The physical fitness room in the Bruxton estate housed an array of equipment that was the equivalent to that found in the grandest hotels. Treadmills, stationary bicycles, rowing machines, free-standing weights and power machines were spaced around a wall-mounted, theatre-sized TV screen. Mary Bruxton labored on a treadmill at a pace of three and a half miles per hour. Her back and underarm areas were damp with perspiration; her cheeks flushed; her neck glistened with sweat, and her face was drawn from exhaustion.

Approaching briskly, Melinda, her personal secretary, covered the mouthpiece of a cell phone and extended it to her.

In a voice quivery from the treadmill, Mary asked, "Who is it, and what do they want?"

Melinda whispered, "It's Ellie Bissell."

Mary's shoulders sagged. "For chrissake, I don't want to talk to her. Make up some excuse."

"She insists on talking to you. Says it's very important. Has to do with the estate."

Mary shut off the TV, stopped the treadmill, and grabbed a towel from the side support to wipe her neck. "Give me the damn phone." With unconcealed annoyance, she said, "Yes, what is it?" She listened for a moment, then muffled a sigh. "All right, meet me for lunch at the Las

Palmas in Rancho Mirage." She looked at her watch. "It's 11:30. Give me an hour and a half to shower and dress. No, I won't bring anyone with me, and by the same token, I don't expect you to bring anyone with you."

Ninety minutes later, Mary Bruxton emerged from her persimmon colored convertible in an iridescent teal pantsuit selected especially because it complemented the color of the vehicle. The valet walked around the vehicle to assist her, noting her personalized license plates, which read: MB'S MB. "Hello Mrs. Bruxton," he said as he offered her his hand. "Welcome to the Las Palmas."

"Thank you." She handed her keys to the valet, and nodded briefly to the doorman who also greeted her by name; then she took quick steps, producing a clickety-clack from stiletto heels that struck the Mexican tiles of the lobby as she walked toward the dining room.

"Good afternoon, Mrs. Bruxton." The maitre d' bowed and rendered the obsequious smile reserved for patrons who were known as generous tippers. Mary looked for Ellie Bissell in the elegant dining area with its dark mahogany wood-paneled wainscoting, Currier and Ives prints, white linen napery, and tall wine goblets. Single long stem red roses in slender silver vases adorned each table.

Seated next to a window overlooking the gardens, Ellie waved tentatively. Her face, devoid of makeup, seemed diminished by a stiff bouffant hairstyle that might have been in vogue several decades ago, but was certainly not au courant. It resembled nothing less than a junior-size shako helmet. Her flower-patterned cotton dress reached the mid-neck line in a graceless fashion consistent with deep Southern Baptist protocol.

Mary, impatient, and unaccustomed to small talk, tried to sound casual as the waiter assisted her into her chair.

"Ellie, good seeing you again. How are you feeling, and how long before the blessed event?"

In a distinct Oklahoma twang, Ellie said, "I'm fine,

now that the morning sickness is over. I'm due in about six months, ma'am."

The waiter approached to take their drink orders. Mary ordered a vodka gimlet, Ellie a glass of milk.

Placing her elbows on the table, Mary hunched forward. "All right, Ellie, what can I do for you?" Mary fully suspected that lawyers had coached Ellie.

"Well," Ellie started her rehearsed lines, "you know, your late husband...." She stopped then added quickly, "He forcefully violated me a number of times."

Mary's brow arched. "Do tell, and where did these lovers' trysts occur?"

"I beg your pardon?"

"Where did you two have intercourse?"

"Well, we went to the Springs Hotel most of the time, but sometimes in his office on the sofa and on his chair. I would sit on his lap...."

Mary shook her head and put up her hand. "Please spare me the sordid details." She glanced around, hoping there were no eavesdroppers. "From your description, it occurs to me that the activity was consensual."

"I'm not sure I know what that means, ma'am."

"It means you both agreed to it, and you probably enjoyed it." Mary snapped a strip of celery like an exclamation mark. She closed her eyes momentarily and thought to herself, *this creature is completely illiterate. How in the hell did she function as a secretary? No wait. That's a really stupid question.*

Ellie affected a look of innocence. "Oh, no ma'am. Mr. Bruxton said that doing *it* was just another way of pleasing the boss, and if I expected to advance in my job, I had to...."

Mary cut her off again. "So you were forced to go to his luxury suite any number of times and accept his invitations to fancy dinners. Tell me, did he give you any gifts?"

"Yes, ma'am. He bought me a darling little VW convertible since my old car was kind of rickety, and he bought me this lovely watch." She advanced her wrist to show Mary a Rolex with a diamond-studded bezel.

"Seems like you were pretty well compensated. That means he paid you well." *Either this gal is demented, or she's the shrewdest cookie in the jar.*

"Yes ma'am, but I'm pregnant now, and I just don't know what I'm going to do. I can't have an abortion. My daddy being a Fundamentalist, is against that, and I can't afford to keep it."

"What do you want of me?"

Ellie studied the tabletop and straightened an imaginary crease in the tablecloth. "Could you pay for the baby's delivery and other expenses?"

"What would you consider reasonable payment?"

"About five hundred thousand dollars or so?" Her naïve voice escalated with the question.

"That may be reasonable to some but not to me."

Mary's response did not surprise Ellie. "My attorney said that a court might award me a million dollars."

"Oh, he did, did he? Tell me," Mary's eyes locked onto Ellie's, "did you have intercourse with anyone else before your pregnancy?"

"Why, no ma'am. Why would I do that?"

Mary ignored her question. "What did your preacher father expect to do when he ran into Mr. Bruxton's office with a gun? Did he demand money for your pregnancy?"

"Well, I guess so, or he expected Mr. Bruxton to marry me since he was the father-to-be."

"The presumptive father-to-be."

"I—I, don't know what you mean, ma'am."

Mary leaned across the table and with a deliberate icy incisiveness said, "Listen to me closely, Ellie. You could have had intercourse with Peter Bruxton a thousand times, and you'd *never* become pregnant."

Ellie tilted her head, and with a quizzical expression said, "I'm sorry, ma'am, I'm not sure I understand what you mean."

Mary sat back, sipped her drink, then dabbed the corners of her mouth with her napkin. "Mr. Bruxton, for all his stud-like activity was no more effective at siring offspring than a gelding. You're a farm girl, you know what I mean."

Ellie, with open-mouth wonder, nodded and followed Mary's every syllable.

"That's right, Ellie, a gelding, a sterile horse. After your baby is born, a DNA test will prove that my deceased husband whose DNA was preserved, by the way, was not and never could have been the father of that child. Do you understand? He had no sperm." Again, Ellie nodded absently. "So you can tell your attorney to fish in other waters or face a hellish countersuit, and you can tell your holier-than-thou father, as soon as he gets out of jail, that he can start pointing his shot-gun elsewhere."

Ellie lowered her head, wiped tears with her napkin and placed her hands in her lap. In a hoarse whisper she said without looking up, "That man, that preacher, is really not my father." Mary studied Ellie and waited for an explanation. "He's my mother's special friend."

"You have my sympathy. Care to tell me who the real father is?"

Ellie hesitated, and continued to look down while twisting the napkin in her lap. "It was him, my mother's friend—the preacher."

40

Compared to landings at Los Angeles or San Francisco, the approach to Bozeman International Airport was always welcome to the sophisticated traveling experiences of Mary Bruxton; it was delightfully uncongested.

The Lear Jet taxied toward a hangar at the far end of the airport where a black Chevrolet Avalanche waited. When the plane door opened, Mary appeared, clutching the mink collar on her full-length coat. She took a deep breath, and shut her eyes as the wind whipped her face and tousled her hair. How wonderful not to be assailed by the industrial and automobile fumes that were so much a part of LAX. The faint fragrance of harvested wheat took her back to her childhood on the farm in eastern Montana.

That uncomplicated farm life, shared with doting parents and two older brothers who treated her like a princess, evoked sweet nostalgia. She had never known such encompassing love and affection since. Although her parents had died years ago; her older brother had been killed in Viet Nam, and her younger brother had died in a blaze as a volunteer firefighter in western Montana, she still felt deeply rooted to this fertile valley. When her husband, Peter, suggested creating a resort here in a remote forested area twelve years ago, she was elated, but disagreed with him on policy. She wanted a development accessible to many; he insisted on an exclusive enclave for the rich and famous, arguing that they needed an escape from the prying, gawking slobs and paparazzi. Besides, he'd said, the profits from the sale of luxury homes would be much greater. She agreed, but only reluctantly. Peter had always shown a keen business sense, that is, until recently.

Mary's younger brother's only son, Matt, emerged from the Avalanche and hurried towards the plane. At six feet, wearing a worn leather jacket, stocking hat, Levis and mud-encrusted boots, he looked the part of a prototypical Montanan.

Mary smiled as she descended the steps and held on to the wire handrail. Jim Keyes emerged from the plane behind her, carrying her luggage. On the tarmac, she stood on her toes to put her arms around Matt to hug and kiss him.

Jim placed the luggage on the back seat of the Avalanche, then helped Mary. She took the front seat, and Jim closed the door for her, then climbed into the back seat next to the luggage. Matt got in the drivers' seat and started the vehicle. Once they turned onto the low-trafficked highway, Mary turned to look at Matt. "How are things going since I talked to you last?"

Matt's boyish charm and light-heartedness changed. "I'm not sure Uncle Peter left you any great income resource with this project, Aunt Mary. We've had a number of cancellations on our home-sites in the past weeks, and a few of the buyers have defaulted on their payments."

Biting her lower lip, Mary listened to Matt, who was the overseer in charge of construction. He continued, "We need an infusion of about twenty-five million to pay suppliers, tradesmen, and employees to get the club through the ski season. The banks are playing hardball; they're simply not lending. But of course, you know all that."

She had been keenly aware of everything he was saying, but hearing it only made the dreadful financial crisis more poignant. To add to the gloomy atmosphere, snow flurries gathered on the windshield. "At twenty percent interest plus points, those blood-suckers want to steal our property, plain and simple."

"Aunt Mary, we're already in hock, up to our eyeballs— almost four hundred million, and those Swiss bankers are tightening their purse strings. You know, of course, they flatly refused our last request for additional funds."

Mary looked askance. "But our assets are worth almost twice that!"

"Not really, our assets are in undeveloped land, and in this rotten economy, there aren't many takers for lots or homes. Let's face it, we're being boxed in." He paused then glanced at her. "Whatever happened to the two hundred fifty million Uncle Peter got from Credit Suisse and put into a private account?"

Mary stiffened and turned to look at Matt. "How did you know about that?"

"Everybody around here knows. It's been in *The Chronicle* every day, and our creditors want the public to know. They say we've mismanaged our resources. They're making statements to the press about foreclosing unless we make payments soon. Their lawyers say that you and Uncle Peter received four hundred million dollars and two hundred and fifty million of that was in an unsecured loan Uncle Peter stashed into a private account."

Mary turned aside and muttered, "Those bastards, nothing's sacred to them." She hesitated before continuing, "Unfortunately, much of that money has been spent. Your uncle bought properties he was sure would increase in value. I doubt if we can sell them at half of what we've paid. I think we're closer than ever to bankruptcy."

"We've got quite a few ticked-off buyers who've already ponied-up three hundred thousand dollars each as down payments. Bankruptcy of the lodge would only make them angrier."

She turned aside and huffed. "They're not losing nearly as much as I am. I've taken out a loan of forty million secured by the Rancho Mirage property, and I'm trying to sell my castles in France and England." She paused and sneered. "Isn't that a laugh? I figure I need castles now like I need menstrual cramps. No one is standing in line for them, either."

They traveled along Highway 191 toward the project, fifty miles south of Bozeman. Mary turned to look at Jim Keyes, who had said little, but occasionally nodded or shook his head to indicate agreement. Mary reached back to place her hand on his. "Your investment in this project is in jeopardy, too. If Peter were alive he might have figured out some way of protecting your money."

"Yeah, money was his thing," Jim said.

The Avalanche stopped at the handsome stone archway entrance of the Sunburst Club. A uniformed guard emerged from his quarters; he gave Matt an okay sign then looked across the seat and smiled broadly at Mary. "Good seeing you again, Mrs. Bruxton. Enjoy your stay."

Mary nodded and looked away. "I shudder to think that over four hundred people will be losing their jobs if this place folds." She thought: how did we ever fall into this shitty abyss? And to think, we contributed thousands to two campaigns of that idiot president who had no more sense than a billy goat about finances, or anything else for that matter. He's the one who's responsible for this damn recession and for all our troubles. Mary was jolted from her thoughts when the truck struck a jarring pot-hole.

"Sorry about that, Aunt Mary. This road is in bad need of repair. Some of these holes could swallow a Mack truck."

"Matt, this road is less than ten years old...."

"Right. I hate to be constantly carping, but if Uncle Peter hadn't skimped on materials and had used good construction techniques, this road would have held up. This shoddy work would have been unacceptable to the county inspector of roads, but since we're not in the county, our construction doesn't come under county jurisdiction.

We're falling apart before we really get started."

This added to Mary's frustration, and she sighed wearily. "Matt, dear, just drive me to my chalet, so I can go over the loan papers. I'm facing a new group of lenders tomorrow, and I want to sound as though I know what I'm talking about."

Hoping to point out a number of problems needing attention, Matt was reluctant to tell his aunt at that point that he and six other engineers had not been paid in over three weeks. Although he would not quit, he knew the other men were hurting, and had threatened to walk off, claiming that unemployment compensation was better than the shaky promise of back-pay and questionable job security.

Matt lifted his aunt's suitcases out of the back of the extended cab while Jim Keyes took his overnight bag off the vehicle hanger. Carrying his aunt's suitcase toward the large alpine chalet, Matt was stopped by Jim who said, "I've got it, thanks anyway."

Mary kissed Matt and said she would call in the morning, but for now, she needed to peruse the papers, make some calls, have a drink and rest her weary bones.

"I understand." he said, and turned to leave.

Jim removed his shoes and followed Mary into the spacious home. The great room, with its exposed log-beamed vaulted ceiling and furnishings, was enormous, and suggestive of a cattle baron's estate. As they passed the fireplace, Mary pointed to it. "Jim, could you get a fire going?"

"Sure Mary," he replied.

Jim deposited Mary's luggage in her bedroom, then returned to the great room and placed three logs from a bin next to an oversized fireplace made with river-washed rock; he started the fire, then carried his own overnight bag upstairs.

Mary, once settled into her bedroom, undressed, threw her garments on the bed, then stood sideways in front of the full-length mirror. She inhaled, and pressed her palms on her slightly protuberant abdomen before walking into the adjoining bathroom with its large, open, marble-walled shower stall. She turned the water on, stepped inside, and began to let the steamy water spray forcefully upon her head, neck and back. Jim Keyes came into the room carrying two goblets of red wine. He set the glasses on a dresser and looked over at his lady boss, her skin covered with cascading soapy lather.

She turned to look at him, and called out above the sound of the splashing water, "Don't just stand there. Get out of that uniform and get in here to scrub my back."

Jim smiled. He quickly disrobed, and hurried into the shower. He stood behind her while she handed him her soapy washcloth. Gently, he moved the cloth over her back, then moved closer to her. His engorged member pushed against her derriere. Coming even closer, he dropped the washcloth and touched her breasts. The water splashed on their heads. Mary raised her face and closed her eyes to allow the water to spill onto her face. She reached forward to shut the water off, then grabbed two large terry cloth towels. She kept one for herself and gave the other to Jim. "Let's finish this on the bed," she said. They both toweled off as they made their way into the bedroom. Mary lay on the bed, placed a pillow under her pelvis, and spread her legs. "Now show me how hard you can drive."

Sexually fulfilled, Mary rolled off the bed, stood up, and glanced back at Jim Keyes's nude body lying spread-eagle on the king-sized bed. Impatient, she threw a towel at him. "Get up," she said.

Mary stood before the mirror in her robe, brushing her tousled hair after the fête d'amour. Jim, still in the nude, walked up behind her, nuzzled her neck and filled his senses with the silky softness of her skin, and the delicate fragrance of her body lotion. She ignored him and continued to brush her hair. With her elbow, she jabbed his abdomen. "I told you to get dressed before someone comes."

"Want me to put on the black mariah uniform?" Mary

did not respond. He continued, "I want you to know that I care for you more now than I ever have. I don't mean just this thrashing around in the sack—although that's great, don't get me wrong. I'm just thinking of all the nice things you've done for me over the years: gifts at holiday times, bonuses, you know—things like that."

Mary scarcely acknowledged his comments.

Jim had always been protective of Mary; even before they started their affair. He'd always thought she deserved someone better than Bruxton, and Jim was definitely better, at least morally. Jim felt an enormous pride in his secret relationship with this fabulously wealthy and attractive woman whose picture appeared often on the society pages of the local newspaper. She was head of this charitable organization and that one, and she hosted the governor and both state senators at social gatherings. Hell, she could have had any damned good-looking guy she wanted, but she had chosen him, at least from time to time, and for that he was grateful. Of course, he was unable to brag about their intimacies for obvious reasons. Theirs was a kind of secretive beauty and the beast relationship— not that he was ugly, in fact he was still good-looking for a guy in his mid-fifties. Much of his hair was intact, even if it was getting gray, and receding a bit. Being her part-time love slave wasn't all that bad either. Sure, he'd cater to her every whim, and he'd protect her with his life, if he had to. And though he was a widower, he didn't mess with other women. She knew that—hell, she insisted on it. Truth is, she could get real wild in bed like she was starving for it. No one could compare with Mary on that account.

He often fantasized about marriage to her. That would be his ultimate wish come true. In fact, he wanted her as his wife more than anything in the world, if only she could be more serious about him. Jim could just see himself married to Mary. Why, he'd be like a prince consort, accompanying her here and there, and shaking hands with this big shot and that one, helping her select clothes and planning trips—things like that. Those thoughts had fueled Jim's dreams for years. Without them, his life would have been like a road going nowhere, and ultimately facing a cul de sac.

Of course, there was that tinhorn actor-cowboy, Frank Parma, who had come on the scene for awhile, but fortunately, he seemed to have worn out his welcome with Mary in pretty short order. Jim would have asked Mary about that relationship, but she was sort of funny that way. She refused to discuss personal matters with him. He had so much that he would want to have shared with her if only she'd let him. But she'd made it clear from the start; she wanted no lingering emotional attachments. She wanted only the release from tension that sex provided.

Jim knew Mary had had other affairs after Bruxton started ignoring her appeals for affection. But in the end, she always came back to old reliable Jim, and he knew that one day, she would see how much he meant to her, and return his long spurned affection. He deserved her, and she deserved him. She deserved everything after having put up with Bruxton all those years. Bruxton was a fool to have cheated on Mary. More the fool, because she was such a treasure. But that was most likely a large part of the problem for Bruxton. He couldn't handle having an equal as a spouse. He needed to dominate. That was why he'd sought out ever-younger women—women who were easily impressed with his wealth, and over whom he could exercise dominance.

If Bruxton was aware of Mary's liaisons, he made no mention of them. On the other hand, Mary was well aware of his philandering, and constantly worried that his escapades would jeopardize the estate. There had already been an attempt at a paternity suit, and a near fatal confrontation with a jealous husband or lover. The possible publicity and notoriety from such events would have caused Mary unthinkable hardship. Jim wanted only to protect her. If her character was flawed, he did not see it. She was his personal 'high-on-a-pedestal goddess,' and he worshipped her. Her most demanding requests, such as going to the casino in the wee hours of the morning, he obliged without the slightest hesitation. When she was lonely and craved intimacy he obliged eagerly. Theirs was a relationship that made no deep incursions into the psyches, needed no explanations, and carried no regrets—at least for Mary. And she set the rules. Aside from those moments of physical intimacy, they lived separate and highly unequal lives. To outsiders, they appeared to have a normal employer/ employee relationship. Their clandestine affairs were a way of avenging their common nemesis, Peter Bruxton. Paradoxically, they both owed their financial stability to him, yet they detested him for the way he had always demeaned them, made them feel inferior, and dependent. Not even in death did he warrant their forgiveness. In fact, from Mary's standpoint, the entire funeral ceremony was a sham, just a pile of unmitigated bullshit. The recital of Bruxton's sins she thought would have been far more entertaining than the false praises heaped upon him. His sins could have curled the hems on those Episcopalian robes.

41

The door chimes were followed by three loud knocks. Mary, in her robe, shouted, "Just a minute." She hurried to help Jim gather his clothes, and then told him to go to his room upstairs and remain out of sight. She walked quickly to the door and found her nephew holding several large envelopes.

"Sorry to disturb you, Aunt Mary. I forgot to give you this mail. It was delivered to our office yesterday. Might be important; some of it looks sort of official."

Mary pulled the robe tightly around her neck as the cold wind whipped around the door. "Come in Matt. We'll talk for a few minutes over a cup of coffee."

Matt removed his muddy boots and left them at the door. Together, they walked towards the kitchen. As they passed the living room stairwell, they both noticed a pair of men's Jockey shorts lying at the foot of the stairs. Mary reached over and grabbed them, crumpled them into a ball, and shoved them into the pocket of her robe. Neither she nor Matt said a word.

"Let me make the coffee, Aunt Mary. I've gotten pretty good at that lately." Matt shuffled around in his heavy socks, searching through several kitchen cabinets in search of the coffee and coffee cups.

"Matt sit down. I'll make the coffee. I know my way around a kitchen. Did you know I was a short order cook, and a waitress for some years before I met your uncle? I can still sling hash with the best of them, even though I haven't had to in over twenty years. On occasion, just for the hell of it, I'd prepare my own breakfast in the mornings in that thirty thousand square foot barn I occupy in the desert. I say occupy because I don't know how much longer that place is going to be mine—legally mine, that is. I've got to sell some property to raise enough cash to keep this place afloat and out of the hands of those money lenders."

"Aunt Mary, if I'm not too nosey, would you mind telling me what properties you have that you can turn into cash?"

After mulling the question over, she said, "A lot of them. Unfortunately, I don't have nearly enough to offset my liabilities." Looking at the vaulted ceiling she began to enumerate: "Two jets, twelve automobiles, a grand estate off the French Riviera, a drafty castle in Scotland, a casa grande in Mexico, and believe it or not, a private island in the Caribbean." She sighed. "God, we never spent time at any of those places."

Matt whistled low.

"And of course, there's my jewelry and wardrobe. All of which will bring in about ten cents on the dollar."

"Can't you protect your assets by declaring bankruptcy under Chapter 11 or something like that? I ask without really knowing what I'm talking about. I've just been hearing that kind of talk around here."

Mary smiled wanly. "Bankruptcy relief isn't possible when you're the owner of millions in assets, but I'll let my lawyers work that out with the Federal bankruptcy court. In the meantime, I've got to figure out a way to keep this fourteen thousand acre wonderland from becoming a financial albatross."

She reached for the mail on the table and stacked the envelopes, then in rotation read the return addresses. "Just look at these letters: attorneys, contractors, building suppliers. Every one of them making payment demands.

Just a few months ago this resort was valued at four hundred seventy-five million. Our debt was about four hundred million. She scoffed, "And now we can't seem to sell any of it."

Matt listened, stared into his cup of coffee, and, with his middle finger, slowly outlined the rim of the cup. "If you had to, Aunt Mary, would you or could you just walk away from this project?"

With a smile of resignation, she said, "Hardly. You mean like Sarah Palin walking away from the governorship of Alaska—not while my personal assets are valued in the millions and workers and suppliers have to be paid. And then there is the problem of one hundred six irate owners who have made sizable down payments. The U.S. bankruptcy judge would order the sale of all my assets, including my personal treasures, to pay off...." She stopped when she noted a return address on a special delivery envelope that read, *Regional Office of the Western States AFL-CIO, O. Brazilowicz, Director.* She reached for her reading glasses in the pocket of her robe. Speaking softly aside, she asked herself how in the hell did Brazilowicz know she was in Montana, then as in a reply to her own question, she remembered that she had talked with Deena a week ago. Deena must have told her boyfriend Johnny, who in turn must have told his father.

Mary tore away the envelope edge and scanned the letter, then read a portion to her nephew. She shook her head and scoffed as she explained that Oscar Brazilowicz was aware of the financial difficulties existing at the Sunburst Club and was indicating that he'd be happy to direct union investment funds to the Club in exchange for a major share of the ownership. The amount under consideration would be fifty million. The union would control all future development of the recreation area, and all existing debts would be assumed. Mary looked at Matt. "I can imagine how that buffoon would settle debts."

Reading a personal note, a P.S., she leaned back in her chair and laughed. It was a welcome respite from all the gloomy talk. "Why that old S.O.B., that overblown horny goat is propositioning me. Says he'd like to invite me to a weekend in Cancun where we could explore business opportunities." Mary folded the letter and replaced it in the envelope. "What he means is that he'd like the opportunity to explore *me* and give *me* the business."

Matt, who had never thought of his aunt as an object of physical desire, said, "Aunt Mary do you think this guy Brasil... whatever his name is, could have possibly been the one who ordered the murder on Uncle...." Matt stopped the conversation when Jim Keyes appeared at the kitchen entrance. Both turned to look at him.

"I just heard the word 'murder' and wanted to know what was going on."

Matt was taken aback at Jim's casual appearance, a plaid shirt, jeans and loafers. Matt's opinion of Jim was that of a stand-offish hired hand functioning unobtrusively in a proper uniform; one not involved in family affairs.

Mary gave Jim a disapproving look for interrupting a private matter. She did not want him to be a part of this conversation, and, under pretext, asked, "Jim would you call the garage and have them bring a car around? I want to tour the properties."

Jim raised his right index and middle fingers in an abbreviated salute, nodded and left the room.

With Jim out of ear shot, Matt said, "Aunt Mary, I'd be happy to do that with you."

Mary sipped her coffee, then pushed the envelopes on the table aside. "I want to see what's going on around here, and I don't want to take you away from your work. Besides, that will give Jim something to do. He was a loyal employee to your Uncle Peter over the years. Their friendship went back years before I married Peter. Whenever I asked Peter about their friendship he became evasive and would change the subject, and if I persisted, he became hostile. After a while I gave up asking."

Mary gathered the envelopes and looked at the return addresses again. She selected two and shook her head. "Here are two letters from the Federal Bankruptcy Judicial Department. They're as much a pain in the ass as the Swiss Money lenders."

Jim drove the company's four-wheel Hummer cautiously to avoid potholes and construction barriers. A light dusting of snow had fallen on the undulating row of framed houses in various stages of construction. They formed a strangely mournful site in the approaching dusk: open kegs of nails, bales of electrical wiring, scattered pvc pipes on raw flooring, porcelain tubs, sinks and toilets; some in unopened cardboard containers. The skeletal framework provided see-through visibility of winding stairwells, rock-faced fireplaces, vaulted ceilings and slabs of marble—all indicators of luxury homes moldering after sudden work stoppages.

Mary shook her head. "I hope to hell this doesn't become a graveyard with my epitaph written over these wooden coffins."

42

At the Pioneer Town movie lot, Scooter stomped through the louvered swinging doors of the dreary canteen that reeked of whisky, beer and cigarette smoke. He removed his rain-soaked, oily misshapen cowboy hat, slapped it against his chaps and hollered, "Whoo-ee! Goddamn, it's comin' down like a horse pissin' on a flat rock." He ambled past several cowboy extras seated at the bar, all of whom greeted him with abbreviated high signs. At a rear table, hunched over a mug of coffee, a somber Frank Parma waved him over.

"Howdy, Frankie Boy. You reserve this seat fer me, didja? Well, I sure thank ya. Ain't this a helluva mornin' to strike a set? Just a couple more retakes, if this damnable downpour ever stops, and we can quit this here memorable cin-ee-matic triumph."

Frank rubbed his eyes and stifled a yawn.

Scooter signaled the waitress for coffee. "Have you made peace with the lady of that fancy house, Frankie? You should be having clear sailing now that the old man's daid, right? 'Course, from all I read in the local newspapers, things ain't looking too good for her—not with that Montana Lodge facing bankruptcy and the home you're staying in offered for sale. You thinking the Bruxton gal's got too much on her mind for romance? Maybe she's just a mite bit tired of your pussy pettin? If she is, you might wind up with nothing more substantial 'n a horse's fart in a hurricane." He thanked the waitress for his coffee.

Parma shook his head and sighed. "Scooter, you've got a colorful way of talking. For your information, we had a little misunderstanding, that's all. Besides, Mrs. Bruxton reassured me that she had her lawyers draw up a codicil to her will giving me access to a fund for producing films, whether she lives or dies, and whether or not she remains competent. Given all that, I think I'm fairly secure." Frank sipped his coffee and shifted his eyes toward Scooter, expecting his pithy comments.

Scooter pushed his mug aside and spoke slowly, "Frankie, everything you're saying is all well and good, but this here old fool finds three bear traps with gapin' jaws, just waitin' to snare you." He put three fingers on the table and started to count off: "Number one: if there ain't no money left in the till, there ain't no money for you no way. Y'understand what I'm saying? Number two: a will can be changed at any time, yes sir, anytime. Number three: if you buy anything with her money, well, my boy, it's still her money and possession is nine-tenths of the law. If she doesn't like the way things are going, she can bring the curtain down on the show, maybe on the first act, just like that." He snapped his fingers. "You'd be a mite wise to make some kind of permanent arrangements, like gettin' hitched, and do it before she changes her mind or the credi-tors do it for her."

Frank leaned on the table, supported his chin in his hand and nodded slowly. "Yeah, you make a good case for closing a deal. Maybe I'll just fly up to Bozeman and have a chat with her."

"That's right. Have a little parley with her. You got a cell phone. Go on, call her now."

Frank pulled out his phone and punched in Mary's number. "Mary? It's Frank. I miss you terribly Baby. This

place is nowhere without you. I've just got to see you."
He listened. "What do you mean, that's not a good idea?
There's no room? You've got to be kidding. Sure, I understand people are more conservative there, and with me
staying with you.... Baby, this is the twenty-first century,
c'mon, you're putting me off—okay, okay, I won't argue. You
can put me up in a charming bed and breakfast, the Fox
Hollow Inn in Bozeman on Mary Road? Heh, heh, I'll bet
the road was named for you." The edgy tone of the conversation was relieved by his last comment. "What's that? A
memorial service for Peter in one week? Sure, I'll come, but
why there? You've already held one in Palm Desert. I see.
Okay, baby, till next week. Prepare your little friend for a
real workout."

Scooter who had been listening, asked, "Who'd she go
up there with, Frankie?"

Parma looked at him with a blank expression. "I don't
know. Does that matter?"

Scooter raised his brows. "Yeah, it might.... it just might."

Mary, leaning to one side, placed her left hand on her
hip, grumbled as she moved slowly to the couch facing the
fireplace. "This damned back of mine is out of kilter again
and hurts like hell. What did I do to aggravate it?" She
called out, "Jim, get the pain medication from my dresser,
and make me a vodka gimlet chaser."

Jim Keyes came into the room and stopped to look
at her. "Should you be taking pain pills and an alcoholic
drink? The doctor warned...."

Mary stopped him. "Don't go flitting around me like
an old hen. Just do as I say. I wish Dr. Josh were here to give
me an injection. That last one really helped." She grunted
as she sat up to take the two pills offered by Jim and swallowed them with a sip of the vodka gimlet. She looked at

the gimlet. "I think this is more helpful than the pills."

"Do you want me to call Dr. Harrington? It's three o'clock our time, two o'clock their time; they should be back from lunch."

"Get that pillow at the end of the sofa and place it in the small of my back." She adjusted her sitting position with the pillow in place, but the frown on her face indicated continued discomfort. She became pensive and soliloquized. "Here I am one of the wealthiest broads in the country, if you discount this temporary financial reversal, and I'm not exercising my rights and privileges for relieving this damned pain." With a note of determination, she called out to Jim, "Phone Dr. Harrington's office and tell his girl I want to speak to him."

"Josh, darling, this is your pain-in-the-ass patient, Mary Bruxton. I'm in Montana. My back pain has come roaring back. I need you to fix it. No, sir, forget that. I won't let anyone here touch it. Let me propose a plan: how would you and Maggie like to spend a long weekend here? Now wait, hear me out before you say no. I'll put you up in a luxury cabin and you can ski, cuddle up before an open fire, toast marshmallows, and make love under a goose down blanket. Don't tell me you can't take the time. Sign out to someone as though you had an out-of-town family emergency. I'll send one of my jets to Palm Springs. That's right. If you don't have warm clothing, there's plenty of Peter's stuff around here, and Maggie can wear some of my winter clothes. We'll pick you up at the airport here. And for heaven's sake, don't forget your syringe and needle."

43

One week later, Frank had an hour and a half stopover at the Salt Lake City International Airport on his way to Bozeman. He walked around the busy airport thinking how he had missed the princely luxury of the Bruxton private jet that could have whisked him from LAX to Bozeman, in less than two hours. He had become accustomed to the ease and comfort, and thought his return to a plebeian lifestyle was absolutely unthinkable.

He worried about Mary's cool attitude toward him and wondered if she had become permanently indifferent toward him. He hadn't slept with her in several weeks. Didn't she miss that as much as he did? Frank felt for the Viagra in his shirt pocket and was reassured. He had not lost his desire and certainly not his virility, but the blue pill was good insurance. Again, he searched the deep recesses of his mind trying to understand what he might have done to displease her. Could it still be the blackout incident at her home when he stood behind her with the fireplace poker? But he'd explained all that. Surely she must realize that it was just coincidental.

Perhaps Mary no longer found his clever comments or his off-color jokes as amusing, but what the hell, that kind of dust settling happens in every love affair. Was it possible that somebody was horning in on his territory?

Mary wouldn't allow that—would she? Of course, she wasn't exactly a shrinking violet, and she did have a lusty sexual appetite. If anyone is beating my time—well, the old Sicilian knows all about vengeance. He was only three generations removed from the marauders who roamed the hills of Sardinia.

In his first-class seat, Frank had been nursing his second scotch and water and enjoying the warmth and mellowness that suffused his innards. He loosened his collar and pushed his back support to rest in the semi recumbent position. This was the lifestyle he did not want to relinquish. Although not as luxurious as a private jet, it was a hell of lot better than the kind of travel he had used several years ago. No more second class for him, no sir, that was for struggling slobs.

The people Mary introduced him to were refined and wealthy. They knew the good life. Okay, maybe some were less than completely honest, maybe they fudged on their taxes, skimmed profits before declaring them—so what? I still want to be a part of that scene, Frank thought to himself. I want the applause and the praise when I go to a charitable function and take a seat at the head table. I want to smile and nod and give a royal wave to the masses who look on while the cameras are flashing, and I still have a damned good smile.

I enjoy wearing my own custom-tailored tux, not a rented one doused with deodorant spray to cover up someone else's stink. But how far would I go to protect my position with Mary? Would I commit murder? He paused, looked out the window, moved his tumbler of scotch and soda in a small circle and mused, "You're fucking-A right I would."

Frank turned to watch the movements of the flight attendant and tried to clear his thoughts. He fantasized her in the buff, maybe wearing a thong but no bra. When she leaned toward him to ask if he wanted a refill, he imagined her bare breasts yearning to be caressed. He thought...but then he found himself thinking again about Mary Bruxton. Mary, whose breasts were ample, and only slightly pendulous. He knew he could fix things with Mary. After all, she had always enjoyed their intimacies. It was just a matter of rekindling the romance. Again, he touched the Viagra vial in his shirt pocket. Hell, he really didn't need it, but he knew the sustained action pleased Mary.

Stepping through the door of the Delta Airliner, Parma pulled his light gray Stetson rakishly over his left eye, his leather sheepskin jacket with a turned up collar and burnt-orange leather gloves made him appear rugged, like the Marlboro Man. His tailored Levis were cut to expose custom-made Italian alligator boots with pointed toes and elevated heels. He descended the stairs with a leather bag and looked around, hoping to see a familiar face. On previous visits with Mary, Matt, Mary's nephew, met them. This visit was decidedly different; there was no one to cheer his arrival, or to help with his luggage. What the hell, he had learned from his stage experience to project an open face to an unresponsive audience. His sunglasses protected his eyes from a gusting wind, and added to his imagined grand entrance.

Frank threw his bags into the back end of the rental Jeep, then looked at the sky. It had turned a foreboding dark gray in just the last few minutes, with heavy cumulus clouds seeming to boil in. To add to the gloom, the air was punctuated with light snowflakes and small pellets of hail that pinged on the top and hood of the Jeep. With directions on the passenger seat, he started for the Fox Hollow Inn.

After about fifteen minutes, Frank turned onto the street indicated by the directions. Off to his left, a sign with a running fox indicated the location of the Fox Hollow Inn.

Several small cottages surrounded one large house, all set in a verdant patch cleared of trees. Parma parked the Jeep, checked in with the proprietor in the main house, then made his way to one of the tidy cottages. He heaved his bag on the bed, opened it and turned it upside down to empty the contents. When the clothing and toilet articles were removed, he unzipped a false bottom, reached in and pulled out a leather holster from which he removed a gleaming chrome-plated .38 caliber Colt Python. Examining the safety, he rubbed the barrel lightly with his handkerchief, and then tossed it on the bed. Stepping into the shower, he stopped when he heard a knock at the door. Grabbing a terrycloth robe from a hook, hr hurried to the door to find the lady innkeeper with several nubby bath towels.

"Sorry to bother, Mr. Parma, these towels were supposed to be in your room before your arrival." She handed the towels to him and glanced at the revolver on the bed.

Parma, following her eyes, said, "We had target practice here the last time. This time I brought my own weapon."

"You know it's illegal to shoot firearms within the city limits," she said.

Parma replaced the gun in its holster. "I know. I'll be firing in the unincorporated area. I don't intend to knock anyone off—unless I'm forced to." He laughed openly. The lady innkeeper responded with a brief smile and left.

Parma reached for his cell to call Mary. He got her voicemail. "Mary," he said, "I'll be leaving here shortly, and I should be at the lodge in about an hour. I'm giving you fair warning: get rid of any male sniffers. I won't tolerate competition. I brought my six- shooter, and I'll use it if I have to." Parma intended to be humorous.

Mary, who had not answered the phone, but was listening to the message, was not amused.

44

"Josh, I sat in on a most interesting class at the senior citizen center last night before I conducted the First Aid class. You would have loved it." Maggie's ebullience was part of the charm that made her so endearing. Josh pushed aside a medical report and watched his animated wife explain further. "An elderly woman with a decided English accent was lecturing on the derivation of Anglo-Saxon surnames. She had two large reference books, and took names submitted from the audience. She gave the history of some of them without even referring to the books. Isn't that remarkable?"

"Yeah, I guess so."

"Anyway, I submitted my maiden name, Ballard, which she defined without hesitation as a medieval English nickname for a bald man, a transformation from the word, ball. Isn't that fascinating?"

Josh, said without enthusiasm, "Yes, fascinating."

"Do you know the origin of your name?"

He shook his head.

"Well, wait till you hear what she had to say about Harrington. She referred to one of those large reference books."

Josh cocked his head and raised one eyebrow in anticipation. Maggie, looked at her notes and read, "Harrington is derived from the ancient English, Hoe ferr, which is a nickname meaning, male goat." She stopped to giggle, then continued, "The name was given to those who came from Harrington in Northamptonshire, England. So, my dear, your name is derived from a male goat."

"My name may be derived from a male goat, but I really only develop horns when you're around."

Maggie smiled and put her arms around his neck. "I like it that way. You're my favorite horny goat."

"What other names did you explore?"

"I was so intrigued I bought a book on the derivation of common surnames." She reached for the book she had placed on the shelf and placed it on Josh's desk. "It'll be fun to use at our parties." She thumbed through the book and said, "Here for instance is the name Kurtz. Let me read what it says: its German derivation was given to those who were short in stature." Maggie continued to thumb through the first part of the book. "Here, Bruxton is probably derived from the Old English, Braxton...." Maggie noticed Josh stifling a yawn. "Am I boring you?"

"No, Love, I've got early morning surgery. Please forgive me. What you had to say about the origin of names is quite interesting, and I'm sure I'll enjoy looking through the book." Josh held Maggie to give her a goodnight kiss. His hands slid down her backside and gently but firmly squeezed her buttocks.

She smiled. "That's exactly what I'd expect from a horny old goat."

"I'm only half goat; a satyr, and I'm lecherous only with you."

"Show me." Maggie's playful command came as a challenge.

He scooped her up in his arms and carried her toward the bedroom while she giggled. "All right, my little woodland nymphet. I'm taking you to my lair where I'll have my way with you."

She covered his face with repeated kisses. "Oh, I do hope so."

Mannheim pushed aside several folders on his desk to allow space for the latest homicide reports; there were several from Desert Hot Springs. The L.A. gangs had established an outpost for their extended activity in the desert, approximately a hundred thirty miles from their base in the south end of L.A. While murders most often involved rival gangs, innocent people were being killed in the cross fire. Mayhem most often resulted from drug wars, robberies and hold-ups.

While studying several mug shots, Mannheim chatted with Oliver, who had been completing reports at his desk less than ten feet away. "Damn, these assholes are ugly looking dudes, and their tattoos don't help."

"Not all killers are ugly," Oliver said.

Mannheim called over his shoulder, "Excuse me, Mr. Absolute Correctness, I didn't mean to offend your sense of fairness regarding the socially derelict, deprived and depraved. I'd like to be around when one of those assholes fires at you. Then you and your holier-than-thou attitude can..."

Just then the phone rang. "Mannheim here. The Springs Hotel? Yeah. The report on Mr. Short's occupancy of room 1230.... I see. Did anyone with the first name of Melinda register that night?" After a pause, he said, "Okay, thanks."

Oliver approached Mannheim. "What did you learn?"

"That was the reservations clerk at the Springs. The suite next to Bruxton's on the night he was murdered was occupied by a Mr. Lawrence Short and his wife."

"What're you thinking, Tim?"

Mannheim studied the jottings on his scratch pad. "I'm thinking Larry Kurtz and Lawrence Short are one and the same. What do you think?"

"Relying on my German 101, I'd say, yes."

45

Bonnie Ouvray stood in the doorway wearing a bathrobe. She had a towel spiraled on her head. "Fresh from the shower, I see," Mannheim said as he came walking up the sidewalk.

Bonnie's smile, warm with anticipation, broadened as she replied. "Ah, my Prince Charming calls upon his lady fair with a lovely bouquet." She made a short curtsy. "Welcome to my humble abode, dear sir."

Bonnie took the flowers from Mannheim then kissed his cheek. "Did you like my greeting? I rehearsed it. I couldn't be sure whether you'd bring flowers or candy, so I had something planned for both." She led Mannheim into the living room and placed the bouquet in a vase on the coffee table.

"You're not only clever; you're also a good actress. Suppose I had brought nothing, were you prepared to say something about that?"

Bonnie tilted her head, smiled and placed her arms around Mannheim's neck. "I would have said, 'goodbye' and would have told you to go home, because I had a severe headache."

Mannheim was not quite sure whether she was teasing.

Bonnie burst out laughing. "Had you worried, didn't I? Poor baby, I was only teasing, no chance of that happening, my love. Why don't you make yourself comfortable? I'm going to dress. Give me fifteen minutes."

Mannheim gave her an abbreviated salute.

She stopped to face him and opened the top of her robe to expose her well-formed breasts. When he reached forward to touch them, she closed her robe, and backed away quickly, giggling in retreat. She turned and ran to her bedroom shouting, "Mustn't touch, yet."

Mannheim looked around the living room. The place had taken on a homey atmosphere he would be proud to call home. He looked at the pictures on the wall and the framed photographs on the mantel. He picked up a snap-shot-size photo and studied it. It showed a young mother on a porch swing with her arms around the shoulders of two children, a pretty girl of perhaps five and a boy about eight or nine. Another framed snapshot revealed two young adults in side-view kissing.... the woman caressing the side of the man's face; partially obscuring his features.

Mannheim picked up the photo and studied it closely, comparing the features of the woman in the second photo to the one in the first photo with her arms around the children. He decided she was the same person. He couldn't help feeling that she looked familiar. This had to be Bonnie's mother—same light brown pigmentation, dark hair, bright eyes and winsome smile.

Mannheim was replacing the picture on the mantel when Bonnie came into the living room wearing a short black skirt and a white sweater with a double strand of pearls. He whistled, and then smiled as she whirled about to model her outfit.

"Were you able to identify the people in those old photos?"

Mannheim guessed the identities of her parents, and Bonnie as the pretty little girl. He pointed to the boy and looked at her. "The boy is..?"

"That's Jackie, my brother." She held the snapshot of the adults kissing. "Those beautiful people, as you've already guessed, are my parents."

"What happened to your mother?"

Bonnie looked at the picture of her mother and father, then placed it against her chest. "Mother died when we were quite young. Even now when I think about her I sometimes cry. Dad refuses to talk about her death. But I knew even as a child that he was hurting something awful."

"Had she been sick?"

"All this happened when we were quite young. After her death, Jackie and I stayed with my dad's parents. We returned after several months to the loneliest home in the world. I was told mother had an incurable disease. But I never could get Dad to talk about it until many years later."

"And your father, what does he do?"

"Dad drives for a large corporation."

Mannheim placed his arms around her and brought her close. He kissed the top of her head. "I'm grateful to your parents for giving me such a beautiful and loving child." He lifted her chin and kissed her lips. He brought her hands to his face, then kissed her palms.

She took his hand and pulled him to the sofa. They sat facing each other holding hands. Mannheim's curiosity compelled him to ask more questions. "Did your father re-marry?"

"No. After mother's death, he sort of moped around for a while. At times he became despondent; he became angry, he'd punch the furniture, or he'd chain smoke cigarettes. Now I can understand the depths of his depression. He would sit and stare out the window. Tears would well up, and at times he cried openly. He was unable to work because of his terrible sadness, and without a paycheck, we were forced to go back and stay with his parents again. We didn't like living with our grandparents. Jackie cried, and I tried to console him by telling him that one day we would be rich, and have everything we wanted. Even though Jackie was older than I, I would act like his older sister and comfort him."

"So did your dad eventually get over his depression?"

"Dad, as a veteran, was given psychiatric treatments for a number of months at the army hospital in *Los Angeles*. After he was discharged, he made regular visits to the psychiatrist and seemed to recover passably well. He got his current position, and thank goodness, a wonderful salary. Jackie and I were able to come home, and we were a family once again.

Mannheim reached forward, held her arms and looked at her. "And everything went well from that time on?"

"Yes—more or less. Dad would brood and have his periods of sulking but those periods alternated with longer episodes of normalcy. When I grew older, that is when I was a junior and senior in high school, we would sit at the kitchen table at dinner and talk about future plans. That was so much fun."

Mannheim placed his arms around her. "And what plans did you and your father make for the future?"

She looked at her watch and put her finger against Mannheim's lips. "That's enough chatter for now. Take me to dinner; I'm famished. Let's go to a steak house. I want a shrimp cocktail, a sirloin steak with garlic mashed potatoes, crisp vegetables and a tall glass of Cabernet Sauvignon."

"You haven't mentioned dessert. Will I do?"

"Only if the steak is juicy and the wine is smooth."

46

Mary sat at the computer in the chalet den, and clicked on Skype. She dialed the Rancho Mirage estate. Her assistant, Melinda answered.

"Melinda, I want you to send invitations for the memorial service to the following people, get your pen and pad ready: Dr. Josh and Mrs. Harrington. I've already talked with them, but send them an email invitation anyway. My daughter Deena, Larry and Lucy Kurtz, and Susan Bird Song. They've all been notified by phone but send them email invitations to remind them, and extend the invitation to Sven Bruxton as well, even though I know he won't be coming."

"I'm going to arrange for all of them to spend a long weekend here at the lodge. I'll provide the transportation with my own jet, flying out of LAX and Bermuda Dunes. Tell them there'll be skiing, tobogganing, ice-skating and target practice. They can bring their own guns. We'll have our chef prepare gourmet dinners, and we'll show movies in the evenings. My nephew Matt has all the winter sports equipment. Make the invitation sound appealing, and don't take 'no' for an answer. In addition to the email invitations, call all those people by phone. If anyone is reluctant or makes an excuse, let me know. You know the date and time, now get going."

Early, the following morning, Melinda was on the phone to Mary. "Mrs. Bruxton, we have our first refusal."

"Who?"

"Your daughter, Deena."

"My daughter? What's *her* problem? Never mind, I'll call her right now. Is there anything else you have to tell me?"

"No—no. It can wait."

"There is something else, isn't there? I can tell by your voice. Keep yourself available, I'll talk to you later."

Mary punched in Deena's number at the exclusive home she lived in just off the USC campus. Deena answered on the second ring.

"Deena, what's going on? Yes, dear, I know, but this is a memorial for your father. You must be here. We'll have a spectacular weekend. You'll be able to ski, toboggan, and roast marshmallows...what's that? You won't come without Johnny? Look, Dear, you're not engaged to him. You can't occupy a cabin together. That's not acceptable. What's that? Mr. Parma is *not* going to be in my cabin, he's staying at a B&B in Bozeman." With a sigh of exasperation she continued, "All right, bring Johnny, we'll figure out sleeping arrangements for him. Call me back tonight, to confirm."

Mary called Melinda again on Skype. "Melinda, a call came in on my personal phone from Detective Mannheim. He asked for your unlisted number at the Rancho Mirage estate." Melinda blanched and put her hand to her mouth. "Does this have anything to do with what you hesitated telling me earlier?" Mary watched Melinda's troubled expression.

"No, it's nothing—nothing."

"Melinda, that detective is from homicide division, so don't tell me it's nothing. Does this have anything to do with my husband's murder?" Mary was not going to be put off by Melinda's hesitation again. "Tell me what the hell is going on, because I'm going to call Mannheim and find out anyway."

Melinda's mouth contorted, she sobbed openly, and her shoulders heaved. Between sobs, she said, "Larry, that is, Mr. Kurtz, and I were at the same hotel the night Mr. Bruxton was murdered. The police want to question us about that." She blurted out, "But we had nothing to do with Mr. Bruxton's murder. I swear."

"I'm not sure I understand. You and Larry Kurtz were together at the same hotel that night?"

Melinda sniffed and wiped her eyes. "Yes."

"Wait a minute. Are you saying you two are lovers?"

Melinda froze, then nodded slowly. "We were in the suite next to Mr. Bruxton's. Larry said those two suites were leased by the company."

Mary stared at Melinda's image on Skype. She responded with a studied, "I see."

Melinda's eyes were pleading, and her voice became tremulous. "Oh, Mary, you can't believe we had anything to do with your husband's murder. Please, please, believe me, we're innocent."

"Yeah, innocent, like two cats screwing away the night while my husband gets his brains blown out next door." Mary's face hardened, and her voice grew brittle. "That makes for a lovely children's bedtime story. Did Kurtz leave you at anytime during the night?"

Melinda thought for several seconds. "Once for about five minutes to get ice."

In a direct and tactless way, Mary asked, "How long have you and Larry been cheating on your spouses?"

"It isn't like that at all—maybe six months." Mary waited for Melinda's further explanation. "Larry was lonely. His wife wouldn't let him get near her, and you know, my husband drives a truck cross-country, and is gone for weeks at a time. When he comes home he wants to sleep, drink beer and watch TV. He expects me to love him, but he's sloppy fat and treats me badly. Larry treats me like a lady. He's gentle and kind."

"That scenario sounds familiar. Tell me, when you two weren't pawing each other, what did Kurtz say about my husband? Don't spare the details. I want to know how that mismatched team ever found enough common ground to work together. Peter never confided in me about his association with Larry."

Melinda sniffed intermittently, dabbed her eyes and wiped her nose. "Larry told me that he and Peter, that is Mr. Bruxton, were in Viet Nam together, and that something terrible happened that he couldn't talk about. He hinted that he and another soldier saved Mr. Bruxton from going to jail. I asked him what happened, but he wouldn't say. He said he had taken an oath never to discuss it. After they were discharged, Larry and Mr. Bruxton had become partners."

"Did Larry ever express a strong disliking for Mr. Bruxton? Did he hint that he wanted to kill him?"

"Oh, never, never. Larry is too gentle and caring; he could never hurt anyone."

"Uh-huh. So he was perfectly kind and a loving sweetheart."

Melinda did not respond to Mary's obvious sarcasm.

"Where did you think your rendezvous would lead? Were you aware that your Mr. Nice Guy has a gambling addiction, and that he owed my husband thousands of dollars? Did you know that my husband owned the mortgage on his home? Did your kind and gentle Mr. Kurtz, ever tell you that my husband had an affair with his wife? Or that he threatened to kill my husband?"

Mary waited for Melinda to stop shaking her head.

Melinda said nothing.

"Well, it's all true. So don't tell me your sweet, loving Romeo couldn't be a prime suspect in my husband's murder. I just want you to be prepared for Detective Mannheim's questions. That scarecrow is looking to hang a murder rap on the first suspect he can find. I'm sorry, Melinda, I have to go. I am totally disgusted, and my cell phone is ringing. It's

Deena." Mary clicked the disconnect button and Melinda's face disappeared from the Skype screen. "Hi Deena. No, I'm glad you're coming with Johnny. What's that? The old man? Oh, for heaven's sake, why? Well, quite frankly, because I don't know whether he wants to make sure that you and Johnny get married, or whether he wants to diddle me. What? Yes, Dear, I'll extend an invitation to him—under duress."

Mary closed her cell and thought about Oscar Brazilowicz. He could have put a hit man on Peter to make sure there would be no opposition to his son's marriage to Deena. He probably has delusions of coming into billions of dollars with that marriage. What that bastard doesn't know is that the whole goddamned Bruxton enterprise is currently in a financial free-fall, and that, unless some miracle turns things around, his son is going to be marrying a poor, little poor girl.

47

Maggie was packing her suitcase. "I'm happy I never gave away my long handle underwear. I suppose subconsciously I figured on going back to the windy city one day during the winter season. The thought of walking along Michigan Avenue with that icy wind blowing off the lake makes me shiver. These clothes will be fine in Montana." She looked at Josh, who was packing his clothes also.

"Remember our first date on that cold night in Chicago? Oh, Josh, I was so much in love with you I tingled all over just being near you. The temperature could have been fifty below, but my love for you kept me warm. I thought about you all through the day and couldn't wait for the evenings to be with you.

"You were handsome as an intern and resident, but you belonged to Sally. How I envied her. I think all the nurses did. Besides, you didn't even know I existed. I made every excuse to be near you when you were on my ward. Couldn't you tell?"

Josh, in his shorts and undershirt, came over, wrapped his arms around Maggie and nuzzled her neck. "I just thought you were efficient and friendly. If I had known you were hot to trot I might have arranged a tryst or two."

Maggie pushed him away playfully. "That never would have happened, and you know it. You were a goody-two-shoes, and I was a virginal Florence Nightingale."

"Were you really a virgin?"

"Yes—practically—well almost."

They both laughed and Josh gave her an open-mouth kiss. She eagerly reciprocated, and he unfastened her bra. She threw it over her shoulder, then rumpled his hair and reached for his tumescence. She took his hand and led him to the bed where she pushed the luggage aside. With Josh lying on top of her, she held his face in her hands and kissed him rapidly and excitedly.

Following their frenzied movements of magnificent intimacy, Josh, exhausted, lay spread eagle for a moment before turning on his side to face Maggie. "Have I told you lately that I'm madly in love with you?"

Maggie turned to face him. "After this little party, that's good to know. That gives you favored status over all my other lovers." Maggie bounced off the bed and bent over for her panties and bra. Josh made a swipe at her buttocks and missed as Maggie scooted away. "Josh, you're incorrigible. If you had your way, you'd be making love twenty-four hours a day."

"You give me too much credit, my love. I simply don't have the stamina." He stood next to her, naked, and kissed her again.

She pushed him away gently. "Take a cold shower, then we can finish packing for our trip." Maggie continued placing her clothes in the suitcase then stopped to look at Josh. "Were you serious about low back pain with frequent intercourse? I ask because of Mary Bruxton. Do you think that's the cause of her back pain?"

"I made those comments with tongue in cheek, half-jokingly. Why are you concerned about Mary?"

"Rumor has it that she and Frank Parma are no longer a couple. So if her backache is a result of frequency and intensity, who is her lover?"

"Maggie, you have a fertile, suspicious and

lascivious imagination. I'd suggest you occupy your mind more advantageously."

"Fine. The next time you feel the need to swap juices, I'll tell you I'm too busy reading *Chaucer's Canterbury Tales* or Shakespeare's, *As You Like It*, or...."

Josh hurried to cover her mouth with a kiss, then smiled. "You win, and I don't know who Mary's latest lover is."

48

Frank parked the Jeep in front of Mary's large Alpine chalet. He ran up the two steps to the landing, and stood in front of the double doors with their ornate leaded glass panels. He stomped the snow off his boots and squared his shoulders, then rang the doorbell, and pushed the brim of his Stetson upward. Through the wavy distortion of the leaded glass a male figure approached. The door opened and an unsmiling Jim Keyes stood before him. Parma's smile disappeared as he stepped forward and walked past Keys. "Where's Mrs. Bruxton?" He was clearly annoyed and the animus between him and Keyes was palpable.

"She left for the airport with her nephew Matt, to meet her guests."

"Hell, I could have picked them up, if she'd told me. When are they expected back?"

Jim looked at his watch. "In about an hour—more or less."

Parma groused as he made a quick survey of the lower floor of the home. "This place could sleep a half dozen. I don't know why she insisted that I stay elsewhere." He walked toward the stairwell. "What's upstairs?"

Jim answered flatly, "A bedroom and a den."

"Who the hell occupies those rooms?" Parma eyed Keyes suspiciously.

"I do."

"You do? Well, I'll be damned. Parma's jaw muscles tightened and his eyes narrowed as he stared at Keyes. "And where does Mrs. Bruxton sleep?"

"Here, on the main floor, in the master bedroom."

Parma took the full measure of the chauffeur, eyeing him from head to toe. "Aren't you out of uniform, buddy?"

"Not really, we're less business-like here."

Parma was seething with resentment over Keyes's insolence, coupled with Mary's failure to meet him or have someone meet him at the airport, or provide quarters for him at the lodge.

Keyes turned his back on Parma and walked toward the kitchen.

Parma read Keyes' attitude as clearly hostile, and a deliberate show of insubordination toward an employer— well, a potential employer who could be responsible for his future earnings. Who in the hell did this hired hand think he was?

He shouted, "Hey, fella, how about bringing me a Scotch on the rocks?"

Keyes stopped momentarily but did not turn around. He continued to walk toward the kitchen. Parma watched him approach the refrigerator, open it and remove a can of Coke. Keyes moved to the kitchen table, spread the newspaper before him to read and sat down with his drink.

Parma's face reddened; he grumbled under his breath. Nobody ignores me; much less a servant. His heavy steps pounded the parquet floor, and he charged into the kitchen. "Hey, fella, are you deaf? I asked you for a Scotch on the rocks. His face darkened, and scowl lines deepened around his mouth. His eyes grew small and mean. He leaned across the table into Keyes's face.

Keyes looked up blandly at the fuming Parma. In a lightning move, Parma snatched the can of Coke and poured the contents on Keyes' head. Keyes did not react immediately. Then in movements like a slow motion film sequence he flicked the fluid drops from his face and shoulders, then stood. He gathered the wet newspaper in front of him and surveyed his wet shirt and trousers, then pushed his chair back and looked at Parma.

In a flat voice, he said, "I'm sorry you did that."

Parma, his hands on his hips, pressed his face next to Keyes's and in a nose-to-nose confrontation said, "What are you going to do about it?"

In a movement Parma never saw, Keyes threw a straight power piston jab to Parma's face. The blow sent Parma scrambling backward across the kitchen, slamming him into the oven door. He slid down to the floor in a daze. Keyes approached him, grabbed his lapels and pulled him up. Parma placed his hands over his face to protect it as Keyes kneed his groin. Parma moaned and bent over to grab his crotch. Keyes delivered a roundhouse uppercut, throwing Parma's head back against the oven. Parma pitched forward, allowing Keys to deliver a chop to his neck. Parma sprawled forward, hitting his face on the floor with a thud.

Dazed and suffering excruciating pain, Parma lifted his head and shook it. He got on all fours thinking that dumb chauffeur bastard got in a few lucky punches. Well, he'll pay for that as soon as I get my bearings.

Keyes watched as Parma struggled to stand. A small pool of blood formed on the floor from Parma's bleeding nose and lip. Keyes reached forward to help Parma stand. The unsteady Parma looked at his bloody shirt and reached for a handkerchief from his back pocket. He held it to his bleeding nose and walked unsteadily toward a chair. Keyes reached out to steady him.

Parma jerked away and with muffled sounds through his handkerchief, said, "Get your fucking hands off me, you sonofabitch. I could have killed you in a clean fight." Parma bypassed the chair and staggered out of the house, holding his bloodied handkerchief to his nose.

Keyes cleaned the mess on the floor and table, then went upstairs to put his head under the faucet to wash away the syrupy cola that matted his hair. Standing in his shorts and combing his hair in front of the mirror, he stopped and squinted to see Parma's grotesque image approaching; his one eye already swelled and discolored; his hair disheveled and blood caked below his nose and chin.

"Don't move you sonofabitch." Parma's hoarse voice was filled with loathing. "Put your hands up and turn around slowly. Make one stupid move and I'll blow your fuckin' head off." The gleaming Colt Python held in both of Parma's hands quivered. He glanced at a chair in the adjoining bedroom and ordered Keyes to sit on it. He kept the revolver trained on Keyes chest. "Put your hands on the armrests where I can see them. Make a funny move and I'll kill you, I swear it. You took advantage of me downstairs. Well, you're not going to be as lucky this time. Don't say anything until I tell you to. I want you to answer my questions and don't bullshit me. If I think you are, I'll put a bullet through your heart."

Keyes stony countenance irked Parma further. Keyes said calmly, "You can't get away with killing me, and you damn well know it."

"Shut up! Don't talk until I tell you to. I've got my alibi for killing you. I'll tell them I found you rifling through Mrs. Bruxton's belongings, and when I put the gun on you, there was a scuffle and you were shot accidentally. Simple as that. The cops will take my word for it, especially after they find some of Mary's jewelry in your pockets. Now answer my questions. Look at me when I talk to you. Are you sleeping with her?"

Parma extended his gun further, his hands still revealing a fine tremor and his eyes bored into Keyes'.

"No." Keyes answered without hesitation, and without emotion. "Why don't you put that goddamned gun away? You know you're not going to use it. To begin with, Mary

Bruxton will never buy that story."

"What the hell makes you so damned sure?"

"Because she knows me too well." He stood and turned his back to Parma , then walked back into the washroom. "I'm going to finish cleaning up, then I'll put some clean clothes on. You'd better do the same. Wash some of that dried blood and snot off your face and get rid of that bloodied shirt." He pointed to the closet. " Bruxton's clothes are in there, put some on."

Parma, although still angry, recognized the futility of his threats, and gave no further argument. The unexpected beating and humiliation had depleted his superior attitude, but not his rage. He responded reluctantly to Keyes suggestion and placed the gun on the counter top of the double basins. Leaning into the mirror, he studied his bloodied nose and the dried mucous clinging to his lips and chin. He immersed his head and face in water. He touched the tissue around his black eye and jerked his head back from the tenderness.

Parma seethed at Keyes' image in the mirror they shared. "You came after me like a fuckin' commando. I didn't know what happened. Where in the hell did you learn to fight?"

Keyes, combing his hair, spoke to Parma's image. I did some boxing as a kid in the CYO. In the army I was division champ, but hell, that was a hundred years ago. I've kept my hand in it by coaching at the Y and working out at Golds. I still do some bag punching and sparring. Pete, that is, Bruxton, wanted me to stay in shape."

"Why did he care if you stayed in shape?"

"Same reason he sent me to the Bondurant School for Defensive Driving. To keep him safe from his enemies, I suppose."

"What kind of enemies?"

"Just enemies. All rich people have enemies of one sort or another—goes with the territory."

49

From his module, a mere ten feet from Mannheim's, Oliver walked to his partner's desk. "What're you thinking, boss? With that far-away look, I can't tell if you're mulling over some ideas on the Bruxton murder, or if you're just thinking about the Ouvray gal."

Mannheim's chair was tilted back; his long legs extended onto his desk top and crossed at the ankles, revealing his wrinkled white athletic socks, the kind that come three pair in a package at the dollar store.

Oliver felt the urge to taunt him. "I've heard that too much intercourse can cause deafness and loss of sight."

Mannheim turned slowly to look at him. "What'd you say? I can hardly hear you, and you seem to be going in and out of focus." He smiled, pleased with his retort. "What a great way to lose one's senses."

"You certainly seem pleased with yourself."

Oliver studied the usually phlegmatic Mannheim. "Old Daddy Long Legs has captured the heart of Miss Mocha Latte, who in turn has stolen his common sense and dignity."

"What dignity?" Mannheim leaned forward, picked up a pencil from his desk and threw it at Oliver. "Buster, contrary to what you may be thinking, I've got a few thoughts about that murder that keep ricocheting in my brain."

"I'm your partner, remember? Tell me about them."

"Only if you stop making smart-ass comments about my relationship with Bonnie."

"Hey, come on. I'm only kidding."

Just then, the Fax machine started jigging. Oliver walked over to it as a report from the forensic lab came out. It was directed to the Homicide Division: Attention, Sgt. T.A. Mannheim.

Oliver read aloud, "Examination of a .22 caliber bullet fired from a Glock automatic...." He looked up. "Hey, that's Susan Bird Song's piece."

"That's right. What's the conclusion: yea or nay?"

Oliver glanced at the bottom of the report. "...bullet markings not identical to those found in head of corpse and casing markings noticeably incompatible."

"Too bad. Bird Song was a damned good suspect. She had motive, opportunity, and means," Oliver said, flipping the report onto Mannheim's desk.

Mannheim glanced dismissively at the report. "I never felt strongly about her involvement. She was getting damn good regular payoffs from Bruxton, and as far as him threatening to fuck her, hah, that's a lot of crap. That little squaw would have chopped his nuts for granola before he got his pecker out of his pants. Opportunity and means, maybe, but motive? Uh, uh."

"So she's off our list of suspects?"

"Not completely." Mannheim picked up the desk phone, punched in the front office, balanced it between his shoulder and neck, and said, "Hello, Gorgeous, when are you going to send me a photo of you in a bathing suit? Preferably in a topless one." He looked at Oliver and signified large breasts with his hands. "Do me a favor: call Mrs. Bruxton's place."

"Melinda? Is the boss lady in? Bozeman? She's preparing a second memorial service for Bruxton? How nice. She wants to be sure he gets a good sendoff. Who's all going to be there? Hold it, let me get those names on my pad." Mannheim wrote rapidly and asked when Mrs. Bruxton planned to return. "I see, thanks." He replaced the phone on the cradle and looked at Oliver. "We may have to get an out-of-town warrant for an arrest. How would you like to take a trip to Montana?"

"How're you going to finagle that?"

"I'm calling the D.A. to give him my suspicions and findings. If I can convince him, he'll get the governor's office to request the Montana governor's office to issue a warrant."

Oliver turned in his seat and stared incredulously. "Wait a minute: who in the hell are you going to arrest?"

"The murderer, who else?"

"The murderer? Who the hell is that? Don't clam up. Talk to me."

Josh and Maggie drove to the Bermuda Dunes Airport about five miles from their home at the east end of 42nd Street. Josh pulled into the parking lot of the privately owned airport that catered to owners of small and mid-sized aircraft. When tournament tennis matches were played at Indian Wells, or PGA championships were held at one of several valley courses, the airport was quite busy. A five thousand dollar air taxi tab for a half-day sporting event was not unusual.

At 8:00 A.M. and fifty degrees, the rising sun had already placed a bright wintry glow on the mountaintops, with snowcaps jutting vividly against a cloudless azure sky. Josh and Maggie pulled their rolling suitcases into the store-front type waiting room and were met by the captain and co-pilot of the Cessna Citation XLS+ turbine aircraft owned by Bruxton International.

Josh walked out of the waiting room to get a closer look at the plane, when he saw Larry Kurtz parking the Jaguar Vanden Plas. Lucy emerged carrying only a shoulder strap Chanel bag while her husband struggled with three suitcases.

Josh walked over and introduced himself, although they had met briefly on one occasion some months ago at the Bruxton estate. "Let me help you with these." He took one of the suitcases while Larry reached into the trunk again to remove a rifle sheathed in a black plastic case. Josh's quizzical expression evoked a hasty explanation from Larry.

"This is for target practice." He hoisted the gun against his shoulder and held the stock like a G.I. standing at attention. "If I'm lucky, my wife will step in front of the muzzle when it accidentally fires. I keep it loaded in case the opportunity arises." He laughed. "Just joking."

Susan Bird Song arrived with an overnight bag and looked about the airport waiting room expectantly. She approached Maggie and asked if she were flying to the Bruxton memorial service in Montana. Maggie responded enthusiastically, and launched easily into conversation.

When Lucy entered the waiting room, Maggie extended her hand, and then turned to introduce Susan Bird Song. Lucy responded to both women with a cold-fish handshake, and a condescending smile.

"This should be a wonderful trip," Maggie said with her usual ebullience. "I've never been on a small jet before. Have you? I understand the flights are fabulous."

Lucy intended to establish her role as dominant female immediately, and regarded Maggie's comments as so much country bumpkin talk. She said with nonchalance, "I've flown many times. I became one of the first gals in our group to join the *mile high club.*"

Maggie shrugged and looked askance. "I beg your pardon?"

"It's a name given to those who fuck while in flight."

Maggie gasped and held her hand to her mouth. Susan Bird Song's eyes widened, she cleared her throat and turned away. Lucy continued her patronizing air. "Some years ago I got chummy with a pilot in flight. I sat on his lap, unzipped his fly and maneuvered his joystick while the co-pilot took over the flight. I was a little loopy from three martinis. But, let me tell you, up there in the wild blue, with every little bounce, the sensation was magical. The old guy I was with was flat-out drunk and unconscious in the cabin. The flight cost him a fortune, but hell, he could afford it, and he was too old and limp to be interesting. We were on a four hour trip, and I would have been bored to death without the action."

Maggie listened with blinking eye amazement. Susan Bird Song had discreetly distanced herself.

Lucy continued, "I like to mix it up every now and then. Don't get me wrong. I love my husband. It's just that he isn't as romantic or hungry as he used to be, and he can't respond ...."

Just then, Josh and Larry came through the door of the waiting room with the luggage. The captain and co-pilot came up and relieved them of the suitcases.

The captain counted heads. "Are we ready for take-off?" He asked.

The five responded eagerly. "Last chance for washroom relief until we're airborne." The captain looked at Larry's encased gun. "Is the chamber empty?"

"Huh? Well, yeah, I think so. Why?"

The captain reached for the gun and removed it from its sheath. He checked the chambers and emptied the cartridges. "I'll take these and place them in the forward compartment. The gun will go in the external baggage bin."

Larry mumbled to Josh, "What the hell's the big deal here? These guys just have to show their authority. Besides, I didn't like the way he looked at Lucy."

Josh knew he had it wrong. It was Lucy who had been sizing-up the pilot.

The five passengers accompanied the two pilots as they walked about one hundred yards out on the tarmac to the sleek plane. The captain opened the air stair door and had the women enter first. With the passengers on board and the pilot on the ground inspecting the tail end of the plane, the young co-pilot spoke into the captain's ear. "I watched the tall slender dame go up the stairs. I don't think she's wearing anything under her skirt. Do you think she plans to do anything like, well—you know?"

"She can do whatever the hell she wants to do as long as she's wearing a seatbelt and the other passengers don't complain."

"But that's lewd, and well, sort of socially unacceptable." The young co-pilot looked to the captain for agreement.

The captain showed little concern. "If it doesn't interfere with our flight pattern, and no one objects, are you going to take it upon yourself to reprimand her?"

"Well, no, I just thought...."

"These are privileges that come with wealth, and as long as no FAA, state or company policies are violated, what our passengers do is not our concern. Right, Bucko?"

Maggie, stepping into the passenger compartment, held her breath as her eyes scanned the unimaginable luxury of the cabin with its tall, buttery leather seats, richly stained wood trim, plush carpeting, and individual TV screens and telephones. Still in awe, she walked toward the rear to marvel at the Corian-topped galley with overhead cabinets filled with crystal stemware. She turned to express her wonder to Lucy who was noticeably blasé.

"It'll do," Lucy said as she tested the comfort of the abbreviated sofa on the port side of the plane. She looked around, then asked of no one in particular, "When's Captain Kirk going to feed us on this junior space ship?"

Maggie pointed to a refrigerator with a wood finished door and a microwave oven. A box of a dozen sandwiches, each individually wrapped in plastic, had been placed on the counter below the oven.

Josh and Larry occupied seats on the starboard side.

The seats were captains' chairs, and the men conversed easily across a pull-up table until the roar of engines drowned out conversation. Susan sat aft, reading a current issue of *People* magazine.

Once the plane reached its designated altitude, the co-pilot walked among the passengers to offer drinks and snacks. Maggie, sitting with Lucy on the sofa, requested white wine; Lucy ordered a margarita. Josh ordered a glass of Cabernet Sauvignon and Larry, a Scotch on the rocks. Susan Bird Song ordered a Coke. Lucy sipped the margarita and turned a sour face. "This goddamned stuff is swill." She spat in her glass and called out to the co-pilot, "Bring me a gin and tonic that doesn't come out of a can." She crossed her long legs and pulled her hem above her sun tanned mid thigh. Josh turned to look out the window, hoping she wasn't attempting a flirtation with him, then turned to Larry. "What is your take on Peter Bruxton's murder? If I recall correctly, you knew him longer than most. Weren't you in the service with him?"

"That's right, and for thirty-six years I was his business partner." He pointed to his glass for a refill as the co-pilot passed through the aisle. Then he looked around as though someone might be eavesdropping. He leaned toward Josh and spoke softly, "Peter was a strange man—a really queer sonofabitch."

"In what way?" Josh had his own thoughts about Peter's personality; after all, he too had known him for about thirty years, even though they socialized infrequently. But he was still curious to know Larry's impression.

"When we were GIs, we had bull sessions in the tents after evening chow, and we swapped stories late into the night. Pete had the gift of gab and usually hogged the conversation. He told how his dad died and left the family penniless when he was a kid. I think that really fueled his insecurity. Making money became an obsession; he absolutely hated being poor and was embarrassed by it. He vowed one day he'd be a bloody millionaire. While we were slogging through the Mekong, he'd talk about how he was going to make a pile of money in timber, and how he was going to have every goddamned thing he ever hoped for. And that included women."

Larry sipped his Scotch and in subdued tones said, "Jeez-uz he loved to fuck, and for sure, didn't discriminate. Some of the ugliest, pock-marked, wizened, bandy-legged gooks were fair game. As long as they had a snatch, they qualified."

Larry smiled in anticipation of his next thought. "Pete went to the field dispensary more times for the treatment of *clap* than anybody else in the whole division. I remember one night he got up to piss and couldn't. He cursed with agonizing pain. He just about crawled to the dispensary, where the medic gave him an injection of antibiotics and passed a catheter to get rid of a gallon of piss. He screamed like a banshee when the catheter was passed. But hell, do you think that stopped him? No, siree. The next time he had a hard-on he was out there looking for another broad. His sexual appetite never changed, but his preference in gals overtime definitely improved." Larry threw his head back to finish the Scotch. He held the tumbler, swirled the ice cubes and glanced at the other passengers to be sure no one was listening. Then he leaned forward again.

"Sometimes he acted crazy with broads, kind of sadistic; he beat the shit out of some of them. Then he'd throw money at them so they wouldn't squeal."

Josh nodded but said nothing.

"Pete was designated point man in our platoon, our fearless leader, the one looking to find the enemy first. He was aggressive and vindictive as hell. When he shot a gook, he didn't stop there—he riddled him. For his kill rate, he earned his stripes fast, but then he lost them just as fast."

"Why?"

"Insubordination. He once told a commissioned officer

who ran the fighting from behind his desk to go to hell...
that he didn't know squat about field conditions and ought
to get his ass out to where the action was."

"He could have been court-martialed for that."

"You're right, and he would have been, but the company
commander gave him company punishment instead. That
amounted to nothing more than a slap on the wrist. Pete
accounted for the most enemy kills in our company, and
our commanding officer needed those numbers."

"What kept your friendship strong? Your personalities
seemed so different."

Larry Kurtz took a moment to look at his wife, and
motioned for her to pull her skirt down. In her state of
inebriation, Lucy ignored him and lifted her skirt higher.

"Actually, Pete and I weren't all that different. We
were close in age; we both came from the northwest, and
our families were poor, dirt poor. We wanted a better
life style after our discharges. The difference was that he
was a hell of a lot more ambitious than I was, and I guess,
more committed to the business at hand. He could make
deals with anybody who had something he wanted. That
included politicians of every rank: senators, congressman,
and, I know he even got the president's ear at one point."

Larry blinked; the drinks were beginning to alter his
vision. He moved his tumbler in small circles on the table
and tried to get the attention of the co-pilot for another
drink. When he could not, he said, "Hell with it. Where
was I? Oh, yeah, Pete was an emotional guy; kind of crazy,
you know? Sly as a fox when it came to making money.
But when it came to women? Absolutely nuts." Larry was
becoming more and more talkative, and although his enun-
ciation had become less precise; his thinking still seemed
largely coherent.

"There were four of us who buddied-up in the service,
you know, like kids often do. We protected one another
like the three musketeers, plus one. We did everything

together—shot craps, smoked pot, got laid—well, you get the picture. Then one day on patrol on the Mekong Delta, one of our buddies steps on a booby trap. Got his goddamned face and the top of his head blown off, I mean completely blown off. His arteries are shooting blood like geysers. Pete sees this and goes berserk. I mean shittin' crazy. He takes his M1 and fires a burst into a nearby hootch, killing all the gooks standing there. A whole goddamned family." Larry had begun to sweat and breathe deeply. His bloodshot eyes made rapid side movement, and his face reddened as he relived the ghastly sight of a thirty-five year recurring horror.

Josh studied Larry's tormented expression, but withheld comment.

Larry finally turned his gaze down, and shook his head slowly as he battled memories that clearly wracked his emotions. "You gotta forgive me, Doc.. Every time I think about that, it's like I'm living it all over again." He reached for a handkerchief in his back pocket, wiped his brow and blew his nose. "The three of us swore never to reveal anything to military intelligence or anyone else about what happened. We were grilled a number of times, but we told them nothing. We denied every damned thing. Pete promised to take care of us after the war if we kept our mouths shut. Hell, we had no intention of telling anything to anyone. We were afraid we'd be dragged into the mess and get blamed."

"What happened to the third man?"

"You mean Old Peckerhead? He's...."

At that moment, Lucy interrupted. Unsteady, she held her tumbler of gin and tonic over her head and dropped onto Larry's lap, then embraced him with one arm around his neck. "You're ignoring me, Love Boat." She kissed him on the mouth; he placed his hand on her outer thigh and ran it up her bare buttocks.

His brow shot upward. "Baby, you're ready for action."

"Excuse us, Doc."

Lucy grabbed Larry's hand and pulled him towards the lavatory at the rear of the plane. En route, she placed her drink on the liquor counter, announcing loudly, "I'm going to inaugurate this raw recruit into the *Mile High Club*." After pulling Larry in, she closed the pocket door and locked it.

Thereafter, giggling preceded raucous laughter that came from behind the restroom door. Rhythmic grunting, and a number of explosive exclamations invoking the name of the Almighty followed that.

Maggie, sitting opposite Josh, rolled her eyes and whispered, "Now, there's a touch of class."

Josh nodded, "Yeah, really."

50

The early morning sun created a glow that reflected off the brilliant white fuselage of the Hawker 900 XP. It was poised like a sleek missile on the tarmac at LAX.

Deena walked, elfin-like, between the two colossal figures as she approached the pilots. "Captain Hansen and Mr. Gilroy, this is my fiancé, Johnny Brazilowicz and his dad, Mr. Oscar Brazilowicz. Do you think the plane seats are large enough to accommodate these men?" She smiled her little girl smile.

The captain returned a weak smile. He wasn't quite sure if she had intended to be humorous. "I'm sure your guests can be made comfortable, " he said, finally.

The three passengers pulled their luggage behind them as they followed the captain and copilot to the private jet. Deena's bags were hoisted into the external baggage compartment along with those of her male companions. With the pilots out of hearing range, Oscar Brazilowicz whispered to his son that he had his custom-made disassembled 20-gauge rifle concealed in his bag. "I don't want the pilot messing around with this expensive gun by emptying its chamber. Just don't say anything about it to anyone."

Captain Hanson reached up to open the air stair door and watched as Deena ran up into the plane. She plopped into one of the oversized leather chairs, turning it toward the aisle like a child at play while kicking her legs alternately against the bottom of the seat.

She threw up her arms with impish joy and sang out, "I love this plane. It's so neat; it's my very favorite."

Oscar Brazilowicz lumbered up the stairs and filled the doorway from side to side and from top to bottom. The plane seemed to actually tilt as he stepped into it. Johnny followed his father and negotiated the steps easily, but had to lower his head to clear the entry.

The pilots checked the pre-flight procedural list while Oscar Brazilowicz managed to squeeze himself into a seat facing the young couple. A foldout table separated the couple from Johnny's father.

A message from the pilot came over the P.A. system. "Please fasten your seat belts and keep them on except when you get up to stretch or go to the lavatory. Federal aviation laws prohibit smoking. If all goes according to schedule, we should arrive in Bozeman at approximately one o'clock, about ten to fifteen minutes behind the arrival of our other plane leaving from Bermuda Dunes. Now sit back, relax and enjoy the flight. Mr. Gilroy will serve drinks once we're in the wild blue yonder. There's also a box of fresh snacks, salads, and Danish, as well as a variety of beverages, including coffee, tea and milk."

The Hawker taxied to the runway and idled until the tower gave the all-clear signal. With a burst of speed that brought wide-eyed responses from its two male passengers, the plane made an arc over the Pacific shoreline, then headed in an East North East direction. In the relative quiet of the cockpit, the co-pilot made a quick backward glance at the passengers, then leaned over toward the captain. "Can you imagine that 300 pound gorilla diddling that delicate little girl? There's no way he could get on top of her without crushing her to death. No sir. Either she lies on it or sits on it."

Without looking at his young co-pilot, Captain Hanson,

adjusted the controls and said, "Gilroy, you sound like a goddamned adolescent."

Nothing was said for several seconds; the chastised co-pilot looked and felt humiliated.

Captain Hanson turned toward him and started to laugh. "You're so gullible. For your edification, and I speak from years of experience, a stiff prick will usually find its mark in any situation and get help from the screwee, if necessary. Now do me a favor and think about something more prosaic like landing this baby safely before the snow forces us to land outside of Bozeman."

Oscar Brazilowicz was on his third Chivas Regal on the rocks, and participated in light banter with the two lovers. He had removed his jacket, placed it on the back of the chair, loosened his tie and unbuttoned his collar. With flushed jowls and eyes taking on a mellow glaze, he watched Deena when she excused herself to go to the lavatory. He leaned on the table and spoke softly to Johnny. "For chrissakes, don't let that little girl out of your gun sight. Look around you: see this spiffy jet? Pretty damned nice, ain't it? Probably costs twenty-five to thirty mill if it costs a red cent. Hell, not even the union can afford that.

"And this is just peanuts to her family. Hell, once you're married, and if you still want to go to college, you can pick your own school and get right on the varsity team; maybe endow a chair, or create a scholarship. Now that her old man's out of the way, she's a lot closer to inheriting his moolah, and she'll be even closer once the old lady's iced." His eyes shifted around the cabin, and he whispered, "I have plans for her, too."

They had been in the air for approximately one hour when the pilot's voice came over the P.A. system, "Folks if you look out to the left side, you'll see the Great Salt Lake."

Oscar turned his head for a cursory glance then sat back, continued to sip his drink, then leaned forward to give his son the benefit of his worldly wisdom. "Take those people down there; when the men want a change in bed partners, they take on another wife. In their religion, that's kosher, ya see? When you got a lotta dough, you can do the same. Only in your case, you can't marry more than one at a time. To do that, you got to belong to their religious franchise. I think they're called Moroons or something like that."

"That's Mormons, Dad."

"Whatever. The point is, you gotta get yourself into that Bruxton family." He pointed toward the lavatory and spoke in a coarse whisper. "You get that little girl in a family-way, and the old lady'll accept you with open arms. Christ, she'll make a wedding for you so fast, your head'll swim. After you're hitched, I can take charge of your investments, and we can...."

Deena returned to her seat and reached for Johnny's hand. She snuggled against him. "Did you miss me?"

Johnny leaned toward her, held her face in his massive hands and covered it with kisses. Oscar Brazilowicz, like a smiling Buddha, nodded his approval.

51

At the homicide bureau in Thousand Palms, Mannheim and Oliver sat at their desks doing paper work. The main thrust of their efforts remained the Bruxton murder case, which included fending off the constant niggling reminders from the State Attorney General's office, asking for progress reports. The afternoon post-prandial lethargy had sapped Mannheim's energy. He leaned over the papers on his desk and supported his head in his hands.

Oliver walked to Mannheim's side and deposited a tome that made a thud as it struck his desk. Mannheim yawned without restraint and turned his head slowly to look up at Oliver. "What the hell are you dumping on my desk?"

"This is the book on the origin of surnames that Mrs. Harrington left behind. It's kind of interesting."

Mannheim looked disdainfully at the weighty book. "What wonderful information did you get from it?"

"Want to know where my name, Oliver, came from and what it means?"

Mannheim sighed, "Not particularly, but you're going to tell me anyway."

Oliver opened the book to a bookmark, and placed his index finger on the name. "It comes from the British Isles, France, Catalan and Germany. In old French it is *Olivier* and was brought to England by the Normans. It means olive tree." He looked at the unresponsive Mannheim. "Interesting, eh?"

Mannheim intertwined his fingers behind his head, leaned back in his chair and closed his eyes to enter a state of semi-consciousness.

"Let me read about your name—Mannheim. You listening?" Oliver's distracting voice caused Mannheim's eyelids to flutter. "The name *Mannheim* comes from the city of that name in southwest Germany." Oliver's voice barely penetrated the mantel of Mannheim's consciousness, like a distant irritation. "It is a name that was adopted by Jews who occupied that city before the seventeenth century...." The sound of Oliver's voice seemed to grow in intensity.

Several quiet seconds passed before Mannheim sat up wide-eyed. "Huh? What the hell did you say? Gimme that!" He grabbed the book and scanned the page until he found his name. He read the paragraph, then read it again. A constrained smile gave way to a burst of uncontrolled laughter. His shoulders heaved and he guffawed until tears welled.

Oliver stepped back. Mannheim's near hysteria caused him concern. Three other members in the department stopped to stare at Mannheim. The raucous laughter subsided to a staccato-like heh-heh-heh, and Mannheim reached for his handkerchief to wipe his tears. "Boy, that's the best I've ever heard!" He threw his pencil on the open book. "I don't know about the accuracy of that, but it sure would explain a lot about the old man, may God rest his tormented soul. If he was a Jew, he never told me." Mannheim smiled and shook his head, trying to assimilate that information with his father's personna. "Of course that might explain a few things, like his interest in the Jewish philosophers: Maimonides, Spinoza and Heine."

"And why he was interned in a Nazi death camp like a prisoner of war or an enemy alien," Oliver said.

Mannheim looked at Oliver. "You say, "*Interned?* That's a word reserved for civilized people. Nazis weren't civilized. Hell, they weren't even people. They were the lowest form of creature, scum bags of shit spreading their stink, poison and death wherever they goose-stepped." Mannheim's vitriol came to a halt. He nodded, stood and placed his hands in his back pockets, took a deep breath and expanded his chest. A smile curled the ends of his lips. "Maybe the old man imparted some of that ancient Hebrew tribal wisdom to me; some mysterious and uncanny ability that allows me to solve riddles."

"Yeah, like Bruxton's murder?"

Mannheim's posturing quickly faded. "Listen, Buster, I have strong suspicions about the murderer. I just need a little more time to consolidate data."

"Really? How about sharing your suspicions with a less qualified gentile?"

Mannheim responded in his deep monotone, "Wise ass, just for that, you'll wait."

Oliver closed the book, picked it up and walked toward the door.

"Where are you going with that?"

"I'm putting it in my car to return it to Mrs. Harrington."

"Hold it, I've got a few more names to investigate."

52

Mary sat next to Matt in the extended Cadillac limousine as he drove toward Bozeman Airport. She looked at the sky through the windshield and wrinkled her brow. "Those clouds are loaded with moisture. Thank goodness the guests beat the snow, or the hail, or the sleet or whatever the hell we're going to get hit with. Let's pray the weather will clear to allow them to leave after three or four days. The thought of entertaining all of them in snow-bound cabins for an extended period..." She trailed off, wrapping the fur-lined leather coat tightly around her.

"Aunt Mary, may I ask why the guests wouldn't be arriving in one jet instead of two? It would seem to me that the LAX-based plane could have swung over to the desert to pick up the other guests."

Mary paused. "This may be difficult to understand, but let me try to make things clear. Uncle Peter received almost four hundred million dollars in unsecured funds from the lending institute."

Matt looked at her quizzically. "I'm not sure I understand. How could the funds be unsecured?"

"Because your uncle insisted on it. Doing it that way, he was not beholden to anyone for the way he spent the money. The lender didn't oppose the deal since the paper was sold immediately to hedge funds and other investors for a handsome profit.

"With that kind of money, plus his profits from the lumber mills, Peter and I, of course, became two of the wealthiest people in the country, perhaps the entire western world; we had well over a billion dollars in assets."

Matt whistled. "How does one spend that kind of money?"

"Your uncle made real estate investments. Some of them turned out to be real sink holes. I gave a large share to charities and still do. You asked about the jets? One of them is leased and used for business; the other Peter bought out-right. Truth is, we used both for business and personal needs. So having two jets, why not use them for our guests' convenience?"

Mary patted Matt's arm. "Don't let all that concern you, dear. The government picks up the tab in the end, anyway."

Matt, stone-faced, said nothing.

She continued, "I'm no psychiatrist, and I don't mean to sound analytical, but as I see it, your uncle's spending ways go back to his early days of deprivation. With his sudden wealth, he was like a kid in a candy store with a pocket full of nickels and dimes—he bought everything he ever wanted, including things he never should have had."

Matt found himself becoming more and more uncomfortable with his aunt's casual description of such obscene wealth and wanton waste; he was eager to change the subject.

"I'll be happy to see Deena again. I haven't seen her in several years. She must be all grown up and pretty." He glanced at Mary. "The last time I saw her, she looked nothing like Uncle Peter; much more like you."

"Thank you Matt." Mary thought, 'If you only knew.' Matt's comments were right on target, given the fact that Peter had nothing whatsoever to do with Deena's conception.

"Aunt Mary, forgive me for asking, but what happens to all this property if you should become disabled or die? Would Deena ...?"

Mary interrupted. "She would have financial advisers to help her. However, at the rate we're incurring losses there may be little for her to worry about. All this might collapse like a house of cards. If I can get my lawyers to convince the judge in the Federal Bankruptcy Court to give us an extension, we might be able to scare up enough investors to save this project," she hesitated, then said softly, "but that's a big *if.*"

The Cessna Citation descended swiftly out of the clouds. Its thrust reversers created a roar as it touched down gracefully and sped past the airport terminal. Making a U-turn turn, it taxied to the deplaning area.

After parking the limousine, Matt walked with Mary to the tarmac in time to see the plane air step descend. The captain waved to Mary and stood at the foot of the stairs to assist Maggie, who was followed by Lucy Kurtz, Susan Bird Song, then Larry and Josh. Maggie and Josh hurried to embrace Mary who was holding out her arms to them.

"How are two of my favorite people?" She eyed Josh's medical bag. "I hope you brought something for my pain in the ass—sorry, I meant to say my lower back." They all laughed.

Josh nodded. "I did."

In a line behind Maggie and Josh, Susan Bird Song stepped forward and was met warmly by Mary, who hugged her. Lucy, waiting to greet the hostess, gave her a perfunctory peck on the cheek and walked on. Larry stepped forward and ostensibly whispered to Mary but loud enough for all to hear, "You're still a good looking broad. Got anything exciting planned for tonight?" He winked and kissed her cheek.

Mary, sighing with exasperated tolerance, pushed him away.

Matt hauled the passenger bags to the limousine then returned to the second floor coffee bar where the guests and Mary awaited the arrival of Deena and the Brazilowicz men from LAX.

In the waiting room, Lucy studied Matt. "My, aren't you a good-looking young buck." Removing her coat from the chair next to her, she pointed to it. "Sit down, handsome, and tell me all about yourself." She tossed her head back and hand combed her hair. Her dancing eyes devoured Matt as though picturing him completely disrobed and in possession of abundant genitalia.

Larry, aware of his wife's prurient thoughts, frowned and said, "For chrissake, Lucy, pick on someone your own age." His acerbic command left no room for playful banter.

Mary saved Matt from further embarrassment when she placed her hand on his shoulder. "Matt, dear, Deena's plane should be arriving soon. Why don't you go down to meet it?"

After Matt left, Mary gave Lucy a frigid stare. "What you need, girl, is some physical activity that doesn't involve a man and a bed."

Lucy stood, looking down at Mary, and said, "Darling, a bed isn't always necessary." She turned to Larry. "Isn't that right, Sweetie?"

Larry tried to ignore her and looked away.

The Hawker swooped out of the low-lying moisture-laden clouds onto the airfield, and, like the Cessna, taxied to the private jet area. Deena was the first to descend, and ran toward her smiling cousin, Matt, who embraced her eagerly.

"Hey, ding-dong Deena, you're all grown up." He held her at arms' length. "You're pretty, just like your ma."

Oh, Matt, if you weren't my cousin, I'd marry you right here and now."

He looked beyond her, and, seeing Johnny standing in the plane's doorway, whispered, "Where'd you find the giant?"

Before she could respond, Matt saw Oscar Brasilowicz behind Johnny. "That must be the giant's keeper."

Without turning around, Deena said, "Matt, you be nice. Johnny's my intended, and that's his father."

The two goliaths ambled towards Matt to shake his hand.

"Welcome to Big Sky Country, gentlemen."

Matt asked about their trip and made the customary small talk as he led them to the terminal, then to the elevator to the second floor to meet the other guests. As soon as the elevator doors opened, Deena ran to her mother's open arms and held her firmly.

Maggie, meanwhile, had pulled Josh away from the others. They peered out the window onto the airfield that had turned eerily quiet. The sky was filled with dark clouds that descended ominously low, transforming the last hour of daylight into the somber blackness of night.

Maggie put her hand in Josh's and spoke softly, "Josh, I have a creepy premonition about this whole thing—like something weird is about to happen."

53

The cavernous limo accommodated the seven guests easily, even the senior Brazilowicz. With its well-stocked bar built into the back of the chauffeur's seat, the vehicle took on the cozy merriment of a college alumni group before the homecoming game. Mary struck the side of a crystal glass for attention.

"Just a word to thank you all for coming to our mountain retreat to enjoy a few winter sports and to say goodbye, once again, to Peter. He would have been pleased, knowing you're all here, even if it meant drinking his liquor and free-loading his hospitality, but you know I'm only kidding." She paused to accommodate the sparse laughter. "I'll tell you briefly about the program for tomorrow." She outlined the outdoor events including skiing, target shooting and bobsledding.

"After lunch, at approximately two o'clock, the mayor of our little city will be delivering the eulogy, and anyone who cares to say something nice about Peter is welcome to do so."

Deena waved her hand frantically. "Mother, I'd like to say something about my daddy 'cause he was very good to me, even if he did object to my seeing Johnny." Johnny, embarrassed, looked down, studying his size fourteen Nikes and said nothing.

Oscar Brazilowicz, swirling a tumbler of Scotch on the

rocks that clinked over his bulging abdomen said, "I heard Mr. Bruxton, God rest his soul, was a good business man who invested in waste management companies, which goes to prove he was pretty damn smart. I know he stood up to the SEC and the IRS when they accused him of fraud and financial crimes. On that basis alone, I would be proud to say something good on his behalf."

Oscar was not entirely correct on several counts, but no one challenged him.

Lucy Kurtz, embarking on a new round of inebriation, held up a premixed Martini unsteadily and announced, "Here's to old Pete, who loved life and died like few men do—satisfying the pleasures of a stiff and wild cock." The comment evoked gasps and snickering.

Larry poked her in the ribs and in a hoarse whisper said, "For God's sake, Lucy, shut up!"

Mary stared at Lucy with searing hostility, then looked away. "Does anyone else wish to offer a sentiment or two?" The silence was profound. Mary continued, "I think Peter would have enjoyed this gathering and would have given his own weighty rebuttal to that last comment." She glanced at Lucy again. "*He* probably would have been more selective with *his* guest list. But on to other matters."

"We've arranged to have four furnished A-frames for all of you. Deena will stay with me, Dr. and Mrs. Harrington will occupy the cabin next to ours, Larry and Lucy will be next to them, and Johnny and his father will occupy a cabin just beyond." She craned her neck to see Susan Bird Song huddled in a seat at the far end of the limo. "Ms. Bird Song will occupy a cabin at the end of the block. Our meals will be served in the community center. We've brought our own chef from the desert, who incidentally, flunked a course in calorie counting." A few polite laughs followed. "Drinking before or during skiing is dangerous and quite frankly stupid. Après ski will be held in the community hall where we'll enjoy a roaring fire and an open bar.

"Our first ski run tomorrow morning will start at eight. We should be off the slopes by noon. All participants will be fitted with new skis and poles, courtesy of Sunburst Lodge. Those of you requiring instructions will have professional trainers to guide you through the basic elements and start you on the bunny slopes.

"After lunch, we'll assemble in the great hall to attend the memorial service. Some townsfolk have been invited, and a number of TV, radio and newspaper people will probably be milling around. Please don't arrive in lounging robes or plan to sleep during the eulogies. It's a small town. If you sleep, the cameras will focus in on you, and probably turn up the audio if you snore." She paused until the chuckling stopped, then continued, "Matt will help you with your luggage and answer any questions about your accommodations."

Deena followed her mother as she stepped out of the limo and walked toward the large A-frame. Mary stopped momentarily to look at the Jeep parked curbside, then thought it could probably be Frank Parma's rented vehicle. She said nothing until Deena asked where Mr. Parma and Jim, the chauffeur, were staying.

"Mr. Parma has rented a room at a B & B in Bozeman. Jim Keyes is occupying our loft. You and I will sleep in the master bedroom on the main floor."

Deena stopped, placed her hands on her hips and in a challenging tone, asked, "Why is the chauffeur staying in *our* chalet?"

Mary continued walking, and did not respond immediately. "I had to give Susan Bird Song a chalet. I don't have another empty one for Jim, and besides, what difference does all that make? He occupies the loft, and we have the entire downstairs."

Deena, walking behind her mother, continued to carp, "That's not fair. Johnny and I could have occupied the loft and...."

"Deena, that's enough! You and Johnny are not married,

and it's just not proper...."

"Mother! Please don't talk to me about being proper. You know..."

Just at that moment, Jim Keyes opened the door and stepped forward to greet the arrivals. "How are you Ms. Deena? Hope your trip was pleasant." He looked at the sky. "I think you just missed a storm."

Standing behind Jim, Frank Parma, wearing sunglasses, squared his shoulders and controlled his smile to avoid reopening his lip laceration. He stepped in front of Jim and leaned forward to kiss Mary, who turned her cheek. She regarded him without warmth, noticing that he was wearing Peter's clothing and using his distinctive after shave fragrance.

Jim carried Deena's overnight bag into the bedroom, with Deena following. Mary remained in the living room, walked toward the fireplace, hugged her arms and shivered as she faced the blazing logs. Frank followed closely even though she maintained an air of aloofness. She said dryly, "I see you've made yourself comfortable in Peter's clothing and toiletries."

"I hope you don't mind. I can explain that later." He moved in front of her, then took her arms and held her hands to look at her with a pleading sadness. "Mary, I've missed you terribly. Why are you so standoffish? Have I done something to offend you?"

Before she could respond, he pulled her into his arms and covered her mouth with a kiss. She squirmed, and attempted to push him away as Jim entered the room.

"Everything all right here, Mrs. Bruxton?"

Frank looked disdainfully at him and released Mary. Inadvertently, Frank removed his sunglasses.

Mary stared at the blue-black swelling that produced a mere slit for the eye opening. "Don't tell me you walked into a wall."

"What happened isn't important." He replaced his

sunglasses quickly.

Jim Keyes had watched the scene for a few seconds before walking to the front door and stepping outside.

Frank's eyes followed him, then looked at Mary. "He sure as hell is a protective watch dog. I don't know whether that's loyalty or something deeper."

"Don't concern yourself about him." Mary turned away as Jim, coughing, stepped back into the large room.

"Heavy snowflakes falling," he said. "Maybe Mr. Parma ought to be thinking about heading back before the road gets impassable. Snow plows might not get out here for a few hours."

The thought of Frank driving sixty miles to Bozeman through a snowstorm seemed ridiculous. Whatever hostility Mary felt toward Frank, she could not justify turning him away. "We'll make accommodations for you here at the club," she said, then she thought for a moment. "If you don't mind sharing space with the Brazilowicz men, you can stay in their cabin. There's a hide-a-bed in that cabin. In the morning you can have breakfast in the club house with the other guests."

Frank responded without enthusiasm. "Yeah, I suppose I could do that."

"I'll have Jim help you with your bag."

"No, no! I can manage. Just call the Brazilowiczes and tell them I'm on my way."

Josh and Maggie were absolutely thrilled with their accommodations. Josh bent over the fireplace and looked upward to be sure the flue was open. With a long match-stick, he lit the pine logs and watched as the fire started. The pungent fragrance of pine filled the room, while the dancing flames grew higher, and the crackling, popping and sparking of the burning logs transformed the coolness of the room into warm coziness. Maggie placed her arms around his waist and held him closely but without her usual display of joyfulness.

"Why so pensive? This should be a wonderfully romantic moment." Josh reached behind her with both hands and felt the firm, rounded contours of her derriere. He squeezed her gently but firmly.

Maggie pulled his hands away. "That's not romantic, silly. Can't you be loving without becoming so—so physical?"

"Oh, oh, that's not like you. What bothers you, Love?"

Maggie took a deep breath and released it slowly. "Something about all of this—all these people with their guns and their concealed hatred for Peter Bruxton bother me. I really think we may be the only sane people around."

"All right, what's the blip on your radar screen?"

Maggie put her index finger to her lips. "That Parma character; he's kind of smarmy. I was surprised that he was even invited, especially if it's true that Mary's cooled her affair with him. Honestly, I think he could have killed Bruxton to get to Mary."

"No argument there."

"Then there's that Jolly Green Giant and his Pillsbury Dough Boy son. I don't trust them either."

"Sweetheart, you're tired and hypercritical. What you need is a little loving."

"How can you think of intimacy at a time like this?"

Josh ignored the objection and started to unbutton her sweater. "It's part of my genetic make-up. A gift from my daddy. This is who I am, and what you should expect of me."

His humor finally disarmed her. She smiled and shook her head with mock disapproval. "You're so fiercely hetero-sexual, and I suppose I should be grateful." Her eyes glistened, taking in all of his face. She looked longingly into his eyes, and put her arms around his neck. "Whenever you commiserate with your dear departed daddy, be sure to thank him for me."

54

Oscar Brazilowicz, with Johnny standing behind him, opened the door, and watched as Frank brushed the snow off his jacket and slapped his hat against his side. "Thanks for taking in a lonely transient, fellas," he said as he walked in and dropped his leather bag on the living room floor. "Hope you can put up with me for a day or so."

Oscar studied Parma's face after he removed his sunglasses. "What the hell happened to you? Have an argument at the union hall?" He laughed, and his abdomen shook.

"It's a long story, and not important."

"Yeah, sure, I understand. You can put your stuff in the hall closet."

Oscar smiled and rubbed his hands at the prospect of having a drinking partner. "How about a little something to warm the gizzard?" He held up a pinch bottle of Haig and Haig. "This stuff is so smooth you'll think you're drinking ambrosia—the drink of the *ditties*."

"That's nectar, Dad, and it's the drink of the *deities*," Johnny said as he walked with his father to the kitchen.

"Whatever." Oscar tilted his head back to project his voice toward Parma. "Send a kid to college and this is the kinda crap they learn 'em." In the kitchen, he opened a cupboard for two tumblers and poured four ounces of Scotch in each. He called out over his shoulder, "A little water or ice with that, Mr. Parma?"

"A little water'll be fine—and call me Frank."

Oscar turned to Johnny. "Sonny, pour some water into these tumblers and bring them into the living room." He hadn't offered Johnny hard liquor, not because he cared if his son had a drink or two, but rather because Johnny had been on a strict abstinence order from his football coach.

Oscar approached Frank who had seated himself in a club chair. He grunted with the effort of lowering himself in a twin chair that faced Frank. "I understand you're some kind of actor, is that right?"

"That's right."

"What was your connection with old man Bruxton?"

Before Parma could answer, Johnny handed the tumblers of Scotch to both men. The tumblers had been filled to the brims with water.

Oscar grimaced. "Jeezuz, Sonny, that's hundred-fifty buck Scotch you watered down with piss."

Johnny's face reddened.

Aware of his son's embarrassment, Oscar attempted quick amends. "Aw, forget it Sonny, I know you meant good."

Johnny sulked off to the seclusion of the den and the TV.

Oscar shook his head. "Sometimes you gotta take these kids by the hand and show 'em zackly what to do." He leaned close to Frank. "I hope to hell he knows what to do with that little Bruxton gal. I don't want to be around on their nuptchual night calling signals." He pushed back in his chair, smug with his sagacious comments. He intertwined his fingers on his chest and said, "Like I was askin': what was your connection with Peter Bruxton?"

Frank raised his tumbler to click with Oscar's. "Happy hunting." He sipped the Scotch then looked at it. "Damn good stuff, you've got excellent taste."

Oscar nodded, but waited for Parma to answer his question.

Parma paced his reply with a bit of drama, as though acting out a role. "Actually, old boy, I never met Bruxton.

I've seen photos of him, and of course, I knew about him through his wife, I mean Mary, his widow."

Oscar's eyes grew flinty. "Zatso? How well do you know the widow lady?"

The change in Oscar's demeanor did not escape Frank. "I've actually had the privilege of knowing her quite well."

"Oh, yeah? Well enough so that you were planning on getting spliced?"

"The idea's crossed my mind." Parma's index finger outlined the rim of his tumbler. "However, I'm not sure Mary is entirely comfortable with that at the moment."

Oscar exhaled audibly—a smile transformed his scowl. "Guess there's a chance for this old shit kicker to move in, then, eh?" He reached across the table to punch Parma's shoulder playfully.

Parma regarded him with a tight smile. "If you're thinking of making a play for her, you'll have to fight me off."

Oscar put his drink down. His stare bore into Parma's eyes. "Beating the competition is what I'm good at."

55

The alpine chalets had been built to withstand the accumulated tons of snow that could bury them in a severe storm. Situated well beyond the possible ravages of avalanches and the destructive forces of battering northerly winds roaring down from Alaska, they appeared to be hunkered down into the snow-covered landscape. From the outside, the chalets appeared rustic, but inside, they had all the conveniences and luxuries of modern living. The Bruxton chalet, in particular, had been furnished with only the most luxurious materials. The five thousand square foot domicile was filled with personally selected accessories: English bone China, fine Irish linens, stout German appliances, and handsome Scandinavian furniture.

At six-thirty a.m., Jim was already at work, making the kitchen ready for Mary and Deena. He'd decided to set the table in the kitchen since the dining room was not as cozy or conducive to intimate conversation. He spread the linen tablecloth and hand smoothed it, then at each setting, he placed folded napkins in the classic fleur-de-lis configuration. He held each of the crystal juice glasses to the light and hand wiped them with a kitchen towel. The silverware, examined for water spots, was also hand wiped, then aligned along each delicate plate. Once the table was set, Jim went to the fridge, took out a grapefruit, halved and sectioned it, and then topped off the halves with mara-schino cherries and a sprig of mint. He placed an assort-ment of imported jams and jellies, plus butter and cream cheese in small porcelain containers. Finally, he started the drip coffee maker, and gave it time to make a full pot before walking to the closed door of the master bedroom. He put his ear to the door, heard nothing, then knocked gently to announce that breakfast was ready.

Mary, in a nubby housecoat, sleep still in her eyes, came out of the bedroom. A yawning Deena, wearing an oversized USC sweatshirt and running pants, followed her. Both shuffled into the kitchen with fluffy house slippers. Jim pulled back Mary's chair.

"Mm-mm, that coffee smells wonderful," Mary said. She scanned the beautifully arranged table and clasped her hands. "Oh, Jim, this is absolutely lovely. She picked up her napkin and said, "This is folded magnificently. Where did you learn to set a table like this?"

He shrugged. He was not about to tell her he learned all this in a class for domestic skills on the neuro-psychiatric ward at the V.A. hospital. She touched his arm while she slid into the chair that he pushed forward gently. Deena had already picked the cherry off the grapefruit, chewed it noisily and licked the tips of her fingers.

"Mrs. Bruxton, do you have a preference for toast? Sourdough, white, whole grain, bagels?" Jim's manner was properly starchy in Deena's presence.

"Half a bagel toasted would be fine."

Deena said, "I'll have the other half plus a slice of sour-dough. I could eat a horse."

Mary turned her eyes upward and silently prayed that Deena's appetite did not arise out of a pregnant condition.

She turned to Jim who was pouring coffee in her cup. "Would you care to join us this morning on the slopes?"

Deena looked at Mary. "Mother, is your back well enough for skiing?"

"That injection Doc Harrington gave me last night worked wonders. I know he wouldn't approve, but I intend to ski anyway." She looked at Jim again. "You're sure you wouldn't like to join us?"

"No, ma'am. I don't know the first thing about skiing, and I'm not about to learn. Besides, I'd like to do some hunting around the property."

"Hunting?" Mary set her cup on the saucer and regarded him sternly. "You be sure you're a long way from the ski run. I don't need any more gunshot deaths. I'm not even sure this is deer hunting season, and you don't have a license."

"No need to worry, ma'am."

Deena, chewing her bagel slathered with strawberry preserves, asked, "Oh, Mother, speaking of shooting, can I use your Perazzi skeet gun?"

Without hesitation, Mary shook her head. "I don't deny you much, but in this case, the answer is a definite no, N-O, and please don't ask again."

Deena pouted. "Mother, you know full well, I'm qualified to shoot that weapon as well as a lot of others."

"That magnificent weapon and scope cost over fifty thousand dollars, and no one gets to shoot it but me. After I'm gone, you can have it, along with everything else I own, but not until then."

56

Matt, who had been responsible for the skiing arrangements, drove his Hummer on the road dusted overnight
with a new layer of snow. After parking in front of Mary's
chalet, he stomped his boots on the welcoming mat before
entering the house.

He stopped in the entryway and looked at Mary. "Wow,
Aunt Mary, you look great in that jazzy ski outfit." Looking
beyond Mary, he saw Deena in casual clothes. "Hey, Ding-
Dong Deena, aren't you skiing with us?"

Mary answered for her petulant daughter. "Not this
morning. She's going to play hostess to her boyfriend and
his father. They don't ski. There'll be six of us for the slopes.
You have equipment for everyone?"

"Sure do, no problem."

Mary, with Matt close behind, stepped outside in the
bright cold sunshine. She blew steam vapor into the air and
looked at the sky with an almost childish delight. "When
I was a youngster, I remember these gorgeous blue skies
after the snow fall....puffs of white clouds like giant cotton
candy that I wanted to pull down and eat. In the summer,
I'd run up a hilltop and look at the green fields for miles
and miles around. Some days, my brothers and I would fly
kites, and when my daddy thought I was old enough he'd
allow me to go out with the boys to shoot critters." Mary

gazed at the sky with longing. "This would be a perfect day for target practice, too."

Frank Parma, approaching them in a bright red ski suit with matching Norwegian ski hat and wrap-around goggles, hailed Mary and Matt. In his best theatrical manner, he called out, "Hello, there." Then, as though approaching center stage, he held out his arms to show his skiwear.

"Peter's outfit fits him pretty well, don't you think? The goggles do a good job hiding his shiner, too," Matt said.

Mary turned her back partially, and did not comment, although she knew he looked better in Peter's clothes than Peter ever could. She still harbored troubling doubts about him, and could not erase the image of him standing behind her with the fireplace poker poised above her head when the lights came on suddenly that horrible evening at the desert estate. She questioned her thinking over and over— if he turned off the lights, who turned them on? She had difficulty rationalizing the sequence of events. Was she being guided by emotion rather than reason? He'd been too passionate a lover to want to harm her; he could not have play-acted those torrid love scenes that were so intense... and yet, he was an actor.

Part of her wanted to forgive him and resume a relationship; the other part would not allow her to become so foolishly involved again. Almost imperceptibly, she shook her head as though trying to clear her confused thinking. She was annoyed with herself for having promised to provide him with funds for his movie-making venture even in the event of her death. But, she thought quickly, her team of lawyers could always reverse that clause.

57

Detective Brad Oliver looked at his watch—5:30. He gathered the papers on his desk and stacked them neatly, then replaced them in a file cabinet at the far wall. He reached for his jacket on the back of his chair and reflexively touched the holster under his left shoulder. He remembered being reminded repeatedly at the police academy, a phrase that still rang in his head: the weapon will be your best friend or your worst enemy. The admonitions that the gun was to be fired only in self-defense, or in the defense of others, were mere words. He knew that when and if he had to use it; he wouldn't need the law enforcement officers' manual to advise him of the obvious.

Unlike many of his fellow officers, Brad thought of himself as liberal; one who could exercise more patience with a perpetrator and could identify the compromised social background of the criminal. That kind of thinking, in his opinion, gave him an edge. Then he thought about his partner, Mannheim, who had bitter contempt for most suspects, and certainly for all confirmed crooks. But he also knew that Mannheim was a conscientious investigator whose arrest rate was among the highest in the county. What he lacked in civility, he compensated with dogged determination.

The most recent example of his partner's determination was the out-of-state arrest warrant he'd gotten in the Bruxton case. Oliver did not fully understand how Mannheim managed to get it, but somehow, he did. On the other hand, in this particular case, he'd had some help. The local newspaper was still carrying on a relentless campaign, reminding the public of the shameful unsolved murder. It almost seemed as if the editor of *The Desert Times* conducted a personal vendetta against the Riverside County Sheriff. The editorials had become more blatantly overt and vitriolic, with complaints of deficient crime control and the need for broad organizational change, not to mention personnel replacement. The sheriff had been feeling the heat of growing public resentment and had, in turn, been pressuring his local departments to get the "goddamned murderer." The order, of course, fell ultimately on the shoulders of Mannheim and Oliver in homicide.

Oliver walked out of his cubicle and peered into Mannheim's. Mannheim was poring over scattered reports on his desk and had reached forward with his lanky frame, his head down and his rump up, reminding Oliver of a praying mantis.

Startled by Oliver's appearance, Mannheim jerked up, then looked at his watch. "Leaving so soon?" A wry smile curled his lips; he knew the shift had ended an hour and a half ago.

Oliver inhaled deeply and noisily. "Hm-mm, replaced your Old Spice aftershave with expensive cologne? A little gift from the princess?"

Mannheim straightened and brought his shoulders back. "For your information, she did buy me Ralph Lauren Polo. I use it when we're going out on a date, and that happens to be tonight. Besides, the cologne is better at covering up fart smells that get trapped in my pants."

Oliver shook his head. "You're giving me much more information than I want." He looked at a travel itinerary on Mannheim's desk. "We all set for our trip to Montana tomorrow?"

Mannheim collected the papers on his desk and reached for an attaché case leaning against the bottom drawer. He jammed some papers in it and said, "Don't forget to pack your Kevlar vest and your winter underwear."

"I don't have winter underwear."

"Better get some or you'll freeze your balls off."

Oliver nodded tolerantly. "What in the hell does that good looking gal see in you and your uncouth mannerisms?"

"Oh, I can be quite couth when I'm with her. I'll be especially couth tonight since I won't be seeing her for a few days. Know what I mean?" He winked.

At the doorway, Mannheim presented Bonnie with a bouquet of red roses. She clasped her hands and asked, "For me?"

He looked around. "Who else?"

She took the roses and held them off to the side, tilted her head upward to kiss him, then led him to the sofa to sit beside her. "How's my big, handsome detective?"

"Your big handsome detective gets big every time he sees you."

Bonnie elbowed his side. "You're naughty, but I suppose I should be flattered. Well, what bold plans have you made?"

"For tonight? I'd like to make love to you. I gotta confess, Baby, being near you causes my *cajones* to ache."

"Really?" She stood with her hands on her hips. "How subtle and suave you are." She smiled disingenuously, picked up the bouquet from the cocktail table, and put the roses in a vase.

Mannheim's deep-set eyes followed the supple movements of the youthful woman whose curvaceous body and exotic skin tone evoked such a strong male response in him. Everything about her was soft, feminine and desirable.

His carnal craving had almost embarrassed him, so much so, that he resolved to project a more mature and discreet image. He did not want her to think this relationship was merely a series of sexual encounters, but on the other hand, he doubted that he could ever actually resist her physically.

He engaged in the yin-yang of soliloquy. *Hadn't we talked intelligently about our families and backgrounds? Of course we did, for hours. However, she may not have been altogether forthcoming. She spoke of her family in casual, terms — nothing extraordinary or scandalous. Hell, families don't exist in vacuums. But for that matter, I didn't tell her everything about my past either. How would she react if I told her I clubbed a number of black assholes when I was a cop on the beat in South L.A.? Yeah, I beat them probably as much because they were black, as I did for resisting arrest, and I stupidly wore my prejudice like a badge of honor back then.* He shrugged in resignation. *But after twenty-five years I've learned that perps come in all colors, shapes and sizes, and that's no Pollyanna bullshit.* He thought of Bonnie's beauty: her exquisitely toned café-au-lait skin, her enchanting smile and voluptuous form. *She's perfect, and I couldn't love her more. Hell, I'd marry her tonight if she'd have me.*

Bonnie returned with two goblets of red wine and handed one to Mannheim, who stood to receive it. She tilted her head, and with that innocent little girl smile, toasted their love. They sipped the wine, then Bonnie closed her eyes as though making a wish. Mannheim watched her, then took her glass, and, with his, set them on the cocktail table. He reached for her and held her firmly, pressed his body against hers, and planted a long open-mouth kiss on her eager lips.

She became limp and slumped in his arms, then regained her equilibrium with a start. She opened her eyes wide and shook her head. "Whew! If that was the wine, I'm ordering a case of it." She took his hand, and they both sat on the sofa again.

Mannheim's heart pounded like that of a young lover

anticipating the excitement of concupiscence.

Bonnie held off his advances. She removed his hand as it surreptitiously came up around her side to cup her breast. She said she wanted to engage him in meaningful conversation and not have him treat her as an object of mere sexual fulfillment. With her arms folded across her chest, she pushed back into the sofa. "Tell me what you did today. Did you solve any horrible murders?" When Mannheim shook his head, she continued, "By the way, what progress is there on the Bruxton case?" She looked for any nuanced changes in his expression.

Bonnie's insistent questioning had caused Mannheim's libido to sink to almost unrecoverable depths. He reached for the goblet, swirled the wine and took a gulp. Piqued and frustrated, he blurted, "Oliver and I are flying out to Bozeman tomorrow morning to pick up the murderer. How does that grab you?"

Bonnie sat upright. "You're doing what? Who in the world are you picking up?"

Mannheim gave no immediate response.

"For heaven's sake," she continued. "Don't just sit there, tell me!"

"Whoa, slow down, girl. This is a hush-hush deal. I shouldn't have even said anything about it. And for chrissakes, don't breathe a word of this to anyone."

"I won't. I swear!" Her eyes danced with anticipation. "Now, tell me, who is it?" Before Mannheim could respond, she said, "This is the guy who murdered Bruxton, but probably also saved *my* life, remember?"

Mannheim nodded, but said nothing.

"Oh, come on. At least give me a hint."

Mannheim shook his head again. "Uh, uh, nothing doing."

Bonnie punched his arm. "Let me have three guesses."

Again, Mannheim shook his head and placed his wine glass on the cocktail table.

Bonnie jumped up and pursed her lips. "Well, if that's

the way you're going to play, don't expect any favors from me tonight. Either you tell me who the murderer is, or you can go home with your aching *cajones*." Her brief forced laughter did not conceal a very real underlying note of irritation.

Mannheim took her hand, trying to lighten the mood, and started to pull her toward the bedroom. "Come on, Dearie, *maybe* I'll tell you after we make a little love."

His attempt, however, came across to Bonnie as smug condescension, and it only provoked her further; she pulled away and picked up the roses from the vase, walked smartly toward the front door, opened it and raised her chin.

"Sorry, Mr. Keep-it-all-to-yourself-detective." In a tone totally devoid of friendliness she said, "Good night."

Mannheim followed her haltingly, silently cursing his reckless utterance about picking up Bruxton's murderer. "Look, I'm sorry, but I can't tell..."

Bonnie thrust the roses at him. "*Maybe* we'll visit after you get back into town." She hesitated then added, "But be sure to phone first—I may be busy."

She waited for him to take the roses, then stood mutely and resolutely as he walked out the door and down the sidewalk.

58

The morning sun began its ascent behind the Madison mountain range, producing a glow of subdued pink, then a golden orange, and finally a burst of brilliant yellow. Mary waited outside the chalet with Matt and Frank Parma, their breaths produced plumes of steam in the chilled air. Jim emerged from the chalet in a hunting jacket, stocking hat, knee-high boots and sheathed rifle. Mary was actually glad he'd decided not to join them on the ski slope. Best to keep him and Frank separated; they could have killed each other in their kitchen brawl, and, given the hostile looks they gave each other they still might.

Mary thought, they had each filled an important role in her life; Jim, for many years as her sometimes lover, and Frank, as her recent sexual conquest and social companion. It was sad, in a way, that Jim was socially inferior to her. He satisfied her as an occasional lover and was fiercely loyal and protective. But he could never be her constant companion. Too many differences existed between them that could never be bridged. A relationship with a chauffeur would be scandalous and ruinous in her social milieu, no matter how good the sex might be. Frank, on the other hand, might have made a good companion. He was like a satyric lover; one who consistently satisfied her, but he created an uneasy doubt in her mind. There was the incident with the poker, and his insistence on the financial arrangements for his filming.

"Frank, you'll have to forgive us," she said. "Matt and I are going to test the snow pack and our timing on ski run number one, before the rest of the gang gets here."

She turned to look at Jim who held the muzzle of his rifle down and admonished him again, "You be careful with that."

He walked away and casually raised his left hand to acknowledge her warning.

On his cell, Matt notified the tower that Mrs. Bruxton and he were coming up.

Seated in the open lift chair with Matt, Mary gazed at the splendid expanse of the landscape, the vastness of the blue skies, the immense evergreen areas blanketed by the predawn snow that clung to the tree branches like looping, billowy waves concealing the sharp outlines of the firs and the jagged mountain arêtes.

A tower attendant greeted Mary and Matt at the top, and advised them that skiing conditions were fast, and the visibility, excellent. Mary adjusted her glasses, checked her bindings, then moved to the starting point where she crouched and waited. The starter looked at the wall clock, raised his hand then dropped it, and shouted, "Go!" She pushed off with her poles and headed down the fall line with the ease and grace of one who knew and loved the slopes. Mary reveled in the breath-taking excitement of careening downward at an ever-faster pace, leaning and weaving to guide her turns. The sound of the icy wind whipping about her head and the shushing of the skis was all she heard.

Three minutes later, Matt stood at the starting platform in a slight crouching posture, moving his skis back and forth. He flexed his torso then straightened, then flexed again, holding the poles in push-off position. The starter raised his hand, lowered it and gave the command, "Go!"

Matt edged too far on his right ski and bobbled, almost falling before he regained his balance. He tucked the poles under his arms and attempted to make up for lost time.

"Crack!"

A piercing gunshot jarred the serenity of the valley, and its echo reverberated over the slope. A cascading shower of snow fell from one of the trees about a hundred yards before him. Matt looked around anxiously. Beyond that tree, a dark form appeared to the right of the slope. *Was that a downed animal?* Approaching at rapid speed, he banked sharply to stop, causing a heavy spray of snow. He approached the figure cautiously, only to discover that it was his Aunt Mary sitting in a slight depression off the ski run. Her right ski had been thrown off, and she was rocking back and forth in grimacing pain.

Matt kicked off his skis and hurried to her side. "What happened? Are you hurt?"

She nodded impatiently. "Of course I'm hurt. Give me your hand and help me get up. I heard that shot and edged too much, then lost my balance. My damn ankle hurts like hell and my butt stings."

"You think that shot was fired at you?"

"Hell, I don't know, but I swear something whistled right past me."

Matt bent over her and removed her left ski. "Stay down, don't try to stand; turn on your belly and move farther to the side of the run where the land dips." From her belly-lying position, Mary raised her head to look about. Neither of them could see far because of the undulating and curving contour of the run and the forested areas to either side.

In a quivery voice, she said, "Do you suppose someone was really shooting at me?"

"I don't know, but let's not make ourselves easy targets." Matt scooted closer to her and pushed her deeper into the depression. "Don't move." In the prone position, he reached for his cell and punched in 911. "Operator, someone is shooting at us on the number one ski run at Sunburst Lodge...about four to five hundred yards from the tower. Mrs. Bruxton injured an ankle. Get someone out here now."

Before he replaced the phone, Mary shouted, "Don't have them send an ambulance! It's only a sprain, and I don't want to make a big deal of this and frighten everyone. If the first aid men have an elastic bandage, they can apply it, and I'll ski down."

Matt relayed the request.

Mary rubbed her ankle gently, then asked in a plaintive voice, "Why would anyone be shooting at me? What have I done?"

"Some crazy jerk is probably going to tell us he thought he was shooting at a deer," Matt replied.

The distant wail of a siren brought some relief to their anguish. "I hope to hell the police arrive before that madman fires off another round," Matt said. He raised his head slightly, looked around, and then whispered, "Whoever's shooting has stopped—I hope."

A snowmobile with two men, one holding a first aid kit and a splint, were making their way up the slope where Mary and Matt lay huddled.

One of the first aid men jumped off and crouched low to examine Mary's right ankle. "Could be sprained or maybe fractured," he said.

"Just wrap it up so I can ski down to the finish line."

"Sorry, Mrs. Bruxton, we'll do this our way." The splint was applied and an army blanket wrapped around the leg. The two men carried her, and Matt acted as a shield to Mary's exposed side as they placed her on the snowmobile. One of the men, an instructor, said, "We're going to cancel all skiing for the rest of the day."

"Is that really necessary?" Mary asked petulantly.

"Yes, Ma'am. We've been in touch with the police and those are their orders."

Matt put on his skis and said he would meet them at the finish line.

Word of Mary's fall and the gunshot caused anxiety and excitement among the guests who had already congregated at the bottom of the ski run. When the snowmobile arrived, the guests converged around it. Mary, in the semi-recumbent position, smiled and raised her hands in a triumphant gesture. She leaned on Matt's arm and stood, placing only partial weight on the injured ankle. "All of you dear people please understand that I'm all right. My fall was my own klutzy fault. Sorry the ski run will be closed."

Lucy Kurtz called out, "What about the gun shot?"

Mary shook her head, and waved her hand dismissively. "That was probably some over-eager hunter who thought he saw a deer or an elk or whatever. I'll talk with the police, then we'll all meet at the clubhouse for lunch at noon. After that, we'll hold the memorial service." Mary said, eager to quell the mounting anxiety and leave the scene.

One of the uniformed police approached Mary. "Would you like us to drive you home, Mrs. Bruxton?"

"No, but if you're planning to ask a lot of questions, you can follow us home. I'll be able to elevate my foot, and one of my guests, Dr. Harrington, can take a look at it."

Elbowing his way past the other guests, Frank called out, "Mind if I tag along?" He moved up and insisted on holding Mary's arm to support her. She was reluctant, at first, to have him do so, but when Matt offered to support her other side she accepted. She patted Matt's hand. "You'll never know how much I love you for protecting your old aunt." She leaned over to kiss him.

"Aunt Mary, I'm not such a noble guy. While I was protecting you, I was protecting myself. Let's hope the s.o.b. who caused this is nabbed before he does something else." The three of them proceeded slowly to Matt's Hummer. Mary, with the two men supporting her, was hopping to avoid having to put pressure on the ankle. Exhausted, she stopped before reaching the vehicle.

Frank ran to open the Hummer door, then returned to lift Mary onto the front passenger seat. When he bent forward to fasten the shoulder/lap harness, two bullets dropped out of the upper pocket of his jacket and fell onto the floor of the vehicle.

59

In the kitchen, Mary sat exhausted, with her leg propped on a chair, while Frank and Matt sat at either end of the table, and the two officers stood to one side.

Officer Smith removed a spiral notebook from his shirt pocket, then apologized for taking more time as he started questioning. "Mrs. Bruxton, can you tell us exactly what happened on the slope?"

Mary explained the events hurriedly, but grew restive and looked at Matt. "Darling, tell these officers what they want to know. I need to get out of these clothes and freshen up. Call Dr. Josh and ask him to come over to look at my ankle." She glanced at her watch. "Give me about fifteen minutes." She moaned with her first step, but held up her hand to resist help from Matt, then continued to limp toward her bedroom.

Frank was talking with the officers when Jim Keyes came in from the outdoors. He placed his encased rifle against the corner of the entryway, then removed his snow-covered boots and placed them on a mat. His outer clothes went into the hall closet before he walked into the kitchen. Seeing Frank, Matt and the officers, he stopped and asked, "What the hell's going on here?"

Officer Smith looked at him. "Who are you?"

Keyes identified himself, and Sergeant McGowen

asked, "Where were you during the past hour?"

"Trying to bag some game." Keyes became impatient. "Will someone tell me what the hell's going on here?"

"Looks like someone attempted to shoot Mrs. Bruxton or Matt on the ski slope," the senior officer said.

"What? Where is she? Is she all right? Did anyone see who did it?"

"No one saw a goddamned thing," Parma interjected, then turned his back on Keyes.

Keyes's jaw muscles tightened. He faced Parma and glowered. "Where were you?"

Parma stood abruptly and squared off. McGowen hurried to separate them.

Mary limping back into the kitchen called out, "Jim, calm down! Frank was nowhere near me." She took her seat at the kitchen table; Matt hurried in with another chair for her to prop her leg up.

"Well, he should have been keeping an eye out for you." Keyes groused and turned his back to Parma.

The senior officer pointed at Keyes. "You were hunting, eh? What did you shoot?"

Keyes, still chafing under Parma's dismissive attitude, grumbled, "Nothing. I had no luck."

"Let's see your weapon." McGowen said.

"Suit yourself." Jim left the kitchen and returned with the rifle in its carrying case. When he started to unzip the case, McGowen reached for it and said, "Hold it! I'll do that." He removed the rifle, opened the chamber, looked inside and sniffed. He pushed the gun back toward Keyes. "This was just fired. I thought you said you had no luck."

Jim snapped, "That's right. I didn't bag anything, but I got a round or two off."

"What were you shooting at?"

"A coyote or some such critter."

"Were you anywhere near the ski run when you fired?"

"Hell, no way. I was out at the perimeter firing in the

opposite direction."

"Where'd you get this Browning automatic?"

Before Jim answered, the officer said, "I had one like it in 'Nam. Were you in the service?"

"Yeah, that's right."

Officer McGowen turned to look at Mary. "Mrs. Bruxton is it possible that someone outside the club could have gained access to the ski run?"

Mary shook her head. "No—no, I don't believe so. This is a gated community, and the perimeter is secured by an eight-foot Cyclone fence...."

"So, there's a better than even chance that someone on the club grounds fired that shot?" McGowen kept his eyes on Mary, who was clearly troubled by the question.

"I suppose that's possible." She hesitated, then frowned. "You can't be thinking that any of my guests—they're all people I know. They're my friends." She turned towards Matt, and in a subdued voice, said, "I can't imagine any of the employees wanting to harm me, either. They're getting paid well in this rotten economy."

Matt said nothing, but was keenly aware that the remaining employees had taken a cut in salary, forfeited benefits, and, to the contrary, were generally quite unhappy.

Mary continued, "Truth is, I don't even know the workers, except for my nephew, Matt, here."

"How many people are employed at the club today?" McGowen asked.

"We're way down to a skeleton crew—maybe two dozen," Matt said.

Parma interrupted. "Officer, can you get the names of all employees who are registered gun owners?"

McGowen gave him a sideways glance. "Mister, you're in Montana. At least eighty percent of the people in the State are registered gun owners. The other twenty percent just haven't gotten around to it."

Mary smiled as Josh and Maggie arrived. Josh carried

his black bag and a pair of aluminum crutches he'd found in the lodge's first aid room. Mary put up her hand to suspend the police interrogation. "Sorry, fellas. You'll have to allow time for my examination and treatment." She pulled up her pant leg.

Mary watched as Josh set his bag on the table. "Oh, boy, am I ever glad to see you two. So far, Doc, you've had to treat my back and now my ankle. Should I be worrying about a broken arm or a fractured spine?"

"If you had taken my advice, you wouldn't have skied."

"If I had taken good advice all my life, I wouldn't have done a thousand things I've done, and I wouldn't have had half as much fun." Mild laughter followed Mary's remarks, thereby relieving a bit of the tension in the room. Josh, busy with his examination of Mary's ankle, noted the swelling and the bluish-pink discoloration on the outer side of the ankle. He applied light finger pressure until she complained. "Without x-rays, I can't say there isn't a fracture, but at the very least, it's a bad sprain. I'll tape it and give you some pills for pain...."

"Save the damn pills," Mary interrupted. "I've got my own remedy for pain, and I'll enjoy it a helluva lot more." More laughter followed.

Josh adjusted the crutches for height and demonstrated their use.

60

Beyond the entrance to the enormous clubhouse with its bizarre neo-gothic architecture framed in heavy timbers, a section had been cordoned off, and a sign posted for the memorial service. The Honorable John Q. Clark, mayor, was to deliver the eulogy. The red-faced portly man stood at the speaker's stand and appeared to have been fortified by the likes of Jack Daniels or one of his brethren.

Mary sat in the front row reserved for family, close friends and dignitaries, such as the district congressman, the postmaster, the fire chief and the chief of police. Even with the crowd that had gathered, the interior of the clubhouse had a daunting awesomeness with massive beams of cedar and pine supporting the vaulted ceiling with gabled outcroppings.

Notice of the memorial service had appeared in the local newspaper daily for one week. This was an event of significance since the exclusive clubhouse was to be opened to the public for the first time, and locals were eager to pay their respects to a man they knew only by reputation. The offer of free refreshments didn't hurt either.

Mary looked about anxiously for Deena and the two Brazilowicz men. She had reserved four seats to her right, thinking Oscar might require two. Frank Parma sat on her left and reached for her hand; she pulled it away.

In a troubled whisper, Mary asked an imaginary third

party, "Where are they? Why does she aggravate me like this?" She looked at her watch. "It's 2:15. She knew the services were starting at 2:00."

Frank leaned toward her. "They may have gone for target practice and just forgot to notice the time."

Mary gave him a perfunctory glance. "Ridiculous. She doesn't have a gun."

Frank leaned closer and whispered, "But Oscar Brazilowicz does—an expensive rifle with a powerful scope."

Mary's tone reached a stage one panic level. "Would he permit her to use it?"

"He'd do cartwheels for her—if she asked him to."

Mary stood on her crutches to scan the entire clubhouse for Deena and her two guests. Her shoulders drooped with relief, and she gave an audible sigh, when she saw Deena leading the two burly men from a side entrance. Mary waved eagerly.

Deena, in a down-filled jacket and heavy boots, clomped with each step to hurry to her mother. Seeing Deena's ruddy cheeks and broad smile, Mary's anxiety melted and she hugged her daughter. Now, she thought, the memorial services could begin, and she would be at ease, despite the gunshot episode and her painful ankle.

Wearing a frontier-styled suede jacket over an open-collar flannel shirt with a loose hanging bolo displaying a US flag shield, Mayor Clark cleared his throat. He looked at his notes, tilted the microphone up and read, "We are gathered here to commemorate, to honor the memory, of a distinguished member of our fair community, one who had the rare foresight, the vision to create this magnificent retreat in the heart of our Lord's bountiful wonderland. Although we are facing uncertain economic times, we know this magnificent project will endure and flourish to bring Peter Bruxton's dream of an exquisitely planned refuge for the deserving...."

The mayor, clearly enjoying his own verbosity,

hooked his thumbs into his suspenders and expanded his chest. Deftly he escaped the solemnity of the eulogy to segue into the political stump.... "And so my friends with the mournful passing of that great American philanthropist, Peter Bruxton, we can look forward to his legacy of conservancy in this great green belt, and the wholesome environment of lands set aside for future generations to enjoy and treasure.

"I, John Quentin Clark, as your duly elected mayor, am committed to the ideals of that late great man whose memory shall forever be emblazoned upon our hearts. To keep his ideals in perpetuity, we need to maintain a political base, the tenets of which run parallel to mine...."

Finally, Mary signaled for the Mayor to cut it short by indicating the letter "T" with her hands. The mayor acknowledged her signal and concluded. "May his soul rest in the Pantheon of Gods who espouse peace and goodwill among Republicans everywhere—Amen. And now we shall hear from one who was very dear to the heart and soul of Peter Bruxton, his charming daughter, Deena." The mayor pulled the microphone down while Deena clambered up the three stairs to the stage and stood behind the speaker's podium.

"Thank you, Mayor Clark. I just want to say a few things about my daddy." She looked over the audience of several hundred; her eyes began to tear, and she cleared her throat. "My daddy was wonderful to me. He bought me just about everything I ever wanted, well, practically. Maybe he did that because he couldn't spend much time with me, but I understand all that now. All I ever wanted was to be with him; to know him better, and later, to try to understand what it was that had driven him to work so hard.

"I know he loved me, and yet he spent so little time with me and Mommy. Not until I took classes in Psychology 101 and 102 at the university did I begin to understand some of the things that accounted for his behavior. By definition, he suffered from an obsessive/compulsive disorder with oral tendencies, as well as an abnormal heterosexual sex addiction."

Mary stared at Deena with disbelief. With an audible *ahem*, she ran her index finger across her neck.

Deena broke off her pseudo-analytical eulogy in mid phrase, then concluded with, "I will miss him very much. Although he did not always approve of my friends, I think he would have liked Johnny, once he got to know him real well." She looked upward toward the rafters. "Daddy, we forgive you your transgressions, 'cause we know you couldn't help them."

The mayor moved the microphone upward and said, "Thank you, Ms. Bruxton, for those words of wisdom. I am honored to announce that through the generosity of our dear hostess, Mrs. Mary Bruxton, there is a bountiful buffet in the dining area awaiting your pleasure. Thank you all for your attention. Now enjoy your vittles."

After the eulogy, Mary dabbed her non-tearing eyes with a facial tissue, then stood, placing her crutches against her chair. Almost immediately, a queue formed; extending out the door, and around the clubhouse. The long line of visitors waited to shake Mary's hand and express condolences, before heading over to the buffet. This was the sort of activity Mary had been accustomed to, and even enjoyed, up to a point. She maintained a fixed and melancholy smile, but after several hundred hand-shakes, her response developed a noticeable insincerity. The bobbing of her head had become mechanical, metronome-like. A crick developed in her neck, her fingers grew numb and her ankle had begun to throb with every heartbeat. She no longer saw identifying features, but a blur of faceless mannequins. She prayed silently that the line would end soon.

The last hand she shook was cold, the fingers spidery and gripping; she jerked her hand away reflexively. Looking up at the pale, angular face with its brooding deep-set eyes, a shock, like an electrical current, zinged through her head, causing momentary dizziness. She tottered, and was grabbed before she fell. Regaining her balance, she adjusted her crutches and stared into the gaunt face of the one who had caught her. In a hoarse whisper, she said, "Mannheim, what the hell are you doing here?"

Mannheim thought her question carried an element of fear and anxiety. His smile, more like a sneer, preceded his answer. "Detective Oliver and I thought we'd pay our respects."

Mary's day, already marred by unhappy events, was aggravated further by the appearance of these unwanted gumshoes. *What could they possibly want?*

Mannheim looked around, then asked Mary if she could step away for a moment.

Jim Keyes, at a distance, studied the three as they left the crowd. He walked slowly, deliberately toward them. "Mrs. Bruxton, is everything all right? Is there anything I can do?"

"I'm fine Jim. I need a few minutes alone with these detectives."

He left reluctantly, but turned twice to look at the three as they huddled in conversation.

Mannheim waited until Keyes was out of earshot. "We've learned from talking to the local police that your day was jinxed by your injury on the ski slope after a gunshot firing."

She regarded him suspiciously. "That's right—but that's *not* why *you're* here."

"No, Ma'am, we're here to pick up a suspect in the murder of your husband," Oliver said.

Mary's eyes widened. "What?" Then her surprise turned to indignation. Before the detectives could explain, she said, "What the hell are you waiting for? Why didn't you have the local police pick him up?"

Oliver said, "The chief didn't want any long-distance muck-ups resulting in further delays. The last time he wanted a murderer that was being held in another state, there were too many legal hoops. He swore he wouldn't go that route

again. Besides, he's getting flak from the Sacramento polit-
icos who need publicity for the next election."

Mary's eyes locked onto Mannheim's. "You mean to tell
me you *know* who killed my husband and that person is *here?*
In this very room?" She threw her right arm out in a sweeping
motion toward the gathering. "That's absolutely perverse!"
She raised one crutch and slammed its end onto the floor.
"For God's sake get him the hell out of here." The detectives
remained poker-faced while she became more distraught.
"What the hell are you waiting for—another murder?"

"No, Ma'am. But first, we'd like to ask your guests some
questions, just to be sure we've made no mistakes in our
calculations. Do you mind?" Mannheim said.

Mary, seething, experienced another episode of vertigo
and took an unguarded step backwards, bumping into
Frank Parma, who, upon seeing her lose her balance, had
hurried toward her. He grabbed and steadied her. She
made a half turn and shrugged off his support.

Frank backed off. "Sorry, Dear, I meant to give you
some reassurance."

"Reassurance? Reassurance from what?" She became
snappish, then turned to face him. "Sorry, all this has made
me a little crazy. Give us a few more minutes of privacy,
would you?"

Frank retreated. "Certainly."

Mary, still peevish, said, "As soon as my guests finish
eating, I'll have them convene at my chalet, and you can ask
your questions there. Then I'll expect you to take your killer
and get the hell out." Her eyes bore into Mannheim's. "I
hope you know what you're doing...with everyone carrying
a firearm...."

"Don't worry ma'am, the local police will help us collect
all the guns."

"If you make a false arrest, there'll be hell to pay." she said.

Mannheim nodded. "I'm well aware of that. Our jobs
are on the line if we screw up."

61

Mannheim and Oliver stood on either side of the entrance to the Bruxton chalet as the guests arrived from the clubhouse. Standing with them were Officers McGowan and Smith, who conducted a pat-down search on the men. Officer Liz Weiel had been called in to do the same on the women: Deena, Lucy, Susan Bird Song, Maggie and Mary.

As Oscar Brazilowicz entered, Officer McGowen stopped him at the door, took his rifle, and then removed it from its sheath. He inspected the chamber, sniffed it, and then looked at Brazilowicz. "This gun has been fired recently."

Brazilowicz gave the officer a deprecating glance. "That's right. That's what guns are for."

"But not for attempted murder." The officer took the rifle, replaced it in its sheath and propped it against the wall.

Brazilowicz snorted but said nothing until he was well beyond the officer, then he mumbled, "Fuck you, copper."

Mannheim, still standing at the front door of the chalet, addressed the group,

"Do we have the firearms belonging to Kurtz, Parma and Ms. Bird Song?'

"My .357 magnum is in my vehicle," Parma said.

Kurtz raised his hand. "My rifle is in our chalet."

"Mine is in my hall closet," Susan Bird Song said.

Mannheim put up his right hand. "All right folks, you'll

need to get your firearms and bring them here. One of our local officers will accompany each of you, and take possession of the firearm. I'd like you all back in ten minutes so we can get on with the meeting."

Within minutes, the guests returned, accompanied by the local police officers. Their firearms were checked, then placed in the entryway closet.

Mannheim shook his head, and in an aside to Oliver said, "Well I see that this little exercise didn't help one goddamned bit. All these firearms show signs of recent use. Okay, the hell with it, let's get on with the show."

The chairs had been arranged in a semi-circular pattern around the 52" TV set in the den. Mannheim and Oliver stood with their backs in front of the TV and faced the seated guests. Only Mary had any knowledge of the detectives' true mission, but she attempted to appear nonchalant; only her fidgeting with the tassels on her woolen shawl suggested nervousness.

Mannheim remained impassive. He stood behind his chair, his hands buried in the pockets of his rumpled trousers. His deep-set eyes perused every guest, who in turn, followed his eyes. With deliberation, he took a spiral notebook from his back pocket and flipped pages. The group grew quiet when he cleared his throat and began,

"Folks, thanks for assembling here. We bring apologies from the Riverside County Sheriff's office for disrupting your visit. Some new orders issued from Sacramento had placed an urgent need to pick up the murder suspect of Mr. Peter Bruxton." He paused. "We have reason to believe the killer is here among you." A collective gasp arose from the women, and the men squirmed, and cast suspicious glances.

Larry Kurtz, sweating profusely, removed his snowflake-patterned knit sweater. He wiped his brow with a handkerchief and sat on the edge of his chair. His temporal arteries pulsated, and his eyes darted around the room. Lucy, beside him, attempted to pull him back.

"For God's sake, relax. You're nervous as a cat. None of this concerns you." She looked at him sideways. "Does it?"

Larry leaned toward her without taking his eyes off Mannheim and whispered, "You don't know these guys. They can find you guilty of almost anything."

"I doubt that." Lucy crossed her arms over her chest and sat back, secure in the knowledge that her husband couldn't be found guilty of anything exciting—and certainly not murder.

The group, intent, sat quietly except for a nervous cough or two. Larry's anxiety mounted until he could no longer sit. He jumped up and blurted, "I don't know what kind of game you guys are playing, but I, for one, don't like it. Seems to me you're into some kind of stupid guessing game, hoping someone will make a confession. If you knew who Pete Bruxton's killer was, you wouldn't be here conducting this damned charade—you'd grab him and get the hell out of here!" His eyes darted at both detectives. "Well? Wouldn't you?"

Lucy tugged at his shirtsleeve, and, in a whisper loud enough for most to hear, said, "Sit down for pity's sake, you fool."

Larry sat back down rigidly and found an ally in the senior Brazilowicz, who called out, "Atta boy, you tell 'em!"

While Kurtz spoke, Mannheim pushed his hands deeper into his pockets, closed his eyes, then croaked, "There's some merit in what you say Kurtz. Unfortunately, several of you are prime suspects, as you'll soon see. We have our suspicions, based on solid findings, as to who the murderer is. What we plan to engage in here is an exclusionary process."

Mary sat up and cast a suspicious eye. "What the hell does that mean?"

"By that I mean, we want to be sure we eliminate the innocent."

Kurtz, finding nothing reassuring in Mannheim's

words, called out, "I'm certainly not a suspect, and if you don't mind, I'd like to return to my chalet. All this crap is giving me palpitations." He stood, prepared to leave.

Mannheim, with pen in hand, pointed at him. "If you can, I'd like for you to bear with us for just a few more minutes. In fact, I'd like to discuss *your* role in this matter."

Kurtz stopped as though his shoes were bolted in place. "What the hell do you mean, *my* role in this matter?"

Mannheim read from his notes. "Springs Hotel, 8:15 p.m., January 18th."

His deep-set eyes, shielded by bushy brows, stared at Kurtz.

Sinking slowly into his chair, Kurtz stared dumbly at Mannheim. Tension in the room became palpable. Lucy's expression grew dark; she glowered at her husband, then at Mannheim and Oliver.

"A man fitting the description of Mr. Larry Kurtz was seen at the registration desk of the Springs Hotel in Palm Desert by Detective Oliver and me."

Kurtz bolted. "That's a lie! You have no proof of that."

Mannheim remained stolid. "Actually, we do. You occupied a luxury suite, number 1230, next to the one occupied by the late Peter Bruxton."

"That's absurd! I never...."

Mannheim interrupted.

"That suite and an adjacent one were rented on a yearly basis by Bruxton Enterprises. According to hotel records, the name of the person occupying the suite was a Mr. Lawrence Short. We learned from hotel housekeeping that two people occupied the suite that night as well as on a number of other nights." He looked at Mary Bruxton. "As a matter of fact, Mrs. Bruxton verified that her personal secretary, Mrs. Melinda Ortiz, had confessed to an intimate relationship with you, and also confessed to being in that suite with you on the night Peter Bruxton was murdered."

Lucy Kurtz glared at her husband, her eyes flashing her nostrils flaring, and with her lips drawn in ugly grimace, murmured, "You rotten sonofabitch." Larry reddened; he looked at the floor and said nothing.

"The point of interest to the police, in this matter, was the connecting door between your suite and the one Peter Bruxton occupied. A slip through that door by the killer.... well, you can see why you're a person of interest."

Kurtz mumbled, "Go to hell, I had nothing to do...."

Mannheim continued, "This may not be important, and I'm not much on the origin or meaning of names, but a book lent to us by Mrs. Harrington states the origin of the name Kurtz comes from the German, meaning *short*. The name Larry is often the abbreviated form of Lawrence. In a court room your position of complete innocence could easily be challenged." His eyebrows arched when he looked at Kurtz. "A motive for murder was made by your own admission. You recall telling us you owed a ton of money to Peter Bruxton, but more importantly, you told us that you harbored a festering resentment about his affair with your wife."

"I don't remember ever saying that."

"We have that on a recording, Sir. I think you can see that your position of complete innocence becomes quite shaky. Before you leave, I'd like to ask you a few more questions after we talk with some of the other guests."

Lucy turned her back to her husband.

Mannheim next turned his attention to the senior Brazilowicz, who was leaning back in the club chair, which he filled completely. The position of his head against the back of the chair accentuated the multiple fat folds on his chin and neck. His open collar allowed a display of several gold chain necklaces. Gripping the side arms like royalty; he regarded the detectives as mere jesters and rewarded them with a smug grin. His air of complacency irked Mannheim further.

"Suspicion against you, Brazilowicz, is hardly subtle. You knew Peter Bruxton objected to his daughter, Deena, marrying your son. Mrs. Bruxton made that clear to us.

You wanted your son to marry into the Bruxton family for the obvious reason of controlling Deena's inheritance. You could have removed a serious obstacle to your son's marriage by getting rid of Peter Bruxton."

Brazilowicz, no longer amused by the scarecrow Mannheim, grabbed the arms of his chair and hefted his massive bulk upward with a groan. Jabbing his unlit Havana Supremo at Mannheim, his contorted fleshy lips moved before his hubristic outcry.

"Let me warn you, copper: watch your mouth. I'll sue you for anti-defamation of character. You got no right to...."

Oliver held up his hand and interrupted. "Forgive us for impugning your sterling character. In spite of your protests, you're ranked high on our list of suspects."

Brazilowicz poked his cigar toward Oliver. "And don't *you* make any smart-ass cracks either." He pulled the sides of his jacket over his bulging abdomen, his jowls shook as he looked around the room for approval but got none. He fell into his chair with a grunt.

"Thank you for sharing your thoughts with us, Mr. Brazilowicz. Rest assured, if we think you're implicated in the murder, we'll haul you in—as a matter of fact, we can cite you for making threatening remarks to officers of the law."

Turning crimson, Brazilowicz started to stammer; spittle formed at the sides of his mouth. "You think I'd be so goddamned stupid as to kill someone in a hotel room? Huh? Answer me that!"

"No, Sir. I think you'd be inclined to have a hit-man do that."

Brazilowicz, almost apoplectic with rage, was rendered speechless.

Johnny pulled at his father's sleeve and whispered, "Don't say any more, Dad." Brazilowicz scowled and jerked his sleeve away. His chest heaved, and he chomped down on his unlit cigar.

Mannheim, surveying the room, locked onto Frank Parma. Parma swallowing hard, was drawn in by the cold, penetrating stare of the detective. He reached for Mary's hand that lay in her lap; she pulled it away.

Again referring to his spiral notebook, Mannheim said, "Parma, your innocence in this murder has not been firmly established either."

"What the hell does that mean?" Parma glared at Mannheim.

"There are lingering questions that need to be addressed."

"I don't know what you have in mind, Detective, but I can tell you, there is *no way* you can implicate *me* in that murder."

"We're not trying to implicate you, sir," Oliver said. "We just need more information to establish your innocence."

Parma crossed his arms over his chest, cocked his head. and challenged Oliver. "Go ahead, ask me—ask me anything."

"Where were you on the evening Peter Bruxton was murdered?"

"Jeezus, how many times do you have to be told? I was with Mrs. Bruxton. You already know that. You saw us both that night at Mrs. Bruxton's estate."

Mannheim's eyes bore into Parma's. "As a matter of fact, when we questioned Mrs. Bruxton again two days later, she remembered being at a council meeting of the Desert Angels. She didn't get home until 8:45."

Parma turned his head to look at Mary, who looked away.

"I can't remember where I was every damned hour and every damned minute. Hell, I had nothing to do with Bruxton's murder. Why would I want to kill him? Mrs. Bruxton was planning to divorce him, anyway."

"That may be, Sir, but no divorce papers were drawn up. With Mr. Bruxton's death, Mrs. Bruxton inherits a large estate. Now, if you were to marry her, you'd come into a lot of...."

Parma, becoming abrasive and defensive, pointed a finger at Mannheim. "You're engaging in a lot of bullshit speculation, mister. You're fishing in the wrong pond. You can't prove a goddamned thing and you know it. By the way, have you figured out how I was supposed to get into Bruxton's locked suite?"

Mannheim turned slowly toward Oliver. "I don't remember saying the suite was locked, do you?"

Oliver shrugged and shook his head.

Parma, with a show of resignation, sighed, then dropped onto the sofa. Low-level chatter ensued as Mary inched forward, reached for her crutches, and stood. She looked about, then announced, "How about a break— maybe some coffee or tea?" She pointed to Jim Keyes, Matt and Deena. "Why don't the three of you prepare some refreshments? That all right with you Detectives?"

Mannheim nodded. "A short break'll be fine."

The guests stood, formed an irregular circle, and talked among themselves. Mary, on crutches, approached the detectives. "I didn't know you were going to engage in these melodramatics. How much longer are you going to play twenty questions? I thought you came here to pluck the rotten apple and take off with him."

"With *him* or with *her*," Oliver said.

Mary rolled her eyes. "All right then, with *him* or with *her*. You're acting like the prosecution. Aren't you exceeding your authority?"

"No, ma'am, I don't believe so. We have every right to ask our questions if it helps us make a positive ID," Mannheim said.

Annoyed, Mary said, "If you're attempting to embarrass my guests, you're succeeding—big time. How many more of them are you putting on the hot seat in your clever mock trial?"

"Maybe two or three," Mannheim said. "We know the killer is here, either as a lone operator or as a partner. We have only a few points to clarify, and someone is going to do that for us, willingly or otherwise."

"Do you suspect anyone you've already talked to?"

Mannheim swallowed, and his Adam's apple made its

long excursion. "Rather not say at this point, ma'am." His penetrating eyes bored into hers.

"For heaven's sake, don't look at *me* that way. You know damned well, I'm innocent."

He nodded, closed his eyes and pushed his tongue against his hollow cheeks, then answered absently, "Yes, ma'am."

Within fifteen minutes, everyone returned to the seat he or she had previously occupied. No one smiled; all communication ceased. Once again the air became strained. Side-glances darted about. Finally, all eyes focused on the dark inquisitor standing before them. Oliver stood three steps behind him.

Mannheim surveyed the guests, then shifted his gaze to Susan Bird Song. She was projecting an aura of almost angelic innocence, but Mannheim knew too much to dismiss the possibility that she could be the shooter. To begin, she detested Bruxton, and by her own admission had fantasized about killing him a number of times. As head of hotel housekeeping, she had access to Bruxton's suite, and as a trophy-winning shooter she had the expertise to have hit a head-sized target at twenty or more feet.

Mitigating circumstances of her involvement were Bruxton's regular and generous payments to her for procuring prostitutes. She used that money for her husband's medical care. It really didn't make sense that she would eliminate that source of revenue. Besides, ballistics failed to make a match with her ammunition and the bullets found in Bruxton's skull. Conversely, though, she may have had other guns that were not tested. She also couldn't be absolved as a suspect in the ski slope shooting incident. However, a motive was not at all clear. Mannheim decided to wait, and question her later.

Mary, growing more impatient with Mannheim, said, "So far, you fellas haven't spared anyone, and unless I failed to understand your little game, you're not coming up with any great revelations. Are you hoping for a last minute confession; maybe a thunder clap—a kind of epiphany?"

Before either detective could respond, Jim Keyes disrupted the intense mood with a paroxysm of prolonged coughing that produced phlegm. He collected it in a tissue, then stood and quietly excused himself as he headed toward the kitchen.

Mannheim's eyes followed him. "We'll need you to answer a few questions when you get back."

Keyes, without looking back held up his hand, and between coughs said, "Right. Wouldn't want to miss this for anything."

Mannheim directed his attention once again to Larry Kurtz who sat rigidly, totally immersed in the proceedings. Lucy, seated next to him, leaned away as though avoiding a leper.

"Kurtz, you told Detective Oliver and me that you were in the military service with Mr. Bruxton. Is that right?"

Kurtz nodded. "That's right."

"I'm going to read some notes taken from a conversation we had at the Rancho Mirage sheriff's office, on January 6th. You spoke of your wartime experiences in Viet Nam. You said you were on patrol in the Mekong Delta with three of your G.I. buddies when one of them got his head blown off by a Claymore mine. You recall saying that?"

Kurtz nodded.

Mannheim continued, "When Peter Bruxton saw his buddy's head blown off he went berserk. He picked up his rifle and gunned down a family of Vietnamese who witnessed the deadly explosion. Is that right?" Several of the women gasped. Mary sat up; her expression filled with revulsion as she lowered her head and buried it in her hands. Mannheim paused just long enough for the emotional impact to subside.

"You, Bruxton and your other buddy, someone you called Jake, or Pecker Head, made a pact never to discuss Bruxton's killing of the Vietnamese family, right?"

Kurtz nodded.

"To show his appreciation, Bruxton made an offer to you and Jake to join him after your military discharges. He promised each of you a partnership in lands that he intended to acquire. Bruxton told you he could purchase forested acreage in Washington and Oregon with his mustering out pay and a bank loan. You went along with the idea. Did this other person join you two?"

Larry looked around before answering. "After we were discharged, Jake was offered a one-third partnership but declined. He thought the deal was too risky. Besides, he wanted to settle down, get a salaried job, marry and have a family. That was okay with Bruxton as long as Jake kept his mouth shut about the killing."

Agitated and sweaty, Larry wiped his brow before continuing. "Jake, like the rest of us, had no special skills and took odd jobs for several years, but never made any real money. I guess, he finally became desperate enough to call on Bruxton, hoping to get steady employment. By that time Bruxton Industries had become really big."

"How do you know all this?"

"We kept in touch through the years."

Mannheim, his hands in his back pockets, and his head bent forward, paced slowly back and forth. "So Jake came to Peter Bruxton, hat in hand, so to speak, to ask for a job, right?" Mannheim stared at Kurtz, whose eyes began to shift from side to side. His fidgeting quickened and his breathing became more rapid.

The uniformed police standing against the back wall of the room listened intently as the interrogation became more heated. Mannheim gave Kurtz no respite. "Is this Jake person still in the Bruxton organization?"

Kurtz's expression begged relief from the probing. He said nothing.

Mary, eager to relieve the tension, stood and faced Mannheim. "Where are you going with these questions?

Isn't it time you stopped this stupid cat and mouse game? Why don't you just grab your damn killer and leave?"

"I second that motion!" Parma shouted.

Mannheim's eyes looked up from under his bushy brows. "Just a few more minutes folks, and I think we can conclude our meeting." His placid composure contrasted to the tautness of those seated before him.

At that moment, Jim Keyes returned to his seat with a glass of water. Mannheim looked at him and said, "Keyes, your name on your military discharge—that document on your office wall in the Bruxton garage...." He looked at his notes. "It read, *Jacobius James Keyes*, right? Now, Jacobius is one helluva moniker, difficult for most G.I.s, I'd think, so I'd guess they called you *Jake* for short." He paused long enough for the *ah-ha* recognition by the group. "You were one of the G.I.s in that forward patrol on the Mekong Delta when Peter Bruxton shot and killed that Vietnamese family—right?"

Keyes stiffened and glared at Mannheim.

Mannheim continued, "A review of your military records indicated that your army discharge was delayed several months because you suffered from post-traumatic stress disorder. You were released from the neuro-psychiatric ward at Walter Reed, then you returned to your parents' home in Los Angeles." Mannheim paused to look at Keyes, whose face was drained. "You were in and out of the V.A. hospital at Sawtelle for almost a year. While in L.A. you met a girl, married her, and fathered two children." Mannheim stopped again. "Is our research correct?"

Keyes did not respond, but looked at his interrogator, this time, with deep hostility. "Apparently you had difficulty making ends meet, and according to Mr. Kurtz's account, just a few minutes ago, you approached your old war time buddy, Peter Bruxton, and asked for a job. All that took place about fifteen years ago."

Keyes's stony demeanor collapsed like an unstrung

puppet; he folded and bent forward in his chair. This diabolical character was exposing secrets he and his former G.I. buddies had suppressed for years. Keyes took a deep breath, coughed, then took a sip of water.

"We think you had the means and the opportunity to kill Bruxton. We're not completely sure about the motive, but we've got a suspicion or two."

Mary Bruxton, sitting on the edge of the sofa, her heart pounding against her chest wall, listened as Mannheim chipped away at the armor that had concealed Keyes' past. She realized how little she actually knew of his background. He had tried to speak of his former life to her, but the few times he tried, she had shown no interest and brushed him off.

Keyes reached for his back pocket. The movement alerted Officer Smith, who moved toward him, then stopped when Keyes took a handkerchief out to wipe his brow. He sat more erect and summoned his courage to redress Mannheim's comments. "You have no right to accuse me of killing Peter Bruxton. We were like brothers, honor bound to protect each other...."

Mannheim's cell phone rang. He excused himself, and said he needed to take the call out of the room. Every eye followed him, and whispering among the guests began. When Mannheim returned, he leaned toward Oliver and whispered, "Jack Locke, our missing bellhop, the one who handled Bruxton's bags the night he was murdered, is in Vegas. The cops picked him up for questioning, but released him." The detectives whispering heightened the guests' curiosity.

Mary stood leaning forward on her crutches. "Look fellas, these theatrics are really getting to be too much for me. Either you take your killer and leave with him, or just admit you're only fishing here, and leave without him. Either way, I want you to stop harassing my guests. You've practically indicted everyone here, and now you're casting suspicion on Jim Keyes, who has been a faithful employee and friend for all these years." Mary, fearing that Jim, under duress, might reveal his intimacy with her, wanted to take some of the heat off him. God knows she didn't need that kind of exposure right now. It could ruin her, both financially *and* socially. She became edgy, looked at her watch, and shook her head.

Mannheim, acutely aware of her displeasure, nodded slowly. "We need just a little more time to button things up." He ignored her remonstrations and continued to interrogate Keyes. "You have children?"

"That's right, so what?"

"Their ages?"

"I resent these questions, and I don't know what they have to do with anything...." He stopped. "I want to talk to a lawyer. I'm not saying any more." Another coughing spasm gripped him; it took his breath away and turned his face crimson. He placed a handkerchief over his mouth.

Mannheim waited until he caught his breath. "You can talk with a lawyer, Mr. Keyes, but let me tell you what we know first."

Keyes frowned, and between gasps, stammered, "I don't need to hear what you know." He started to move out of his chair but was stopped by Officer Smith. Keyes looked askance at the policeman. "What the hell is this? Do you mind if I use the washroom?"

Mannheim motioned for Officer Smith to accompany him as they left the room. Sergeant McGowan went out the front door.

Mary Bruxton, standing, leaned on her crutches and faced Mannheim. "I think you owe us an explanation, and when Jim returns you can apologize to him. Why was it necessary to badger and humiliate this poor man in front of everyone?"

"That wasn't my intention. We're looking to get our dominoes lined up before the push. This visit to your exclusive winter playground is our last excursion, and our reasoning leads us to believe...."

She cut him off. "You're reasoning doesn't concern me one damned iota. You've done nothing but tell us how clever you are. Well, if you ask me, I don't think you know your ankle from your elbow—and that's putting it politely."

Mannheim cupped his chin in his hand and laced his comments with more than a shading of sarcasm. "Thank you, Mrs. Bruxton, for your valued and considered opinion. However, we haven't even had the chance to discuss another very likely candidate who might have murdered your husband."

The statement caused an immediate cessation of sound and movement, like a stop-action freeze in a motion picture.

62

Bonnie arched her back to allow the fine, warm spray of the shower to splash off her shoulders and her firm round breasts. She took a step back, and the water played on her pubic escutcheon, then she turned around and raised her buttocks to rinse her backside. She turned again, and held her breasts to the water and gently stroked her nipples to indulge in sensuous imaginings like the ecstatic thrills she'd felt when Mannheim suckled them.

But all those vicarious, little sensitive and erotic pleasures hardly satisfied her essential sexual desires; they only stimulated her passion for male companionship, and that meant being with Mannheim. His maturity and experience made her love and appreciate him even more. He was so unlike some of the impatient and insensitive young fools she had dated. With Mannheim, lovemaking had been kind of poetic and unhurried. What's more, she took pride in knowing how to please him.

She turned her face up toward the shower, closed her eyes and enjoyed the soaking of the final rinse. Becoming pensive, she wondered if her love for Mannheim reminded her of her love for her daddy. Unconsciously, she shook her head. She could never love her daddy in a sexual way. Incest was a sin of such unspeakable depravity, and yet, in her confused thoughts as a child....

The phone rang. She turned off the shower, grabbed a towel, wrapped it around her and hurried to the phone. A broad smile transformed her face as soon as she heard the voice. "Hello, how are you, Darling? I haven't seen you or talked with you in the longest time—of course I think about you—I miss you terribly—what's that? Am I still seeing that old dick?" She laughed. "I hope to tell you I am—what kind of naughty question is that? What does he have that I find so attractive? For one thing, I think he's crazy about me, and with a little persuasion, I think I can get him to propose and even think about raising a family—something you never seemed to care much about. I know you love me, and I'll always love you—take care and call me again soon."

She placed the phone back on the cradle and walked back into the bathroom, with its large wall mirror. She removed the towel from around her and used it to dry her hair, then ran her hand through it. She studied her nude image and was pleased. When she raised her arms, her breasts appeared even lovelier, more provocative and saucier. She studied her frontal view, then turned to look at her profile. She knew that men found her attractive, and that too pleased her.

But her moments of pleasure were frequently spoiled by thoughts of that bastard, Bruxton, whom she could never forget; his image haunted her. Every time she thought she was done with it, it would reappear to spoil her serenity. That awful pig, and that horrible evening, would be an ever-lasting and recurring nightmare. She relived the horror in detail. He had attacked her, drunk and slobbering, throwing her on the bed, tearing her clothes, then straddling her, before forcing his thing into her mouth. When she fought, he put his hands around her throat, choking her until she lost consciousness. Before that moment, she wished him dead. Perhaps she shouldn't have. Her Maker might judge her, but she would defend herself, arguing that Bruxton intended to kill her when she refused to suck his penis. She would be forever grateful to whomever....

Looking in the mirror, she saw her eyes well with tears as she ran a brush through her long, lustrous tresses. She brushed the back of her hair, and a little smile changed her expression as she remembered how Mannheim ran his hand through her hair and kissed the top of her head. Loving a man completely and knowing that he loved you, allowed acts of consensual sexual freedom without inhibition or guilt.

When frightful moments of insecurity and dread returned, she thought of Mannheim. He represented strength, kindness and protection. She felt completely safe in his presence and reassured in his arms. How happy she would be to hear his voice now. Instead she worried about him being away in a hostile environment. Then she remembered the unkind things she said to him before he left. Why had she been so stupidly insistent on learning the identification of the killer when he could not reveal his name to her?

Bonnie wiggled into her panty hose and hiked them up. At the edge of her bed, she sat and raised her legs, smoothed wrinkles in the hose, then lingered just long enough to admire the curves in her calves and thighs. Mannheim had complimented her on the lovely shape of her legs, and she enjoyed having him explore their contours.

Looking at an arrangement of pictures on her dresser, she focused on one: a photo of a young police officer in dress uniform, complete with visored hat, white shirt and black tie. To others this might have been a photo of a handsome, youthful graduate of the police academy, but to Bonnie, this was the image of her love as she saw him even now. The inexorable changes associated with aging did not exist to her. She did not see the gaunt, hollow cheeks, the deep lines extending from the outer edges of the nose to pull the sides of his mouth downward causing a cynical expression, nor did she see eyes that were deeply recessed and overshadowed by bushy brows. To her, his expression, and his bearing, inspired only gentleness, understanding and a loving nature.

In her fantasy, he was her knight, her very own protector; the one who would slay a dragon seeking to harm or molest his fair maiden. She would cling to her hero's side while he fought valiantly to protect her. In a less fanciful moment, she compared him to her daddy, who she also loved dearly, and yet deep down, she saw Mannheim as more independent, more forceful, and less beholden to others.

Bonnie slipped into a skirt and studied her image once again in the mirror. She brought her hands down along her sides as though to compress a slight bulge around her hips. An adjustment to her bra made her think of Mannheim's hairy chest and its possible exposure to gunfire. She hoped he was wearing his Kevlar vest. She gave a silent prayer for his safe return.

63

Mary glared at Mannheim's cynical expression. "All right, Mr. Detective, who is this prime suspect who murdered my husband?" When Mannheim hesitated, she persisted. "Or is that question too direct for your stalling tactics?"

Mannheim dug his hands into his pockets, looked at the floor, then brought his head up slowly, and in measured cadence, said, "That person—ma'am—would be you."

Mary's eyes flashed, she paled, drew in her breath, then shouted, "Me?" She laughed nervously. "Why you—you are the most stupid, the most incompetent, half-witted ..."

Before she could hurl another insult, Mannheim nodded, and put up his hands. "You may be right on all accounts, dear lady, but tell me, who would stand to gain the most from Peter Bruxton's death?" His brow creased. "You don't have to be a Rhodes scholar to figure that out." His deep-set eyes stared at Mary, who glowered back at him. "You, Mrs. Bruxton—you had the motive and the opportunity. Getting access to the suite was easy, and firing two rounds into the back of your husband's head at about twenty feet was a cinch, given your shooting expertise. What's more, you were able to get home long before the police got to the crime scene."

Mary tapped the crystal on her watch. "I'm giving you five minutes to bring this farce to an end." She leaned on the armpit supports of her crutches, then brought her wrists forward. "Here. Go ahead. Put your handcuffs on me and arrest me. But I warn you, if you do, I'll sue you and that cockamamie Riverside County Sheriff's Department for every last penny in their treasury. Now, for the last time, either you make an arrest and take your prisoner, or I'm breaking up this party, and you can go straight to hell."

Mannheim remained unresponsive to the ultimatum, and spoke with a casualness that further annoyed Mary. With a penetrating stare into Mary's eyes, he said, "You had strong reasons for murdering your husband." Infuriated, Mary was rendered speechless and turned her head forcefully to the side to ignore him. Mannheim continued as he scanned the room . "Others on the outside may have had their reasons for wanting him dead, but we still believe the killer is in this room." The mood remained tense. Furtive glances darted as Mannheim put his foot on the seat of his chair and leaned forward on his bent knee. "Firstly, we figure the killer had to know the victim and his movements pretty well. *He* or *she* had to have first-hand information to anticipate his activities. Secondly...."

BAM! A gunshot jarred the chalet. The already edgy guests jumped in their seats, then froze; all turned in the direction of the sound that came from the bedroom. Mannheim shouted, "Get down! Everyone—flat on the floor!" Both detectives reached for their guns then moved hurriedly but cautiously toward the bedroom. Muffled shouting and cursing from the outside were coming through the walls of the chalet. The front door burst open, and a wild-eyed Keyes ran in holding his right arm. In close pursuit, Sergeant McGowan ran in with his pistol held in his extended arms.

Keyes ran toward Mary Bruxton, looked back over his left shoulder, then tripped over her crutches, and lay sprawled on the floor in front of her.

"Hold it right there!" McGowan, breathing heavily,

stood over Keyes.

"What the hell's going on?" Mannheim demanded as he and Oliver ran in from the bedroom area.

McGowan said, "Our friend here, cold-cocked Officer Smith and was making his way out of the washroom window with Smith's weapon. When he aimed at me, I shot him. He dropped the gun. I told him I'd kill him if he picked it up or if he started to run. The crazy sonofabitch ran anyway, like he was challenging me to kill him." McGowan tilted his head toward the bedroom. "One of you guys better check on Smith in the john."

Blood seeped down Keyes's torn jacket sleeve onto his right hand.

He was helped to his feet by Mannheim and was ordered to sit. While the other guests were still lying face down on the floor, frightened into a state of near paralysis, Josh Harrington rose and walked toward Keyes. He removed Keyes' jacket and shirt, and examined the smaller point of the bullet entry and the larger exit wound near the insertion of the right deltoid muscle near the middle of the arm.

Keyes complained of pain and gave Josh an anxious look as the arm was rotated and assessed for neurological damage.

Mary, limping without her crutches, hurried to the linen closet and returned with a stack of towels that she handed Josh. He applied a firm pressure dressing over the arm to stanch the bleeding. Mary bent over the pale and frightened Keyes and ran her hand through his tousled hair. "Don't worry, Jim, we'll get this straightened out, and you'll be fine."

With a deprecating look she said to Mannheim, "I want you and your Keystone Kops to get the hell out of here. You can play your cop and killer game elsewhere"

"We'll leave soon, Mrs. Bruxton." Mannheim replied, "But Keyes will be leaving with us." He looked at the guests still lying on the floor, then turned back to Mary. "Why don't you take your guests to another room while we talk to

Keyes and wait for the ambulance." Mary, although reluctant, did as she was told. The guests also began to move out, giving wide clearance to Keyes and the police as they walked toward the kitchen.

At about the same time. Oliver came in with the dazed Officer Smith, who was holding a bloody handkerchief to his head.

"What happened to you?" Mannheim asked.

"While that sonofabitch was pissing, I was standing right behind him. Too close behind him, I guess. All of a sudden, he elbows me in the gut, knocks the damned wind out of me, and before I got my bearings, he snatches my gun, then whacks me on the head—jeez, my lights musta gone out. The next thing I know, Detective Oliver here is shaking me and helping me to my feet."

Mannheim looked at Keyes. "Well, Jake, or Jim, or whatever you call yourself, you're facing some serious charges: assaulting an officer, resisting arrest and stealing a firearm with attempt to commit murder." Mannheim stood with his legs apart, facing Keyes, while Oliver stood behind him and Sergeant McGowan stood off to one side. Mannheim told Oliver that he wanted a few minutes with Keyes alone, and asked him to take the two policemen with him.

Mary lingered at the door after her guests had all moved into the kitchen area. She clearly didn't want to leave Jim alone with Mannheim. Finally, though, she turned to leave.

Something bothered Mannheim about all this. He was having difficulty reconciling Keyes as the murder suspect since he seemed so fiercely loyal to Peter Bruxton all those years, not to mention the fact that he was also so clearly faithful to Mrs. Bruxton. Mannheim's tongue poked into his cheek as he studied Keyes, then happened to turn in the direction that Keyes was looking and saw Mary's backside, her hips shifting as she left the room.... *Wait a minute, he thought to himself, Wait one goddamned minute...back up...is it possible? Oh, man! Yeah, it's possible. How the hell could I have missed this one? And what about that tinhorn cowboy? Could she be taking on two? Some broads are like that...hell, they're no different from guys who need more than one. Could she have conspired with Keyes to whack Bruxton? Maybe...just maybe.*

Mannheim pulled up a chair, sat opposite Keyes, and leaned toward him in a non-threatening mano-mano attitude.

" Okay Jim, let's start from the beginning."

Keyes, holding his arm, turned his head and attempted to speak but started to cough. When he stopped, he said, "I'm not saying anything."

"Fine. Let me put it together, and you tell me if I'm wrong." Mannheim reversed his chair, then sat and leaned on the backside. "You and Kurtz, plus another buddy who got his face blown off in Viet Nam, were pals with Peter Bruxton. After Bruxton mowed down a family of Vietnamese, you, Kurtz and Bruxton entered into a conspiracy of silence." Mannheim waited for a response from Keyes. "Am I right, so far?"

Keyes maintained his silence; his poker face conceded nothing.

"Following your discharge from the army, you were approached by Bruxton and asked to join him and Kurtz as a partner in a logging company in the Northwest. You chose not to join them, but you came on as an employee several years after Bruxton's company was well-established." Mannheim brought his face closer to Jim's. "What I can't figure out is why you wanted to kill your old buddy? And why did you choose a time when he was getting laid or getting a blow job?" Mannheim paused. "That's some serious vindictiveness, Jim."

Keyes looked up slowly and sneered; his eyes narrowed, and the lines in his face deepened into an ugly scowl. "Listen to me, Copper. That sonofabitch was forcing himself on her. He was choking her to death! Can't you understand that?" He was murdering her while his dirty cock...." His spittle flew onto Mannheim's face.

Mannheim reared back. He was listening to what amounted to a confession to the murder of Peter Bruxton. He needed to learn more but didn't want to compromise his advantage by appearing too eager. "So you shot him to protect the girl from being choked to death?"

Again, Keyes turned away from Mannheim, his vitriol subsided. He spoke softly, "That's right, I had no choice."

"What do you mean, you had no choice? You knew Bruxton was a womanizer and had probably forced himself on lots of dames. Hell, he probably laid broads in the back seat of the limousine you chauffeured, and we know for a fact he had prostitutes in his hotel suite. Why was this occasion so different that you felt compelled to stalk him and then kill him?"

Keyes raised his head, glared at Mannheim, as though he were about to respond, then changed his mind.

Mannheim placed his hand on Keyes' shoulder. "Look, you've already told me you shot and killed Bruxton. Let's go on from there. Tell me how you did it." Mannheim wanted a full confession; he needed Keyes to believe he was understanding... impartial...maybe even forgiving...almost like a priest at confessional. He had used this method of coaxing many times before.

"If there were extenuating circumstances, a smart defense lawyer could soften the blow. I'll do my best to see that the prosecution gives you some consideration, but you've got to give us the complete story. Hell, everyone knows Bruxton was a sonofabitch. Not too many out there mourn his death. The defense might even make you out to be a sort of hero: you know, saving the young girl from rape and certain death." Keyes nodded slowly without emotion. Mannheim continued, "Did you have a key to his suite?"

Keyes gave no reply. His jaw muscles tightened and relaxed alternately.

Mannheim brought his head closer to Keyes, who stared at the floor. Slowly Keyes brought his head up and murmured, "You'll never know how rotten that sonofabitch was."

"Suppose you tell me."

Keyes attempted to clear his throat, but the effort initiated another coughing spell. Mannheim waited patiently.

"Years ago, my wife committed suicide." Keyes anguish resulted in his fractured speech and intermittent coughing. "The kids were young; her death was awfully painful to them. It was a terrible time. I did my best to raise them, but I was out of work, and we were on public assistance. I was still having emotional problems, and getting help from the VA." Tears welled, and his chin lay on his chest.

Mannheim reached over and patted Keyes' shoulder. "Take your time, Jim."

"My wife had a history of depression—severe depression. One day, she took an overdose of anti-depressant and pain pills and never regained consciousness. But it wasn't just the pills that killed her; she was emotionally dead for a long time." He looked around, fearful that he might be overheard.

"The day she took her life, I was out looking for a job; the kids were in school. When I returned, I found her crying, and I asked her what happened. She refused to tell me at first, and walked away. I followed her and insisted she tell me. I kept nagging until she confessed that Bruxton had been there, and then she clammed up. I didn't know what to think, but I didn't like it. I hadn't seen him in some years, although I knew about him through Larry Kurtz, his partner, who kept in touch with me. I tried coaxing her to tell me what happened, and all the while I'm fearful about what she might tell me."

"And what did she tell you?"

"She said that Bruxton had heard from Kurtz that I was desperate and needed a job. Then she clammed up again. I knew something happened between her and Bruxton; I pressed her for details. I had a terrible suspicion that Bruxton had raped her" Keyes remained quiet and squeezed his eyes tightly to avoid further tearing. "After her death, I found a stack of ten one hundred dollar bills in her dresser drawer under some clothing."

Mannheim slowed the pace of his interrogation. "So you don't know for sure that Bruxton...."

Keyes cut him off. "I knew all right. I knew for goddamned sure. There were signs: there was the smell of men's cologne—expensive stuff—not like mine. Before I left home that morning she had showered, and when I returned home, she had just come out of the shower again. She went into a deep funk, a really deep funk. It all added up. I knew she did it for the money to keep our family together. But she could never forgive herself."

"So you harbored a deep resentment towards Bruxton all those years?"

"Resentment? Hell, I wanted him dead!" He hesitated, then added, "I was going to make him pay and pay good. I vowed I'd make him lose it all—his fortune, his wife— everything he valued. I didn't know how I'd do it, but by God, I was going to do it, no matter how long it took. I thought about revenge every day of my life after that. Some things you can't ever forgive or forget."

Mannheim stood and took a step back. "How did you get into his hotel room that night?"

"I had a card key; I used it when he wanted me to bring things from the estate or office."

"Do you usually carry a gun?"

"Always. A Ruger .22 caliber pistol. I wasn't only his chauffeur. I was also his bodyguard."

"What made you go into the hotel suite that night?"

"After I left Bruxton and his secretary at the hotel, I went into the coffee shop for a sandwich. When I finished, I returned to the limo, looked in the passenger compartment and saw Bruxton's briefcase. I remembered he told me he was going to take care of some business in the room, and I figured he probably needed it. I grabbed the case and went to his room. When I got to the door, I heard screaming. I used the card key and opened the door. The screaming was coming from the bedroom. Christ, it sounded like someone was being murdered. I reached for my .22 and saw Bruxton sitting on top of her, choking her. I got a bead on the back of his head and fired two rounds."

Mannheim stopped writing and looked up. "You intended to kill him?"

"When I saw what he was doing, I went crazy. I wanted to kill that sonofabitch then and there. All those years of anger and frustration just sort of blew up, and I lost it."

Mannheim scratched his head. "Jim, why didn't you just tell him to stop? Why did you have to kill him?"

"Maybe if I had been able to think straight, I wouldn't have. Sure, like you say, I could have warned him, but.... I knew one day Mary was going to divorce that sonofabitch. She wasn't going to put up with his whoring around forever. Then, when she divorced him, I'd step in. I knew it was a long shot, me being her chauffeur and all, but believe it or not, I bedded her a number of times, and she liked it all right—even with my cigarette breath."

The confession was interrupted by another coughing spell. He pulled out the handkerchief Mannheim had given him and spat into it.

"Things were going good until that phony cowboy came along. I shoulda wasted him too." He shook his head, then asked for a cigarette. Mannheim said he had none, and besides, Mrs. Bruxton wouldn't have approved. Keyes shrugged. "What the hell does any of that matter now?"

"What's the rest of this magilla, Jim?"

Although reluctant to continue, he knew Mannheim expected more, and the confession was having a kind of cathartic effect, a release from those years of hate, frustration and the need for vengeance.

"It all seems so goddamned stupid now." Keyes shook his head. "I gotta wonder now how I ever concocted such a dumb plan. Talking about it now makes me feel ashamed."

"You're doing fine, Jim. Keep talking."

"Okay, but you probably won't like what I'm going to tell you."

"Try me."

"My plan was to have my daughter cozy up to Bruxton and get him to divorce Mary, with the intention of marrying my daughter. After being married to him for a while, she could divorce him for a settlement that would give her security for a lifetime." Keyes' shoulders sagged. "I know it wasn't the noblest thing in the world, but it seemed like a good plan at the time. I had trouble convincing my daughter. She never really accepted the idea, at least, not whole-heartedly. But she did finally consent to it. She knew I had sacrificed so much for her and her brother, and she trusted my judgment. Hell, nothing turned out the way I planned it. You can see, it all turned to shit."

Mannheim was seized by a kind of torpor. Startled into momentary silence, he grew cold, his skin prickled, and his tongue cleaved to his pallet. He leaned slowly forward and with a searing stare into Keyes's eyes, asked in a hoarse and condemning tone, "Your daughter is *Bonnie Ouvray?*"

Keyes smiled sardonically. "You couldn't figure that out? Hah! Mister. I guess you're not as bright as I thought you were."

Mannheim suffered momentary disorientation. Either he failed to fully comprehend what he was hearing, or he refused to believe it.

Keyes, sensing Mannheim's emotional upheaval, felt a surge of triumph in his desperate moment.

Mannheim backed away. Every fiber in his body seized up; the creature sitting before him repulsed him. His usually expressionless face began to twitch. The corners of his mouth drew downward, his nostrils flared. His eyes bore into Keyes' eyes. Then he spoke slowly and caustically, "What kind of animal throws his daughter to a fucking monster and allows her to be treated like a whore?" His voice became more menacing as he brought his face close to Keyes' face. He grabbed him by the lapels and jerked him forward. "And on top of everything else, you had the goddamned nerve, to fire a gun, knowing you were putting your daughter's life at risk?" He released Keyes' lapels and pushed him back into the chair. "You're disgusting! You're one sick, fucking miserable sonofabitch."

Keyes, looked down and nodded. "Maybe I am."

Mannheim turned his back, then whirled around and pointed his finger at Keyes. "Did you fire those shots through the window of Bonnie's home the night I called on her? Look at me! Don't even think about denying it. It was you, wasn't it? Were you trying to kill me too?"

Keyes' plaintive voice begged for understanding. "You read me wrong. I was only trying to protect my child from more abuse. I had no intention of shooting you."

"Why the hell should I believe you? You already killed one man...."

"If I wanted you dead, you'd be dead. From where I stood, you were an easy mark. I just didn't want Bonnie to get hurt any more. I sat in my car and waited outside her home every night until I thought she was safe in bed. When you called on her that night I worried."

"You worried? What kind of bullshit is that? Why would you worry about my being there?"

"When I saw you get near her, I didn't know what you intended to do. All I could see was your back as you went toward her. In my crazy head, I thought you were going to force her to take your.... Christ, I couldn't stand the thought of that happening again. I figured I'd save her, and fired over your head—way over it. You were never in danger of getting hit. I knew you'd be too damn busy wondering about the gunfire and cleaning up the mess afterward to do anything else."

The bright ceiling lights revealed beads of perspiration

that glistened on Keyes' brow and upper lip; he took a deep breath, mucous rattled in his chest, and he coughed with a shuddering fierceness. His face reddened and his breath was labored. He diverted his gaze from Mannheim's unrelenting stare. Then he paused to catch his breath before saying, "There's something else you should know."

"Go on. What other surprises have you got for me?"

"The bell hop, who brought Bruxton's bags to his room the day he was killed is my son."

"What? Your son? You've got to be kidding."

"No, I'm not. His name is Jack Locke. He changed his name from Keyes so as not to be linked to me. He's innocent of any wrong doing."

"That's not exactly true. He's facing charges of pandering—procuring prostitutes for Bruxton. We know where he is now, and we'll be picking him up soon." Mannheim scratched his head. "Keyes and Locke I understand, but what's their connection with the name Ouvray?"

"Bonnie chose that name herself; said it came out of her high school French class. Something about a verb meaning he or she opens, as in a door. The word was changed from Ouvrez to Ouvray 'cause that's the way it's pronounced in English. So, we had the lock, the key and the opening—maybe to a door of opportunity for all of us."

"How clever." Mannheim shook his head. "Whose creative mind conceived all that?"

"All three of us collaborated on family matters. We always have." He hastened to add, "But my children know nothing about my killing Bruxton." He sighed and turned away. "Now you know everything you need to know. I've got to hope some court-appointed attorney will plead my case, and claim that I went crazy, absolutely nuts when I saw my daughter being strangled during a vicious sex act. That should be the crux of my defense—that and something like justifiable homicide. Hell, no jury in the world is going to convict a father for that, are they?"

Mannheim shrugged. "I'm no lawyer, but I think your case is probably defensible. Not that it makes me feel like you're any less of a monster for what you did to your children. While you're coming clean, Jim, tell me, was it you who fired that shot at Mrs. Bruxton on the slopes this morning?"

He answered slowly, "Yes—and no."

"What the hell does that mean?"

"That means I fired my rifle all right, but I sure wasn't aiming to hit Mary or her nephew. I waited behind a large pine at about a hundred yards, and when they came down the slope I fired over their heads—way over their heads. I never intended to harm them."

"Really? How thoughtful." Mannheim fought to maintain his equanimity but found that difficult.

"Your role in all this becomes more difficult to justify."

Gripped by another coughing paroxysm, Keyes brought his head and shoulders forward and expectorated into a handkerchief; his eyes were bloodshot and his face reddened with the effort.

Mannheim walked into the kitchen and returned with a glass of water. Keyes looked at him with appreciation.

Mannheim came forward in his chair and leaned closer to Keyes. "Getting back to your shooting on the slope this morning.... Why?"

"I wanted Mary, that is, Mrs. Bruxton to become frightened. I wanted her to think someone out there wanted her dead. I wanted her to leave, so she wouldn't spend any more time with that slimy, fake cowboy. I didn't want her getting used to having him around again. Truth is, I might have been tempted to pick him off if he had been skiing with her."

Mannheim jotted notes, but made no further judgmental comments. He warned himself to refrain from criticism while Keyes was opening the floodgates of confession.

All of a sudden, a barely perceptible smile transformed Keyes' otherwise troubled expression. "Did Mary tell you about the night the electricity went off at the Rancho Mirage estate in that windstorm?"

"She did. Were you responsible for that, too?"

He nodded. "That was the damnedest thing. I knew she was alone that night and just plain scared of the dark, with all that wind howling and blowing things around. I figured I could come off like a hero and comfort her. I pulled the circuit breaker and disconnected the generator. Then I planned to come around with a candle and start a fire in the fireplace, kinda cozy and romantic. She'd be grateful and maybe...well, you get the picture. About the time I unlocked the front door, the damned wind whipped the door wide open, and it struck the wall with a bang. With the fireplace poker in her hand, she groped her way into the entryway to see what the hell was wrong. At one point, she got so close to me, she even touched me—frightened the hell out of her. She screamed and dropped the poker.

While she found her way back to the sofa, I went through the kitchen door, into the garage and turned the electricity on. Little did I know that while I was turning the lights back on, her fancy-pants cowboy had arrived and picked up the poker. I guess he was standing behind her looking for all the world like he was getting ready to do her in when the lights came back on. That's what she thought, anyway. I never told her otherwise. Hell, I didn't want to spoil my chances of staying in her good graces, and I was hoping it would cool things off with the cowboy actor."

When the distant sound of a siren grew louder, Keyes stopped talking. He lowered his head, then looked up. "Well, Copper, this is where I get off. It's been one hell of a ride—kinda bumpy at times, but all'n all, I suppose I can't complain. How many bozos get to kill the sonofabitch who raped his wife and tried to strangle his daughter, and in the process, get paid a pretty good salary, get to bed his wife, one of the richest and prettiest gals in high society, and drive a limo worth a damn fortune."

Mannheim said nothing.

Keyes shut his eyes, shook his head and spoke quietly, "Shit, if it weren't for you, everything might have turned out all right."

Just then, the door opened, and Oliver, accompanied by the officers with their guns drawn, and two paramedics came into the room. The paramedics approached Keyes, looked at the arm wound, and redressed it. When they finished, Oliver draped Jim Keyes' shirt and jacket over his shoulders.

Keyes walked out between the paramedics, then stopped at the door, turned and faced Mannheim. "Copper, I'm trusting you to take good care of my little girl."

Once the California State Attorney General's office was notified that the suspect was in custody, and had given a full confession, they told Mannheim that he and Oliver were to return with the prisoner ASAP. In the process, the detectives were to take every means of avoiding publicity. Nothing was to be said to the media about the confession until it was documented, and the pigeon was caged at the Indio lockup.

Three loud raps followed the melodic sound of door chimes. Inside, a distant female response called out, "Hold on, I'm coming." Mannheim, weary from the past thirty-six hours, waited impatiently as Bonnie opened the door as far as the chain restriction allowed.

She peered into Mannheim's unshaven, haggard face. "I thought I asked you to phone me as soon as you returned from Bozeman." With a trace of humor, she said, "I'm not quite sure I want to see you just yet."

"Open the damn door."

The chain was released, the door opened, and Bonnie, in her robe, stepped aside as Mannheim walked in, looked around, then glanced at the bewildered Bonnie. "We have a few matters to clear up before your place is swarmed over by newshounds."

"What are you talking about? What's this about news-hounds? And why aren't you kissing me and telling me how happy you are to see me?"

He gave her a perfunctory peck on the cheek and said, "Throw some clothes on. Let's get the hell outta here. I'll explain later. "

She hurried to her dressing room and shouted, "Should I take my make-up?"

He yelled, "Yeah, and a change of clothes and pajamas."

"Oh? Are you sure you don't have something sleazy in mind? A little adult-type entertainment—maybe?"

"C'mon, put some speed into it."

Mannheim tossed Bonnie's overnight bag into the rear of the car and held the passenger door open for her.

"Thank you, I see that you're still a gentleman even if you are grumpy. Are we going on a treasure hunt?" Her cheerful attitude was diametrically opposed to Mannheim's foul mood. After he climbed into the driver's seat, she reached over and hand-combed a few stray hairs on the back of his head. He said nothing, leaned forward to turn on the ignition, and dialed up the heater. In a flat tone, he asked, "Are you comfortable?"

"Uh, huh, but I'd be more comfortable if I knew what this was all about."

They drove on in silence for several minutes, Mannheim's jaw muscles tightened and relaxed alternately as he drove along the dark street intermittently lit by the occasional street lamp. Without turning his head, he said, "Aren't you curious to know what happened up in Bozeman? Who we picked up? Who the murderer is?" He turned to look at her for an instant.

"Yes, of course, but I was afraid to ask. You were so angry when I asked you about it before you left, and I was certain you'd chew my head off if I started asking about it again."

Mannheim delayed his response. He stared forward; his chin jutted upward. "I think you knew who the killer was all along."

Bonnie turned to face him. "What's that? What did you just say?" Her tone evinced more anxiety than curiosity. "Say that again, please."

With a note of condescension, he said, "Either you're the world's greatest actress, or you're naive beyond belief."

"What are you talking about?"

"Jim Keyes is your father."

Bonnie remained silent for a moment; she squared her

shoulders, pushed back into her seat, then in a defiant tone, said, "All right, so what?"

"So what? I'll tell you so what. He's also our murderer."

Only the soft blowing sound of the heater fan could be heard. Several seconds passed before Mannheim looked at Bonnie. He did a double take. Her head had fallen on her chest. Her mouth drooped and saliva was collecting at her lower lip, dripping onto her blouse. "Bonnie!" He shouted. There was no response. He pulled to the curbside, jumped out of the car and ran to the other side, yanked the door open, pulled her head back and patted her face, then released the shoulder restraint. "Come on Baby. Come on, wake up!" With his handkerchief he wiped her chin and reached for her wrist pulse.

Her eyelashes flickered, then her eyes opened slowly; she attempted to focus and peered at Mannheim's concerned expression. She shivered and wrapped her arms around her chest. Mannheim removed his jacket and placed it over her shoulders. "You okay?" She nodded. "You're sure? You had me worried, Baby." She nodded again, but said nothing.

Mannheim buckled her seatbelt, walked around the car and slipped back in behind the wheel to drive off, turning to look at Bonnie every few seconds. She remained quiet and stared through the windshield, then in a voice without emotion, asked, "Where are you taking me?"

"Some place where we won't be bothered by prying snoops."

"Where's that?"

"My place. We've got a lot to talk about."

She looked at him and shook her head. "Mannheim, I hardly know what to say. I can't possibly imagine that what you told me about my father is true. This is like a horrible nightmare."

"I'm sorry I hit you with that without preparing you. Maybe after a drink or two, some of this will be easier to take."

"You know I don't drink hard liquor, and nothing will make this easier to take."

Mannheim placed his arm around Bonnie's waist and helped her climb the stairs to his second floor apartment. He opened the door and flipped the light switch. Bonnie stopped in the doorway to look into the room; she shook her head slowly.

"This place looks awful." She picked up two discarded beer cans and placed them into a wastebasket, then started to collect newspapers and magazines strewn next to a recliner. She stacked them neatly on the floor.

Mannheim bent over and took her hand. "For chrissakes, stop cleaning my damn pig sty. Now sit down and let's talk."

Bonnie cleared space on the sofa, sat with folded hands and watched the agitated Mannheim.

He sat next to her and reached for her hands gently, trying to atone for his brusqueness. "Sorry, I don't mean to hurt you further, but there are some things I simply do not understand."

Bonnie looked at him with a sorrowful and questioning expression.

"I find it difficult to believe that you had no idea your father was Bruxton's murderer."

Her eyes beseeched his. "I swear to God, I never knew. You must believe me. I still can't believe it."

Her sincerity made Mannheim doubt any suspicions he might have had about her complicity.

"I gotta say I still don't get the whole damn picture. I listened to your father tell me how he hated Bruxton, and yet he wanted his daughter to have sexual relations with the sonofabitch; even convince him to marry her—more than that, he said it was all with her, err, I mean your consent."

"Hold it right there, Mannheim! That never happened."

"Really? It pains me to remind you that your teeth marks were found on Bruxton's penis at autopsy."

"That's not fair!" she shouted. "He forced himself on me, or have you forgotten? He strangled me...." She stopped, her shoulders heaved, and she wept openly; her hands covered her face.

Mannheim handed her a tissue, then knelt beside her and pulled her hands away from her face. He kissed her gently on the forehead and then on her lips. "Baby, forgive an old fool for shooting his mouth off."

Bonnie reached for his arm, then patted the sofa cushion next to her. Mannheim placed his arm around her shoulders and held her protectively. She snuggled into his arms; her eyes pleaded for understanding.

"I really need to tell you more about my family." She cleared her throat and swallowed. "My mother was a beautiful, loving woman.... large dark eyes, long black hair and a wonderful smile."

"That explains where you get your beauty."

She continued, "My father told you that Jack Locke is my older brother." Mannheim nodded. "Mother adored Jack and me when we were children." Bonnie became contemplative. "But as we grew older, we sensed a change in her. She had become distant; kind of detached. That change concerned us, and later her personality became so disturbing that it frightened us. Her behavior became erratic, and we, of course, knew nothing about clinical depression. She would lock herself in her room for hours, and we could hear her crying. We were too poor to get medical help, and Dad was frequently gone from the house, looking for work or working at some poor-paying temporary job. He had his own problems." Bonnie hesitated, as though reluctant to continue.

"Please go on."

"One incident was a painful turning point in Jack's life, I guess, in all of our lives, really. He came home from school one day and ran up to mother's room all excited to tell her how he scored the winning goal in a soccer match. He burst into her room, only to find mother on the bed, stark naked, with a strange man on top of her. When mother saw Jack in the doorway, she screamed and bolted upright. Jack ran down the stairs and out of the house. He ran as fast as he could down the street until he couldn't run anymore. When he finally stopped, he sat on the curb and cried. He told me he cried until he had no more tears.

"I believe that incident scarred Jack's psyche for the rest of his life. He said nothing to father about it, and he avoided mother almost completely. Mother committed suicide shortly after that by taking an overdose of her medicine. Jack blamed himself for her death, and confided in me that he believed that if he had never seen her doing that, she might not have...."

Mannheim shook his head. "The poor kid could hardly blame himself for that. Besides, your mother was unstable."

Bonnie nodded and sighed. "As Jack got older, he too suffered bouts of depression. When I look back, I'm convinced there must have been some sort of hereditary tendency for this. I think both Dad and Mother suffered from depression. Anyway, by the time Jack graduated high school, he was able to control his wide mood swings with medication. Dad found a way to use his VA benefits to get Jack in to see a psychiatrist who diagnosed him with clinical depression. They helped, but he still wasn't particularly stable. He went from one job to the next: pizza delivery, flipping burgers, bell hopping—that sort of thing. Still, through all of that, he remained close to me and Dad. He always regarded me as his kid sister who needed protection."

"That gives me at least a little insight into the family dynamics."

Bonnie turned to Mannheim and said, "Darling, I'm so tired, so weary, so terribly hurt. Do you mind if I turn in?" She reached for her overnight bag next to the sofa.

Mannheim started to unbutton his shirt. "Use my bed. I'll sleep here on the sofa."

"Oh, no you don't! If ever I needed your love and security, I need it now. And don't bother with pajamas. I want to hold and feel all of you."

65

Six weeks after Jim Keyes had been charged with the murder of Peter Bruxton, he remained imprisoned and awaiting trial. His respiratory symptoms worsened, making breathing difficult; his illness ravaged his body, creating a gaunt, sallow face. Medical reports from the prison hospital ward confirmed he was suffering from advanced metastatic lung cancer. His treatment was palliative.

Dark ringed, sunken eyes opened slightly as the nurse approached to adjust his IV fluids. He asked, "No letter today?"

"Sorry, nothing—not even junk mail."

"Shit."

Mannheim sat at his desk scanning the closed circuit reports for recent homicides, suicides and accidental deaths. To his surprise, the name of Jack Locke of Palm Desert appeared on the screen. He moved closer to the monitor and clicked in for further details. Locke had been killed in a highway collision near Las Vegas at 4:05 a.m. The report indicated that he had been traveling alone at excessive speed when his vehicle struck a roadside palm tree. Jaws of life had been used to extricate the body. Mannheim, seldom fazed by even the most gruesome accidents, was

shaken. He read further: Locke was born John Josiah
Keyes, twenty-seven years ago in Los Angeles, the son of
Josiah J. Keyes and Corinne Keyes of Los Angeles. He had
no criminal history and no DUIs, but was being sought
for questioning in connection with prostitution charges in
Rancho Mirage.

Mannheim grabbed his desk phone and punched in
Bonnie's number. Her phone rang six times, and he was
about to give up when her voice came on, softly punctuated with sobs. She had been informed earlier that morning
of her brother's death by the Nevada State Highway Patrol.

Mannheim's heart went out to her, and he expressed
his desire to be at her side. "Look, Baby, if there's anything
I can do...."

She thanked him and said she had planned to drive to
Vegas to make arrangements for her brother's burial and to
pick up his personal effects.

Covering the mouthpiece of the phone, Mannheim
walked over to Oliver's cubicle. "You'll have to cover me for
the next forty-eight hours. I'm driving up to Vegas. When
the chief returns, tell him I went to see a dying aunt. I've
got a ton of overtime I can cash in."

"Going alone?"

Mannheim ignored the question, looked at his watch and
spoke into the phone again. "I'll pick you up in one hour."

When he saw that Mannheim had hung up the phone,
Oliver smiled and said, "Don't forget your little blue pills."

"Listen, Buster, I'm going on an important mission—
besides, what the hell makes you think this experienced
cock needs pills?" Mannheim slipped into his jacket and
felt for a vial in his side pocket.

The straight, but undulating route, I-15N to Las
Vegas could have been tedious, but with Bonnie at his

side, Mannheim felt empowered. He put in a Sinatra CD. Somehow there was just nothing like listening to Sinatra singing nostalgic and schmaltzy love ballads. Bonnie, conversely, maintained a somber attitude and occasionally dabbed her teary eyes. Manheim brought his right arm over the back of her delicate neck and shoulders and patted her gently to let her know it was all right to cry. She reached for his hand and kissed it.

She murmured, "I'm all alone now...it's so frightfully lonesome."

"Not while I'm around, Baby." He turned down the volume on the music and glanced at her. "Tell me about Jack. What kind of kid was he? Was he ever in trouble?"

Bonnie smiled wistfully. "I've already told you, Jack was the apple of my mother's eye—that is, until that dreadful incident when he saw her in bed with that stranger. Of course, my father doted on him, too." She added, "Although I know Dad loved me more."

Mannheim nodded and smiled. "That's understandable."

"Jack was a wonderful brother; he always had a kind of special protective attitude toward me."

"Why was that?"

"When I was quite young, I was diagnosed with grand mal epilepsy. My parents told Jack he had to look after me. Fortunately, I've mostly outgrown the condition." She paused. "Actually, I've had very few episodes in the last few years." She was eager to change the subject. "But getting back to Jack: he was a hard working kid in high school who got by on Cs and Ds, but what he lacked scholastically, he made up in athletic ability. He ran track, lettered in baseball and basketball, and got to state finals in skeet and trap shooting."

"So, he was an athletic jock, and knew how to fire a cannon."

"Yes, but with his manic/depressive illness, he never succeeded in pursuing any one career."

Mannheim drove the Taurus slowly to check the addresses in a row of high-rise apartment buildings massed like giant toy blocks in colors of desert sand and desert flora. He pulled into the parking lot of one of the high-rises located several blocks off The Strip. He escorted Bonnie through a double doorway, and into a broad foyer with walls of stylized murals depicting desert scenes. They stepped into one of four elevators that moved noiselessly to the eighth floor. Mannheim stepping onto the cushy carpeting in the hallway asked, "This is kind of ritzy for a bell hop, wouldn't you say?"

Bonnie said nothing. She pulled out an envelope from her purse, removed a card key and pointed to the right. "Room eight thirty-six."

"How did you get the key?"

"Jack sent it to me some weeks ago. In his sweet, thoughtful way, he told me to use it and bring a friend. He said he'd find a room for himself elsewhere during my stay."

Mannheim knocked at the door and waited a few seconds before inserting the card key. Opening the door slowly, he stepped into a short foyer that led to a spacious living room.

He whistled. "Get a load of this, will ya?" He named objects as though he were a tour guide pointing out the obvious to a make-believe group of gawkers. "Here we have a Steinway grand, big enough for a concert hall, a giant TV that could play in a theatre," he said, sweeping his arm around the room, "and enough antiques to fill a museum." He turned to Bonnie and smirked. "Now, don't tell me he was a successful gambler who furnished this place with his winnings."

"I never questioned Jack about his income; he always seemed to manage, and to my knowledge, never asked Dad or anyone else for a handout. Of course I could never have imagined something like this...." She walked around the living room, admiring the furniture and decorative touches. "This is lovely; it had to be done by someone with excellent taste, maybe an interior decorator, wouldn't you say?"

Mannheim nodded absently. He picked up a framed 8x10 studio photo on top of the piano showing an attractive woman posed coquettishly, looking over her shoulder with one hand on her hip. Her evening gown and hairstyle were reminiscent of the sixties. He replaced the photo and studied the entire room: the Persian rugs, the gilt-framed art work, the eclectic assortment of French, Italian and Bavarian antiques, as well as paintings of the masters and modern art. Walking toward an alcove with a marble topped bar and shelves of fine crystal stemware, he said, "Not exactly your corner saloon." His nose wrinkled as he sniffed. "Fancy smells too, a lot of refined touches here." He looked at Bonnie. "Was Jack gay?"

"Oh no! I'd say quite the contrary."

"A gigolo?" Mannheim studied a signed Picasso lithograph and an original Tarkay.

"A gigolo? I—I don't know—maybe."

Mannheim followed Bonnie into the master bedroom. He stood in the doorway and looked around. "Pretty fancy bunk bed here." He rubbed his chin. "Why would a single guy need a four poster oversized bed?" Bonnie shrugged. Mannheim opened a louvered door to a walk-in closet.

One side held men's outerwear: sport jackets, slacks and suits arranged by color. There were also three tuxedos. The other side held compartments filled with folded shirts, sweaters and ties. Mannheim fingered the fabric of a cashmere jacket, then looked at the Italian label. "Expensive rags." He placed his hands behind and beneath the stacked sweaters and shirts.

"What are you looking for?"

"Guns... ammo... drugs...anything that might explain all this."

Mannheim opened an adjacent closet door to discover a double row of women's clothing with lingering scents of delicate fragrances. He walked back into the bedroom toward an ornate Italian bombé dresser. He opened the drawers and patted down the underwear, stockings and undergarments. "No guns, ammo or drugs here, either."

The framed photos atop the dresser drew his attention; he picked up one to study it. Bonnie looked over his shoulder and pointed to the young man in the company of an older woman seated at a nightclub table. "That's Jack. Wasn't he handsome?"

Mannheim nodded. "Who's the old broad next to him?"

Bonnie brought her face closer to the picture and shook her head. "I don't know. Do you think Jack might have been her boy-toy, and all this belongs to her—a wealthy widow—a dowager?"

Mannheim's lower lip protruded, and he nodded. "I think you've entered the realm of possibility." They walked into a den, dominated by a turn of the century seven foot mahogany secretary with a slanted cover/desk top. Mannheim attempted to open it but could not. An ornamental escutcheon surrounded a keyhole near the top of the slanted door. Using his multi-bladed Swiss knife, Mannheim selected a thin blade, then inserted it into the lock, jiggled it and pulled the top down, releasing a musty odor of wood polish and perfumed stationery. A number of slots and a locked central compartment required more of Mannheim's dexterity. The small central compartment revealed a packet of letters held together with a rubber band.

Bonnie reached forward, took the packet out of his hands, removed the rubber band and glanced at the return addresses. She had gone through six envelopes before looking up to tell Mannheim that all of them were recent, and had been sent to Jack by her father from the prison. Her brother and father had been communicating largely by mail rather than phone, since her father had limited phone use and no computer availability. Bonnie pulled up one letter with French postage and an address written in a distinctly female hand. She removed the letter and read aloud:

Mon Cher,

Having a simply marvelous time in gay Paree, revisiting all the museums...the new section of the Louvre, the D'Orsay and strolling along the Champs Elysée revives my youthful yearning for love and romance. I am constantly reminded of those nights in Vegas when you made love to me again and again. You were so naughty, and I loved every precious moment of it. Unfortunately, as that old Cole Porter song goes: 'It was too hot not to cool down.' When you had that bout of depression, I thought it was something I said or did. I felt terribly rejected and needed to get away. No matter, my dawrling, ours was a brief but exhilarating ride, and I loved you for it and always shall.

I do also have a confession. Dear Boy, don't think ill of me, but I've met another wonderful young man who opened up yet another world of excitement and thrills. He has taught me the meaning of true French love. Ooh-la-la. I've decided to spend at least six months with Marcel as my guide. As I recall, the lease on the Vegas apartment is paid for the next three months. Feel free to use it as you wish.

Toujours l'amour, toujours,

Belle

Bonnie folded the letter and replaced it in the envelope. She looked up at Mannheim, who was bent over her. "That letter must have been enough to push Jack's emotional equilibrium right off a cliff," she said. She picked up a stamped, but unsealed envelope addressed to her father, James Keyes. She opened that envelope, removed the hand-written letter and read aloud:

Dear Dad:

I know you are ill and probably suffering despite the fact that you wave off my concerns and refuse to complain. Your being in jail makes me feel terribly guilty—I think about it more and more every day, and keeps me awake at night. I don't know whether I'll be able to live with our shared secret or not, but in accordance with your wish, I will not confess to the murder of Peter Bruxton. While I understand your argument that you want to take the blame because you will die soon, it still does not relieve me of the guilt I feel. I have been having recurring nightmares. I see Bonnie lying in bed choking and gagging like she was having one of her old seizures and I see that monster on top of her, strangling the life out of her. I was grateful I had my .22 with me at the time. I got rid of it, though, and now no one will ever find it.

The guilt over you, and your need to take the blame for what I did, and the guilt over driving Belle away, have left me in a very sorry state. I simply cannot shake the depression. Maybe I inherited more of the family's tendency toward mental illness than I thought. Sometimes I think I'd be better off dead. My antidepressants don't seem to help. I don't think I've felt this way since mother committed suicide. May the good Lord forgive us all.

Your loving son,

Jack

Bonnie put the letter down, and cradled her head in her hands; her shoulders heaved, and she sobbed uncontrollably. Mannheim took her in his arms and held her tightly.

66

Mannheim accompanied Bonnie into the cold, stark whiteness of the county morgue where she identified the barely recognizable battered face of her brother. She removed a ring from his little finger, an onyx gem. She looked at Mannheim, and said tearfully, "I saved money from babysitting and waiting tables, then bought this ring on a payment plan. I gave it to him on his twentieth birthday." She kissed the ring and slipped it on her middle finger, then clasped her hands to her chest. "I'm ready to go."

On the road home, Bonnie remained somber, and introspective as she looked out over the desert landscape.

"What's on your mind, Baby?"

"I was thinking of Father. He'll die when I tell him Jack was killed."

Mannheim said nothing.

"We won't have to tell him, will we?"

Mannheim had a troubled expression. "Your brother's letter was essentially a confession."

Bonnie, agitated and frustrated, stared at Mannheim. "I'm so confused—so devastated—I just don't know what to think or do."

"Bonnie, we have two confessions to the same murder: your dad's oral confession and your brother's post mortem document. I don't have to make any legal decisions. My obligation is to inform my chief, then let him and the prosecuting attorney decide what to do."

In the prison hospital ward, Bonnie and Mannheim looked in on the emaciated Jim Keyes. He lay motionless, with IV fluids and a nasal oxygen tube. His eyes, retracted in dark sockets, moved slowly from Bonnie to Mannheim.

Bonnie placed the back of her hand gently on his sunken, bewhiskered cheek, patted it, then leaned forward to kiss his brow.

He looked at her and spoke in a raspy, barely audible voice. Bonnie put her ear to his mouth as he said, "I don't have much time, Darling. Tell your brother he can come home now." His eyes moved toward Mannheim. He labored to inhale slowly to gather enough breath to whisper, "Copper, I'm trusting you to take good care of my little girl."

About the Author

After serving in the Pacific Theatre as a field and hospital medic in the U.S. Army, Alvin J. Harris, M.D.F.A.C.S. graduated from the University of Illinois, College of Medicine. He completed an internship and residency in Orthopedic Surgery at the Cook County Hospital in Chicago, Illinois, where he instructed medical and nursing students as well as physicians in post-graduate courses.

In Los Angeles, California, he served on the staff of the Children's Hospital, guiding residents in clinical and surgical techniques. While tending to his private practice, he served as chief of the orthopedic section at the Presbyterian Hospital in Van Nuys and the Holy Cross Hospital.

He practiced for twenty years in Washington State and founded the Sequim Orthopedic Center. As an expert witness, he has testified in litigation resulting from vehicular and industrial accidents, as well as physical abuse, and trauma.

When he isn't writing, Al attends lectures at the university or researches information for his novels. He occasionally squeezes in a game of golf with his wife, Yetta.

Other Novels

Did you enjoy Death in the Saddle? Be sure to pick up more A. J. Harris, M.D. novels at amazon.com. Paperback and ebook formats are available.

A. J. is currently working on his fifth book, the story of a maverick in the day of McCarthyism, intrigue and government corruption. Available in the spring of 2013.

CPSIA information can be obtained at www.ICGtesting.com
Printed in the USA
LVOW111748180312

273619LV00001B/1/P

Preaching to Pluralists

How to Proclaim Christ in a Postmodern Age

CHRIS ALTROCK

CHALICE
P R E S S
ST. LOUIS, MISSOURI

Biblical quotations, unless otherwise noted, are from the *New Revised Standard Version Bible*, copyright 1989, Division of Christian Education of the National Council of the Churches of Christ in the United States of America. Used by permission. All rights reserved.

Quotations marked Message are from *The Message* by Eugene H. Peterson, copyright (c) 1993, 1994, 1995, 1996, 2000, 2001, 2002. Used by permission of NavPress Publishing Group. All rights reserved.

Cover art: Detail from stained-glass window, St. Norbert Abbey, De Pere, Wisconsin. Copyright The Crosiers.
Cover design: Elizabeth Wright
Interior design: Stet Graphics, Inc.

This book is printed on acid-free, recycled paper.

Visit Chalice Press on the World Wide Web at
www.chalicepress.com

10 9 8 7 6 5 4 3 2 1   04 05 06 07 08 09

Library of Congress Cataloging–in–Publication Data

Altrock, Chris
    Preaching to pluralists: how to proclaim Christ in a Postmodern Age / by Chris Altrock.
        p.   cm.
    ISBN 0-8272-3000-1
    1. Racism–Religious aspects–Christianity. 2. Race relations–Religious aspects–Christianity. 3. Race relations–United States. I. Title.
BT734.2.B73 1998
261.8'348 — dc21   98-37398
                                                                    CIP

Printed in the United States of America

Contents

Acknowledgments

Thank you Steve Williford for coaching me through the rewrite of a doctoral dissertation into something beneficial for people who don't sit on doctoral committees. Your thoughtful and encouraging advice was priceless. I would not have embarked on this writing journey without your prompting.

Thank you Harold Shank, Dave Bland, and John York for reading each chapter as it was written and providing enormously helpful suggestions. You made this a much better book.

Thank you members of the Highland Street Church of Christ who sharpened this material as it was taught and preached over the last three years.

Chris Altrock

CHAPTER ONE

Something's Missing

Bring Your Neighbor Day. Ten years ago. Las Cruces, New Mexico. Our college students brought ten of their unchurched friends from the university across the street. Kendra and I had our non-Christian neighbors, a young married couple, sitting beside us on the pew. A recent convert to a non-Christian religion smiled, shook hands, and sat down beside her coworker and friend, a core leader of our church who had invited her to attend our church on this special day.

After several songs, I stepped up on stage and stood at the pulpit. Quickly scanning the five hundred faces before me, my heart rate sped up. My eyes filled with dozens of faces I didn't recognize. Faces of people our church members had invited. I realized that several were present this morning who had never responded in faith to the message of Jesus.

Expecting God to do great things today, I launched into the message. I had wrestled with it and prayed over it for twenty hours during the last three weeks. The message was a simple yet potent presentation of the gospel. Just hours earlier in our study at home, I had prayed for God to lead our non-Christian guests to respond in faith at the end of my message, and for God to lead many others to respond in the days and weeks to come.

For twenty minutes I preached passionately. As I came to the conclusion, I felt that I had rarely preached so effectively. I explained to our guests how they could, this very minute, through faith and baptism, ask Jesus to be their leader and forgiver. I invited them to come to the front of the auditorium to indicate their desire to follow Jesus. I also told them that I'd be willing to meet with them after the service or during the week.

The church stood and sang. I walked off the stage to the front aisle, praying, hoping, for some non-Christians to respond.

Stanza one.

No responses.

Stanza two.

No responses.

Stanza three.

No responses.

Disappointed, I walked to the back of the auditorium. I consoled myself with the hope that many of those who didn't respond by coming forward would respond by talking privately to me after the service, or by calling me later that week.

After the closing prayer, I shook five hundred hands while people exited the service. None of them belonged to a seeker wanting to talk further about Jesus.

In the days and weeks after, I stared expectantly at my office phone, hoping with each ring that it was a non-Christian from Bring Your Neighbor Day wanting to talk about Jesus. The call never came.

In the "funk" that followed, a gnawing realization began to stir in the back of my mind: something's missing in my preaching. Don't misunderstand me. I knew that Paul said that wise and persuasive words were not what would win people. It was only the proclamation of Christ crucified that would win people (1 Cor. 2:4). It was the power of the divine gospel, not the power of my human words, which would draw people to faith. Still, I felt that I had just preached Christ crucified. Yet, I felt that I had preached it in a way that was ineffective. I had preached Christ, yet, for some reason, no one was won.

I had read the stories in seminary. Jonathan Edwards. Charles Finney. Billy Sunday. Thousands upon thousands of non-Christians responding to the gospel preaching of old. But few lost people were responding to my own preaching. Why? I was preaching the same gospel they had preached, I thought. Why wasn't I experiencing the same results?

That Bring Your Neighbor Day was my first suspicion that something was wrong with my preaching. Somehow, I was getting in the way of God. Somehow, I was inhibiting God's work of conversion and conviction. Somehow, Christ crucified wasn't what our guests were hearing.

And that suspicion wouldn't go away. It hung on like a bad flu. It clung so tenaciously that I was compelled to investigate it. For the next ten years, I threw myself into finding an answer to that question: why? Why wasn't my preaching as effective at reaching lost people as the preaching of the great revivalists and evangelists of years gone by? For the last ten years I've searched for the answer to that question.

Along the way, I discovered that I'm not alone. *With some exceptions, not only is there something missing in my preaching; something's missing in the preaching of the Western church. It's not as effective as it could be.*

The Harvest Is Plentiful

In Matthew 9:37, Jesus states that "the harvest is plentiful, but the laborers are few." Something's wrong, Jesus says. But the problem is not with the harvest. The problem is not with the lost. The problem is with the saved. The laborers, Jesus says. That's where the real crisis lies.

In the last ten years, I've reached the same conclusion. The problem is not with the harvest. The problem is not with the lost. The problem is not that I have fewer or more hostile non-Christians to preach to today than Jonathan Edwards or Charles Finney had in their day. The problem is not that the Western church can only find a handful of people in desperate need of Jesus to whom she can preach. If anything, the harvest facing the Western church is even more plentiful than the one facing those early preachers of the eighteenth century.

And we've known this for years. In his 1995 book, *Evangelism That Works*, George Barna presented the results of a study to determine the religious beliefs of Americans. While half a decade old, the findings are sobering. Consider this: approximately 1.1 million Americans die each year outside of Christ.[1] Barna determined this figure by asking American adults if they were "Christian." He defined *Christian* as "those who say they have made a personal commitment to Jesus Christ that is still important in their lives today and . . . those who believe that when they die they will go to heaven because they have confessed their sins and have accepted Jesus Christ as their Savior."[2]

Only 35% of American adults met these criteria. This suggests that nearly two-thirds of the American adult population in 1995 did not adhere to even these minimal Christian characteristics.[3]

When asked this question in 2001, only 41% of American adults met the criteria. When asked in 2003, only 38% met the criteria.

Thus today about 60% of American adults do not subscribe to even these minimal characteristics.[4]

The harvest is plentiful.

When the question is made more specific, the harvest becomes even larger. Barna searched for American adults who met the criteria above as well as who met the following criteria: their faith was very important in their life today; they believed they had a personal responsibility to share their religious beliefs about Christ with non-Christians; they believed that Satan exists; that eternal salvation is possible only through grace not works; that Jesus lived a sinless life on earth; and they described God as the all-knowing, all-powerful, perfect deity who created the universe and rules it today. Only 7% of American adults in 2001 met these criteria. Ninety-three percent of Americans did not.[5] *Ninety-three percent of Americans are not what we might describe as evangelical Christians.*

The harvest is plentiful.

Barna is not alone in painting such a picture of North America. Over ten years ago, George Hunter III offered this image:

Imagine a football team playing every game on its home field . . . During the 'Christendom' era (from Constantine's conversion to the Renaissance) the Western Church scored for a thousand years like a football team with perennial 'home field advantage.' The Church even defined the game, announced the rules, and briefed the referees, and the Church's team always had the crowd behind it, and the wind as well. All of that has changed. If the Church plays today, it plays on opposition turf . . . Once, the countries and peoples of Europe and North America were 'Christian' and the countries and peoples of the Third World were mission fields. The picture today is starkly different. Today a higher percentage of Angolans are active professing Christians than Americans, a higher percentage of Koreans than Canadians, a higher percentage in Fiji than in any country in Europe. *The USA has become the largest mission field in the Western hemisphere, and many countries of Europe are almost secular wastelands.*[6]

The harvest is plentiful.

Similar descriptions are given by missiologists who suggest that we are in the midst of a paradigm shift in missions. No longer is the dominant direction for missions from the first world (e.g., Europe) to the third world (e.g., Africa). It is now reversed. In 1900, 50% of the world's Christians lived in Europe and 2% lived in Africa. In 1980, 25% of the world's Christians lived in Europe and 15% lived in Africa. In 2000, approximately 20% of the world's

Christians lived in Europe and 20% lived in Africa. *In Europe and North America, an average of 53,000 people leave a Christian church from one Sunday to the next, while in Africa, an average of 115,000 join a Christian church from one Sunday to the next.*[7]

Darrell Guder calls attention to two "great new facts of our time": 1) Christianity has become worldwide with churches in every continent and in every major cultural group; and 2) Christianity in America has experienced a loss of numbers, power, and influence.[8]

David F. Wells argues that America is in a "unique cultural moment." He suggests that most otherworld cultures (and past American cultures) have religious assumptions behind them (Hindu, Muslim, Christian, etc.). There are no such assumptions behind the public culture of America today, however, and this is the first time any major civilization has attempted to build itself in this way. Our public life finds neither its justification nor its direction from a divine or supernatural order.[9]

The harvest is plentiful.

Leonard Sweet states that there are 120 million "pre-Christian" people living in the United States who are fourteen years old and above. There are only two countries with more non-believers: India and China. *The United States is thus the third largest mission field in the world.*[10] Indeed, Craig Van Gelder states a "great new fact of our day" is this: America is a mission field.[11]

The harvest is plentiful.

The location of the Christian church with the largest attendance? Korea, with the second largest in Nigeria. The location of the world's largest Buddhist temple? The United States. The location of the world's largest Muslim training center? The United States.[12]

These facts are difficult to believe. I recently presented the information above to a gathering of preachers and students. Afterwards, one of the preachers shook his head in disbelief, "America is a mission field?!" This was news to him.

Yet there is no denying it. The harvest is indeed plentiful.

The problem is not with the harvest.

The Problem with Preaching

The problem, it seems, is with us: the harvesters, the preachers. We work hard. We preach hard. Our lessons aren't entirely ineffective. They bear some fruit. But not the kind of fruit they could. Something's missing.

The evidence?

In the year 2000, 3,750 churches in America closed their doors. Half of the approximately 350,000 churches in America did not lead a single person to faith in Christ all year.

My own fellowship, Churches of Christ, lost forty-eight churches between 1997 and 2000.

In my own state, it took ten Tennessee Churches of Christ to reach one new person a year between 1997 and 2000.[13]

The harvest is plentiful. But the workers are few—or at least ineffective. Much of our preaching is missing the mark. Ninety-three percent of Americans admit to being non-Christian, yet 175,000 churches in America did not reach a single one of those millions of Americans in 2000.

There are sufficient numbers of lost people. There is a lot of preaching. But the preaching doesn't seem to be making much difference.

The problem, however, is not with preaching in general. Some may take the information above and conclude that preaching itself is outdated and ineffective. You'll never reach lost people today through preaching, they might say. I disagree. The problem is not with preaching in general.

After all, it was preaching which God used in Acts 2 to lead three thousand people to confess Jesus as their Lord. And it is preaching that God is still using today. While most churches are not reaching lost people in significant numbers, a handful are. Thom Rainer analyzed part of that handful. In a survey of the most evangelistic churches of the Southern Baptist Association, he found that they shared three things in common. One of those things was this: effective evangelistic preaching.[14] Preaching can make a difference.

But why wasn't it in my church ten years ago on Bring Your Neighbor Day? And why isn't it in hundreds of thousands of churches today? *Why did it take the combined preaching of ten churches in Tennessee to win one lost person, when the preaching of just one man in Acts 2 won 3,000 lost people?*

The Challenge of Postmodernism

The answer to that question, I believe, lies in the analysis of those to whom we preach. *What's missing, I believe, is an adequate understanding of the non-Christians we long to reach through our preaching.* We do not know our audience. As a result, our approach to scripture and to preaching creates messages that miss their target.

The more I've prayerfully researched my own ineffectiveness with preaching, the more I've realized that the Western world around me has changed. Ten years ago, I thought I was preaching to non-Christians who shared the same values, held the same worldview, dreamed the same dreams as non-Christians have for decades. Today, however, I realize how wrong I was. Today, I feel like a preacher who fell asleep and woke up in a foreign country. And the preaching that connected in that old world of Jonathan Edwards won't connect in this one.

A few years ago I flew to Ukraine to preach in two of our church plants. I boarded the plane in Memphis, Tennessee. I sat down in my seat and closed my eyes in a world I knew, a world where I spoke the language. I ate the food. I knew some of the history.

But hours later, I opened my eyes and we had landed in Amsterdam. Suddenly I was in a world full of people who spoke a language I did not speak, held values I did not, ate food I could not pronounce, and shared a history foreign from mine. While I slept, my world changed completely.

That experience is a parable for preaching. While we preachers may have stayed the same, the non-Christian world around us has changed. It is as radically different from the non-Christian world of decades ago as the world of Memphis was from Amsterdam.

The problem is that we are still preaching as if we live in Memphis. Meanwhile, Amsterdam is showing up in our services. And our lessons, geared to reach Memphis, leave Amsterdam confused, unconvinced, and, in some cases, not even understanding the language in which we are preaching.

This book explains this radical change and the kind of preaching which best connects in this brand new world.

This world-change has happened because North America and Western culture is in the midst of a cultural shift from modernism to postmodernism.

Western culture can be divided into three epochs, each characterized by a different worldview. The first epoch, pre-modernism, was dominated by a pre-scientific worldview in which meaning was determined by tradition. The worldview was communicated through myths. The second epoch, modernism, commenced with the Enlightenment. It was dominated by respect for science. The empirical method was the primary arbiter of truth.

The third epoch, postmodernism, came into its own by the 1970s. It places limits on modernism's reliance upon science for truth. Its primary characteristic is that it denies the possibility of impartial objectivity in human knowledge. It affirms that all knowledge is subjective and the result of interpretation. As a result, pluralism and relativism are the hallmarks of postmodernism.[15] Postmoderns believe in a plural number of truths (Christianity may be right for some, but not for all) and that all truth is relative (you may not want to engage in homosexuality but that doesn't make it wrong for me to).

Another way of viewing postmodernism is suggested by Marva Dawn in her book *Is It a Lost Cause?*[16] The real difference between the three worlds of pre-modernism, modernism, and postmodernism comes in the beliefs held by its leadership. In the pre-modern world most people, especially the leadership of society, believed that God was truth. In the modern world most people, but especially the leadership of society, believed that science was truth. In the postmodern world most people, especially the leadership of society, believes in many truths. It's not simply that pluralism is found among people in the postmodern era; it's that pluralism is espoused by and validated by the political, media, literary, and other forms of leadership.

The postmodern era could also be called post-Christian or anti-Christian. The Boomers (ages thirty-six to fifty-four), Busters (ages twenty to thirty-five), and Net-Gens (ages twenty and younger) are the transitional generations within this cultural shift.[17] The highly publicized differences between these generations can thus be attributed to factors beyond simply generational differences. Their differences are largely the result of the varying degrees to which they have been raised in postmodernism.[18]

This cultural shift, which will be explored in detail in later chapters, has brought about significant changes in the worldviews of the non-Christians to whom we preach. *The non-Christians within homiletical earshot today are simply not the same as those within earshot fifty years ago. Few churches and preachers realize the radical degree to which our audience has changed. I didn't. For this reason, much preaching has ceased to be effective in reaching them.*

While our audience has changed, our preaching methods have not. Many of us rely on preaching methods and strategies that worked fifty years ago, but do not work in a postmodern setting. We've been trained in preaching styles that reached those from the modern epoch, but are impotent to reach those in the postmodern epoch.

From the day of Pentecost to the twenty-first century, preaching has played a pivotal role in the church's evangelistic growth.[19] While it is not the church's sole method, preaching has historically ranked among those methods that consistently reap a harvest.[20] Postmodernism, however, presents a unique challenge to preaching. Its greatest obstacle is found in how it questions the existence of absolute truth and authority and therefore weakens the potency of preaching, which makes radical claims about absolute truth and authority.[21]

The problem is not with the harvest. It is as plentiful in the Western world as it ever has been. The problem is with the workers, with our preaching. We put our preaching scythes to the stalks of the lost, and it's like trying to cut steel with a butter knife. The homiletical strategies which once cut cleanly and swiftly through the stalks do not do so any more. Postmodernism has created the need for a different scythe to reap the plentiful harvest.

The problem is that my preaching was geared towards winning barbeque-eating, blues-music-listening, English-speaking, lost people (to return to my earlier parable). But those who showed up were cheese eating, Dutch-speaking, lost people.

Seven Faces of Postmoderns

In the succeeding chapters we'll explore seven basic characteristics or faces of postmodernism. These seven characteristics are critical to understanding the new audience to whom we now preach and hope to reach. In the last ten years, I've found these seven qualities not only in literature, but also in the lives of those non-Christians closest to my preaching ministry. As we walk through the seven qualities, you'll recognize them in the lives of the non-Christians in your church and community. In summary, here they are:

Postmoderns are *uninformed* about the basics of Christianity. They are the first generation with little to no Christian memory. They do not know the stories, doctrines, and vocabulary of the gospel and the Bible.

Postmoderns are interested in *spiritual* matters. Unlike their Modern counterparts, who embraced science or reason over spiritual issues, postmoderns are highly interested in spirituality.

Postmoderns are *anti-institutional*. While they are attracted to spirituality, they are repelled by institutional religion. While community appeals to them, organized religion does not. They like Jesus, but not the institution of his church.

Postmoderns are *pluralistic*. This is the dominant characteristic of postmoderns. They do not believe in the existence of one absolute truth that applies to all people at all times. Thus they do not believe that one religion can claim to have a monopoly on religious truth.

Postmoderns are *pragmatic*. They are not interested in life after death as much as they are interested in life before death. They do not want to hear theology for theology's sake. They want to know "So what?" They want something that is going to work in the here and now to make life better.

Postmoderns are *relational*. Where Moderns could be characterized by the old television show *The Fugitive*—one man alone against the world, postmoderns can be characterized by the more recent show *Friends*—a community of people supporting and encouraging one another.[22]

Postmoderns are *experiential*. They trust what can be experienced over what is simply reasonable or logical. They are more persuaded by a personal encounter with something or the story of someone's personal encounter than by an analytical argument. They long for an encounter with God, not just for information about God.

Of course, individual non-Christians and even groups of non-Christians before the postmodern era have possessed some of these qualities. For instance, as a rule, non-Christians have almost always been uninformed about basic Christianity. And generally, they have always tended to shy away from the church, even when attracted to Jesus. *However, no generation of non-Christians, has, as a whole, been characterized as deeply by these qualities as the postmodern generation is.*

For instance, while other non-Christian generations in the Western world have been uninformed, none has been as broadly and as deeply uninformed as postmoderns are. In addition, since its founding, never have a greater percentage of Americans been as hostile to the institution of the church as the postmodern generation is.

For some of these seven characteristics, it is the depth in which they are held, and the vast number of people who hold them, which distinguish postmoderns from other generations who may have shared similar qualities in the past.

In addition, some of these qualities are particularly unique to postmoderns. Their reliance upon experience over reason, and their pluralistic bent cause them to stand out from other previous generations in the Western world.

We are missionaries who find ourselves preaching in the foreign country of Postmodernity. As we step on stage and stand at the pulpit, these are the qualities predominant in the lives of lost guests in our service: uninformed, spiritual, anti-institutional, pluralistic, pragmatic, relational, and experiential.

How do we preach to such people in a way that draws them to Christ? After reviewing these seven characteristics, we'll explore the answer to this question. We'll go back through each of the seven characteristics, noting specific strategies for preaching evangelistically to people characterized in each of these seven ways. In a nutshell, here are the strategies we'll explore:

Evangelistic preaching will address postmoderns' *uninformed* status in at least two ways: 1) in general, by using vocabulary, illustrations, and images which do not assume prior knowledge of the biblical story; and 2) specifically, by preaching messages designed to tutor them in the basics of the gospel and the biblical story.

Evangelistic preaching will address the postmodern interest in *spirituality* in at least two ways: 1) by preaching in ways designed to facilitate an encounter between the lost postmodern and the saving God; and 2) by preaching in ways designed to equip lost listeners to daily experience the presence of God.

Evangelistic preaching will overcome the *anti-institutional* bias of postmoderns in at least two ways: 1) by preaching messages designed to reveal the benefits of belonging to a faith community; and 2) by partnering with efforts which enable them to experience those benefits first hand.

Evangelistic preaching will address postmoderns' *pluralism* by preaching at least three kinds of messages: 1) those which reveal the inclusive and tolerant nature of the gospel; 2) those which explore the uniqueness of the gospel and Jesus (and thus the basis for their exclusivity); and 3) those which highlight the inaccuracies and inadequacies of pluralism.

Evangelistic preaching will address postmoderns' *pragmatism* by preaching at least two kinds of messages: 1) those which show how the gospel "works" in dealing with practical issues of daily life; and 2) those which reveal how the gospel brings a better life before death, not just after death.

Evangelistic preaching will address the *relational* nature of postmoderns in at least three ways: 1) by preaching messages which reveal the community which is available in church; 2) by preaching messages which reveal the help the gospel brings to practical matters in relationships; and 3) by partnering with efforts to help the listener connect in meaningful relationships with Christians.

Evangelistic preaching will address the *experiential* bias of postmoderns in at least four ways: 1) by leading the listener to experience the gospel through inductive and narrative preaching; 2) through testimonies; 3) through worship which engages multiple senses; and 4) by enabling them to observe the gospel lived in community outside the worship service.

It will be helpful for me to note at this point two important items. First, throughout this book I'll refer to non-Christian postmoderns. Clearly we all could identify Christians who have certain postmodern qualities. This book, however, is about non-Christian postmoderns. I am not identifying non-Christians by whether or not they attend a particular denomination or hold a specific theological view. For the sake of simplicity, I'll define non-Christians as those who identify with the characteristics of the postmodern worldview listed above and from the basis of this perspective do not accept the truth and validity of Christianity as a basis for their own beliefs, actions, and way of life.

Second, I've purposely chosen to use the word *non-Christian* rather than *unchurched* or *seeker*, or some other term in order to force us to remember the fate of those to whom we are preaching. The more we think of these individuals as non-Christian, the more deeply convicted we may be to consider how to preach evangelistically to them. This term, however, is meant to be "insider" language. It would not be effective in a sermon for a preacher to state, "Now, to all you non-Christians out there who are pluralistic, let me explain why pluralism is not a credible way of life. . . "

It's my prayer that these seven descriptions of postmoderns will drastically affect your understanding of the non-Christians to whom you are or could be preaching. It's my hope that the seven characteristics of preaching to postmoderns will deeply affect your preaching.

And ultimately, it's my prayer that this book will so sharpen your scythe, that Sunday mornings find you praising God for the harvest reaped rather than cursing yourself, as I did that one Sunday ten years ago, for the harvest which remains untouched.

CHAPTER TWO

Postmoderns Are Uninformed and Spiritual

Packing for Postmodernity

Monica, our missionary in Kiev, Ukraine, had invited me to preach and teach in Kiev for a week. Our missions committee made the arrangements and soon I was packing for Kiev. It was my first trip overseas since being in preschool. It was my first time to preach in a foreign country. Most importantly, it was my first time to preach in Kiev.

Knowing that the Ukrainian culture and people were different from my Memphis crowd each Sunday, I asked Monica to brief me on what to expect. Through e-mails and an Internet brochure she had prepared, I learned a great deal. I also met with two Highland staff members who had previously preached in Kiev. How should I prepare? What sticking points to faith will they have? What won't they understand? What's different about preaching in Kiev versus preaching in Memphis?

As I packed for Kiev, I realized that I was about to enter a new world. These men and women helped me prepare to preach in a way that would have the best potential for being used by God effectively.

Imagine that you are packing for a foreign country for an extended preaching campaign. Imagine that you know little about this country, except that the people and culture are radically different than the one you are used to.

That country is America. And that culture is postmodernity.

For a moment, put aside all you think you know about the lost in America. Picture yourself as I was, preparing to speak in a country I had never been in, to a people I knew nothing about. Imagine you are a green missionary about to come to America. What follows in the next three chapters is a briefing. Here's what you can expect. Here's what characterizes these people. Here's the culture into which you'll be going.

As we cover each of the seven characteristics of postmodernism, think as a missionary thinks. Ask the kinds of questions a missionary asks. If you were traveling to a foreign country whose people were characterized in this way, what impact would this have on your preaching?

By the way, the information in this briefing comes from two sources. One source was an analysis of evangelical literature on postmodernism. Simply put, I read as much evangelical literature on postmodernism as I could during the last ten years. I surveyed church growth and homiletical literature and tracked the frequency with which authors mentioned various characteristics of postmodernity. The seven characteristics discussed in this and the following two chapters were the ones most often mentioned by these authors. According to these veteran missionaries, the seven characteristics in this and the next two chapters are central to understanding postmoderns.

A second source for these characteristics is the non-Christians I interact with in my preaching ministry at Highland. Specifically, I worked in depth with a small group of non-Christians over a period of three months. I interviewed them at length on their beliefs and attitudes toward Christianity. They also provided responses to evangelistic sermons preached at Highland. During these detailed interviews, these seven characteristics rose to the top.

For the sake of brevity and conciseness, I'll describe more than one characteristic in this and the following two chapters.

Uninformed

David is a high school senior at Highland.[1] Last year, he and some friends started a teen Bible study in a home near their high school. Evangelistic by heart, they invited several friends each week to the study. More and more friends came to the study. Finally, David and the core group decided it was time to confront these lost teens directly with the gospel. One night, David's high school friend spoke at length to a packed living room of lost teens. He slowly walked through the events of the last twenty-four hours of Jesus' life. He kept it simple—telling the events as they unfolded in the four gospels. David was uneasy about the approach. After all, this is Memphis, Tennessee. These lost teens are growing up in the belt-buckle of the Bible Belt. Surely, they've heard this all before, David thought.

But when the teen stopped speaking, David was shocked. Guest after guest came up and told David that they had never heard anything like this before. They had never listened to the events of the last day of Jesus' life. They had no idea what Jesus went through. The old, old story was fresh and brand new in their ears.

The experience illustrates the first characteristic of postmoderns: *they are uninformed about basic Christianity.* George Hunter III has spent years studying postmoderns. At the top of his list of characteristics which make up postmoderns is this: they know little about basic Christianity.[2]

Recent studies of American adults support this observation. According to George Gallup:

Only 34% of adults know that it was Jesus who gave the Sermon on the Mount.

Fewer than 50% of adults can tell you that Genesis is the first book of the Bible.

Most adults struggle to name more than two of the Ten Commandments.[3]

Another survey found the following:

Nine out of ten American adults cannot accurately define the meaning of the "Great Commission";

Nearly seven out of ten have no clue what the term "John 3:16" means;

Barely one third know the meaning of the expression "the gospel";

Only 4% are able to correctly describe the meaning of all three terms: the gospel, John 3:16, and the Great Commission;

More adults are capable of accurately naming the top-rated prime time television shows than of correctly describing the meaning of all three terms.[4]

In one of his "Jay Walking" episodes, comedian Jay Leno asked people to name one of the Ten Commandments. One person replied, "Freedom of Speech." Leno then asked people to complete the sentence, "Let he who is without sin ..." Someone replied, "Have a good time." Finally, Leno asked, "According to the Bible, who was eaten by a whale?" One person replied, "Pinocchio."[5]

I recently attended a movie that was a legal thriller in which the lawyer, at one point, compares his battle against corporate lawyers to King David fighting "that big guy [Goliath]." A twenty-something woman in the seat next to me leaned over and asked her friend, "Who's this David guy?"

Such comments are not surprising given the fact that postmoderns more often get their information about God and spiritual matters from films and music rather than from church and organized religion.[6] In her book *Seeing and Believing: Religion and Value in the Movies*, Margaret Miles puts it this way: "Where do contemporary Americans receive our values and our images of ourselves and one another, of our social world, and of our relation to the natural world? As a society, we do not primarily get our informing images from the walls of churches as historical Christians did; we get them from the media culture in which we live."[7] Miles is saying that in the absence of a strong religious influence in their lives, most non-Christians build their values and beliefs with images they receive through contemporary music, novels, television, and movies.

Each year the Barna Research Group surveys the religious practices of Americans. Not surprisingly, many of the findings are low. For instance, in 2003, only 39% of adults read the Bible during a typical week. Only 43% attended a religious service.[8] Postmoderns are uninformed about basic Christianity.

I've seen this in my own non-Christian friends at Highland. Several of them have told me that their own lack of understanding of Christianity is an obstacle keeping them from becoming Christians. One, Rob, claimed to have a high level of understanding of Christianity. But the more I talked to him the more I realized how little he actually understood. He once summarized his view of Christianity to me in this way:

God created us as imperfect and then punishes us for being imperfect? It's like hanging a candy bar around a child's neck and slapping him each time he touches it. What is our crime? The crime of being human? Why was reconciliation necessary? God made us this way, so why do we need to be forgiven?

Rob thought he knew what Christianity was about. But years of reading liberal religious authors and a handful of negative encounters with Christians had left him misinformed. He didn't have a clue as to what Christianity was truly about.

Another non-Christian friend of mine, Harry, was raised in the Jewish faith. He has actively attended Churches of Christ with his Christian wife for twenty-three years. Harry has heard a lot about Christianity. Still, when I recently asked what was keeping him from becoming a Christian, Harry mentioned that he simply did not possess enough knowledge, especially to compare Judaism with Christianity and make a choice of one or the other. Ironically, he found himself as void of understanding about Judaism as he was about Christianity—after twenty-three years.

In the past few years we've had many young married Christians and non-Christians come to Highland. Our preaching apprentice Josh recently spent several weeks teaching from the Gospel of Matthew to a mixed young married group on Sunday mornings. After one morning, several of them came to him and said, "We realize that we don't know anything about the doctrine of Christianity. Would you take some time and go through some of the basic teachings of Christianity with us?" Some of those asking were non-Christians. Others were Christians who had been raised in a churched setting. Even the preaching they had heard growing up had left them uninformed about basic Christianity.

That's why for the last three years we've offered an "ABCs of the Christian Faith" class and an "Old Testament/New Testament Survey" class once a year. The classes are not just for our own members. Each time we offer them, they draw a handful of non-Christians (we advertise these classes) and new Christians who want to "fill in the gaps" of their knowledge about Christianity. Betty, a non-Christian, attended our last "ABCs of the Christian Faith" class. She was interested in Christianity, Judaism, and Islam and wanted to learn more about Christianity.

But classes like these are not enough. Any evangelistic preaching which we do in this postmodern setting will need to account for and strategically compensate for this lack of understanding.

Obviously, non-Christians have always been uninformed about basic Christianity. That's part of what made them non-Christians. But never have more people in the Western world known less about Christianity than postmoderns do today. Never before could we so easily and accurately label so many people as ignorant about the central teachings of Christianity as we can today.

If you were a missionary preparing to enter a country whose citizens were largely uninformed about the basics of Christianity, how would you approach preaching?

Spiritual

In spite of their ignorance of Christianity, however, postmoderns are deeply attracted to spiritual issues in general and into Jesus in particular. They may be uninformed. But they are not necessarily uninterested.

For instance, in his comprehensive study of the pop culture of Generation X, Tom Beaudoin concluded that Gen X is strikingly religious, just not Christian.[9] Pollster George Gallup, Jr. states that the dominant trends in society today are 1) a search for deeper and more meaningful relationships, and 2) the search for spiritual moorings. From 1994 to late 1998, Gallup found that the percent of Americans feeling a need to "experience spiritual growth" rose from 54% to 82%.[10] In 1999 that number dropped slightly to 78%.[11] Thus, approximately 80% of American adults feel a conscious need to experience spiritual growth.

This interest in spirituality is perhaps best seen in a 2003 study that found that, similarly, over 80% of American adults have prayed to God in the last week.[12] If we accept Barna's statistic cited in chapter one—that only one-third of Americans meet a minimalist definition of being a Christian—these numbers are astonishing. *Only thirty percent of Americans are "born-again" Christians. Yet almost 80% want to experience spiritual growth and over eighty percent have prayed during the last week.*

Not only are postmoderns interested in spiritual issues in general, many are interested specifically in Jesus. Compared to much of the third world, North American culture is widely open to Jesus Christ. In the late 1980s, nine out of ten Americans said that Jesus had some kind of positive impact on their lives.[13]

A survey of postmodern culture reveals just how interested in spirituality postmoderns are. In 2002, of the top twenty-five grossing movies, 92% had at least some positive moral or biblical content, according to the Christian Film & Television Commission.[14] Several of the all-time-highest grossing movies feature spiritual plots, such as *Star Wars* (second all time), *The Sixth Sense* (fifteenth all time), *Raiders of the Lost Ark* (twenty-sixth all time), *Signs* (thirty-third all time), and *The Exorcist* (forty-fourth all time).[15] Margaret Miles, in her book *Seeing and Believing*, concludes, *"Movies are for the masses what theology is for an elite."*[16]

The same could be said for some popular television shows. The television network program *Touched By An Angel* proved to be one of the most popular prime time shows of the 1990s. It was the first explicitly religious drama to break into the Nielsen Top Ten in the forty-six-year history of Nielsen.[17] More surprising is that at least one out of every three episodes of *The Simpsons* contains at least one religious reference. In many ways, the Simpsons are defined by their religion. They attend church every Sunday and say grace before meals. Their next-door neighbors are committed Christians. When faced with crisis, they turn to God and pray.[18]

Postmoderns are more open than the moderns before them to the possibility of the transcendent. To the modern person, science was God. There was no need for the transcendent. Logic, reason, and the scientific method could provide all that humanity needed. Postmoderns, however, have reacted against this over-reliance upon science. They hunger for the spiritual and transcendent.[19] To a large extent, postmoderns are very religious. They believe in God, pray, and consider themselves spiritual.

Yet, as we explore in the next chapter, they do not join a church. North American religiosity is pluralistic, individualistic, and private.[20] Postmodern spirituality is just "between me and God." It rarely manifests itself in a commitment to an organized religious body. It infrequently expresses itself in any public way.

In addition, Darrell Guder calls postmoderns "spiritual secularists."[21] That is, they like to live in both worlds: the spiritual world and the secular world. They can, at the same time, hold deep transcendent values and shallow worldly values. They will pray to God in the morning and commit adultery in the evening. They will express awe at the view from the foot of the cross but will then sacrifice everything to get to the top of the corporate ladder.

Vicky, a Highland teen, told me recently that this was the most difficult thing about trying to evangelize her postmodern peers. "They want to be religious, but they don't want to give up their sinful life. They don't want to give up their drinking, smoking, and cussing." They are spiritual, yet secular.

Perhaps most importantly, while interested in spiritual issues in general, and in Jesus in particular, they are not necessarily interested in Christianity. Leonard Sweet explains the distinction in this way. In postmodernity, if Christians try to evangelistically engage postmoderns by saying, "I'm a Christian," postmoderns will often turn a deaf ear. They don't want to hear about Christianity. If, however, Christians say, "I'm a disciple of Jesus," postmoderns may lean in and want to hear more.[22] In other words, we must not mistake the postmodern interest in spirituality and in Jesus for an interest in Christianity. For postmoderns, Christianity and the church may not be "hot," but God and Jesus are.

Eight of my non-Christian friends admit that they are non-Christians. But each of them also considers themselves spiritually minded. John, a medical school applicant, believes Jesus is the Son of God and that God created the universe. Larry, a local physician, believes in the existence of a higher being who is in control of the world. He sees prayer and meditation as an important means of gaining strength. Lou, a financial analyst, believes in God as a Creator who sent his son Jesus to earth. He views the church as a place of spiritual enlightenment.

At one point, I even asked these non-Christian friends to rate themselves on an instrument called the Engel Scale. The Engel Scale suggests that non-Christians fall on different parts of a continuum represented numerically by an 8 to a 1:

- An 8 non-Christian has an awareness of a supreme being but has no knowledge of the gospel.
- At 7, the non-Christian has an initial awareness of the gospel.
- A 6 non-Christian is aware of the fundamentals of the gospel.
- At 5, one grasps the implications of the gospel.
- At 4, one has a positive attitude toward the gospel.
- At 3, the non-Christian personalizes the gospel and understands personal sin as a problem which is solved by the gospel.
- At 2, there is a decision to act.
- At 1, the individual repents and comes to faith in Christ.[23]

Presumably, a person with no interest in spiritual matters would rate him/herself at an 8. *My eight non-Christian friends all rated themselves between 5 and 2.* While this is anecdotal, it illustrates the larger truth that postmoderns *are* interested in spiritual issues.

It was an interest seen in my opening story. The surprising thing about David's teen Bible study is not just that so many teens that came had never heard the events of the last day of Jesus' life. The surprising thing is that they came at all to a Bible study to hear about those events. In the modern world, such a Bible study would have fallen flat on its face. It would have been David and his Christian friends in an empty living room. But in the postmodern world, things are different. Not only are teens and postmoderns uninformed about Jesus and his way of life. They hunger to learn more and to experience the life Jesus came to give.

Imagine you were a missionary preparing to enter a country whose citizens had this dominant characteristic. How would it affect your preaching?

CHAPTER THREE

Postmoderns Are Anti-institutional and Pluralistic

Characteristic Three: Anti-institutional

Doug struck up a conversation with his classmate in study hall. After they chit-chatted, the topic of God came up. Doug told him about Highland and some of the spiritual activities on the church calendar. The conversation, which had been quite positive to that point, suddenly turned negative.

"Look, I believe in God. I believe in Jesus. But I hate the Bible. I think it's pointless. I think most of it was just made up. And, I see no point at all in church."

"Why?" Doug asked.

"That's just the way I feel."

"Did you have a negative experience in some church somewhere?" Doug prodded.

"No. That's just how I feel. I just think that church is pointless."

When I asked Doug recently how his non-Christian friends at school reacted to the idea of church, this is the story he told me. Doug's friend is typical of postmoderns. God is great. Jesus is good. But the church? It's pointless.

The previous chapter suggested that postmoderns are uninformed, but are enthusiastically seeking spirituality. The remaining five characteristics reveal the kind of spirituality postmoderns are seeking. Characteristic three is the first of these: *postmoderns are seeking a non-institutional spirituality. They generally reject institutional religion.*

In 2001, approximately one-third of the people in the United States were unchurched. This means they had not attended a Christian church service, other than a special event such as a wedding or holiday service, in the past six months.[1] Ironically, one in seven unchurched Americans define themselves as born-again Christians who have made a personal commitment to Christ.[2] Postmoderns have not rejected Christ, but they *have* rejected his church. In 2003, while over 80% of American adults had prayed during the week surveyed, only 43% had attended a religious service during that same week.[3]

Postmoderns' rejection of church seems to have two causes. *First, they view the church as irrelevant* (or "pointless," as Doug's friend put it). They no longer value the church as important to the social and moral order of our culture.[4] The church has nothing to offer by way of improving the morals of our culture or the social relationships we share in our culture. This thinking is seen in the fact that 62% of those not attending church think that church is irrelevant to their needs, spiritual or other.[5] Postmoderns want whatever works in making their daily lives better—and in their estimation, church does not work in improving daily life.

Oddly, they even view church as irrelevant to filling their spiritual hunger. Church exists, at one level, as a way of filling the spiritual hunger of people. Yet postmoderns believe that they are more capable of filling that hunger themselves than the church is. Thus they are often more likely to worship God alone on a mountaintop than to attempt to fill their spiritual hunger through a church service on Sunday morning. They simply doubt that the church can do better than they can in filling their spiritual hunger.

Alex, one of our teens at Highland, had a friend who came with him to worship services at Highland for a few weeks. Then, Alex's friend stopped coming. Alex asked why. His friend explained that he had decided he could worship God best by himself. He had no problem with our doctrine or teaching. But he had concluded that the best way he could grow closer to God was to worship God privately, apart from organized church. He had come to view the church as irrelevant to meeting his spiritual needs.

Another reason postmoderns seem to reject church is that they are skeptical of the church's claim to have absolute authority in spiritual matters.

Pre-moderns assumed the validity of the authority of the Bible, the church, and the preacher. Something was true because the church said it was true. The church said it, I believe it, that settles it.

Moderns conceded to a preacher's or church's authority—if the preacher or church could provide empirical or rational evidence for their spiritual claims. Something was true because the church proved it was true. This helps explain why Christian apologetics were so popular during the modern period. They provided a way for the church to logically prove its spiritual claims.

Postmoderns, however, recognize no universal standard of truth—no matter who says it or what kind of empirical or rational evidence backs it up.[6] They are skeptical of *anyone* claiming absolute authority in *any* area, including spiritual areas (a trait directly tied to the pluralism discussed below). As a result, they are likely to reject church. The church's message which is founded on universal claims about the sinfulness of all humanity, the uniqueness of the biblical God from all other Gods, and the absolute necessity of finding salvation in Jesus and Jesus alone run against the grain of the postmodern preference for "what's right for you isn't necessarily right for me, and what's right for me isn't necessarily right for you."

Because of these two issues—a sense that church is irrelevant to meeting one's needs, including spiritual needs; and a dislike for the universal and absolute claims of the church's message—postmoderns reject institutional Christianity. Indeed, in his study of the music, television, and literature of Generation X, Tom Beaudoin found four themes, all of which signal a rejection of institutional Christianity:

- a deep suspicion of religious institutions
- a challenging of religious institutions in general
- a specific assault against the Catholic church
- an attempt to pit Jesus against the church[7]

Where the faith journey of the modern person may have once begun with an awareness of the church and a neutral attitude toward it, the faith journey of the postmodern person often begins with (best case scenario) ignorance of or (worst case scenario) hostility toward the church.[8]

In a very real sense, postmoderns are "high on God" but "low on church."[9]

Often this rejection of institutional Christianity can be traced to more personal reasons than just a sense of irrelevance or of skepticism. I found this to be especially true with my non-Christian acquaintance, Rob. He once mentioned to me an event that permanently altered his view of church. Rob served on the financial committee of a Methodist church when their missionary had to come back to the United States before his prescribed time. The committee had to determine what to do with the remaining money that had been allotted to that mission. Rob suggested that they use it to support a non-Methodist missionary with whom he was familiar. The committee scoffed at him.

Rob remarked to me, "Christians love to talk about 'agape,' but they don't live it." That event marked his permanent separation from church. He once told me that the church has "created" the need for God and that the church has "fabricated guilt to justify its existence and power."

"Power, not love, drives the church," Rob said.

This, perhaps, represents a third reason that postmoderns reject church. While the previous two reasons may be specific to postmoderns, this is a reason shared with countless generations before them. Postmoderns have sadly experienced, through the media and in their own lives, churches or preachers who stumbled morally or spiritually or who otherwise negatively impacted them. These experiences have created almost insurmountable obstacles to getting them into (or back into) institutional Christianity.

If you were a missionary bent on preaching in a foreign culture characterized by such anti-institutionalism, how would you preach?

Characteristic Four: Pluralistic

Valerie has been attending Highland for a year and a half. Her mother was killed recently in a tragic and senseless incident. The experience crushed her. Several Sunday mornings, she would leave services with tears streaming down her face. Yet through it all, she never gave up on God. Never left Jesus. Never abandoned Highland.

Because of this, I thought that if anyone had ever come to believe in Jesus as the Lord of Lords, as the one true source of hope and help, it would be Valerie. Surely, I thought, this experience of intense suffering and finding healing in Jesus has led Valerie to a unique loyalty to Jesus. A loyalty that was far beyond what most Christians have.

Yet ironically, she has revealed, in recent months, that Jesus is great—for her. Jesus is the right answer—for her. Jesus is what helped *her* through suffering. "But," she has said in private and during Sunday school classes, "if you chose Mohammed, that's great too. Or if you choose Buddha, he'll help you just as much." For Valerie, Jesus is *a* lord, but not *the* lord. He was a good choice for her, but he's not the only choice.

Valerie represents the bulk of postmoderns. Postmoderns reject the possibility of universal and objective truth. This is seen in a recent study in which less than twenty percent of Americans stated a belief in an absolute moral truth—a moral standard which applies to all people in all times.[10] In another study, more than two out of three adults and more than four out of five teens argue that truth is always relative to the individual and the circumstances.[11] This rejection of absolute truth in general, carries over to religion in particular. In postmodernity, no single religion is considered absolute—true for all people in all times. Three fourths of Americans think that more than one religion offers a true path to God. Just one in six Americans thinks their religion is the best path to God.[12] As a result, postmoderns are open to many religious faiths.

This pluralism is due, in part, to globalization and urbanization. Globalization—brought about through high-speed travel, the Internet, immigration, telecommunications, etc.—has brought the cultures of the world to our front door. Postmoderns live in a "global village" which has introduced them to a diverse world of alternative cultures and faith traditions.[13] The religions of Hinduism and Islam are no longer mysterious faiths practiced by people living thousands of miles away. Globalization has created a circumstance in which we now see Muslims on television and in which we live side by side with Hindus in our neighborhood. For instance, for three years, our closest neighbors in Memphis were a Muslim family across the street. This globalization has led at least one person to proclaim that America may be "the most religiously diverse country in the world."[14] In this setting, it has become harder for postmoderns to reject the truth of non-Christian faiths. It was one thing years ago to say "untrue" about a Muslim I read about in *National Geographic*. It is quite another to say "untrue" to a Muslim neighbor as we play basketball together in his driveway.

Urbanization fuels pluralism as well. In 1870, the United States was 20% urban. In 1900, it was 40% urban. Today, it is approximately 90% urban. By bringing different cultures and traditions together in one area, urbanization creates more potential for pluralism to develop.[15]

The result is a culture that suggests that no single faith system is the means to absolute truth. In fact, in postmodernism, spiritual issues are relegated to the private realm of "values/beliefs" rather than to the public sphere of "facts." *In postmodernity, saying, "I believe Jesus is Lord," is no different than saying, "I believe Tennessee is the most beautiful state."* Religious statements, like statements about which state is the most beautiful, are merely statements of personal opinion and feeling. They do not carry the same weight as facts (e.g., It is 11.9 miles from my house to my church office). Therefore values and beliefs that differ radically from one another are nonetheless valid, and people are free to choose their own. Unlike facts, there are no right or wrong values/beliefs.[16]

When it comes to choosing values/beliefs, the choice is often made on aesthetic rather than rational criteria. Simply put, postmoderns believe what they like—literally. For example, whether or not there is a hell is beside the point. Whether postmoderns like that belief or not is the point. The point is that postmoderns are unwilling to believe what they do not enjoy.[17] Thus religious matters can never be "true," but only "true for you."[18]

Jesus may work for some; crystals may work for others.[19] It's all a matter of personal preference. All of this has led some postmoderns to adopt a kind of eclectic faith. A friend of one author stated, "My spirituality is drawn from Hinduism, Buddhism, Christianity, and Muslim mysticism, and Native American religions."[20]

In this climate, tolerance is the top cultural value. Those of different faiths are to tolerate one another and respect each other's differences. Even more, those of different faiths are to affirm the truth of one another's beliefs.

Some, however, have declared pluralism, and postmodernity as a whole, dead after the September 11, 2001 attacks on the World Trade Center towers. A culture columnist of the *Chicago Tribune* wrote, "What lies in the mess in the lower Manhattan and in the black gash in the Pentagon and in a field in southern Pennsylvania may be this, the end of postmodernism and its chokehold on the late twentieth century cultural imagination."[21]

Perhaps what the writer meant to say is that postmodern's *ethical* pluralism has died—the belief that there are no absolute moral standards. It *is* hard to stare at the gaping hole in New York City's skyline and still believe that some things are not absolutely evil, no matter by whom they are committed.

Still, not even ethical pluralism has been dealt a deathblow by 9/11. In a response to the attack, a Yale University student wrote of her class's discussion of the events of September 11. Many in the student's class argued that there was, in essence, nothing immoral about the attacks because they were driven not by immorality but by Middle Eastern poverty, America's foreign policy, and noble religious motivations.[22] Such a conversation signals that even ethical pluralism is still alive and well.

Indeed, the events of September 11 may have actually furthered the cause of postmodern pluralism. One religion editor calls Americans to greater religious tolerance in the wake of this tragedy: "Mere tolerance of other religions is not enough...even the acceptance of other religions as valid paths to God is insufficient...What committed Christians and Jews and Muslims must do is find within their own traditions sound theological *reasons for valuing* other faiths . . ."[23]

According to this author, it's not enough for us to simply tolerate the existence of other faiths and those who follow them. It's not even enough for us to say that all religions are valid paths to God. In the wake of September 11, this religion editor says that we must use our own Christian theology to affirm the truth and value of all non-Christian religions. This is pluralism, through and through.

Christianity's emphasis on the exclusivity of Jesus is therefore a major stumbling block for postmoderns. Modernists rejected Christianity because they thought it was not true. Postmodernists reject it because it says it is the only truth. Postmoderns see Christianity as intolerant.[24] In one interview, postmodern couples were asked what was keeping them from becoming Christians. One wife replied, "The whole Jesus-is-the-only-way-to-have-a-relationship-with-God thing really bothers me."[25]

Donald McGavran states that postmodernism exists in the clash between two powerful but opposing forces: cultural relativism which says there are many ways to God and many rights and wrongs, and Christianity which says there is one way and one right—Christ.[26]

Postmoderns are seeking a spirituality with room for their pluralism. This, in my estimation, is the largest obstacle we face in preaching evangelistically to postmoderns.

In conversations with my non-Christian acquaintances at Highland, I've asked them what keeps them from becoming Christians. Recently, Lou, Rob, and Larry all mentioned this issue:

Christianity's apparent intolerance of other religions. I talked at length with Larry about this. When asked about any obstacles keeping him from becoming a Christian, three of the four things he mentioned fell into this general area of pluralism.

First, he objected to the way that churches demand young couples who have fallen in love to remain sexually pure outside the marriage relationship. In his view, such strict and fundamentalist views of sexuality were unhealthy and might force a couple to have a "secret wedding" so they can finally consummate their relationship but not tell anyone about it until the "real wedding." Larry saw Christianity as holding too tightly to an intolerant moral viewpoint that contradicts the natural urges of young men and women.

Second, Larry objected to Christianity's view on homosexuality since it contradicted certain scientific conclusions that suggest that homosexuality is not voluntary. Once again, Christianity was holding too tightly to a moral viewpoint that contradicted the moral tolerance of postmodernity.

Third, Larry said that it would be a great difficulty to raise children who believed in Jesus' claim to exclusivity and yet at the same time teach them to respect other faiths. The exclusivity of Christianity presents a formidable obstacle for Larry.

It is even more formidable for Rob. While believing that God, Jesus, and the church are the "biggest hoax ever placed on humankind," he also told me that if other people wanted to follow it, that was fine. Rob stated at one point, "I don't believe in any absolutes. Moral absolutes. Religious absolutes." Knowing of my conversion to Christ, he said, "I do not deny the reality of your 'Damascus Road experience,' but it's not normative for me or anyone else. Religion is fine for some, but it's not right for me."

If you were about to step into the pulpit in a mission church whose audience was filled with such pluralistic non-Christians, how would you approach preaching?

CHAPTER FOUR

Postmoderns Are Pragmatic, Relational, and Experiential

Characteristic Five: Pragmatic

With her thin-rimmed glasses, neat navy business dress, and short-cropped hair, Brenna looked as if she had her life together. Just months away from finishing her graduate work and having accepted a teaching position at New Mexico State University, it seemed nothing could go wrong.

But everything did.

She and her husband of three months were launching verbal bombs at one another and treating each other like the enemies they never thought they would be. They stood on the brink of divorce.

That pain drove her to the church where I preached. Brenna's mother-in-law was a long-time member of that church. But Brenna rarely came with her. This day, however, she did. Yet she didn't come asking questions about the Trinity, the omnipotence about God, or a biblical question that perplexed her. She came seeking help and hope in the midst of marriage turmoil.

My wife, Kendra, and another woman befriended her, counseled her, and wiped away her tears. In the course of listening, however, they also spoke. They told Brenna of the One who was their help and hope in difficult times—Jesus Christ. After several weeks, Brenna came to see what they saw in Jesus and committed her life to him through baptism.

Brenna's entry into church and into Christianity follows a path common to many postmoderns: the path of pragmatism. *What often draws postmoderns to Christianity or to any faith is its promise to repair and resolve the problems of life.* As we've already seen, many postmoderns are uninformed about the basic doctrines of Christianity. They are, however, enthusiastically spiritual. The spirituality they are seeking is anti-institutional and pluralistic. But it is also pragmatic in nature. They are drawn to any spirituality that promises to fix the problems of their daily lives.

Postmoderns are less interested in theology for its own sake than in how theology can resolve daily problems. They want a spirituality which makes a difference in their daily lives and which helps them make a difference in the lives of others. This is partially the result of a society which has become geared toward the consumer and which argues that "newer is better, efficient is better, what works is better."[1] Such pragmatism is one of the core values in postmodern American society.[2]

Studies of those who are returning to church find that people are looking for values that help them raise their families and endure difficult circumstances. They are not interested in doctrine, but in practical solutions to personal problems. The ultimate question for them is "so what?" They are more concerned about Monday morning than about the "some glad morning" when we'll "fly away" to be in heaven. They want teaching which addresses life *before* death, and care little for teaching which addresses life *after* death.

Postmoderns want help with the here and now, not the hereafter.[3] Consequently, people today are looking to churches for the kind of practical help once offered only by the twelve-step recovery movement.[4] Thus, preachers often have to speak to people's brokenness, addictions, wounds, victimizations, and trauma just to gain a hearing.[5] Brian McLaren suggests that instead of "If you were to die tonight, do you know for certain that you would spend eternity with God in heaven?" the new and postmodern question is this: "If you live for another thirty years, what kind of person will you become?"[6]

Such pragmatism is found in the way many postmoderns reach spiritual and moral decisions. When asked how they decide if something is moral or not, nearly half of American adults say that the moral choice is the choice that will bring them the most pleasing or satisfying results. In other words, something is moral if it is pragmatic—if it leads to pleasing or satisfying results in the here and now. Only about one in four adults base moral decisions on religious principles or the Bible.[7]

In summary, postmoderns do not base moral and spiritual decisions on objective principles but upon pragmatic concerns. They don't choose what is objectively moral, but what they think will produce a better life in the present. They not only do not base their moral and spiritual decisions upon the Bible, but they don't even base them on any transcendent and objective principle.

My acquaintance Rob claimed to reject Christianity for these very reasons. He saw nothing "pragmatic" in Christianity. One afternoon we sat next to one another in his living room. Bookshelves overflowed with scholarly works on ancient history, sociology, and anthropology. With a smile that barely masked the hostility of his words, he looked at me and said, "I never saw a Christian I wanted to be like—and I still don't." He flatly stated, "Christianity has nothing to offer me."

At one point Rob said, "If there was no heaven, Christianity would have never made it." He meant that the only reward Christianity offered people was a better life in heaven after death. It had nothing to offer in terms of a better life on earth before death. Rob believed he had found more help for daily living in the books on his shelves than in the Book about Christ.

Rob also said, "I'd be willing to put my family and our relationships up against any of your church members. It's not the atheists in divorce court; it's the Christians. That's why I'm not a Christian." Rob did not believe that Christianity "works" in improving things such as family and marriage because he had not seen it "work" in the lives of Christians. This proved to be a major obstacle keeping him from faith in Christ.

How would you preach evangelistically in a foreign country where pragmatism was such a dominant characteristic? What would you preach to someone like Rob?

Characteristic Six: Relational

Sam, his wife, and their two boys had attended Highland for years. About six years ago, his wife was baptized. Sam, however, was not ready to take that step. Still he kept coming, not only to our worship services, but also to my Sunday school class of young families. He even came frequently to a small group of young families that met in our house on Sunday nights for Bible study and prayer. Sam also helped each year with a large children's clothing sale held at our church and with our School Store that gives away school supplies to thousands of needy children. An outsider would have assumed that Sam was a Christian committed to Christ and to ministry.

Why did Sam come all those years? It's clear that he was interested in spiritual matters. It's clear that he wanted to support his wife. But if that were all that drove him, he probably would have settled for just attending Sunday morning church. Instead, he became as intimate a member of our community as a non-Christian could. Why?

The relationships he formed at Highland are a major part of the answer. He hung out with us guys in the kitchen after our small group study while the women talked in the living room. He drank coffee with us in our Sunday school classroom before class started. He talked as we assembled clothing racks or handed out school supplies. He came for the relationships as much as for anything else. He came because of the community.

Sam is a typical postmodern. A sixth characteristic of postmoderns is that they are seeking a spirituality that is relational in nature. Ironically, while being anti-institutional, they nonetheless value and seek community.

In some ways this is a return to pre-modernism. Pre-moderns had a communal vision. They saw people, animals, nature, and the divine as interrelated and as part of one relational community (Native Americans come to mind here). The modern world rejected that worldview and declared the individual to be supreme. Everything in the modern world existed to serve the individual. But postmodernism, in reaction to modernism's individualism, has created a longing once again for community.[8] The loneliness of modernism has led them back to community.

Thus where postmoderns may reject church because of its supposed irrelevance and authoritarianism, they may also still value its community. *In fact, of those who are returning to church, many state they are longing for some kind of community.*[9] In a very real sense, "Relationships rule postmodern life."[10]

Relationships are so powerful that postmoderns may convert to Christ as groups rather than as individuals. Many teens, in particular, are more likely to make conversion decisions as a community rather than as individuals. Teens may not come to a Christian outreach event by themselves. Instead, they will bring members of their "tribe" with them to the event. If the tribe likes the event, the next week they will bring more members of their tribe with them. Thus when it comes to conversion to Christ, some of those tribe members will make the decision together.[11]

I've seen this among our Highland Youth Group. Each Wednesday night our teens host an outreach event called Genesis. Several times throughout the year, they host a "Big Event" Genesis, where they really urge the teens to invite their non-Christian friends and they have special speakers and activities. Before one recent Big Event, Vickie invited the entire saxophone section in her school's band. The entire section then huddled up. They all spoke to each other. "Should we go?" "I don't know, what do you think?" "Sounds interesting." "I'll go if you go." They all turned to her in unison and said they would come. When the Big Event happened, however, no one from Vickie's sax section showed up. When she asked about it later, they told her that one sax player turned out to have a conflict and couldn't come. Since he couldn't come, the entire section decided not to come. Postmoderns' decisions about spiritual issues are often strongly driven by relationships.

In a profound statement about his spiritual journey in general and his experience at Highland in particular, Harry once told me "The church pulls me here." I was asking why he, a Jew, continued to come Sunday after Sunday to Highland—even more regularly than some members. "The church pulls me here," he said. When I asked him to explain, he talked about his Sunday school class and the friendships he's made at Highland. Community kept him coming.

How would you approach evangelistic preaching if you were headed to a mission spot in a foreign country where the people placed such a high value on relationships and community?

Characteristic Seven: Experiential

Each Wednesday night our teens organize Genesis, a weekly outreach to unchurched teens. At special Genesis events, they've had as many as 300 in attendance. Many of those were teens with no church home. Each week teens that have not made a commitment to Christ come to Genesis with their friends. When they talk about Genesis, they often mention one of three things:

- the worship music
- the testimonies
- the teaching

A praise team comprised of teens leads a high-energy period of worship in our gym with the lights low and the words to the song projected on a screen. During the service, one or two teens often go onstage and tell the story of their conversion or a story of how God's been at work in their lives. In addition, the lesson almost always involves elaborate visual aids and/or intriguing Power Point presentations. Since implementing these three ingredients into their outreach activities, the youth ministry has seen an enormous increase in unchurched teens attending.

These three ingredients have one element in common: they are all experiential. They all help create an "experience" or rely on the "experience" of trusted individuals. This reliance upon experience seems to be crucial for reaching postmoderns.

A seventh and final characteristic of postmoderns is that they are seeking a spirituality that is experiential. This is true in two senses. *First, postmoderns want to experience God.* They care more about whether a church offers an experience of God than they do about whether it offers the correct doctrine of God.[12] *There is a shift today when evaluating spirituality and church from "Does it make sense?" to "Was it a good experience?"*[13] The "Bible" for the modernist may have been J. I. Packer's *Knowing God*—a rational and linear approach to the doctrine of God.[14] The "Bible" for the postmodernist may be Henry Blackaby's *Experiencing God.*[15] Postmoderns are experiential in that they want to experience God and will choose a spirituality based upon that experience.

Second, postmoderns trust what can be experienced. They tend to value feeling, intuition, and desire over reason. What is experienced (by self and by others) is true.[16] Thus while postmoderns reject the authority of the church, they still respect tradition (the past experiences of the community) and experience (their or the community's present experience).[17] Indeed, "the congregation is most persuaded of the truth of a claim when it is confirmed in the life story of a person or community with whom they can identify."[18] Postmoderns trust a thing which they have experienced or which someone they admire has experienced.

Postmoderns judge Christianity (and other faiths) based upon what they or those they respect experience first hand. These experiences carry more weight in faith decisions than brilliant logical arguments based upon reason and analysis.

I've seen hints of this in the comments of my non-Christian friends. Rob, even as a staunch agnostic, stated, "I would love to have a Damascus Road experience." He told me that such an experience would be the only way he would convert to Christianity. If he, like Paul, could be blinded by the real presence of Jesus and hear the voice of God, that would persuade him of the truth of Christianity. Beyond this, no apologetics or biblical studies could sway him. He would vote in favor of Christianity only if he had a personal experience like Paul.

I once asked Lou why he held certain spiritual beliefs. He said, "I don't really know the Bible or what it says, but I believe this because this is what I *feel*." Like many postmoderns, Lou had based his spirituality less on what he had discovered through academic study of Scripture and more on what "felt" right.

When describing his beliefs, John told me that, "I believe that God created the universe, but not all at once. Because he allows free will, I also *feel* he allows change [evolution] to occur and that he guides it." Postmoderns often make spiritual decisions based upon what feels right, or what experience has taught them.

Conclusions about Postmoderns

We've seen that in many ways, our audience has changed. The target of our evangelistic preaching is drastically different than the Modern audience of fifty to one hundred years ago. Postmoderns are uninformed about basic Christian beliefs. They are interested in spiritual issues, but the kind of spirituality that interests them is private rather than institutional, pluralistic and open to many truths, pragmatic in nature, relational, and experiential.

The question remains: how do we preach evangelistically to such an audience? I suggested in the opening chapter that we would not reach this audience without a change in preaching methods that recognizes and addresses these postmodern characteristics. In my estimation, my failure to do so contributed to my lack of evangelistic fruit ten years ago on that Bring Your Neighbor Day. The failure of the Western Church to do so has contributed to its lack of evangelistic harvest as well.

Perhaps the most helpful way of approaching this issue is through the eyes of a missionary. The next chapter fleshes out this image from a theological perspective. The subsequent chapters then spell out seven suggestions for addressing postmoderns evangelistically in preaching and for helping your church to grow.

CHAPTER FIVE

A Theological Model for Postmodern Preaching

"Why don't you just preach Christ-crucified, like they did in the book of Acts?" That was the response of one of my colleagues after he read a draft of the material in this book. It is a question worth answering.

Why take postmodernism into account at all when engaging in evangelistic preaching?
Why develop new strategies for preaching to postmoderns?
Why not just rely on existing strategies?
Why not just preach the same old rugged cross in the same old way?
Why not preach to postmoderns the way in which we've always preached to the lost?

A co-worker of mine responded similarly after reading some of the suggestions in the following chapters that call for changes in the way we preach to postmoderns. He said, "I can't decide if we can just preach the Gospel and let God do the rest, or if we really should do everything we can to shape the message for postmoderns in a way that connects with them."

These comments illustrate the tension you may feel at this juncture in the book. What has preceded is mere *description*. The seven characteristics described thus far are undeniable. It is hard to argue that many of those to whom we preach are uninformed, spiritually minded, pragmatic, pluralistic, anti-institutional, relational, and experiential. But so what? What do we do with this information? What affect should it have on our preaching, if any?

What follows in later chapters is *prescription*. I will prescribe specific ways in which our message can be re-packaged in order to gain a better hearing in postmodernity. But is change really called for—and if so, what kind? Why not just preach the cross? And if the message of the cross is to be re-packaged, how do we know when we've re-packaged it too much?

Is there a biblical basis for the call to package our preaching in a way that connects with postmoderns? Or is this just another example of bending to the consumer will of our culture?

The Balance between Our Work and God's Work

Paul raises these issues in two key preaching texts: 1 Corinthians 1:18—2:5 and 14:22–25. In the former text, Paul explains that the cross has a scandalous element to it that often leads non-Christians to reject it. He goes on to say that he refuses to remove this scandal in his preaching and that he is content to preach nothing but Christ crucified. He will not rely on wise and persuasive words. He will not depend upon fancy rhetorical strategy to lead people to faith. He relies, instead, on the power of the simple message of the cross and on the work of the Spirit in the hearts of the listeners.

Apparently, therefore, conversion through preaching is always the result of the Spirit's work through the unadorned message of the cross. The Spirit and the cross do not need the aid of our wise and persuasive words. *Conversion has nothing to do with how we preach.*

In 1 Corinthians 14, however, Paul chides the Corinthians for preaching (through "tongues") in ways that are unintelligible to non-Christians and which ultimately lead them to reject Christianity as "crazy." Because of the unintelligible preaching, the non-Christians are saying, "you are out of your mind" (14:23). Paul therefore demands that the church preach in a way that is understandable to the outsider (through "prophecy"). He calls the church to speak with their mind (14:13–17), or "thoughtfully," not just with their spirit. If the church will give thoughtful consideration to the way they present their message, the result will be non-believers in the assembly falling on their face and proclaiming, "God is really among you." (14:25).

Thus, it is possible to preach in ways that hinder the Spirit's work and actually cause non-Christians to reject that message. Further, this rejection had nothing to do with the inherent scandal of the cross, but with the "thoughtless" way in which it was preached. Paul calls us to preach with our "minds," to preach with a "consideration" for non-Christians in the assembly and for what will be "intelligible" to them. Paul calls us to consider how to make the cross "sensible" to our non-Christian audience. Why? *Because conversion has everything to do with how we preach.*

Evangelistic preaching, then, takes place within the tension created by these two texts. On the one hand, conversion has nothing to do with how we preach. It is all God's work. It is the Spirit's work and the message of the cross that win hearts, not our wise and persuasive words. On the other hand, conversion has everything to do with how we preach. Its success is tied to our work. Our lack of attention to preaching in ways that are understandable to the non believer may lead non believers to reject the message for reasons that are completely unrelated to the scandal of the cross.

How do we preach then in the tension raised by these two texts? How do we walk the line between these two seemingly contradictory views of evangelistic preaching?

That is the task this chapter takes up. This chapter provides a theological model that can help us preach in the midst of this tension. It's the one chapter you'll be most likely to skip. Yet in some ways, it is the most important chapter. It stands as a hinge between the chapters that merely described our postmodern audience, and the following chapters that advocate changes in our preaching in order to reach these postmoderns. It is crucial for us to reflect theologically on change, evangelism, and preaching so that our preaching is at the same time fully dependant upon the Spirit's work to convert and yet fully born out of our own work to proclaim sensibly to our non-Christian audience.

God's Role in Relationship[1]

Both 1 Corinthians 1 and 1 Corinthians 14 are rooted in God's desire for relationship. God wants the message of the cross preached, and preached intelligibly, because of his deep longing for relationship with us. This is a fundamental concept woven throughout Scripture. We find it from Genesis through Revelation.

Initially, however, the focus is on God's work in establishing this relationship. It is God, after all, not us, who spoke the world into existence. It is God, not us, who created Adam and Eve. And why did God take this initiative? Part of the answer is found in the theme woven throughout Scripture in which God states, "I will be their God, they will be my people" (Gen. 17:7–8; Ex. 6:7; Jer. 7:23; Zech. 2:11; Rev. 21:1–5). God desires to have a people, a community, who belong to him and to whom he belongs.

Another part of the answer is found in the affirmation that "God is love" (Ex. 34:6; Ps. 103:8; Jer. 31:3; Jn. 15:9; Rom. 5:8; 1 Jn. 3:1; 4:16). God is love and he seeks a family, a community, with whom he can share that love. Thus God created the first human members of that community: Adam and Eve. God not only desired to love them, he wanted them to love him. All through Scripture, God's people are called to love him (Deut. 6:5; Josh. 22:5; Jn. 14:15). Jesus states that the "greatest commandment" is to love God with all one's heart, soul, mind, and strength (Mk. 12:29–30; Deut. 6:4– 5). God seeks a family, a community, whom he can love and who will love him.

But the initiative for this relationship was all God's. God created Adam and Eve. God made them his people. God called them into community with him. The relationship was entirely dependant upon him. He initiated it. He sustained it. Just as in 1 Corinthians 1, the redemption of the lost is completely dependant upon God's work, so here the relationship between God and humans is entirely dependent upon God's work. It is his work alone that leads to the first divine-human relationship in the Garden of Eden.

Our Role in Relationship: Physical Procreation

There would quickly, however, be a critical role for humans to play. The community of two created by Adam and Eve was not enough. God desired that community to expand so that he could share his love with more and more people.

This physical expansion could have been initiated and sustained solely through God's work. He could have continued to "handcraft" more humans himself. Instead, he now called humans to take up an important role in the expansion of the community. We see this role described in the frequent refrain in Genesis for God's people to "be fruitful and multiply" (Gen. 1:28; 9:1; 13:16; 15:5; 17:2,6,20; 22:17; 28:14; 35:11). Just as an earthly family has a child so that they may share their love with another, so God desired humans to procreate so that he could share his love with more people.

Thus we see the roots of the human role in God's redemptive work that is clearly portrayed in 1 Corinthians 14. Just as the redemptive relationship between God and humans would rely on human work, preaching intelligibly, in 1 Corinthians 14, so here the redemptive relationship between God and future humans would rely on human work, procreation. God gave humans a critical role to play in his desire to have relationships with a growing number of people. If humans did not play that role, his desire for relationship with an expanding community would be frustrated.

Our Role in Relationship: Spiritual Procreation

The human role in the divine-human relationship would not only consist of physical procreation. It would also consist of spiritual procreation. God envisioned all of humanity, its nations and its kingdoms, as potential members of his spiritual community. He wanted his community, or kingdom, to spread to every nation, even to the "ends of the earth" (Gen. 12:1–4; Ps. 22:27; 86:9; Isa. 9:2; 49:6; Acts 1:8). This was to be accomplished through evangelism, or spiritual procreation. Israel itself was meant to take on this missiological task and become a "light to the nations" (Is. 49:6) and to be a blessing to all families (Gen. 12:1–3).

Just as the original Genesis community expanded through birth, ultimately God's spiritual community would expand evangelistically through re-birth. Jesus teaches Nicodemus that "no one can see the kingdom of God without being born from above . . . of water and Spirit" (Jn. 3:3–5). John states that through faith in Christ we "become children of God" (Jn. 1:12). Paul counsels that through Christ we receive a spirit of adoption (Rom. 8:15) and that through baptism and faith in Christ we "are all sons of God" (Gal. 4:26). The community of God expands as more and more people are re-born into it through baptism and faith in Christ.

And just as in physical procreation humans played a critical role, so humans played a critical role in spiritual procreation. In Genesis, through procreation, people were "fruitful and multiplied," and in Acts, through proclamation of the gospel, "the number of disciples increased greatly" (Acts 6:7) and "Yet more than ever believers were added to the Lord, great numbers of both men and women" (Acts 5:14; see also Acts 2:41; 4:4; 11:21,24).

Our Role in Relationship: Preaching

Specifically, this spiritual procreation or re-birth would take place through human preaching. God would rely on the spoken human word to bring more and more into his family. Preaching was the primary means of evangelism in Acts.[2] David Larsen suggests, "Acts pictures an unhindered gospel unleashed through the Holy Spirit. The context for this spiritual conflagration is preaching."[3]

In Acts 2, preaching preceded the baptism of 3,000. In Acts 4, preaching preceded the growth in the number of disciples from 3,000 to 5,000. It was preaching which the Jewish religious leaders outlawed, not healing or prayer, for they knew its potential power to draw thousands to Christ (Acts 4). Acts 6:7 makes a direct connection between preaching and re-birth when it says, "The word of God continued to spread; the number of the disciples increased greatly in Jerusalem, and a great many of the priests became obedient to the faith."

Human preaching continues to play a major role in divine conversion today. In a poll of 906 unchurched American adults, people were asked what the church could do that would attract them to come to the church. The top answer given was "provide better/more interesting sermons." Preaching surpassed other seemingly more relevant concerns, such as changing the hours of the worship service, reducing the emphasis on money, and changing the type of music used in worship.[4]

The importance of preaching for evangelism was also confirmed in a 1977 study of thirteen churches of Christ reporting the largest number of baptisms for 1976. The study concluded that the "first and foremost method of evangelism of significance for these churches is that of pulpit preaching."[5]

Thom Rainer, in a study of Southern Baptist churches, revealed similar findings. Of 40,000 Southern Baptist churches in the United States, Rainer surfaced those that baptized at least twenty-five in one year and had at least one baptism for every twenty members. These 1,400 churches were sent a ten-page survey. Five hundred seventy-six churches returned completed surveys. Three evangelistic methodologies were held in common by all 576: prayer, Sunday school, and evangelistic preaching. The preachers of those churches mentioned evangelistic preaching as the number one factor for the evangelistic effectiveness of their churches.[6]

The message preached is God's message. As 1 Corinthians 1 reminds us, it is God's message of the cross that wins hearts. But as 1 Corinthians 14 reminds us, humans play a crucial role in the proclamation of that message. God relied completely upon human preaching of the divine message in order to expand the community of those with whom he could engage in loving relationship.

Our Role in Relationship: Contextualization

God not only relied on the human act of preaching in general in order to expand his community. He did not simply deliver a set script that he expected all preachers in all cultures to preach in exactly the same way. God also relied on humans to contextualize their preaching, to shape the message in a way that best connected with its audience.[7]

We have come to accept this when it comes to missions. When going to a foreign and non-Christian culture, a Christian missionary often addresses the issue of contextualization: How can the gospel be best communicated in this culture?[8] The nationals' language and worldview often affect the way in which the missionary proclaims the gospel. He will use their native language. He will draw upon images and metaphors from their world. He will address certain behaviors or mind sets unique to that culture. The same model is called for when preaching in a postmodern culture.

For instance, my twin brother Craig works for a para-church organization called Let's Start Talking, which shares the gospel around the world in dozens of different countries and cultures. Here are some of the anecdotes he's told me about how American workers have had to contextualize their ministry in a new culture:

An American couple who are "morning people" forced themselves to adjust to a schedule in Brazil where it is typical to stay up past 11 p.m., even on weeknights. Much of the local relationship building and fellowship takes place during these late night hours and the couple adopted this schedule to better reach people.

A socially reserved American who barely greets others with more than a handshake forced himself to begin kissing and touching others in the foreign country where he was working. In that country's culture, it was considered rude not to do so.

Some American workers found themselves in a country where honor was a much greater cultural value than it is in America. As a result, they changed the emphasis in their gospel preaching. Presenting the love and sacrifice displayed by Christ on the cross, which is a typical message in an American church, did not speak as loudly to this foreign culture which valued honor. Thus the American workers stressed the way in which Christ honored God and brought honor to the Father through the cross. This message was met with much greater appreciation in that culture.

In the Japanese culture, the elderly are held in much higher esteem than in America. Thus it became normal for some Japanese churches to ask the oldest member of the church to say the closing prayer each Sunday, even if that person was a woman. American workers had to make appropriate cultural (and theological) adjustments in this regard.

The point is simply that missionaries are used to doing what we American preachers are not: studying the culture and contextualizing the gospel to best address that culture. This is exactly what we must do in order to reach postmoderns.

Lesslie Newbigin calls for such a contextual approach to evangelism in North America. According to Newbigin, postmodernism has made North America a mission field and it must be approached as such. He urges churches to behave as missionary churches and to contextualize the gospel in ways that will connect with a postmodern culture.[9]

George Hunsberger echoes Newbigin's challenge. He calls for the Western church to become a "missional" church that understands the postmodern culture and engages it meaningfully with the gospel.[10] Many others recognize that Western culture has transformed from Christian to post-Christian and they urge the church to reevaluate its methods in reaching the lost.[11] The Navigators, one of the most effective organizations ministering to postmodern college students, summarize their primary response to postmodernism in this way: we need to start thinking like missionaries.[12]

In his book *Foolishness to the Greeks*, Lesslie Newbigin explores what would be involved in a genuine missionary encounter between the gospel and Western culture. What would proclamation of the gospel look like if we treated the West as a mission field? Newbigin offers three conclusions. First, the gospel would be communicated in the language of the receptor culture. Second, the preacher would radically call into question the way of understanding embodied in that language. Third, if the gospel got communicated clearly, it would only be due to the work of God.[13]

Contextualization is not compromise. Newbigin does not call the preacher to pervert the gospel in any way in his attempt to communicate it contextually to the receptor culture. Instead, once the preacher has found a way to "incarnate" the gospel in the receptor language, he then uses that very language to show where the gospel and that culture clash.

Mission authors often speak of two principles. The first, the "indigenizing" principle, affirms that the gospel is at home in every culture and that every culture is at home with the gospel. In other words, the gospel can be proclaimed in a way that connects with every human culture. No human culture is outside the reach of the gospel. The second principle, however, the "pilgrim" principle, warns that the gospel will always put us out of step with every culture.[14] Even though ways may be found to proclaim the gospel relevantly in every culture, inevitably that gospel will be at odds with certain things within that culture. It is the pilgrim principle that keeps contextualization from resulting in compromise of the gospel.

This is the same tension we started with concerning 1 Corinthians 1 and 1 Corinthians 14. The church must translate the truth of the gospel so that it sounds like good news to the society to which it is sent, but it must not compromise the gospel. It must follow the commands of both 1 Corinthians 1 and 1 Corinthians 14. It must preach intelligibly and thoughtfully, but it must only preach Christ-crucified. This is contextualization.[15]

Contextualization is simply understanding the cultural context and speaking the gospel to that context.[16] It seeks to be relevant to culture yet maintain its identity in Christ.[17] Unfortunately, American churches have devoted themselves to developing contextualized missiology to other countries but have given little thought to developing a contextualized missiology for postmodern North America.

What is needed in our current postmodern culture is a contextualized approach to evangelistic preaching which speaks to postmoderns in their language, uses that very language to challenge their unbiblical beliefs and behaviors, and trusts God to let the gospel be heard in spite of cultural barriers.

Incarnation as Solution to the Tension

1 Corinthians 1 and 14 introduced us to the tension in evangelistic preaching, a tension which is seen throughout redemptive history. Conversion is a result of God's work alone. Yet there is an irreplaceable role for human work as well. God has sovereignly tied his work to human work so that both must be done in order for lost people to come to salvation. God created the world and the human race. God initiated his relationship with us and the work of Christ, which ultimately made such a relationship

possible. He relies upon us, however, to evangelize, especially through preaching, in order to expand his family. In addition, he relies upon us to take his unchanging message of the cross and preach in a contextualized way that fits our culture and audience.

The incarnation is perhaps the best illustration of this delicate balance between divine and human activity. God invites us to join his expanding family, which is bound intimately in relationship with him, where he is our God, and we are his people (Gen. 17:7–8; Ex. 6:7; Jer. 7:23; Zech. 2:11; Rev. 21:1–5). In order to bring us into relationship with himself, God has to reveal his intent, character, and love. This revelation comes through the general revelation of nature, history, and the inner person (Rom. 1:18–23; 2:14–16) and through special revelation in which God manifests himself to particular persons at particular times.[18] The ultimate revelation of God's intent, character, and love, however, came in the Incarnation, through Jesus Christ (Heb. 1:1–3).

Evangelistic preaching links arms with God in his effort to reveal himself through his Incarnate son (1 Thess. 3:2). Our part is to preach the gospel, the message of God's incarnation in Jesus, in our attempt to turn people to God, and thus make them part of God's expanding family (1 Thess. 1:9). Evangelistic preaching, however, not only continues the work of God's incarnation by making that revelation known to others, it also imitates God's incarnational method of revelation. Each preacher proclaims the gospel in a unique way, shaped by one's personality, experiences, and communication patterns.[19] In other words, the message of the gospel is incarnated in the "flesh" of the preacher. The same gospel, while retaining its core substance, sounds different when preached by different human proclaimers, because of the "flesh" of those proclaimers. As the gospel is incarnated in different preachers, it begins to look and sound slightly different. Indeed "the Gospel always comes to people in cultural robes."[20]

But the "flesh" of the messenger is not the only "flesh" in which the proclaimed gospel is wrapped, however. The gospel is also wrapped in a "flesh" influenced by the listener's culture. For instance, for the Jews of Acts 13, Paul "dressed" the gospel in the "flesh" of Jewish history. For the Lycaonians of Acts 14, Paul "dressed" the gospel in the "flesh" of cosmology. For the Athenians of Acts 17, Paul "dressed" the gospel in the "flesh" of pagan religious ideas.[21] In each case the core message, the gospel, was the same.[22] It was contextualized or incarnated into a different form, however, for each audience. One author states that, "The Christian faith never exists except as 'translated' into another culture. . .In Pauline churches, Jews, Greeks, barbarians, Thracians, Egyptians, and Romans were able to feel at home. The faith was inculturated in a great variety of contexts—Syriac, Greek, Roman, Coptic, Armenian, Ethiopian, Maronite, and so forth."[23]

Through the Incarnation, God revealed himself in a form that had the greatest potential to communicate to a particular audience. God's revelation dressed in a "flesh" which took into account his audience's language, culture, and history. God's revelation of himself was contextualized in Jesus. It was so contextualized, in fact, that many never even recognized that Jesus had come from God. *Jesus so mirrored the culture of ancient Israel that it was difficult for many to believe that he was actually more than an Israeli, and was indeed the Son of God.*[24]

In a similar way, evangelistic preaching strives to take a form that has the greatest potential to reveal God to a particular audience. It can be dressed in a "flesh" which takes into account an audience's language, history, and culture. It can be contextualized. The question of evangelistic preaching and postmodernism is ultimately a question of incarnation. In what "flesh" should a preacher "dress" the gospel so that God can best reveal himself to a postmodern audience, bring about their conversion, and enfold them into his new family? As I pointed out earlier, one does not compromise the truth of the gospel in order to "dress" the gospel appropriately. One communicates the gospel in the language of the receptor culture and then calls into question the way of understanding embodied by that culture. David Bosch states, "The Christian faith is intrinsically incarnational; therefore, unless the church chooses to remain a foreign entity, it will always enter into the context in which it happens to find itself."[25] He argues, "from the very beginning, the missionary message of the Christian church incarnated itself in the life and world of those who had embraced it."[26] Paul Hiebert calls this "incarnational witness" and advocates it as a strategy by which we allow people to hear the gospel in their "heart language."[27]

Even non-Christian postmoderns understand contextualization. Lou is a twenty-seven-year-old computer specialist. He occasionally attends Highland Street but has not responded to Jesus through baptism. When I talked to him about his growing faith in Jesus, he said, "I think too many churches preach about how to live the Christian life and what Christianity is, but they don't think about the questions people in the audience have that keep them from becoming a Christian. Churches need to tailor their messages to address these issues."

The matter, in principle, is so simple that even non-Christians understand it.

Thus we do not change preaching methods or strategies blindly in an attempt to reach a consumerist culture. We change and adapt with eyes wide open in an attempt to imitate God's own incarnational method of communication. We never anticipate that our work alone is sufficient to draw others to salvation. We trust that if conversion takes place through our preaching, it is solely because of God's work through us. Yet we take seriously that admonition to preach in a way that is "mindful" of our audience, seeking to translate the unchanging gospel into an ever-changing culture.

The remaining question is this: how does one contextualize the gospel to postmoderns? How, as Lou suggested, can we "tailor" our messages to address those issues keeping postmoderns from faith in Christ? The answer to that question is what's missing in much of our preaching. Answering that question will make our lessons more fruitful and more useful to the God who longs to draw all people to him. The next chapters will explore specific ways in which we can incarnate the gospel in a form that can draw postmoderns to faith.

CHAPTER SIX

Preaching Evangelistically to the Uninformed

John is lost.

He's one of the people closest to my heart. And he's lost.

That's why I was so excited when, a couple years ago, he visited the morning worship service in a church near the university he attends. The preacher was an acquaintance of mine. He has a deep passion for evangelistic preaching. I knew that the morning John visited the church, the preacher would preach something that would connect with John. John did not attend church growing up and he could not tell you Genesis from Revelation. But this preacher, I thought, would be able to communicate the gospel effectively to a novice like John.

When I called John to ask him how the worship service went and what the lesson was like, however, he said, "I didn't understand a thing the preacher said. It was way over my head." John never returned to that church.

Today, John is still lost.

The story illustrates the great difficulty facing evangelistic preachers today. *It's one thing to have a passion for evangelistic preaching. It's an entirely different thing to preach evangelistically in a way that makes sense to postmoderns who are unfamiliar with the Bible and Christianity's worldview.*

I've experienced this first hand. Once when studying the gospel one on one with a university professor named Mike, we came to a basic Christian doctrine: grace. I read Ephesians 2:1–10 aloud to him, where Paul says, more than once, that we are "saved by grace." Mike had never studied the Bible before and had attended church only a handful of times. But he did have a Ph.D. in clinical psychology. Anyone who could make sense of Freud, I thought, could make sense of grace. So I launched into some stock illustrations to illustrate what it means to be saved by grace—the kind of illustrations I would use in a sermon. When I was finished, I was ready for the light bulb to go on in Mike's head and for him to have one of those "Aha!" moments. Instead, he looked quizzically at me and said, "Run that 'grace thing' by me one more time."

While admittedly the parallel to twenty-first century postmoderns is not exact, there is a strikingly similar scene in 1 Corinthians 14. Sunday morning rolls around and the church gathers for worship—but there's all this tongue speaking going on. Tongue speaking is just fine, Paul says—if someone interprets or if you do it in the privacy of your own home (14:6,13). But the problem with spiritual truths communicated in tongues, Paul says, is that no one else in the worship service can understand what's being said (14:2). Not even the most mature Christian in the church can make sense of the message being communicated. Worse, when the non-Christian sitting anxiously near the back hears it, he can't make heads nor tails of it either, and concludes that the church is out of its mind (14:16,23).

As a result, Paul commands the church to speak these spiritual truths not just with their hearts, but also with their minds. He calls them to be "thoughtful" about communicating spiritual truth in a way that "makes sense"—even to non-Christians (14:15). If the Christian speakers in the service will use language which is intelligible even to non-Christians, Paul promises that the non-Christians in the service will be convicted, the secrets of their hearts will be laid bare, and they will fall on their faces proclaiming "God is really among you," meaning they will be converted (14:24–25).

Isn't that exactly what we want for every non-Christian within earshot of our Sunday preaching? It's what I prayed for concerning John. It's what I just knew would happen with Mike that day in my office. Yet too often the opposite happens. *These uninformed postmoderns hear our attempt to communicate spiritual truths and it sounds like a foreign language (14:11).* It sounds like we're speaking in tongues. They don't understand us and they conclude that we are out of our minds.

How then do we preach evangelistically in a way that "makes sense" to those who have never cracked a Bible? That is one of the greatest challenges of postmodernity.

Evangelistic preaching can address this challenge in at least two ways:

- In general, by using vocabulary, illustrations, and images that do not assume prior knowledge of the biblical story and the gospel
- Specifically, by preaching messages that tutor them in the basics of the gospel and of the biblical story

Vocabulary, Illustrations, and Images

Ronald Allen suggests that preachers adopt a teaching mode rather than just a preaching mode in postmodernity. In fact, he prefers to call the sermon in postmodern times the "teaching sermon."[1] We cannot assume that postmoderns know what we mean when we use words such as *gospel, redemption,* or even *church.* The sermon must teach them.

For instance, I was in a church on a Sunday morning recently when the preacher wanted to quickly refer to a biblical story to illustrate one of his points. He said, "Now, we're all familiar with the story of Jonah . . ." He did not re-tell the story of Jonah. He simply referred to it in passing as a way of illustrating another point. This was a large church and I'm certain there must have been some in the audience who were non-Christians. I knew the story of Jonah. I could see how it illustrated his point. But any postmodern non-Christians in the audience did not know the story. He had just lost them—because he hadn't taken the time to understand them. They came to the sermon ignorant of most biblical stories. Instead, the preacher should have taken a few moments to re-tell the story of Jonah so that he could have continued connecting with his uninformed postmodern listeners.

Try this exercise: go through your last four Sunday morning lessons and circle every biblical word or concept you used which you did not stop to define. Circle all those "churchy" words you spoke, assuming the audience understood them. Mark places where you briefly referred to a biblical story and said, "Now, we all know the story of…" and then moved on to another point.

Now, consider what a five-year-old would have understood from your lesson. That may be exactly what an adult postmodern listener may have understood. Not because he has the IQ of a five-year-old, but because his knowledge of the Bible is similar to a five-year-old's (or worse, considering the fact that my five-year-old has been taught Scripture for her entire life). Or consider what those in a foreign country would have understood if you had preached that lesson in a mission church and it was interpreted into their language as you spoke. That's exactly what an uninformed postmodern listener would have understood.

I'm not suggesting we "dumb down" our preaching. And I'm not suggesting that we jettison all religious words or concepts. In spite of arguments to the contrary,[2] postmoderns' ignorance of Christianity does not necessitate that Christian words like *sin* and *reconciliation* be replaced with contemporary equivalents such as "mistake" or "reunion." Traditional Christian words and doctrines can retain their presence in the evangelistic sermon despite postmoderns' ignorance of them.

Baseball does not change its language of "fouls," "fly balls," and "strike zone" simply because a person is ignorant of their meaning. It keeps the language, while, at the same time, trying to educate newcomers to the game about the meaning and purpose of the language. Evangelistic preaching can continue to use biblical vocabulary.[3] What it cannot continue to do, however, is use that vocabulary without instruction as to its meaning. Preachers can use the word *sin*, but they must define the word in images from the world of the postmodern. Preachers can use the word *atonement*, but they must take time to illustrate the word's meaning in ways that a novice can understand.

Thus, despite the fact that some evangelistic preaching should be inductive and experiential in nature (as we will see in a later chapter), some of it will also need to be deductive and instructional. There is a place for teaching while preaching to postmoderns.

Tutoring in the Basics of the Gospel and the Biblical Story

Vocabulary, illustrations and images, however, are simply a smaller piece of the larger issue of tutoring postmoderns in the biblical worldview. Postmodernity necessitates that preachers start farther back in the biblical worldview and biblical story than in previous generations.[4] In modern times, it may have been possible to start preaching with the story of Jesus, assuming that people already accepted the idea of a transcendent yet personal Creator who led Israel out of Egypt and promised them a Messiah. At least if the person did not already hold to that belief, it was not too inconsistent with beliefs and a worldview he did already hold. The same is not true today. Postmoderns come to our evangelistic preaching not only ignorant of the biblical worldview, but possessing worldviews that are often radically different than the biblical one. Their concept of God is more likely to reflect Eastern influences rather than biblical ones. They are more likely to believe in a pantheistic type of god who is in all things rather than the biblical God. Their views of morality will be pluralistic rather than absolute.

Given this, it may be difficult for postmoderns to understand the story of Jesus without some larger framework in which to view it. D. A. Carson states, "You cannot make heads or tails of the real Jesus unless you have categories for the personal/transcendent God of the Bible; the nature of human beings made in the image of God; the sheer odium of rebellion against him; the curse that our rebellion has attracted; the spiritual, personal, familial, and social effects of our transgression; the nature of salvation; the holiness and wrath and love of God…one cannot make sense of the Bible's portrayal of Jesus without such blocks in place."[5]

While the situation may not be as drastic as Carson paints (one could certainly conceive of a postmodern coming to faith in Jesus without intimate knowledge of the biblical worldview), conversion to Christ will be easier for the postmodern who is first given this broader context in which to make his or her decision for Christ.

Paul utilized this strategy when preaching to people less informed about the Bible's plot line.[6] For instance, in Acts 13:16–41, Paul preaches evangelistically to Jews, proselytes, and Godfearers in a synagogue in Pisidian Antioch. Most, if not all, of Paul's listeners in this synagogue were already steeped in the biblical text and worldview. Thus Paul narrates some Old Testament history and quotes Scripture to prove that Jesus is the promised Messiah.

In Acts 17:16–34, however, Paul preaches to an entirely different audience, one full of people who, like postmoderns, were ignorant of anything like Old Testament history, Scriptures, and the biblical worldview. The philosophers and leaders of Athens were much farther behind in their understanding of the Bible than the listeners in Acts 13. Thus rather than starting with Old Testament history, Paul begins with the nature of God and the nature of humanity. Here are nine parts of the framework Paul establishes in his sermon, most of which he took for granted in Pisidian Antioch and never had to explicitly state.

Paul establishes, in contrast to the prevailing notion of pantheism, that God is the creator of "the world and everything in it" (17:24). God is distinct from the world and humans are accountable to him as their creator.

Contrary to the cultural assumption that gods rule only over a particular domain (e.g., Neptune and the sea), Paul states that God "is Lord of heaven and earth, does not live in shrines made by hands" (17:24).

Contrary to the polytheistic notion of gods who are limited and who have needs, God is not "served by human hands, as though he needed anything" (17:25). God is self-existent and utterly independent from us.

Paul establishes that we *are* completely dependent upon God: "he himself gives to all mortals life and breath and all things" (17:25).

Paul moves from discussing the nature of God to the nature of humanity. In contradiction to current thinking which may have believed that different ethnic groups came into being in different ways (and thus had different levels of worth and value in respect to each other), Paul asserts that all nations descended from one human (17:26). The bad news and good news of the Gospel therefore apply to all nations and races, not just one.

Paul states that God created all humans to reach out and find him (17:27), implying that many have not reached out and found him. This is the first hint in Paul's speech concerning "sin."

Paul does want to leave the impression that he is preaching a deistic message. Thus he states that God "is not far from each one of us" (17:27). God is not only transcendent; he is immanent. Paul acknowledges that even some "modern" thinkers have rightly reached this conclusion (17:28).

All of the above, therefore, makes the idolatry of Athens highly offensive to God. The Athenians stand in need of repentance (17:29–30).

Paul closes by introducing the biblical notion of time. Many Greeks had a circular notion of time. Paul paints time as linear and warns them that time is drawing to an end and that the time to repent is now (17:31).

Only after establishing this biblical worldview does Paul finally speak something that sounds like the gospel (17:31). Paul starts at Genesis (or before) and retells the whole of biblical narrative to get to the gospel.

The point is that in preaching to postmoderns who are uninformed about Bible and gospel basics, evangelistic preaching will need to imitate Paul's strategy. We will need to introduce postmoderns to the larger biblical narrative and worldview before we introduce them to Jesus. This helps explain why I made such poor progress with Mike when it came to understanding grace. He had no concept of the transcendence and holiness of God, which would demand death for sin, or of the nearness, and intimacy of God, which would provide a substitute for this death sentence. Evangelistic preaching in postmodernity may need to start with Genesis more often than with Matthew.

Below are four ways this could be approached.

Approach One: Campus Crusade

One method is illustrated by Campus Crusade. While the tool described below is used for personal evangelism, it is also highly instructive for evangelistic preaching.[7] Campus Crusade is often known for their use of the Four Spiritual Laws in evangelistic work.

This presentation essentially begins with the gospels and assumes the listener is familiar with the biblical worldview. They began to suspect, however, that such a presentation was ill suited for postmoderns who know nothing of the gospel or the Bible. Thus, they recently devised a new tool that starts much further back in the biblical narrative and attempts to build a biblical worldview before presenting the gospel. Called "Life@Large," the tool divides the biblical story into seven sections using themes (like intimacy, betrayal, reunion), which would touch a chord with postmoderns. These seven sections could be a very fruitful sermon series designed to teach postmoderns the basics of scripture in a compelling way:

- *God Creates—Intimacy* This section establishes that God made us and desires to live in unhindered intimacy with us.
- *God is Abandoned—Betrayal* This section describes how humanity turned from God and how alienation has replaced intimacy with God. It describes sin not only in its affect on our relationship with God, but in its affect on human relationships and even the environment.
- *God Promises—Anticipation* Here the presentation states that even though he was betrayed, our creator did not abandon us. Instead, he promised to send someone who would restore our relationship with him and to each other.

- *God Appears—Pursuit* This promised one appeared, and he was God himself. As the Son of God, Jesus revealed what God is like and what life was meant to be. He confronted oppression and embraced both the powerless and the privileged.
- *God Provides—Sacrifice* This section describes the death and resurrection of Jesus as the means by which relationship with God is restored.
- *God Calls—Invitation* Through Jesus, God now calls to each of us and invites all humanity to enjoy intimacy with God.
- *God Restores—Reunion* This section describes how all those who follow Jesus will together enjoy God for all eternity and experience life without death, sorrow, or pain.

Approach Two: Things That Matter

Another slightly more didactic approach can be found in the Institute of Christian Studies' small book *Things That Matter*.[8] The original version was written in 1991 to introduce the Bible and Christian faith to a Russian audience that was largely uninformed about the Bible and the Christian faith. Its mission setting thus lends itself well to the American mission setting of postmodernity. The book's eight chapters present helpful material for an eight part sermon series to take postmoderns through the biblical story:

- "The Mystery of Life" This chapter raises the question "What is the purpose of life?" and urges readers to seek purpose in life through a relationship with God.
- "God the Creator" This chapter focuses on what Genesis 1–3 teach about the nature of God, humans, and creation.
- "The Story of the Old Testament" With very broad strokes, this chapter paints the Old Testament's storyline, emphasizing God's desire for relationship with humanity.
- "Jesus the Christ" This chapter surveys the four gospels and explains the significance of the life, death, and resurrection of Jesus.
- "The Importance of the Church" Here, the authors debunk myths about church and present the purpose of and community available in church.
- "Why So Many Churches?" Especially for the uninformed, this issue can be troubling. This chapter gives a brief presentation of church history from the early church through modern times.

- "The Christian Life" This chapter discusses Christianity as a life of faith, hope, and love lived in response to what God has done for us through Jesus.
- "Beginning the Journey" This chapter explains how to become a Christian.

Approach Three: Rick Warren

In preaching to postmoderns in California, Rick Warren has developed a class that covers thirteen topics in an attempt to present basic doctrine to seekers and converts. These could be used as a sermon series as well.[9] They include the following:

- *God*—God is bigger and better than I can imagine.
- *Jesus*—Jesus is God showing himself to us.
- *Holy Spirit*—God lives in and through me now.
- *Revelation*—The Bible is God's inerrant guidebook for life.
- *Creation*—Nothing "just happened." God created it all.
- *Salvation*—Grace is the only way to have a relationship with God.
- *Sanctification*—God's will is for us to grow in Christlikeness.
- *Good and Evil*—God has allowed evil to provide a choice. God can bring good even out of evil events.
- *The Afterlife*—Death is not the end but the beginning. Heaven and hell are real places.
- *The Church*—The only true world "superpower" is the church. It will last forever.
- *Prayer*—Prayer can do anything God can do.
- *Second Coming*—Jesus is coming again to judge the world and gather his children.

Clearly there are multiple ways to tutor postmoderns in the basics of the gospel and the Bible. These examples simply point to a few of those ways. I've included them primarily because they represent the work of people and organizations on the front line, those dealing directly with postmodern non-Christians and attempting to educate them about the Christian faith. There are certainly more scholarly and comprehensive approaches than these. These, however, represent the best efforts of some of those making the greatest impact on the front line.

I should point out, however, that series like these are not the end-all of evangelistic preaching. They are part of the much larger fabric of evangelistic preaching which includes topics and issues discussed in the next few chapters. A series like this might not even be the first series you try in order to attract and convert postmoderns. Pragmatic issues may be more likely to draw a crowd than these worldview issues. At some point near the beginning, however, evangelistic preaching will undertake this critical task of tutoring postmoderns in scriptural basics in as creative and engaging a way as possible.

CHAPTER SEVEN

Preaching Evangelistically to the Spiritually Interested

In 1968, American sociologist Peter Berger told the *New York Times* that by "the 21st century, religious believers are likely to be found only in small sects, huddled together to resist a worldwide secular culture."[1] Berger could not have been more wrong. While modernism did cut away at the landscape of religious believers, postmodernism has vastly increased that same landscape. Today there is an astounding resurgence of interest in matters religious and spiritual.

The *World Christian Encyclopedia* boasts 1,600 pages chronicling this interest. *According to the authors, there are 9,900 distinct religions across the world. Two to three new religions are created every day.* Even religions once completely unfamiliar to most across the world are now bulging with adherents. For instance, in seventy countries there are eight million members of the Ahmadis, a messianic Muslim sect. Fifty countries host the three million members of Cao Dai, a religion that combines teachings of Confucianism, Taoism, and Buddhism. Almost two million Zoroastrians live in Iran.[2]

With 9,900 religions to choose from today, you might say that Berger's prediction should have been just the opposite. It's not those *interested* in spiritual issues who are huddled together in small sects to resist a worldwide culture inhospitable to them. It's those *not interested* in spiritual matters who are now found only in small sects and huddled together.

But just because non-Christians are increasingly interested in spiritual issues does not mean they are necessarily interested in Christian spiritual issues. There is no better postmodern example of this than the television show *Oprah*. In 2002, Oprah Winfrey reached twenty-two million viewers in one hundred and twelve countries with her television talk show. Its success is surprising for some, given its overt spiritual tone. As one article described it, the show "creates community, provides information, and encourages people to evaluate and improve their lives."[3] *Oprah* consistently features an inward focus and challenges viewers to apply in their lives the lessons learned on the show. She urges viewers to have faith in a higher power. In one November 2001 show, she stated, "Today, whatever it is you believe most deeply, now is the time to embrace it."[4] Oprah preaches a "gospel" that promises the power to change people's lives and deliver them from negative thinking, relationship problems, and past emotional wounds. *Christianity Today* called Oprah "one of the most influential spiritual leaders in America."[5]

In fact she is so influential as a spiritual leader that when New York City organized a prayer service in Yankee Stadium just twelve days after the September 11, 2001 attack on the World Trade Center towers, Oprah was picked to host it. She closed with this benediction, "May we all leave this place and not let one single life have passed in vain. May we leave this place determined to now use every moment that we yet live to turn up the volume in our own lives, to create deeper meaning, to know what really matters."[6]

In spite of this prominent spiritual focus, Oprah promotes a spirituality vastly different from Christianity. Hers is a pluralistic faith in which many paths lead to God. In addition, Oprah herself has not attended her Christian church since 1995.[7] She is one of the most influential spiritual leaders in America. Yet she has not attended a Christian church in close to a decade.

How then do we preach to an audience increasingly interested in spirituality but not necessarily Christianity?

I believe this is best done by focusing on the areas where postmodern spirituality and biblical spirituality overlap. There is much in postmodern spirituality that is directly at odds with and outside the sphere of biblical spirituality. At the heart of both types of spirituality, however, is this: a desire to encounter and experience the presence of God.

I believe that what postmoderns desire—through their prayer, through their exploration of other religions, through their deep interest in the supernatural—is an encounter with and experience of Something or Someone higher than themselves. In short, they want to encounter God. Their understanding of God may be somewhat different than ours, but their desire is the same. They want to encounter God. That is the hunger that drives their spirituality.

And that encounter is also at the heart of biblical spirituality. The Christian faith affirms that God is present in the now, that this presence can be experienced in an intimate way, and that this experience changes one's life. It liberates people from destructive and unfulfilling ways of behaving and thinking. It transforms one's relationship with nature and humanity. It makes sense of life and gives meaning and purpose to it. And the Christian faith affirms that this presence can be an on going and daily experience, not just a one time experience. While Christianity is about many things, it is supremely about this one thing: encountering the one true God through his son Jesus Christ.

Two recent authors explain this view of biblical spirituality. First, Bonnie Thurston writes, "Spirituality was what the early Christians did to put into practice what they believed. It was what they did to respond to a world *filled with the presence of God and the risen Christ.*"[8] Thurston suggests that biblical spirituality is the awareness of the presence of God and Christ and the response we make to that presence in our daily lives and relationships.

Second, Stanley Saunders suggests that this issue lies at the heart of the Gospel of Matthew. He states that Matthew frames his gospel in 1:23 and 28:20 with the identification of Jesus as Emmanuel… God is with us." The gospel begins with the affirmation that Jesus is Emmanuel (God with us) and ends with the promise that he will be with us always, to the end of the age. Everything in between those two verses is an "extended illustration" of what it means for Jesus to be "God with us." Saunders summarizes by saying that Matthew "is showing those who follow Jesus what it is like to live in the presence of God…"[9]

And this presence of God, Saunders argues, forces us to reinterpret life and relationships. God is present and supplies each day what is needed (Matt. 6:25–33). Therefore there is "no need for social and economic practices based on the assumption of scarcity (14:13–21; 15:32–39; 19:16–30)."[10] God is present. Therefore reconciliation with enemies is possible (5:38–48), as is limitless forgiveness of others (18:21–22).[11]

In a similar way, Ephesians pictures its readers as already raised up with Christ in the heavenly places (2:5–6). It imagines Christians already living in the heavenly places in the presence of Christ and of God. This presence of God then reinterprets the way we live our lives, as Paul spells out in chapters four through six. Life in the presence of God reorients not only one's relations to oneself, but to employer, boss, spouse, child, etc.[12]

My point is simple: biblical spirituality refers to life lived in awareness of and in response to the presence of God. Biblical spirituality is the experience of God on a daily basis and the transforming affect that experience has on a person. This broad definition overlaps what lies at the center of postmodern spirituality. It provides a biblical point of contact between the Christian message and the spiritual hunger of postmoderns.

What implication does this have for preaching? *Preaching can best reach spiritual postmoderns by doing two things.*

First, it must facilitate for postmodern listeners an encounter with God. The sermon itself must strive to bring listeners to the point where they actually experience God through the sermon.

Second, preaching must reveal to listeners the way to experience, on a daily basis, this presence. It must provide tools and perspectives that allow postmoderns, once they've left the worship service on Sunday, to continue to experience God on Monday.

Preaching must not simply be the dissemination of information. It must be the revelation of God himself, who transforms (and not just informs) those who hear. The goal is for the postmodern worshiper to "bow down before God and worship him, declaring, 'God is really among you!'" (1 Cor. 14:25).

In addition, preaching must not simply reveal a code of ethics and morality to be lived out during the week, a sort of "seven keys to effective living." Preaching falls short both theologically and missionally if all it does is equip postmoderns to have better marriages or more fulfilling careers. It must ultimately seek to equip postmoderns to encounter God on a daily basis and teach them how such encounters result in an outward life of simplicity, sincerity, and service.

Finally, the worship of which the sermon is a part can partner with the sermon in helping to create an encounter between listener and God himself.

The rest of this chapter will explore these three issues: 1) how the preaching event can facilitate an encounter with the ever present God, 2) how the worship around the preaching event can facilitate this encounter, and 3) how preaching can equip listeners to experience God's presence on a daily basis in a way that inwardly renews one's heart and mind and then flows forth outwardly in a life of simplicity and service to others.

Preaching That Facilitates an Encounter with God

There are three considerations when it comes to preaching that facilitates an encounter with God. *First, preaching needs to be primarily theocentric.*[13]

A compass and its arrow are good images to use for thinking about preaching. Just as there are four points on the compass (north, south, east, west), so there are four points on the preaching compass. Preaching tends to head in one of these four directions: bibliocentric, anthropocentric, factocentric, or theocentric. Preaching that has the most potential to engage spiritually interested postmoderns is preaching which points north, that is, theocentric.

Bibliocentric preaching primarily seeks to answer this question: What does this text mean? It focuses on the text. Bibliocentric preaching provides an insightful and informative analysis of the literary and historical contexts of scripture. It explores the words and structure of the text. Bibliocentric preaching is like a lab technician skillfully slicing open the text on the table and explaining each muscle, organ, and tissue. Listeners walk away with a richer and fuller understanding of the text's meaning.

Obviously, this kind of preaching is a part of most sermons. Preaching must always be based in the text and must always help listeners understand that text. The drawback with preaching that centers on bibliocentricity, however, is that it treats scripture as an end to itself, instead of the means to an end. *It reveals the text, but not the God of the text.* People walk away understanding the Word but not the One who is the Word.

Anthropocentric preaching (after *anthropos*—Greek for "man") primarily seeks to answer this question: "What does this text call me to do?" It explores the demands the text places on us. Anthropocentric preaching is like a counselor exploring the depths of our lives and revealing dysfunction and calling for change. Listeners walk away with a convicting sense that something in their lives must change, and a plan for enacting that change. This type of preaching focuses on what is often called the "imperative."

Ephesians chapters four through six illustrate this. Here, we find the imperative of the letter to the Ephesians: be humble (4:2); do not let the sun go down on your anger (4:26); live a life of love

(5:2); submit to one another (5:21); children, obey your parents (6:1); slaves, obey your masters (6:5); pray in the Spirit (6:18). Anthropocentric preaching emphasizes these imperatives.

Obviously, most preaching must include some element of anthropocentricity. The gospel receives us just as we are; yet it seeks to make us just as He is. It calls us to walk in His footsteps. *The problem with preaching that is solely anthropocentric, however, is that it divorces human response from divine initiative. It bifurcates the imperative (what we do) from the indicative (what God has done).* This type of preaching, besides not connecting with the postmodern hunger for the spiritual, ultimately suggests a kind of hopeless legalism: "Here's what I must do in order to achieve salvation." Instead of starting with who God is and what God has done for us, it starts with who we are (sinners) and what we must do (repent).

Factocentric preaching is much like bibliocentric preaching. It focuses on a topic (marriage) or a doctrine (baptism) and seeks to answer the question: what is the correct biblical understanding of this fact or topic or doctrine? Rather than laying a single biblical text on the examination table, factocentric preaching lays down a topic or doctrine. Layer after layer is analyzed until the listener achieves a correct biblical understanding of it.

Clearly, there is much in preaching that ought to be factocentric. The problem, however, is one that is by now obvious: it treats the topic or doctrine as an end to itself. The listener walks away with some biblical tools to build a great marriage but not necessarily reflecting on his marriage to God. The listener leaves with an intellectual clarity about baptism but no spiritual passion for the God who empowers baptism.

Theocentric preaching (after *theos*—Greek for "God") focuses instead on God. It primarily seeks to answer the questions: "Who is God?" and "What has God done on our behalf?" *Listeners walk away not having just encountered the text (bibliocentric) or the demands placed on them by the text (anthropocentric). They also walk away having encountered God himself through that text.*

The sermon may include teaching elements concerning the meaning of the text. It may also include a call for listeners to change in some way. Yet these will be the minor notes of the sermon. The major note will be the exploration of God himself. It will focus on what God has done for us before it focuses on what we must do in response. It will center on who God is before it centers on who we are.

Theocentric preaching will follow Paul's strategy in Ephesians. Chapters one through three are the theocentric focus of Paul's "sermon." Paul spends three chapters in the indicative, on what God has done on our behalf. Only after establishing this does he move on to the imperatives of chapters four through six.

Likewise, In Mark 1:15, Mark summarizes Jesus' teaching. It begins with God ("the time is fulfilled, and the kingdom of God has come near"), and only then moves to us ("repent, and believe in the good news"). While postmodern preaching will not ignore the latter, it will emphasize the former. It will seek to give listeners God, which is what they long to have in the first place. Theocentric preaching may have the best potential for reaching postmoderns.

Paul Scott Wilson writes, "The central purpose of preaching is the disclosure of God, an encounter with God through the Word, more than information about God."[14] The purpose of preaching is to facilitate an encounter with God. This purpose is especially important if we seek to take advantage of postmodernity's interest in spirituality. The sermon can provide an encounter with the very One postmoderns say they desire.

This does not mean that we cannot preach on texts or topics other than God. It means that whatever text or topic we are preaching, we strive to tie it ultimately back to God. As we explore the text, we are asking, "What is God doing in the text? What is God doing behind the text? What hope does God offer us in the text? What judgement?" Take, for instance, a sermon from Matt. 7:7–12 and Jesus' teaching on ask, search, knock.

Bibliocentric preaching will merely satisfy itself with exploring the meaning of the words of the text.

Anthropocentric preaching will focus on the commands to ask, search, and knock. We'll leave with a conviction to pray more.

Factocentric preaching will highlight a deeper biblical understanding of the nature of prayer.

Theocentric preaching, however, will recognize that this text is ultimately about God. The motive to ask, search, and knock is found in Jesus' description of God in this text as a Father who knows how to give good gifts. That image of God will be the dominant focus of the sermon. People will walk away with a much fuller appreciation of God as a good Father, and will thus pray more.

Another text from the Sermon on the Mount illustrates. In Matthew 6:25–34, Jesus urges us to not worry about material things and instead to seek first God's kingdom. The verb *worry* is found here more than any other text. The temptation is to do bibliocentric preaching ("Here's what it means to seek first God's kingdom") or anthropocentric preaching ("Jesus is calling you to stop worrying"). But theocentric preaching realizes that Jesus' description of God in this text as the one who provides for the birds and the flowers is the real point of the text. Listeners will walk way amazed at God's care and provision, and therefore seek first his kingdom and stop worrying about other things.

In a spiritually interested climate, this kind of preaching is not only more true to the text and the purpose of Scripture; it is more missional in nature. Postmoderns are interested in spiritual things. Our preaching should strive to meet this interest. It can by more frequently pointing people to God.

A second means by which preaching provides an encounter with God concerns sermon preparation. Many times in preparation, we preachers open the text to be preached and immediately jump to the question: What is God saying to the church/to non-Christians in this text? Translations, commentaries, and personal meditation of the text all seek to answer this one question: What is God saying to my listeners?

But if the preached text is ever to become a window through which the listener meets God, it must first be a window by which the preacher has met God. *Preachers cannot hope to introduce listeners to a God in the text whom they have not already met and done business with through that same text.*

Within the sermon preparation process, the preacher's first concern must be to personally meet God in that word, and only then to help his listeners encounter that same God. He must not first ask: What is God saying to my listeners through this word? He must first ask, "What is God saying to me through this word?" He must be willing to meditate at length on the preaching text asking," What do *I* learn about God here? What is God saying to *me* here? What is it about *my* life that needs this text?"

Another way of putting this is that the preacher must approach sermon preparation as a member of the very community to whom the sermon is addressed. He does not stand outside of that community, as if the Word was sent to them alone. He stands within that community as a fellow recipient of that Word.

Obviously, this means that sermon preparation cannot begin Friday or Saturday night. The preacher must provide a generous amount of time for contemplation, journaling, and prayer with the sole purpose of hearing in that text a word of God to him.

One way of achieving this is through the method of *lectio divina* described below. The preacher will best hear God's word to the church and to the non-Christian postmodern listeners only after he has first heard God's word to himself through the text to be preached. He and his sermon will be best used to enable listeners to meet God if he has first met God through that same text. The sermon preparation should follow this general sequence: discerning God's word for self; discerning God's word for the listeners.

A third means by which preaching can facilitate an encounter with God is the use of prayer as part of the preaching event. An ancient and widely accepted practice for engaging the biblical text is called *lectio divina*. It is a four-fold process by which an individual ingests and internalizes some portion of Scripture. It begins with reflective and slow paced reading of the text. It moves to meditation upon the text: Why is this a word for me? What is it about my life that needs this word? How is God catching my attention here? This is followed by prayer—the direct cry of our hearts to God based upon what we have heard in his word. The cycle ends with a kind of silent prayer in which we rest quietly in the presence of God.

The purpose of *lectio divina* was not to merely gain information from a text, but to encounter God in that text. It enables an individual to hear God's address in the text and to respond directly to God concerning that address.[15]

While *lectio divina* was intended primarily as a model by which an individual encounters God through a text, it also suggests ways in which a community may encounter God through a text. Of particular interest is the aspect of prayer. Half of the four-fold process involves prayer. Once listeners have heard God's address to them in the text, they are given opportunity to address God in prayer.

Yet this kind of prayerful response is often missing in the preaching event. Clearly there are prayers that normally surround the preaching event. During a worship service, worshipers often address God in prayer concerning pastoral needs of the congregation or on behalf of national or local concerns. They may even have opportunities to respond prayerfully to God in response to the words sung in worship. A preacher might even begin his lesson with prayer, but it is usually to request that God lead him as he preaches. Rarely do preachers provide listeners an opportunity to respond in prayer to what God has said to them through the text that is being preached.

As we seek to allow God to encounter postmodern listeners through our preaching, perhaps we should seek to allow them to also encounter God through prayer that responds to that preaching. This kind of prayerful encounter would be best led by the preacher, since he is the one most experienced with the text and with God's address to us through it.

While it might come at any point in a sermon, I think it works best at the conclusion of the sermon. At sermon's end, the preacher could lead the listeners through a time of spoken prayer in which he cries out in hurt if the word has touched our pain; in confession if the word has revealed our sin; in thanksgiving if the word has evoked gratitude; or in praise if the word has sparked our joy.[16] This might be followed by a time of silent prayer in which listeners quietly make their own response to God based on his word to them through the sermon and in which they are encouraged to just rest in God's presence.

You might also begin your sermon with public prayer, not to pray for yourself, but to ask God to make himself known to the listeners through the text and sermon that is about to follow. This type of public praying imitates the *lectio divina* method of engaging the text with the goal of encountering God.

Our urban ministers in Memphis practice what they call "prayer evangelism." They go throughout the neighborhood engaging people in conversation. Rather than simply opening up the Bible or asking if they want a Bible study, these urban ministers pray with the individual. As prayer needs are raised up to God, discussion about Scripture and God naturally flows afterwards. People are seeking spiritual growth and development. By making prayer more a part of the preaching/teaching event, we connect more meaningfully with the innate spiritual desire of postmoderns.

The GREs of Worship

As I'll flesh out in subsequent chapters, the best worship for connecting with postmoderns is GRE worship. When I applied to graduate school, I was required to take the GRE—the Graduate Record Exam. It was a series of items that determined if I was fit for graduate school. In the same way, there is a GRE for postmodern worship, a series of items which help make worship fit for reaching postmoderns. The *G* in GRE stands for *God-encountering*. We have the best potential for reaching postmoderns if our worship is God-encountering. The other two letters in GRE will be explored in future chapters.

How do we make worship God-encountering? How do we best plan worship so that listeners not only encounter God in the preaching, but in the worship itself? Below are six items critical to having God-encountering worship.

Vertical Songs—While songs in particular should follow the biblical direction to teach and admonish one another (Col. 3:16), they should focus more on making music in the heart to the Lord

(Eph. 5:19–20). *The vertical relationship between worshiper and God should be stressed in the songs instead of just the horizontal relationships between worshipers.* Songs might move from those *about* God and Christ to those directed *to* God and Christ; from singing of God/Christ in the third person ("there is a God, He is alive") to singing about God/Christ in the first person ("you are beautiful beyond description…"). Congregational songs sung to God or about God help worshipers encounter God in meaningful ways.

Seasons of Prayer—Prayer is one of the primary ways people encounter God. Besides the prayer time directly tied to the preaching mentioned above, prayer times can be planned throughout the service in which worshipers are led to speak in prayer to God in praise or lament. These "seasons of prayer" could follow or precede certain songs or groups of songs.

Silence and Meditation—Still and quiet moments are often opportunities for personal encounter with God. Instead of filling each moment in the service with sound, short periods of silence and meditation can be provided where worshipers are encouraged to reflect upon, for instance, the words of a song just sung, the words of a scripture just read, the sermon just preached, or upon some other issue.

Dramatic Reading—the word of God is one of the most powerful agents by which people experience God. God still speaks through his word. His word is living and active (Heb. 4:12; 1 Thess. 2:13). Thus, at some point in the worship service, someone could recite a portion of scripture from memory (or simply read it) in a dramatic fashion. Several of the psalms lend themselves to this type of dramatic reading, as do portions of the epistles (e.g., Rom. 8), and sections from the gospels concerning the crucifixion of Jesus. I was recently at a concert when the musician came to the front of the stage and quoted from memory Psalm 139 in dramatic fashion. It was one of the most riveting moments in the concert.

Another twist on this, which concerns the sermon itself, is to find a small line of scripture and to repeat it as a refrain throughout the sermon. This helps plant the word deep in the mind of the listener and creates greater potential for that word to create an encounter between listener and God. For instance, I recently preached from Psalm 9 about the experience of being forgotten by God. Multiple times throughout the sermon I quoted words and phrases such as 9:18: "the needy shall not always be forgotten" and 9:12: "for he who avenges blood is mindful of them." Repeating short lines from God's word repeatedly through a sermon can be helpful in creating a potential encounter.

Special Music—a well-rehearsed soloist or chorus singing a song to God or about God while worshipers listen can aid worshipers in experiencing the presence of God. While congregational singing may be the norm, this type of special music can be incorporated regularly into the worship service. Who of us can't point to a song we heard sung by someone else which moved us to tears, or excited us to action, or touched something deep within us? Special music, done well by a soloist or chorus, can be a powerful tool in God's hand to create a divine encounter.

Lord's Supper—Communion should be given as prominent a place in the worship service as singing and preaching, if not more prominent. Much more than simply being a remembrance of a Lord who once drew near but is now seated at God's right hand, communion is a unique sacrament in which our Lord once again draws near in intimate fellowship with us? We participate in a spiritual reality, in a communion with Christ, during this sacrament (1 Cor. 10:14–22). Paul literally says communion is a "koinonia," a fellowship, with Christ (1 Cor. 10:16). If there is a time when Christ is most present in a worship service, perhaps it is when the bread and wine are distributed and he joins us at this table of thanksgiving.

Clearly those already in Christ can only truly experience this intimate fellowship. But couldn't this presence of Christ in communion, if we truly sought it, anticipated it, and planned for it, be of such magnitude, that even non-Christians would taste the morsels of his presence while we eat the feast?

In some churches, communion has lost this anticipatory sense of the presence of Christ. It has become either a routine tradition robbed of freshness by the same thoughtless prayers and words spoken over it Sunday after Sunday, or it has tended to focus only on the past presence of Christ in his first century body and blood, and ignored the present presence of Christ as the bread and wine are passed. Anything which could be done to elevate the prominence of communion, infuse it with freshness, rescue it from tired and lifeless routine, and change its focus from past remembrance of Christ to present *koinonia* with Christ would be invaluable in creating worship in which people truly encounter God. More will be said later concerning communion and the GREs of postmodern worship.

Preaching That Equips Listeners to Experience God Daily

Postmoderns value spirituality. And while the spirituality they seek is different in certain ways from biblical spirituality, there is still an overlap between the two. I've suggested that the overlap is this: the presence of God. Postmoderns desire to experience the presence of God. Christianity is the response of those who have come to experience the presence of God in Jesus Christ.

One way to connect with this postmodern characteristic in evangelistic preaching is to use the preaching event itself to facilitate an encounter between listener and God. That connection point concerns *how* we preach. A second connection point concerns *what* we preach. While our preaching will not need to give a steady diet of the following, there is one issue of content, which could be approached as part of a larger effort to reach lost postmoderns.

Preachers can preach lessons and/or series that equip and inspire listeners to pursue the presence of God through the traditional spiritual disciplines. For centuries, Christian leaders have taught that the transforming presence of God is experienced through a collection of daily practices or disciplines. These disciplines do not earn you special favor from God. They merely open your heart, mind, and soul to God and his presence. Neither do these disciplines work like a magic formula that guarantees any practitioner a powerful sense of the presence of God. The state of your heart is just as important as your performance of these disciplines. In addition, these spiritual disciplines have been taught exclusively to Christians, not to non-Christians. Given the fact that only Christians, and not non-Christians, have the Spirit of Christ within them, this makes sense. Christians alone have the potential for fully experiencing God's presence on a daily basis through the spiritual disciplines.

Still, non-Christians can also experience the presence of God to a certain degree through the disciplines. It was the spiritual disciplines of regular prayer and giving to the poor that led a non-Christian named Cornelius to experience a vision from God in which he gained spiritual insight and which led him to faith in Christ (Acts 10). It was the spiritual discipline of Scripture meditation that led a non-Christian Ethiopian eunuch to his life-changing discussion with Philip, and his baptism in that roadside water (Acts 8:26–38).

These brief examples make it clear that God reveals himself to and arranges life-altering events even for non-Christians who seek him through the disciplines.

Thus a fruitful series of lessons could be preached which explain the specific disciplines, equip listeners to practice them, and inspire them to do just that in an effort to experience the daily presence of God. Richard Foster's book *Celebration of Discipline*,

Marjorie Thompson's book *Soul Feast*, and John Ortberg's book *The Life You've Always Wanted* and video *An Ordinary Day with Jesus* provide practical and inspiring ways for preaching the disciplines. A series on the spiritual disciplines, however, has the potential to become overly anthropocentric. It may end up focusing solely on what we do to experience God rather than on the grace by which God allows himself to be experienced in the first place, or the God who we desire to experience. For this reason, it may be good for the first part in this series to focus exclusively on God and the grace of his transforming presence and on his desire to be known by all. Each succeeding lesson would try to maintain this focus while explaining each discipline.

Also, the series would hopefully reveal ways in which these disciplines and experience of God's presence have the potential to transform relationships and affect life Monday through Sunday. Touching on the pragmatism of postmoderns, the series would hope to show how these disciplines lead not only to an intimate encounter with God on a daily basis, but how that intimate encounter affects our character and integrity and thus brings about positive changes in our daily lives.

A series that includes all of the spiritual disciplines is, of course, only one way to approach the issue of equipping listeners to experience God's presence on a daily basis. A series could simply take up one of the disciplines, such as prayer, and explore that discipline in depth. There is great interest in prayer among postmoderns. A series on the Lord's Prayer or on prayer in general would be popular among postmoderns. A series could take up the issue of solitude or simplicity in a similar way. The main idea is simply to preach in ways that equip listeners to draw near to God on a daily basis and to experience the inward transformation such an encounter brings.

Looking for God

Larry is one of the most spiritual men I know. He volunteers time regularly at a local medical clinic for the poor. He places a high priority on his extended and nuclear family relationships. He and his wife pray together daily. He attends Sunday morning services at Highland about three of four Sundays per month, and has for almost two years.

But Larry is not a Christian. Still, he is living a spiritual life which I wish some of Highland's Christians would live up to. Once, after meeting together in my office to talk about a project he was helping me with, I moved to indicate the meeting was over and started to stand to open my office door. "Just a minute," Larry said. "Could we pray?" He did not have some huge crisis which he had not told me about and which he now wanted to confess and pray about. He simply wanted to pray. He simply wanted to talk to God. The very thing the preacher should have initiated, the non-Christian did.

Larry is representative of many in postmodernity. Deeply interested in spiritual matters. Prayerful. Service oriented. And while they may have obstacles standing in the way concerning their conversion to Christ (Larry's is pluralism), spirituality is not one of them. Evangelistic preaching can take advantage of this. It should seek to facilitate an encounter between God and these spiritually minded listeners during the preaching event itself. And it should strive to equip listeners like Lloyd to encounter God on a daily basis, in a way that will lead them, as it did for Cornelius and the Ethiopian eunuch, to faith in Christ.

CHAPTER EIGHT

Preaching Evangelistically to the Anti-institutional and Relational

After one of our Sunday worship services I introduced myself to Barb.

"How long have you been around Highland?" I asked (I ask that question on Sundays of anyone whose name I'm not sure of—sometimes they turn out to be members!).

"This is my first time here," she said.

"How did you hear about Highland?" I asked.

"I was at the wedding you conducted here last week for Sherri and Larry (a Highland member and an attendee, respectively)." Barb was a friend of the groom, liked the wedding ceremony, was spiritually searching, and decided to "check us out."

That was almost a year and a half ago. Since that day, the newly married couple celebrated their first anniversary and gave birth to a healthy son. And Barb recently committed her life to Jesus through baptism. Barb's conversion process is typical of many postmoderns—especially those with two qualities: a hostility toward the church, yet a hunger for community and relationships.

Let me give you some more details: shortly after Barb started coming to Highland following her friend's wedding, I asked if she would be interested in studying the Bible. She said thanks, but no. Several months later, I asked again. Same response: thanks, but no. I was beginning to think that maybe Barb wasn't really that interested in becoming a Christian.

But then a few weeks ago, after one of our Sunday services, she approached me. "What does one do to become a member of this church?" she asked. We set up an appointment to meet later that week, met twice over the next two weeks, studied some scripture together, and she decided to become a Christian and a member of Highland.

In many ways, this represents the typical conversion process of postmoderns.

From King First to Kingdom First

Moderns, with their slightly more favorable outlook on church tended to convert first to the Christian message, and then to the Christian community. With moderns, you could conduct an evangelistic series of meetings or door knocking campaign and baptize some who had no prior connection to the church. Then you simply "plugged them into" the Christian community and helped them become active members of a church. The initial obstacle one had to overcome in the conversion process had to do with the message, not with the church. Once persuaded of the truth of the message, they could easily become part of the church.

Postmoderns, on the other hand, with their much more pessimistic outlook on church often must wrestle first with the Christian *community* and then with the Christian *message*. *Their first hurdle is not accepting the validity of the gospel's message, but embracing relations with the gospel's people.*

Like Barb, they may spend as long as a year investigating those people and their community through small groups, Sunday school, worship services, and one-on-one relationships. Once satisfied that the community is not full of hypocrites, and having experienced the benefits of that community firsthand (their faith being strengthened through its teaching; their lives being enriched through participation in its ministries to the poor; etc.), they are ready then to look more seriously at the Christian message.

By this point, if the congregation has acted as a genuine spiritual community to the person, she is often such a "satisfied customer" of church, that conversion to message conveyed by the church comes relatively quickly. Whatever it takes for her to become part of that community in a formal and committed way, she is ready to do.

This seems to have been the case with Barb. After a year in our worship services, Sunday school classes, some small group experiences, and some one-on-one relationships, she and I only met twice in a "formal" one-on-one Bible study. Then she was eager to be baptized.

The benefits of church membership can be so compelling that, in the contemporary conversion process, a person may convert to the community of faith before converting to Christ.[1]

Because of their anti-institutionalism and their hunger for community, postmoderns most likely need to be persuaded of the truth of the gospel as they experience it in the midst of a community before they will be persuaded of the truth of the gospel as it is preached in the assembly. They will most likely first convert to the unspoken gospel lived out in a community and then to the spoken gospel proclaimed in the assembly.

To paraphrase one author, moderns first converted to the King, and then to the kingdom. Postmoderns, however, will be more likely to convert first to the kingdom, and then to the King.[2]

Anti-institutionalism and hunger for relationships are two forces pulling postmoderns in opposite directions when they approach the doors of a church building. Anti-institutionalism tempts them to distrust the church's message, to dismiss the church's relevance, and thus to not enter those doors. Hunger for community entices them to embrace community in the church (if it can be easily found), and thus to enter those doors. Anti-institutionalism pulls them away from the doors, hunger for community beacons them to go through the doors. Postmoderns are caught in this tug of war. Thus if they can find community, they will likely stay and eventually do whatever they need to do to become a permanent member of that community.

Two Strategies

This seems, therefore, to call for a two-pronged evangelistic strategy, both of which are aimed at revealing to postmoderns the rewards of participating in Christian community.

One strategy is informational in nature. Through preaching, we can combat the negative perceptions postmoderns have about church and accentuate the tremendous physical, social, emotional, and spiritual benefits of being part of an organized Christian community.

The other strategy is experiential in nature. We must help postmoderns experience the benefits of Christian community about which we are preaching. *What we proclaim about church from the pulpit must be confirmed by their experience in the pew.* Thus, on a related issue that won't be fully explored here, preaching must prepare the Christian community to embrace postmoderns and to allow postmoderns to fully participate in the community.

Ultimately both the preaching strategy and the participation strategy ground themselves in postmoderns' desire for relationships/ community. Preaching can take up the ways in which church benefits postmoderns relationally. And strategies can be employed to help postmoderns experience warm and authentic relationships with others in the church.

If it is true that postmoderns' first hurdle has to do with the "kingdom" and not the "King," it may well be that these two strategies mark a sort of "second step" in preaching evangelistically to postmoderns. The first step may lie in preaching that centers on "felt needs" or spirituality, since these are two areas postmoderns already have an interest in and which the gospel readily addresses. But the two major hurdles to then be addressed are pluralism and anti-institutionalism. Since pluralism ultimately deals with the "King," and anti-institutionalism ultimately deals with "the kingdom," it may be wiser to start with the anti-institutionalism hurdle first. Postmoderns may be more receptive to the community's message concerning pluralism if they are first persuaded of the relational rewards to be found in Christian community and have been meaningfully engaged in relationships within that community. In other words, once they fall in love with the community, it may be easier for them to embrace the community's hard message concerning pluralism.

Informational: Preaching the Benefits

Evangelistic preaching, therefore, can reveal the rewards that come from embracing, rather than rejecting, the institution of the church. James Engel suggests that people's negativity toward the church may be the largest obstacle to them embracing the gospel. People may not be able to feel positive about the gospel until they can also feel positive about the church.[3]

Evangelistic preaching can respond to this by first honestly admitting the problems with institutional religion. In a postmodern context, honesty and humility are two hallmarks of effective preaching.[4] Tom Beaudoin concludes—after his study of the literature, television, and music of Generation X (a subset of postmodernity)—that we must embrace a humility in ministry that is honest about the church's failings.[5]

Jesus himself critiqued the organized religion and its leaders of his day. Some of these texts could provide opportunities for postmoderns to hear their own critiques of the religious institution echoed in the words of Jesus. This type of preaching might help postmoderns feel a sort of "kinship" with Jesus and thus make them eager to hear more of what Jesus and his followers have to say about church.

Thus, before preaching about what is right with church, we may wish to preach about what is wrong with church.

Evangelistic preaching, however, will not dwell long on the failures of institutional religion. It will seek to reveal to postmoderns the genuine benefits of being part of the Christian community. The very thing that may lead postmoderns to reject the gospel (the church) can also be the very thing that leads them to accept the gospel (if they find genuine community there).

Obviously there are some ineffective ways to approach this strategy. For instance, I recently received a flyer from a church in my neighborhood. One of the sections was entitled "Why Become a Member of——." In the blank was the name of the church (rather than embarrassing them, I've left the actual name out.) Apparently, they thought I was a lost person, and, as part of a bulk mailing evangelistic strategy, they wanted to use the flyer to persuade me to overcome my anti-institutionalism and join their church.

The flyer listed thirteen reasons why I should join their church, thirteen benefits of becoming part of their community. Here are a few of them:

1. It was founded by a scriptural builder—Christ (Matt. 16:18).
2. It was founded on the scriptural foundation—the teachings of Christ (Matt. 16:18).
3. It was founded at the scriptural place—Jerusalem (Acts 2).
4. It was founded at the scriptural time—Pentecost (Acts 2).
5. It is scriptural in its organization (Phil. 1:1).
6. It has the Bible as its only creed (2 Tim. 3:16–17).
7. It is undenominational (Jn. 17:20–21).
8. It teaches and administers scriptural baptism—immersion (Rom. 6:4).
9. It gives scriptural answers to the question, "What must I do to be saved?" (Acts 2:38)
10. It has a scriptural teaching and observance of the Lord's Supper (1 Cor. 11:23–25).

This flyer assumed that I already wanted to be part of a church, and that my primary concern was that it be a scriptural church. Thus, it attempted to persuade me that their church was more scriptural than any other church.

This is not the kind of approach that overcomes postmodern anti-institutionalism. First, postmoderns could not care less about what is scriptural. Second, they don't already want to attend a church, and just need help in deciding which one to attend. Postmoderns are hostile to the church, even if it's a scriptural church. The kind of preaching about the church that will win them will focus on much broader, relevant, and spiritually significant themes than this flyer did.

One of the problems the flyer illustrates is our tendency to focus solely on orthodoxy when describing the church to non-Christians. I'm using orthodoxy here to refer to the right beliefs. The flyer described the church by describing its beliefs. While the beliefs of a church are obviously very important, what is more likely to connect with a postmodern is talk of the church's orthopraxy (its right practice) and its orthopathy (its right passions and zeal).

For instance, preaching might focus on a text like Acts 2:42–47. If there is a picture of church that is appealing to postmoderns, this is it. Rather than focusing on the church's orthodoxy (its beliefs), this text focuses on the church's orthopathy (its zeal and passion) and orthopraxy (its practices).

Notice the rich spirituality present in this church:
"They devoted themselves…to the *prayers*" (2:42).
"*Awe* came upon everyone"(2:43).
"Day by day…they spent much time in the temple…*praising God*" (2:46–47).

Notice the warm fellowship:
"They devoted themselvesto the…*fellowship*" (2:42).
"All who believed were *together* and had all things in *common*" (2:44).
"They broke bread at *home* and *ate their food* with *glad* and generous *hearts*" (2:46).

Notice the sacrificial ministry:
"They would sell their possessions and goods and distribute the proceeds to all, as any had need" (2:45).

Here is an image of church that is both scriptural and appealing to a postmodern world. These themes of spirituality, fellowship, and service connect powerfully with postmoderns. Postmoderns long for this kind of community—they just don't realize the church can offer it.

Or consider Romans 12:15 as a preaching point: "Rejoice with those who rejoice, weep with those who weep." Paul describes the community every church seeks: a family of people connected in genuine relationships which so exceed superficialities, that when one person earns an A in a class, gains a job promotion, gives birth to a child, becomes engaged, or gains victory over a personal weakness, others throw a party in celebration. When one person flunks a class, loses a job, can't conceive children, endures the breakup of a relationship, or stumbles again in a persistent sin, others gather around and mourn with him. This is the community church is intended to be and the kind of community for which postmoderns (and, for that matter, almost anyone) hunger.

Rick Warren has done an admirable job in preaching about the church in a way that is both biblically grounded and evangelistically effective. Started in 1980, the Saddleback Valley Community Church now averages well over 10,000 and has led over 7,000 to faith in Christ in Orange County, California.[6] Warren has taken the five classic purposes for church which are found in texts like Acts 2:42–47 (outreach, worship, fellowship, discipleship, and service), and repackaged them in a way which connects with postmoderns.

He suggests that these five biblical purposes for church meet five basic human needs:
- a *purpose* to live for (outreach)
- a *power* to live on (worship)
- a *people* to live with (fellowship)
- *principles* to live by (discipleship)
- a *profession* to live out (service)

Warren states that the church, therefore, provides five important things:
- a *focus* for living (outreach)
- a *force* for living (worship)
- a *family* for living (fellowship)
- a *foundation* for living (discipleship)
- a *function* for living (service)

Finally, Warren believes that the church offers these emotional benefits:
- Significance (outreach)
- Stimulation (worship)
- Support (fellowship)
- Stability (discipleship)
- Self-expression (service)[7]

Warren has simply taken an understanding of church accepted within Christendom for centuries and repackaged it for postmoderns. This is the kind of creative and biblical thinking which needs to inform our preaching so that it will draw the anti-institutional postmodern into the "institution" of church. When postmoderns understand church in the ways outlined by Warren, they will knock down the door to get in.

Once, my co-worker Harold Shank preached a lesson called "I Believe Jesus Wants Me in Church." The lesson showed one of the major rewards of participating in Christian community: the ability to overcome ethnic, gender, and other barriers that often divide people. The lesson's thesis was that the church is the only organization capable of truly bringing together diverse groups of people in genuine community. It showed how the cross is the great "leveler," putting rich, poor, white, black, young, old, male, and female on equal ground.

After the lesson, I talked with my non-Christian friend Larry. He had one problem with this lesson—its suggestion that the church alone can bring diverse people together in genuine community. Larry did say, however, "I do believe that nothing does this better than the church." Larry went on by saying, "I could see myself as a contributing member at Highland Street." It is this kind of preaching which had influenced Larry, and which will influence other postmoderns, and help them overcome their anti-institutionalism.

Experiential: Participating in the Benefits

The compelling picture of church that we preach from the pulpit must be what postmoderns experience in the pew. If we preach about church being a place where others will rejoice when they rejoice and mourn when they mourn, that had better be exactly what postmoderns find in our pews. Otherwise, they will assume either 1) that our message is fraudulent, 2) our community is hypocritical, or 3) both. Either way, it will drive them further from the church.

That's why we've spent the last six years and millions of dollars revamping our Sunday school program at Highland. While God had led us to some success in creating worship services where people felt as if they were encountering God, we had no church-wide vehicle for enabling people to experience authentic community. Postmoderns could hear about it from the pulpit. But rarely could they experience it.

Thus we prayerfully determined to create such community through Sunday school. We cast a vision for Sunday school in which each class would not only help people study the word of God, but would also enable people to focus on Christ through worship and prayer, form authentic relationships, pursue outreach to their friends, and get involved in meaningful ministry. We summarized this vision in the acronym CROSS:

- *Christ* We will help you experience the presence of Christ through worship and prayer in a way that prepares you spiritually and emotionally for the week ahead.
- *Relationship* We will provide a community of friends that knows your heart and helps you face life's challenges with support and encouragement.
- *Outreach* We will provide a safe place to bring your spiritually hungry friends and help you fill their spiritual hunger with Christ.
- *Service* We will help you find a ministry that enables you to discover and develop your talents and use them in serving others.
- *Study* We will provide teaching that repairs your relationships, enriches your work, and makes sense of God and of life.

We reorganized classes to achieve this vision, reassigned the roles of three staff members to work with the classes in fulfilling this vision, and hired a full time staff member to coordinate it all. As a result, each of the last five years has seen a new all time high yearly average attendance in Sunday school. We've gone from about 65% of our Sunday morning worshipers attending Sunday school to about 85%. *And most importantly, when we ask non-Christians baptized at Highland and Christians who placed membership at Highland why they started coming, the most oft mentioned item is this: Sunday school.* The primary reason they started coming was the genuine community they experienced through Sunday school.

Churches will need to put this kind of effort into creating community so that postmoderns can experience the benefits of church that are being preached about in an attempt to overcome their anti-institutionalism.

It is extremely difficult in our postmodern culture to lead postmoderns to faith in Christ outside the context of caring relationships between them and Christians. In fact, postmodern evangelism might be summed up by one word: relationship.[8] As was stated earlier, postmoderns may actually convert to the Christian community before converting to Christ. *It is unlikely that postmoderns will embrace Christ unless they are first embraced by Christ's people.* The church must seek to help postmoderns to experience the community of the church, not just hear the gospel preaching of the church.

This can be done by involving postmoderns in any of three relational contexts in the church:

- One-on-one relationships with Christians
- Participation in a Bible study small group or ministry small group
- Participation in a Sunday school class or similar sized-group

Whatever the level of community, it would need to be smaller than the corporate worship service. It is unlikely that postmoderns will form any meaningful relationships in the worship assembly due to its size (see, however, below).

There are three levels of community in any church: celebration (worship assembly), congregation (Sunday school class), and cell (small group). Only the latter two are able to provide the face-to-face and heart-to-heart relationships that would connect with postmoderns' value of relationships.[9]

For my friend John, it was the very lack of these relationships that hindered his conversion. He heard the gospel—I presented it to him over the course of about eight weeks in a one-on-one setting. Then he moved over one thousand miles away from me. At his new hometown, he visited several churches where he heard evangelistic preaching. But when I asked him what was keeping him from becoming a Christian, one of the things he mentioned was his lack of strong relationships with other Christians. Besides me, and I was a thousand miles away, he really had no significant connection to Christians. He had heard the Christian message, but he had not experienced Christian community. I suspect that until he does, he will remain lost.

The relational contact non-Christians have with Christians, however, can be both a blessing and a curse. To test the effectiveness of our preaching, Harold and I once gathered a group of non-Christians who would be willing to listen to a series of evangelistic lessons and provide feedback.

My friend Larry rated himself closer to faith in Christ after the series of lessons than before the series. But it wasn't just the preaching which had impacted him. When asked what had prompted his growth toward faith in Christ, Larry said that his relationships with people at Highland and his experiences with them had been very influential. Larry had recently become engaged to a strong Christian at Highland. He mentioned seeing some Christians support the woman's decision to marry him and seeing how this woman's faith upheld her in the face of those Christians who did not support the decision. The relational contacts, according to Larry, were responsible for leading him closer to faith in Christ.

Another non-Christian, Vivian, was baptized during this series of lessons. I asked her what led to her decision. Vivian mentioned several relationships. For instance, she was moved by the sacrifice of time and energy given by her Sunday school class teachers. She was also touched by the women who taught her young daughter in Bible classes. She remarked how much it meant to her that these women would devote themselves to helping her daughter know more about God. She said, "My daughter's little heart is filled with good things, with love," because of those women.

As mentioned in an earlier chapter, I once asked Harry, a Jewish non-Christian, what kept him coming to Highland Sunday after Sunday. He was more regular than some of our members. He answered by talking about his Sunday school class. "The church pulls me here," he said. By "church," he meant his Sunday school class and the relationships he had formed in it.

Sometimes, however, these relationships become the source of faithlessness rather than faith. Once, when I was talking to a non-Christian named Roy, he revealed what was likely the cause for much of his hostility toward organized religion. He told me about a childhood friend of his who still lived in the area. They often spent time together, two old friends with a friendship grounded on years of shared memories.

But recently, the friend had slighted Roy. Roy would not reveal what had happened. Given Roy's hostility toward church and God, I suspect his friend, an active Christian and church member, had criticized Roy for his atheism. Sometimes Roy can be unnerving when he rants and raves about God. Perhaps his friend finally had enough and ranted and raved back at Roy.

Whatever the offense, Roy asked the friend for an apology. But this Christian friend would not give an apology.

Roy said to me sarcastically, "That's Christianity in action! That's why I'll never be a Christian!" Could it be that this relationship had more to do with Roy's hostility toward Christianity than any genuine intellectual obstacle?

It does not seem too unreasonable to suggest that in a postmodern setting, you cannot simply invite postmoderns to a series of lessons and expect them to convert. Preaching is effective in evangelizing postmoderns, but it cannot sustain the weight of evangelism alone. It must be done in partnership with other evangelism strategies, including relationships with Christians. Saving faith in Christ is unlikely to develop without strong and positive relationships with other Christians in one-on-one settings, small groups, or Sunday schools.

The GREs of Worship

One aspect of institutional religion that seems to particularly irritate postmoderns is corporate worship. One reason postmoderns are anti-institutional is due to corporate worship. They see it as irrelevant to their spirituality.

A family member of mine once said, "Just because I don't go to church, doesn't mean I'm not spiritual." By "go to church," she meant, "go to corporate worship on Sunday morning." One of the primary aversions postmoderns have to church is its corporate worship. Part of this may be due to the fact that they are seeking spirituality but not finding it in corporate worship (a fact I addressed in another chapter). But perhaps another reason is this: they are also seeking community and not finding it in corporate worship.

Earlier, I argued that genuine community is best experienced in smaller settings such as Sunday school, small groups, and one-on-one relationships. Corporate worship, however, can also provide a certain level of community. In fact, corporate worship was probably intended to provide more community than we typically allow. In the previous chapter I discussed one of the GREs of worship that is fit for connecting with postmoderns. The *G* stands for *God-encountering*. The *R* stands for *Relational*. Worship that is fit for evangelistic effectiveness among postmoderns will be as relational as possible. Here are five ways in worship can be more "horizontal" in nature.

The Lord's Supper[10] —The "horizontal" nature of corporate worship becomes clear in 1 Corinthians 11–14, the longest extended discussion of corporate worship in the New Testament. Paul critiques the Corinthians' abuse of the Lord's Supper (chapter 11) and of tongue speaking (chapter 14). In both abuses, the Corinthians have allowed the vertical element of worship (God and me) to overshadow the horizontal element of worship (you and me).

In chapter eleven, the setting envisioned is a house with a large dining area. The Lord's Supper is part of a regular evening meal, which would have been typical in other social or religious gatherings in the Greco-Roman world. Outside the church, these meals involved all kinds of social and economic stratification. The best food, seats, wine, and company were reserved for the most affluent or influential.

Apparently, the Corinthians carried the same approach into their Lord's Supper meal. There are divisions among them (11:18), especially along the lines of rich/poor (11:22). The wealthy and influential eat the meal and the Lord's Supper without waiting for the poor (perhaps slaves, who arrive late) (11:21). Paul tells the wealthy and influential to wait on the others (11:33), and for all to judge or discern the "body" when they take communion (11:29).

Paul's similar use of "body" in 10:17 suggests that in 11:29 Paul is not simply speaking of the bread of communion. He is not urging them to silently, privately, and individually meditate upon the significance of the "bread/body" they are eating. He is urging them to take communion in the recognition that they are one body, a community.

He is saying that the way in which they take communion should illustrate the fact that they are a community, not simply a collection of individuals. As they currently practiced it, however, communion was an individualistic sacrament, or, at best, a sacrament revealing that only a subgroup of the church was a community. Paul desired communion to be practiced in a way that allowed the entire church to function as community.[11]

John Mark Hicks summarizes the issue and its application in this way: "As Greco-Roman culture invaded the Corinthian assembly, the Lord's Supper became a moment of socio-economic stratification. Modern culture has invaded the contemporary church so that the Lord's Supper has become an occasion for silent, individualistic piety. Just as the Corinthians, through their supper, divided the body of Christ along the lines of rich and poor, so modern culture divides the body by restricting the supper to the recesses of each individual's mind. If the Corinthians used the supper to maintain social distinctions in the culture, modernity has transformed the supper into a private event. Both distort the intent of the supper as a public, unifying, communal meal. Both deny the communal character of the table. . . When the form of the supper is reduced to bread and wine, restricted to a formal, ritual context, and stressed as a private moment between worshiper and God, then the function of the supper is distorted."[12]

The point is this—in most churches, the focus in communion is solely on one's private (vertical) relationship with God, rather than also on one's (horizontal) relationship with "the body," the other worshipers. Restoring this horizontal dimension to communion not only results in a needed theological corrective, but a needed evangelistic corrective as well. Postmoderns desire community. Communion is intended to be taken in community, to display community, to provide community.

How a church turns what has become a moment of individualistic piety and devotion into an experience and expression of community is an issue that deserves more space than is left in this chapter. A few possibilities are offered here to "prime the pump":

For churches whose worship area is comprised of movable chairs, communion could be a time when groups of five to ten worshipers circle up their chairs, serve one another communion, and pray together.

For churches with fixed seating, a table, or several, could be placed at the front of the worship area, and/or on the sides and back. Groups of four to six worshipers at a time would be urged to approach the table, serve each other communion, pray together, then take their seat.

A simple strategy would be to serve everyone communion, but to ask all participants to hold the bread and cup, waiting until all have been served. Once every worshiper has the elements, they would all eat and drink at the same time—a symbol of the relationship they share with each other.

Divide the worship area into sections. In each section, have an older person go to the front or back, get the elements of communion, and come back and serve communion to those in their section.

Creative Meet and Greet—Not only does Paul address the need for more relational elements in communion, he urges there to be a more relational focus in the worship in general. Paul's critique of the Corinthians' worship in 1 Corinthians 14 reveals this. Vertically, their worship could not be matched. It was filled with worshipers becoming so intimate with God that they became caught up in "mystical" experiences of speaking in tongues. Many left that worship service never having felt closer to God.

This vertical success, however, was insufficient for Paul. In the midst of such intimate personal experiences of God in worship, they had missed the horizontal aspect of worship. Thus he urges them to ensure that worship is done for the "upbuilding and encouragement and consolation" of all who are present (14:3). Rather than edifying themselves, he urges them to ensure that, in worship, they edify each other (14:4). In fact, those who are willing and able to focus on edifying others during worship are "greater" than those who simply have private and intimate encounters with God during worship (14:5). Everything done in worship should be done in a way that is "mind"-ful of how it may or may not edify those present (14:15).

Paul especially criticizes the church because they have given so little thought as to how they might edify the unbelievers who are present in their worship service. If they would focus more on edifying those non-Christians rather than on having intimate and private experiences with God, those non-Christians would likely come to faith in God through that very worship service (14:23–25).

I argued earlier that worship must be a place where postmoderns find God—the vertical. Yet Paul argues here that worship must also be a place where worshipers also find community—the horizontal.

One very effective means toward that end is a creative "meet and greet." At the beginning or end of a worship service, the worshipers can be directed in a time of meet and greet. To best create the potential for Christians to especially interact with guests, the meet and greet can be creatively done. For instance, I've used the following with great results: "You have forty-five seconds to meet two people who were born in the same month as you. Introduce yourself to them, find out what they do, and how long they've been attending worship here." Here's another possibility: "In the next minute, I want each of you to find one person who has visited the state where you were born. Introduce yourselves to each other and tell each other what you like most about worshiping here." These times of creative meet and greets can especially help guests and newcomers realize 1) that they are not alone, there are other guests present, and 2) that there are people just like them in this church. It can help them gain a sense that they would fit in this community of people.

Another twist on this idea is to coordinate other ways for people to meet. For instance, you could ask every person to write down on a piece a paper the name of someone they know who needs a blessing from God. Then each person would be instructed to find someone in the audience they don't know, swap papers with that person, and promise each other to pray for the name on that paper for one month. This type of directed edification creates many relational opportunities in worship.

Horizontal Songs—Earlier I discussed "vertical songs" (songs sung to God) and "horizontal songs" (songs sung to each other). Many worship songs are written as songs of encouragement, admonition, and instruction. Worship leaders can instruct worshipers about the horizontal nature of those songs and encourage worshipers to look around and sing to each other during those songs. A video could be employed showing people in the crowd while the church was singing these horizontal songs.

Antiphonal or Responsive Singing—Songs where part of the worshipers sing, then another part of the worshipers respond, create a sense of community and relationship. For instance, the worshiper could ask the left half of those in the worship service to sing, "What can wash away my sin?" and those in the right half to respond with, "Nothing but the blood of Jesus." Such responsive singing helps worshipers feel less like an individual, and more a part of a larger community of worshipers.

Seating Arrangements—Andrea Buczynski tells of how, typically, every Campus Crusade for Christ group on college campuses has a weekly meeting. In these meetings, they try to expose non-Christian students to the gospel. The most common settings for these meetings is a college classroom with chairs in straight rows all facing forward, like a theater (and like almost every worship area in churches in America). Until a few years ago this worked well. Today, however, the students they are trying to reach hunger for interaction, relationship, and community. Thus Campus Crusade has changed its approach.

More typical today is the Campus Crusade ministry who took a large hall near their campus, filled it with small tables and chairs, painted the walls dark blue, and created more of a coffeehouse atmosphere. This type of setting has proven much more effective in drawing postmoderns in and in engaging them meaningfully with the gospel. Despite a very straightforward and "traditional" presentation of the gospel using the gospel of Mark, roughly 10% of the audience at one Campus Crusade for Christ coffeehouse each week at Baylor University is skeptical nonbelievers. They keep coming because they feel loved and were "responding to people who extend love and grace to them and who are authentic in their beliefs."[13] Perhaps our worship areas at church should undergo the same types of changes in seating arrangements and atmosphere.

Our campus ministry recently revamped their Wednesday night outreach event. Instead of an event where people entered a room with rows of chairs, listened to a speaker up front, and then left, they now enter a room filled with small tables and three or four chairs around each table. The walls have been painted and decorated to look like a coffee house. For thirty or forty minutes, students can order free coffee-drinks, sit around, and talk. Then there is a period of worship followed by a speaker who addresses a controversial issue. Afterwards, the speaker engages in a question and answer period. Since adopting this new format, our campus ministry has seen a three-fold increase in attendance.

Invitation/Ministry Time—At Highland we offer a public invitation each Sunday after the lesson. We invite people with prayer or pastoral needs to come to the front while the rest of the church sings a song. When people come, we then urge others who know them, or who may simply want to encourage them, to come to the front as well. It is not unusual to have several groups of five or six huddled around each person who's come forward—hugging, whispering words of encouragement, and praying over them. This type of one-another ministry could be done at other times in the service as well. It provides a concrete way for people to edify each other and to make relational connections.

This could also be done by giving five or six people in the audience a microphone and have them briefly discuss a difficult issue in their lives. Others would then be urged to write down verses of encouraging scriptures on paper and to get up and give those slips of paper to them.

My point is simply that much of our worship today is like a television on which the vertical has finally been adjusted. We are interested in helping people connect to God through our corporate worship. But the picture continues to swing from left to right because little attention has been given to adjusting the horizontal.

Theologically, we have a mandate to increase the amount of elements in worship designed to create horizontal links between worshipers. Evangelistically, we have an equally strong mandate. Postmoderns are relational and hungry for community. Making worship more horizontal in nature will connect with this need of postmoderns, make worship more biblical, and perhaps help overcome the postmodern anti-institutional bias against church.

Larry made this insightful comment one day to me: "For me, and among other non-Christians, there is a fear of Christians. We get nervous around you in the same way we do around a friend who is an insurance salesman. You golf, eat, and play together. But underlying all that you keep wondering, 'When is he going to try to sell me some insurance?' But my experience with people at Highland has lessened that fear. That's really been a key. Relationships with real Christians are very important."

Another non-Christian friend, Zoe, shared this: "If there is a god," he said, "he loves us more than we can imagine, just like parents love us more than we can imagine." Zoe then told of the time when a Highland member named John was studying the Bible with him on a Wednesday night at the church building. It was raining that night, and some homeless men came to the front door of the church. John gave them some money and offered to drive the men to a place to stay the night. Zoe was moved by this example of love and said, "If Christians love people that much, I can't imagine how much God loves people. When Christians love others, that's the love of God."

His experience is critical to postmodern evangelism. Postmoderns will equate the love they receive from us with the love they may be able to receive from God. If ours is cold and stingy, they may decide that God's will be likewise. But if ours is warm and abundant, they may realize that God has the same kind of love in store for them. The more we love them, the more they'll come to understand God's love for them.

CHAPTER NINE

Preaching Evangelistically to Pluralists

The Gospel's Scandal in Postmodernity

"Do I have to believe that Jesus is the only way to God in order to become a Christian?"

Mike wasn't joking. For eight weeks his wife and I had studied the Bible together in my church office across the street from the university where they worked. His wife first made contact with me over the phone. She explained that two members of her family had been murdered—one, years ago; one, months ago. The most recent murder had resurrected doubts about God which the first murder had given life to yet which she had since mentally buried. Our discussion about her doubts turned into a Bible study with her and her husband.

Having read very little of the Bible, they were amazed at the stories of Jesus we began to explore. For eight weeks their eyes and ears drank in the images and words of the gospel. They grew more and more eager to start a relationship with God through Christ.

But one cloudy afternoon, we hit a snag. Working our way through John's gospel, we came to chapter fourteen. I read aloud through verse six: "Jesus said to him, 'I am the way, and the truth, and the life. No one comes to the Father except through me.'" That's when Mike stopped me: "Do I have to believe Jesus is the only way to God in order to become a Christian?"

I gulped. I knew I was about to lose him. I took a deep breath, explained what I thought Jesus was saying in this verse, and affirmed the exclusivist message of the gospel: Jesus is the exclusive way to God. Mike was silent the rest of our study. It was too much for him to accept.

As noted earlier, less than twenty percent of Americans believe in absolute truth—a truth that applies to all people in all times.[1] Additionally, three-fourths of Americans think that more than one religion offers a true path to God. Just one in six thinks his or her religion is the best path to God.[2] It's common for postmoderns like Mike to believe in multiple paths to God rather than a single path to God.

Therein lies the greatest "scandal" of the cross in the twenty-first century—it is too exclusive. Such exclusivity runs against the two guiding principles of postmodernism: pluralism and tolerance. Pluralism claims that there are a plural number of truths and a plural number of ways to God. Tolerance says that we should therefore affirm the validity of all truths and all ways. It says we should embrace all who believe differently than we do.

And when postmoderns hear words like those in John 14:6, instead of pluralism(many ways)they hear exclusivism(one way). Instead of tolerance(all ways are valid)they hear intolerance(only one way is valid). No matter how attracted they may be to Jesus, postmoderns will likely stumble at this point in the gospel. It is the greatest scandal and stumbling block of our time.

How, then, do we persuade those who worship the gods of pluralism and tolerance to turn and worship the seemingly exclusivist and intolerant Jesus? What follows are seven things I've found helpful in preaching evangelistically to pluralistic postmoderns. They are seven things I wish I had known during those weeks when Mike was not only sitting in my office reading the Bible, but also sitting in our auditorium listening to my preaching.

First: Preach Messages That Highlight the Inclusiveness and Tolerance of the Cross

Christianity has an *exclusive* message of salvation. For instance, read these words: "There is salvation in no one else, for there is no other name under heaven given among mortals by which we must be saved" (Acts 4:12). This exclusive message, however, is offered to all in an *inclusive* way. Read, for instance, these words: "There is no longer Jew or Greek, there is no loner slave or free, there is no longer male or female, for all of you are one in Christ Jesus" (Gal. 3:28). The gospel does not offer its hope to only one race, age, gender or social status. The gospel states "For God so loved the world"—not just whites, not just blacks, not just men, not just women, not just children, not just senior citizens, not just the rich, not just the poor—"For God so loved *the world* that he gave his only Son" (Jn. 3:16).

The place to begin with postmoderns is at this common ground between their pluralism and tolerance and the gospel's affirmation that all humans are valuable to God and its inclusive welcome for all to find salvation in Jesus Christ. Once we've established this common ground and thus created credibility in their ears for the gospel, we can then move on into the riskier territory of the gospel's exclusive message.

One particularly fruitful way of thinking about this in terms of specific preaching approaches is to break tolerance or pluralism into three levels.[3] In fact, merely explaining these three levels to postmoderns can be quite helpful. The first two levels represent specific kinds of messages you could preach in order to highlight the inclusiveness and tolerance of the gospel.

Level One: Preach on Issues Related to Legal Tolerance

Legal tolerance refers to the idea that all people should be legally protected. No one should be discriminated against, regardless of who they are. It doesn't matter what a person believes—he should be given legal tolerance. *Legal tolerance says, "Represent and protect all people."*

While legal tolerance has been valued by generations before postmodernity, it is particularly valued by postmoderns due to their high esteem for tolerance in general. This type of tolerance is also one that Christians and Christianity can embrace.

This is especially true in the areas of social justice and protection of the abused and neglected. There is a strong biblical call for "justice" and for the protection and advocacy of those whose rights are typically ignored. Isaiah 56:1 demands, "Maintain justice, and do what is right." Paul calls Christians to support their secular governments in their attempt to punish injustice: "to execute wrath on the wrongdoer" (Rom. 13:4). One of the great summaries of the biblical faith is, "to do justice, and to love kindness" (Mic. 6:8). The legal code of Moses' day demanded that the Israelites provide for "the resident aliens, the orphans and the widows in your towns" (Duet. 14:29). Proverbs calls us to "Speak out for those who cannot speak, for the rights of all the destitute. Speak out, judge righteously, defend the rights of the poor and needy" (31:8–9). Jesus defined his mission as one that was to benefit the poor and oppressed: " 'The Spirit of the Lord is upon me, because he has anointed me to bring good news to the poor. He has sent me to proclaim release to the captives and recovery of sight to the blind, to let the oppressed go free, to proclaim the year of the Lord's favor' " (Lk. 4:18–19). Jesus' mission even encompassed one of the most vulnerable and abused in ancient society—children: "Let the little children come to me; do not stop them; for it is to such as these that the kingdom of God belongs" (Mk. 10:14). This unmistakable biblical call for the protection of the abused and neglected is closely related to the idea of legal tolerance and thus provides common ground for the postmodern and the Christian message.

Preaching therefore could focus on topics such as serving the poor in general and on serving children in particular. Legal tolerance says, "Represent and protect all people." Christianity has an especially strong element that says, "Especially represent and protect the poor and children." This message finds an eager hearing in the ears of postmoderns because of its underlying affirmation of tolerance. Children and the poor represent two of the most neglected and abused populations in American and across the world. In my hometown, one in five Memphians live in poverty. 3,000 women and children are homeless. Across the nation, one of every three girls and one out of every five boys will be sexually assaulted before they are eighteen.[4] Preaching that calls the church and the community to represent and protect the poor in general and children in particular can be very appealing to postmoderns and will help them understand how tolerant and inclusive Christianity is.

There are many ways to preach on the poor and on children. At Highland, we preach on the poor for about six weeks each fall as preparation for our annual contribution that funds our ministries to the poor. Two years ago, we preached for thirteen weeks on God's view of children. The gospels and the Prophets present an enormous wealth of material for touching on both of these issues. My co-worker's books on the poor, *Up Close and Personal: Embracing the Poor*, and children, *Children Mean the World to God* help provide additional ideas for preaching on these two issues.[5]

Level Two: Preach on Messages Related to Social Tolerance

A second way to highlight the inclusiveness and tolerance of the gospel is to touch on issues concerning *social tolerance*. Social tolerance refers to the idea that all people should be socially accepted and respected, regardless of who they are. It doesn't matter what a person believes—he should be loved and shown social tolerance. Where legal tolerance says, "Represent and protect all people," *social tolerance says, "Love and respect all people."* This type of tolerance is highly valued by postmoderns.

And if there is one strength of the Christian message in the postmodern era (actually, there is more than one), it comes in the area of social tolerance. Jesus himself teaches us to love and respect even those who are the most difficult to love and respect. In Matthew 5:44 Jesus says, "Love your *enemies* and pray for those who persecute you." In 1 Peter 2:17, Peter urges, "Honor *everyone*." The Christian concepts of "grace" and "agape" demand social tolerance. Jesus was often criticized for his social tolerance—eating with tax collectors and sinners (Lk. 15:1–2). The early church accepted into membership women, children, and slaves—those often rejected by other groups during the first century. Preaching on these themes can help correct the postmodern myth that Christianity is intolerant.

Specifically, preaching on diversity and reconciliation can find common ground with the postmodern value for social tolerance. Texts like 1 Corinthians 12:13 ("For in the one Spirit we were all baptized into one body—Jews or Greeks, slaves or free—and we were all made to drink of"), or Galatians 3:28 ("There is no longer Jew or Greek, there is no longer slave or free, there is no longer male and female; for all of you are one in Christ Jesus"); or Ephesians 2:11–22 (which tells how Jesus made the Gentiles and Jews one) offer appealing messages concerning the value of all races, nationalities, and genders and of God's love for all people. Preaching that picks up the Jew/Gentile, slave/free, male/female message will gain a tremendous hearing today because of its overlap with social tolerance.

Level Three: Preach on Messages Related to Intellectual Tolerance

A third level of tolerance can be called *intellectual tolerance*. Whereas legal tolerance calls us to legally protect all people regardless of what they believe, and social tolerance calls us to socially accept all people regardless of what they believe, intellectual tolerance calls us to affirm the truth of all beliefs.

Intellectual tolerance refers to the idea that all people's beliefs are equally valid.

Intellectual tolerance says, "Accept and affirm all people's beliefs."

While we can embrace and find common ground in our preaching with postmoderns in the areas of legal and social tolerance, we cannot do so in intellectual tolerance. Intellectual tolerance says it is always wrong to try to convince someone that his views are wrong (which is in itself a type of intolerance). This type of tolerance runs contrary to the gospel that says that we are all wrong and that only God is right.

Preaching on topics related to legal tolerance and social tolerance can help postmoderns see that there is a very tolerant side to Christianity. Preaching, however, cannot ultimately remove the scandal of the gospel's intellectual intolerance. The remaining points to follow illustrate ways in which preaching can address the issue of intellectual tolerance.

Second: Clarify the Roots of Exclusivism

We have an active ministry to Asian Americans at Highland. Many of them have strong roots in China or Taiwan and moved to Memphis to continue their education. They gravitate to our church not only because we offer to help them with practical issues like finding housing and improving their English. They come because of an intense interest in Christianity.

Yet for many of them, this interest is the fruit of their larger interest in American culture in general. Not having been exposed to much Christianity in China or Taiwan, they associate Christianity with America. Ron Wade, who leads our Asian-American ministry, comments that some of them are surprised to learn that Christianity actually began in Israel and not in the West. These Asians are thus often interested in Christianity initially because they see it as part of American culture.

Postmoderns may have a similar viewpoint when it comes to the gospel's conviction that salvation is found in no one else besides Jesus. They may believe that this is simply an outgrowth of American culture that says, "Our democracy is better than your communism," or "our basketball players are better than yours." It's the same thinking, they believe, which leads to "my religion is better than yours." When postmoderns hear Christians saying, "Jesus, Jesus, Jesus," they may hear echoes of a crowd at an Olympic sporting event chanting "USA, USA, USA."

Postmoderns might therefore suggest that Christian exclusivism flows out of a my-culture-is-better-than-yours type of thinking—and that since this type of cultural-superiority is wrong, so is Christian exclusivism.

But it would be tragic for preachers to allow postmoderns to reject the gospel on the assumption that its exclusivism is rooted in Western cultural rather than on the truth that it is rooted in biblical theology. We do not want postmoderns to refuse the gospel because they refuse the intolerance of Western culture in general. We must force their decision about the gospel to be separate from their decisions about Western culture.

One of the important tasks of preaching, therefore, is to help postmoderns understand that the gospel's "Jesus-only" message is not rooted in culture but in theology. One of the primary ways of doing this is by revealing that exclusivism is part of the entire biblical message. It is not a "Johnny-come-lately." Exclusivism is not a fad that began to appear in the Christian message at about the same time that American rock-and-roll and Western capitalism began to assert their dominance across the globe. Instead, the gospel's exclusivism is older than any human culture. It is as old as Genesis 1 and it finds itself woven in the biblical text from Genesis 1 through Revelation 22. Texts like Isaiah 43:10–12 are unmistakable in proclaiming that the biblical God is the only God and that there is only one way to him:

> Before me no god was formed, nor shall there be any after me. I, I am the Lord, and besides me there is no savior. I declared and saved and proclaimed, when there was no strange god among you.

The major and minor prophets are filled with such language and contain especially strong condemnations of idolatry—the trust in other gods for salvation. While the seminal New Testament texts like John 14:6 and Acts 4:12 cannot and should not be avoided, these Old Testament texts provide a fresh way to approach the issue which also helps postmoderns understand that Christian exclusivism is rooted in Scripture and not in human culture.

Third: Preach Messages That Explore the Basis for Christian Exclusivism

What gives Jesus the right to claim that he alone is the source of salvation? The answer to that question may be the very thing that can help turn postmoderns toward Christ in spite of the gospel's exclusivism.

While valuing tolerance, postmoderns are ultimately intolerant in certain areas of life. For instance, most are intolerant of the belief that a man with a gun should be allowed to indiscriminately fire it into a crowd at the mall. Postmoderns will embrace an intolerant belief, if there are good enough reasons for it (e.g., the protection of themselves and their loved ones from men shooting at the mall). In the same way, postmoderns will embrace the gospel's intolerance if we can help them understand the good enough reasons for such intolerance.

These reasons are ultimately found in those things that distinguish Christianity from other world religions. I once asked my friend John what one question he needed answered before he would become a Christian. Here is his answer: "Why is Christianity better than all other religions?" While we would not want to state the issue so bluntly, that is the very question we must answer in our preaching. What sets the gospel and Jesus apart from other faith systems? What makes them unique? The answers to those questions provide the basis for the gospel's exclusivism.

Tim Keller preaches for the Redeemer Presbyterian Church in Manhattan, New York. Nearly 30% of their attendees are non-Christians. How is Keller preaching evangelistically to them? "I don't directly make the naked claim 'Christianity is a superior religion,' and I certainly don't malign other faiths," he says. "Instead, I stress Christianity's distinctiveness."[6] By helping postmoderns understand what sets Christianity apart from other religions, we help them see that there are good reasons for the gospel's exclusivism. What follows are four ways of stressing Christianity's distinctiveness.

Distinction One: Preach Messages on the Incarnation, Atonement, and Resurrection

Preaching the doctrines of incarnation, atonement, and resurrection may prove particularly fruitful in postmodernity. These three doctrines stand at the core of what sets Christianity apart from other religions. These three doctrines are the foundation upon which Christianity makes its exclusivist claims. No other major world religion makes the bold claims Christianity makes through these doctrines.

The incarnation is critical because if Jesus truly was God-in-the-flesh, then his words and teaching come with divine authority.

If he is truly God incarnate, then his claim that "no one comes to the Father except through me," cannot be dismissed as the misguided ravings of a self-centered prophet. They must be accepted as the words of God himself.

The incarnation, however, provides more than simply logical support for the gospel's exclusivism. It provides an argument that persuades the heart as well as the head. Christianity proclaims a God who has lived in our shoes; a God who knows what it's like to be tempted, tired, and tense. Christianity proclaims a God who cannot only *sympathize* with our humanity and its struggles, but who can *empathize*. The gospel presents a God who refused to be distant and uncaring but who instead came near and lived among us. That kind of God has a certain amount of credibility to say, "If you're looking for salvation, you won't find any better than with me."

The atonement claims that in Jesus all our sins and failures were paid for. As one book has put it, where world religions are spelled "D-o," the atonement spells Christianity "D-o-n-e."[7] Almost every major world religion offers salvation based upon what we "do." If we "do" enough good things, we earn salvation. Because of the atonement, however, Christianity offers salvation based upon what Jesus has "done" on the cross. Salvation is by grace. Such a message is infinitely appealing and can help postmoderns understand why Jesus can claim to be the only means of salvation.

Tim Keller's church, mentioned earlier, is drawing significant numbers of non-Christians to its weekly assemblies. Many of them are New Yorkers still wrestling with the events of September 11, 2001. Keller summarizes the message which is drawing them in this way: "Only Christians believe in a God who says, 'Here I am alongside you. I have experienced the same suffering you have'…Christianity is the only faith that tells you that God lost a child in an act of violent injustice."[8] The message of the atonement is drawing them to church.

The resurrection too is distinctive and critical to leading postmoderns to make decisions in favor of the gospel in spite of its intellectual intolerance. The resurrection claims that death could not hold Jesus; that Jesus rose from the dead never to die again. If Jesus did rise, then he truly is the Son of God and his words of exclusive salvation are of divine authority. In addition, the resurrection provides a compelling pastoral reason to embrace Christianity. If the resurrection is true, there is life after death—an appealing message in the midst of suffering.

Tim Keller says that "Pluralists get stumped by that [the fact that only Christianity offers the things found in the incarnation, atonement, and resurrection] because they realize that they want the distinctiveness of Christianity—a God who has known human pain [incarnation], salvation by grace [atonement], and the hope of heaven [resurrection]—in their times of need."[9]

When postmoderns thus truly come to understand what took place at the cradle, cross, and tomb, Jesus no longer sounds so intolerant for saying, "I am the way, the truth, and the life." It no longer is an issue of "How could Jesus claim to be the only way?" but more of an issue of "How can I have what Jesus promises here? Preaching which majors in these three areas of incarnation, atonement, and resurrection can persuade postmoderns that there are indeed good reasons for the gospel's exclusivism; reasons so good they will long to embrace the gospel.

Distinction Two: Answer "How Can I Know Jesus Is God's Son?"

Ultimately, the gospel's exclusivity rests on the identity of Jesus. My friend Larry struggled with Jesus' identity and thus with exclusivism as well. He once said: "I would have expected God to give a clearer message than just a simple carpenter who gets crucified. I'm still not convinced that Jesus is not a philosopher or a prophet." Larry also said the whole issue of exclusivity for him hinges on "who Jesus is—prophet, Son of God, or carpenter."

Preaching which helps postmoderns overcome objections to Christianity will thus need to focus on persuading them of the truth of the biblical claims about Jesus. If postmoderns can be convinced that Jesus is God's Son, they will also accept his exclusivist claims. While it may be more of a modern than a postmodern approach, Lee Strobel's book *The Case for Christ* provides an example of the kind of topics one might address in preaching which answers "How Can I Know Jesus is God's Son?"[10] Strobel lays out convincing evidence for believing in the biblical claims for Jesus' identity. We've preached material like this at Highland and found a great deal of interest on the part of our guests.

Bill Hybels of Willow Creek Community Church reports that one of the highest responses among non-Christians in their Generation X service was when Lee Strobel gave three messages on "Why I Believe There's a God," "Why I Believe the Bible" and "Why I Believe Jesus Christ Was Who He Said He Was."[11]

How can I know Jesus is the Son of God? Any lesson or series of lessons addressing that question can be immensely helpful to postmoderns dealing with pluralism.

Distinction Three: Defending the Credibility of the Gospels

Some preaching, however, may also have to deal with the credibility of the record of the life, death, burial, and resurrection of Jesus itself. As noted above, Larry did not trust the credibility of the gospels, and thus could not accept their claims about Jesus. It would be beneficial to therefore present an apologetic defense of the credibility of the gospel records. Not only would this be a response to the pluralism of postmoderns, it would be a response to their anti-institutionalism. Postmodern suspicions about the church extend to suspicions about the church's record of Jesus. Evangelistic preaching may, therefore, need to examine the credibility of the gospel account and show that there are indeed good reasons for trusting in those accounts.

Jack is a friend of mine who adheres strongly to a pluralistic worldview. He has explained to me that the primary reason he worships at Highland is that his wife and children have a Christian worldview and he doesn't want to rock the marriage or the family. If not for them, he would have left Highland long ago.

One of the most engaging moments for him at Highland, however, came when I presented a short series that explored the historical reliability of the gospels. I examined whether or not the four gospels were indeed written by those whose names are attached to them. We explored how biographies were written in antiquity and how this accounts for some of the alleged "problems" with the gospels (e.g., they are not always chronological). I highlighted some alleged discrepancies between the gospels and probable solutions to them. We also looked at the dates of the writing of the gospels and compared that to the dates of the writing of other ancient biographies, noting that by ancient standards, the gospels were written extremely close to the events they described. Finally, we examined the way in which the gospel documents were handed down through history and we viewed comparisons between early and later editions of those documents.

It was not a series that everyone enjoyed. But Jack sought me out after several of the lessons, asking questions and making comments. I believe it helped Jack gain a new appreciation for the gospel record and moved him closer to someday accepting the exclusivity of the Jesus described in those gospels.

How can I believe the gospels provide a true witness to the life, death, and resurrection of Christ? Any lesson or series that examines the credibility of the gospels may move postmoderns closer to accepting this witness.

Distinction Four: Answering Objections to Hell

The doctrine of hell will also need to be approached in attempting to overcome the obstacle of pluralism. If there is one doctrine in Christianity that smacks of gross intolerance to postmoderns, it is the doctrine of hell.

Once, when talking to my friend Roy about pluralism and Christianity, he said, "I want you to look me in the eye and tell me what you believe about all those people not following Jesus. Do you personally believe they are going to hell?" When I explained again the position of Christianity, he said, "If all these religious people are going to hell, then your God is a demon god!" He continued, "The major problem for the church today is its claim of exclusivity. It will go down with it. That's why it's losing numbers."

Roy told me the story of his aunt who married a Christian in Nashville, Tennesee. Roy asked her Christian husband, "*Why should I associate with someone who knows I'm going to hell? Why would any non-Christian have anything to do with Christians, with people who think that everyone else is going to hell?*" Roy concluded, "That issue will destroy the church." In fact, Roy saw the Christian claim of exclusivity as incompatible with the Christian command to love. "You cannot love someone and yet say they are going to hell," he complained.

Perhaps the most helpful approach I have found in discussing hell among postmoderns is to stress the inclusiveness of God. I once preached a sermon on hell using the parable of the prodigal son (Lk. 15). Using the image of the father's house, I spent a great deal of time stressing how this is a house where anyone is welcome. Regardless of race, gender, class, or even past failures, everyone is welcome at the father's house. It is not a house where only one race can enter, one gender can enter, or one class can enter. You don't have to be perfect to get in that house.

I then explained that all of us, like the prodigal son, could decide not to go in that house. We can decide to leave the house and live life on our own terms. Even when we do that, we are welcomed back home. But, I explained, there will come a time when the father will leave that house and take everyone in that house with him to another country. If we wait too long, we may return to the house and find it empty. And hell will simply be the result of the absence of God. Hell is what happens when God leaves. Hell is what is left when all of the goodness, kindness, and holiness of God has left and evil and darkness are allowed to take over.

I illustrated this at the end of the lesson with a contemporary Christian song that speaks of a husband who leaves his wife and young child to go and live life on his own terms. She waits and waits for him. But he does not return. In the end, however, like the prodigal son, he comes to his senses. He travels the long road home. But when he arrives home, he finds it empty. His wife and child have moved away. And the man cries out in anguish, trapped in the hell he has created. This approach to hell stresses relational aspects as well as the inclusiveness of God and may be fruitful in a postmodern world.

Why should I believe there is a hell? The age-old objection to hell is still very much alive in postmodernity. Due to the high value of tolerance, it is especially difficult for postmoderns to overcome. Effective evangelistic preaching will address the issue in a biblical fair yet sensitive way.

Fourth: Preach Messages That Reveal the Exclusivism of Other Faiths

A fourth way of addressing pluralism is to reveal the exclusivism of other religious faiths. Preaching can focus on helping postmoderns understand that some otherworld religions are just as exclusive in their claims as Christianity. If postmoderns want to reject Christianity for its exclusivistic teaching, they must also be prepared to reject many other world religions because of their same type of teaching.

There can be no more exclusivist claim than the central tenet of Islam: "There is no god but Allah and Muhammed is his prophet." In the same vein, other religions contain elements of exclusivism. In fact, most world religions claim that they are, if not the only way, the best way to a relationship with God.

Fifth: Preach Concerning the Inaccuracies of Pluralism

Pluralism claims that all religions are essentially the same. The reason there can be no exclusive claim on religious truth is that all religions have the same basic truth. Each individual religion is the same truth just packaged in a way that reflects a certain culture or tradition. Yet this understanding of religions is patently false.

In his book *Dissonant Voices*, Harold Netland shows that there are some similar moral teachings across the religions.[12] But he compares the way Hinduism, Buddhism, Islam, and Shinto answer three basic questions: Who is God? What is humanity's worst problem? What does it mean to be saved? These four religions offer radically different answers to these three questions. For instance, Shinto believes in many gods whereas Islam and Judaism believe in one God. In Hinduism and Buddhism the human problem is not sin against a holy God, but ignorance regarding the true nature of reality. Christians say Jesus is the Son of God, whereas the other religions say he was just a good teacher.

Netland concludes: "But when all is said and done the dissimilarities between Jesus and the other religious figures far outstrip any possible similarities. Jesus was a strict monotheist. The Buddha, and most likely also Confucius, was at best agnostic about the existence of any God(s). Certainly no other founder of a major religion ever claimed to be the eternal creator God. Jesus located the source of the human predicament in human sin. No other religious figure spoke in quite these terms, choosing instead, like Confucius or the Buddha, to identify the human problem with deep-rooted ignorance or various social influences. No other figure claimed to be able to forgive sin. Nor does any other major religious figure call all people to believe in himself and to find salvation in his person, as does Jesus. The Buddha, Confucius, Muhammad, and Jesus all died, but there is no reliable historical record of any of the others, apart from Jesus, being resurrected after death."[13]

Pluralism is simply inaccurate when it says all religions are the same. Preaching can help postmoderns understand this critical truth.

Sixth: Preach Concerning the Inadequacies of Pluralism

Taken to its logical extreme, pluralism is untenable. As much as a postmodern may espouse pluralism, he does not practice pluralism in every area of his life. Preaching can help postmoderns understand that pluralism provides an inadequate foundation on which to live.

For instance, pluralists ask us to say that every religious belief or practice is more or less true. But do they really understand what they are asking? Consider some of the more questionable religious practices in history: the Christian Crusades, Hindu widow burning, temple prostitution, and Aztec human sacrifice. Are these practices really as true and valid as Islamic almsgiving or Christian self-denial? It seems clear that some religious practices are false and immoral. A pluralistic worldview, however, makes it impossible to say that Mother Teresa's Sisters of Mercy are any better than the Heaven's Gate cult, or that David Koresh's compound at Waco, Texas was any worse than an Amish community.[14]

This is especially true when it comes to religious beliefs. *When faced the ultimate questions of life like "Is there a God?" and "Why am I here?" pluralism says to take Buddhism's beliefs or Islam's—it really doesn't matter.* When faced with the death of your young child, pluralism says to take David Koresh's answer or Jesus Christ's—it really doesn't matter. But we know that it does matter. We know intuitively that some religious practices or beliefs just won't work in life. Preaching can help reveal the inadequacies of pluralism.

Imagine that you're a car, and you need religion or spirituality as your fuel. So you pull into Pluralism Pumps and ask for a fill up.

Pluralism Paul at Pluralism Pumps says, "What will it be: milk, water, diesel, or unleaded?"

"Which one will enable my car to perform at its best?" you ask.

"Oh, it really doesn't matter. Just take your pick. They all work about the same, " he replies.

But it's clear that milk, water, and diesel just aren't going to work when your fuel door says "Unleaded Fuel Only."

In the same way, it's clear that some religious choices just won't work in life. They won't answer our questions. They won't bring comfort. They won't provide stability. They'd be like trying to fill a car fuel tank with water or milk. Pluralism says it really doesn't matter what you fill up with. But it does. Christian exclusivism says it does matter what you fill up with. It understands what the fuel door means when it says "Unleaded Fuel Only." It says there is one fuel, one Lord.

In addition, pluralism simply doesn't make sense. It asks us to say that God revealed himself to a group on one part of the world and said, "OK, I am many gods. And the main problem you have is your bad karma caused by your own greed. If you'll deny yourselves most of the pleasures of life I'll make sure you don't come back in the next life as a cockroach." Then God moved to another part of the world and said, "OK, forget everything I just said to that group. Here's the truth. I'm not many gods, I'm just one. There is no reincarnation. You get just one chance in this life. If you'll confess that there is no god but me and pray five times a day, you'll be able to work your way to heaven." Then God moved to another part of the world and said, "OK, forget what I've told the other two groups. Here's the real story. I am just one God. But I'm three in one: Father, Son, and Holy Spirit. And there's nothing you can do to get into heaven. So I've come to earth in the flesh as my Son. I've paid the debt of your sins by dying on the cross. And I've been raised from the dead. If you'll just believe that, you can live in heaven."[15] In this light, pluralism is almost harder to believe in than exclusivism.

Pluralism itself has an intolerant side. Pluralism says that it is always wrong to try to convince someone that his views are wrong. Pluralism affirms the truth of all viewpoints—except the viewpoint that says there is one absolute truth. Pluralism says there is no absolute truth—which is itself a statement of absolute truth. Pluralists believe in the claims of all world religions—except Christianity's claims about Jesus being the only way to salvation. Thus even pluralism has an intolerant side to it. With such, it proves that pure pluralism is an inadequate philosophy upon which to ground your life. Preaching can help reveal some of these inadequacies of pluralism.

Seventh: Approach the Issue As a Process

Pluralism is such a major obstacle that it is unlikely to be overcome in one lesson or one series of lessons. Tolerance is so ingrained into the thinking of postmoderns that it will likely take months and perhaps years to persuade them to adopt such an exclusivist faith as Christianity. Thus preaching on pluralism must be seen as a process. Over the span of a long period of time, lesson after lesson will chip away at this armor of pluralism. We must keep the war in mind, because we will lose a few battles—especially at the beginning.

Sometimes simply presenting the clear statement of Christian exclusivism creates a short-term retreat away from Christianity for postmoderns. We once preached some lessons on the gospel's exclusivism at Highland. Before the lessons, my friend John said that a sense that Christianity is intolerant of other religions was "not an obstacle at all" preventing him from becoming a Christian. Other things were keeping him from becoming a Christian, but one of them was not his sense that Christianity was patently intolerant. After hearing just one lesson on the exclusivism of

Christianity, however, he said the issue had become "somewhat of an obstacle" for him. John may have been unaware of how exclusive Christianity was until he heard it plainly presented.

My friend Larry also struggled with the first lesson he heard me present specifically on pluralism. "For a non-believer," he said, "this was a very offensive sermon." He said that the whole concept of exclusivity is based on a premise that one already accepts Jesus as the Son of God and believes that the gospels are fact. Larry does not hold this premise. *He went on to say that many non-Christians like him want to pursue their faith in God, but Christianity's demand for exclusivity may actually turn away non-Christians from God altogether.*

Like John, Larry stated that the exclusivity of Christianity was actually more of an obstacle to him after hearing this lesson than it was before hearing the lesson. Before the lesson, Larry stated that a sense that Christianity is intolerant of other religions was "an obstacle" for him. After hearing the lesson, he stated that Christianity's exclusivism was "a serious obstacle" keeping him from becoming a Christian. *Preaching which addresses pluralism can thus initially create more problems than it solves.* Ultimately, however, the Spirit of God will convince postmoderns of the truth of Christianity. We must practice patience and endurance until this happens.

Epilogue

Ultimately it is easier to not address pluralism at all in our evangelistic preaching. That is what I ended up doing with Mike, who asked "Do I have to believe Jesus is the only way to God in order to become a Christian?" I sidestepped his question. I did not take time to fully explore the rich doctrines of the incarnation, atonement, and resurrection. I did not make the effort to point out the flaws of the pluralism that was asking that question. I did not expend myself to lead him through a more careful examination of the identity of Jesus. I addressed the question by re-reading John 14:6 and explaining what it meant. We never returned to it or to the larger issue. A few days later, I baptized Mike and his wife. The next Sunday I proudly introduced him to the congregation. The following Sunday I hugged him as he entered the building for worship.

That was the last Sunday I saw him.

Too eager to baptize him, and too anxious to directly address his pluralism, I neglected to help him root his decision for Christ in the deep soil of the cross, the identity of Jesus, the incarnation, and the resurrection. I neglected to inoculate him against the disease of tolerance that would attack him after his baptism. I planted the seed in his heart without first trying to remove the rocks of pluralism. As a result, he heard the word and received it with joy. But he had no root, so he quickly fell away.

Preaching which addresses pluralism is hard work, like preparing a field of stones for a garden. In the end, however, the work and its potential for deep-rooted conversion is far better than the pain of watching someone like Mike, who matters immensely to God, walk away from Jesus.

CHAPTER TEN

Preaching Evangelistically to the Pragmatic

"If Christianity had no heaven, it would have never survived."
Once again I was in Roy's living room with his zealous golden retriever trying to get in my lap. Once again we were talking about Christianity. And once again Roy, a self-proclaimed non-Christian postmodern, raised a red flag.

Roy's take on Christianity was this: it was targeted to the down and out and its only appeal is its promise of a better life after death. It had nothing to do with life before death. It offered no hope for resolving issues in the here and now. But it did offer the hope of heaven and a better life in the hereafter. That was the only thing that drew people to it.

And to Roy, that was blasphemous (well, it would have been if he had believed in God). Why even have a religion if it cannot help people deal with the real stuff of life: broken relationships, work struggles, parenting issues, and finances? According to Roy, Christianity offered heaven while leaving hell on earth. If he was going to sign up, he wanted a faith that would equip him to live a better life here and now, not just in the hereafter.

Roy's concern is a major concern for postmoderns due to their pragmatism. Postmoderns are looking for something that "works" in resolving challenges and raising the level of joy in earthly life. If they cannot find it in Christianity, they will look elsewhere.

111

It's an attitude caught by Addie Banks, an inner city minister in the Bronx. Years ago, she and her husband, Michael, were non-Christians whose marriage was about to explode. Michael was drinking heavily. He and Addie were wounding each other with sharp words. Then one day Addie became a Christian and her whole reaction to Michael changed. This attracted Michael and he soon also became a Christian.

But then he began to despair that God would not be able to repair their marriage. He even suggested one day, "Why don't you go your way and I'll go mine?"

Addie replied with this sentence: *"If God has reconciled us to himself but cannot reconcile us to each other, then the whole thing is a fraud."*[1]

In a nutshell, that's how postmoderns feel. If Christianity only gets us to heaven but cannot fix what is broken on earth, the whole thing is a fraud. This chapter explores how to preach evangelistically to those for whom pragmatic issues are front and center.

The Legitimacy of Preaching on Pragmatic Issues

If the gospel is to gain a hearing in postmodernity, it will need to show ways in which it can deal effectively with common daily life issues. *Preaching will need to show how, at some level, the gospel deals with pragmatic issues often called "felt needs."* They are called "felt" needs because they are often needs which non-Christians "feel" they have, versus the spiritual needs they do not always feel they have.

But preaching that shows how the gospel deals with felt needs like marriage, work, and parenting has often been the object of intense criticism. I once attended a preaching seminar with 140 preachers from over twenty denominations from two countries. It was a fair representation of preachers from North America. During one session, a speaker criticized the postmodern emphasis on pragmatic felt needs and said emphatically and dramatically, "Scripture is not interested in felt needs." There were hearty "Amen's" from across the crowd of preachers. I was not one of them.

Where did we get the idea that preaching on pragmatic issues is somehow beneath us or is somehow unbiblical? I suspect it has less to do with a correct understanding of scripture and more to do with our own lofty notions of what evangelistic preaching should be about.

Scripture, on the other hand, is very interested in felt needs. I wonder what that same crowd of preachers would have said had the apostle Paul been there to read selections from his own epistles:

- "For the same reason you also pay *taxes*, for the authorities are God's servants, busy with this very thing" (Rom. 13:6).
- "When any of you has a *grievance* against another, do you dare to take it to court before the unrighteous, instead of taking it before the saints?" (1 Cor. 6:1)
- "The husband should give to his wife her *conjugal rights,* and likewise the wife to her husband" (1 Cor. 7:3).
- "Do not let the sun go down on your *anger*" (Eph. 4:26).
- "Let no *evil talk* come out of your mouths, but only what is useful for building up, as there is need" (Eph. 4:29).
- "*Husbands*, love your wives, just as Christ loved the church" (Eph. 5:25).
- "*Fathers*, do not provoke your children, or they may lose heart" (Col. 3:21).

Paul preaches about taxes, legal disputes, sex, anger, speech, marriage, and parenting. These are the kinds of earthy pragmatic issues in which postmoderns are interested. Scripture is very interested in felt needs.

One reason many preachers may be reluctant to delve into such issues today is their incomplete understanding of salvation. Many preachers understand biblical salvation to solely refer to heaven. Salvation, in the minds of some, has little to do with earth and everything to do with heaven. Being saved means going to heaven. Period. Salvation refers to what happens after someone dies. It has little to do with what happens before we die. Earth is merely a "waiting room for heaven."[2]

But the biblical idea of salvation is much broader. It not only encompasses life in heaven, but life on earth. For Abraham, salvation included the idea of an innumerable family who would become a blessing to all nations on earth. For Moses, salvation included the idea of release from Egypt. For Isaiah, salvation looked like a new heaven and a new earth.[3] For Jesus, salvation included all the earthly stuff of his programmatic statement in Luke 4:18–19: "The Spirit of the Lord is upon me, because he has anointed me to bring good news to the *poor*. He has sent me to proclaim *release* for the *captives* and recovery of *sight* to the *blind*, to let the *oppressed go free*, to proclaim the year of the Lord's favor."

In the Old Testament, salvation is not about "earthlings going up, but about heaven coming down," in a way that results in just rulers, honest judges, an equitable economy, and peace among nations.[4] In addition, one-third of the references to salvation in the New Testament have to do with rescue from earthly and current troubles.[5] Biblical salvation is not just about getting to live in heaven. It's about living heavenly on earth.

In a way, the struggle over preaching about "spiritual" issues versus "pragmatic" issues mirrors the long-fought struggle over evangelism versus social justice. Should preachers and churches simply talk to people about getting to heaven (evangelism), or about correcting injustices, serving the poor, and showing compassion to the sick, bereaved, orphans, and widows (social action)? Should preaching focus on the hereafter (evangelism), or the here and now (social action)?

Ronald Sider addresses this issue in his book *Good News and Good Works*. Sider suggests that, biblically, one cannot focus *either* on good news (evangelism) *or* good works (social justice). The Bible does not permit this either/or proposition. Instead, he suggests that biblical churches must focus on good news *and* good works. He makes a strong case for this by exploring the biblical notion of salvation. In the Old Testament, he notes, salvation almost always happens within earthly history and is social and communal in nature. Exodus 14:30 is one example: "Thus the LORD *saved* Israel that day from the Egyptians." Sider comments that "For Israel, God's single most important act of salvation was a concrete historical event that liberated the whole community."[6]

Psalm 72 links salvation with justice in the courts when it describes how God desires the judge to "defend the afflicted among the poor and *save* the children of the needy (vs. 4)."[7] In the same way, salvation in the New Testament "meant a total transformation of values, actions, and relationships."[8] In particular, salvation included physical healing, not just forgiveness of sins. One fourth of the times where Jesus' healings are recorded in the synoptic gospels, the word *save* is used to describe it. Those so "saved" include the Samaritan leper (Lk. 17:19), blind Bartimaeus (Mk. 10:52), and the man with the withered hand (Mk. 3:4–5).

Indeed, Luke uses "salvation" to describe the healing of the Gentile soldier's servant (7:3), the forgiveness of a sinful woman (7:50), the restoration of the Gerasene demoniac (8:36), and the resurrection of a dead girl (8:50). Sider writes, "He wants us to understand that this is what salvation is like—new life, wholeness, forgiveness, and healing."[9]

Salvation in both testaments always has at its center a right relationship with God. It is not strictly a horizontal or earthly notion. It has a strong vertical element. *That said, however, it is clear that salvation is meant to affect more than life in heaven. It is meant to affect life on earth.*

Is it thus too far a step to believe that where salvation included food for the poor and sight for the blind in Jesus' day, it also includes reconciled marriages, functional parenting, rescue from anger and depression, and peace-giving financial stewardship in our day? While Jesus may mean something different by functional parenting than our postmodern culture does, certainly Jesus is just as concerned with breathing life into a dysfunctional parent/child relationship as he was with breathing life into a dead twelve-year-old girl. To believe that Jesus is not interested in such practical and pragmatic issues betrays the biblical understanding of salvation.

If God has reconciled us to himself but cannot reconcile us to each other, the whole thing is a fraud. Thus evangelistic preaching can show postmoderns that the gospel and Jesus solve many of life's common and most central problems. Postmoderns want something that works. They can be shown that the gospel indeed "works." Postmoderns can be shown that believing the Bible makes a difference in daily life.

This seems to be one of the points about the book of Proverbs. Proverbs is intended to show how to live life on earth with a minimum of bumps and bruises. It teaches the wisest ways to deal with neighbors, quarrelsome spouses, and enemies. It instructs us how to pick friends. It mentors us in marriage. It guides us in the way to use words in healing rather than in destructive ways. Any person who followed the teaching of Proverbs in his daily life would immediately see what a difference the Bible can make.

Lurking behind the spiritual questions of postmoderns are often questions about the common problems of life. The question "Does anyone care about my spirit?" is often surrounded by other questions like, "Does anyone care about my finances, my divorce, my children, my addiction?"[10] Evangelistic preaching can offer a resounding "yes" to those questions. Gospel salvation is concerned both with the spirit and with finances, divorce, children, and addictions.

While this may appear to be a caving in to our consumer culture, evangelistic preaching simply cannot ignore postmodern pragmatism. *Postmoderns may not listen to our preaching on Sunday if they do not hear something that will make a difference in their lives on*

Monday. While this has always been true of non-Christians, it is especially true of postmoderns due to their intense interest on pragmatic issues.

The Limits of Preaching on Pragmatic Issues

This type of pragmatic preaching, however, cannot be the primary objective of evangelistic preaching. Our ultimate goal is not simply to reconcile husbands to wives, but to reconcile sinful humans to God. Pragmatic preaching is a step on the way to something else. It is not the final destination.

Our task as evangelistic preachers is not to become psychologists "whose task it is to engineer good relations and warm feelings."[11] Preaching, especially evangelistic preaching, must lead beyond the pragmatic and the here and now. The pragmatic and the here and now, however, can be a starting point. Pragmatic preaching can open the door to further discussion about the gospel and its larger implications concerning the hereafter.

Indeed neither a "secularized church" (one only concerned with pragmatic here-and-now issues) nor a "separatist church" (one only concerned with preparing people for the hereafter) can faithfully achieve God's mission for the church.[12] Both aspects of the gospel must be preached.

This is a lesson learned long ago by missionaries planting mission churches. Over the centuries, there have been three major shifts in missionary ideology: colonialism, anti-colonialism, and globalism.

Colonial missions focused only on the ultimate needs of humans for salvation (e.g., heaven).

Anti-colonial missions focused solely on the felt needs of humans (e.g., food, material well-being, and self-esteem).

Global missions attempt to do both, to be comprehensive in meeting physical, emotional, and spiritual needs. Such global missions may start with felt needs, but then move on to the ultimate needs of salvation, reconciliation, justice, and peace, which the gospel alone can satisfy.[13]

In this chapter, I am calling for global or comprehensive evangelistic preaching that not only prepares postmoderns for heaven but also equips them for life on earth.

James Engel provides a helpful model for putting this type of pragmatic preaching into perspective. His Engel Scale suggests that non-Christians fall on different parts of a continuum represented numerically by a –8 to a –1. Each number represents a different stage in faith, with 0 representing saving faith that culminates in conversion.[14] A person at each number has a slightly different need, which must be addressed in order for that person to move down the scale to 0. For instance, those at –8 don't even believe in God and thus need a different kind of preaching than those much closer to 0 who do believe in God, in Jesus, and the gospel.

Engel suggests that to move a person to a –5 or –4 on the scale, the preacher will need to show that the gospel does indeed meet some "felt needs." Part of helping an individual grasp the personal implications of the gospel (thus arriving at –5, according to Engel's definition of that level) and helping a person have a positive attitude toward the gospel (thus arriving at –4, according to Engel's definition of that level) involves enabling that person to see how the gospel relates to problems of everyday life, problems "felt" readily in life.

People may not listen to the gospel initially unless they see how it speaks to a felt need. This type of preaching can show how the gospel relates to needs such as physiological, safety, love, and esteem needs. Engel suggests it will be extremely difficult to lead a non-Christian beyond this point in the scale without such attention to felt needs.

But, again, speaking to felt needs is not the end of evangelistic preaching. It is simply a way to move people to a –5 and –4. Once there, they will need to be moved to a –3, for example, where they understand the fundamental (and often unfelt) need the gospel addresses: the need for salvation from sin.[15] "Pragmatic" preaching must be seen, therefore, as one step in a much larger process. It is not an end in itself. It is one step of many (the other steps being the other types of preaching covered in this book) toward a greater end: conversion.

The gospel is not simply a miracle drug that heals what ails you, be it depression, school difficulties, or marriage woes. The gospel transcends our common problems and, in fact, can *create* problems for those of postmodern persuasion. William Willimon chides much contemporary evangelistic preaching for starting with the non-Christian's felt needs rather than with the gospel. Instead of showing how the gospel can provide five quick steps to dealing with depression, for instance, Willimon argues that one might show how the gospel can lead to depression in the first place.

The Bible, states Willimon, could often care less about our problems (as we define them) because many of our felt needs are inevitably rooted in sin.[16] One problem with focusing too much on felt needs (how to solve depression) rather than real needs (how to live in the kingdom) is that "the gospel will be voted up or down on the basis of how well it relates to those needs."[17] Willimon complains:

> we have so little trust in the power of the gospel, through the enablement of the Holy Spirit, to evoke the listeners that the gospel deserves, that we either simplify, simplify, reducing the gospel to a slogan for a bumper sticker, or else we poetically describe, describe, obfuscating the gospel with some allegedly 'common human experience' that is not the gospel.[18]

Willimon's critique of preaching on felt needs is overstated, but still a needed word of caution. Preaching on these pragmatic issues cannot be the sole diet we give to hungry postmodern non-Christians. It must be one course in a multi-course meal.

Evangelistic preaching will show the radical dichotomy between life lived in the postmodern world and life lived in the gospel world. It will show the problems that one of postmodern persuasion will have living in the gospel world. It will not seek to remove the offense of that gospel world, but will instead boldly reveal that world and invite postmoderns to join it, in spite of its challenges. Evangelistic preaching will show postmoderns that there are certain crosses to carry if they wish to embrace Christ.

It will need to demonstrate the radical call to discipleship that may turn one's life upside down, rather than placing everything in life right side up. Evangelistic preaching will show, that far from simply solving common problems such as conflict within families, the gospel can in fact "set a man against his father, and a daughter against her mother" (Matt. 10:35). Evangelistic preaching will be honest about the disciple's life as one who becomes a slave of all (Mk. 10:44).

In addition, as it seeks to show that "Jesus works," evangelistic preaching will seek to avoid the conclusion "Jesus works, therefore he must be true." Postmoderns might come to this same conclusion about other faiths or philosophies that appear to work. Ultimately, evangelistic preaching seeks to elicit the significantly different conclusion, "Jesus is true, therefore he works."

With these limitations in mind, however, preaching on pragmatic issues is a critical part of evangelistic preaching in a postmodern world. If someone is sitting in a dark room and you turn on the light switch and flood the room with light, the person in the room will wince, close his eyes tightly, and turn away from the light. But if you walk into the same dark room with a candle, the person in the darkness will be attracted to the light. Gradually, then, you can increase the intensity of light as the person becomes accustomed to it.

Sometimes we take the floodlight approach in evangelistic preaching; we enter the dark room of postmodernism with a floodlight. We preach the most intense heaven and hell doctrines we can. But this approach may simply blind the listener. For someone who has little understanding of the Bible and the gospel, a gradual approach that allows for progress to the point of interest in and receptivity to the light of the gospel message may be better. It may be better to enter the darkness with a candle.[19] One such candle is pragmatic preaching.

Ideas for Preaching on Pragmatic Issues

A specific category of common "earthly" problems evangelistic preaching can deal with effectively is that of relationship problems. While postmoderns seek community, they often have difficulty initiating and sustaining community. As a result, preaching which shows how the gospel can lead to authentic community and authentic relationships may be very well received.[20]

This postmodern difficulty with community may be partially the result of the modern era that valued individualism. Such individualism led to alienation and the inability to relate. This issue therefore provides an opportunity to show how gospel gives both solutions to relationship problems and how it transcends the issue by showing how we must be part of a spiritual community.[21] In postmodern times, one of the aspects of the gospel that is truly "good news" is this: Jesus reconciles people to people and community to community.[22]

Two recent studies suggest a number of other areas where evangelistic preaching might wade into pragmatic waters. In the first, over 1,000 adults (age eighteen and over) were asked to describe the most pressing challenges and difficulties they face in life today.[23] Among the four out of five adults who could identify a problem in their life, the most common difficulties identified were these:

- finances (listed by 28%)
- health (listed by 19%)
- career concerns (listed by 16%)
- parenting struggles (listed by 11%)
- family relationships (listed by 7%)
- personal goals (listed by 7%)

A series or sermon on what Jesus says about finances or personal goals, or what Paul taught about parenting and family relationships, or what God has to say about career or health, would quickly connect with postmodern listeners eager to hear a practical word about their weekday lives.

More specifically, this study was broken down demographically. The following distinctions were found:

Men
Much more anxious about career issues than women.
Women
Nearly twice as likely as men to mention parenting issues
Much more concerned than men about personal health
Adults under 35
The most worried of all age groups about finances
The most worried of all age groups about career issues
Adults 35–54
Prioritized finances
Prioritized health issues
Adults 55 and older
Rated health factors as the top worry by a three to one margin over finances
Blacks
Racial group most concerned about finances
Racial group least concerned about parenting
Hispanic
Twice as concerned as other racial groups about career issues
Whites
Most likely racial group to prioritize financial issues
Most likely racial group to prioritize health issue

These distinctions can be kept in mind in order to target a pragmatic sermon or series to a specific demographic group.

This same study also identified national issues that concerned American adults. Those of greatest concern included the following:

- Fears about terrorism (52%)
- Economic issues such as the strength of the economy, taxes, cost of living, etc. (30%)
- Moral decline of the nation (19%)
- Unemployment and job issues (15%)
- National security (14%)
- Government performance (9%)

- Education (8%)
- Poverty (6%)
- Racism (5%)
- Health care (4%)

Once again, a sermon or series could take up some of these issues in an attempt to connect pragmatically with postmoderns. The issues of fear and anxiety are woven through several of these national concerns and could provide the basis for an effective series.

A second study uncovered factors that hinder a restful night's sleep (just one in four Americans says their sleep quality is very good or excellent).[24] According to the study, here are what American adults say keep them up at night:

- Anxiety about jobs/finances (46%)
- Aches and pains (43%)
- Thoughts of war (30%)
- Relationship issues (22%)

A short series might take up these issues with a title like "Sleep Like a Baby: What the Bible Says About the Top Three Things Keeping You Up at Night." It could show how the gospel relates to anxiety about finances, war, and relationships.

Finally, different life stages of families bring with them predictable challenges and issues that could be addressed from a preaching perspective.[25] Consider these possibilities:

- Issues for couples without children
- Separating from parents
- Sexual bonding
- Establishing couple rules
- Career beginnings
- Issues for couples with preschool children
- Pregnancy
- Birth of first child
- Career building/interruption
- Parenting
- Issues for couples with school-age children
- Balancing multiple roles (work, mate, family, school)
- Involvement in community
- Job and income needs
- Instructing children
- Issues for couples with adolescent children
- Mid-life evaluation

- Independence of children
- Couple relationship
- Advising children
- Issues for couples who are launching children
- Letting go
- Being a consultant to children
- Rediscovering spouse
- Caring for aging parents
- Financial concerns/college
- Issues for couples with an empty nest
- Relinquishing authority to children as adults
- Financial evaluation
- Work/career options
- Grandchildren
- Death of parents
- Health issues
- Issues for couples in retirement
- Couple freedom
- Friendships with adult children
- Grandchildren
- Lifestyle changes
- Facing death and serious illness

These are the kinds of issues on the minds of listeners to whom we are preaching. Finding ways to address them from a biblical viewpoint can be very instrumental in the larger task of evangelistic preaching to postmoderns.

In fact, pragmatic issues may be the door opener in evangelistic preaching. They may be the very things that first attract non-Christian postmoderns to Jesus and which leaves them open to hearing more about Jesus. My friend Larry indicated this to me once when we were talking about Jesus' teaching on relationships. He said, "If I believe Jesus can improve my relationships, yet still question if he is the Son of God, I can still respond and follow his example. *There is a group of us out there who wants to accept Jesus as an example for living, but can't accept him as the Son of God. The Bible and Jesus get me back on track [in my daily life]. And in that sense I am a Christian. I call myself a Christian in that I accept and follow Christian teaching about how to live.* In that sense, I'm more Christian than Jewish or Muslim."

It was a remarkable confession coming from one who for over a year had resisted my best efforts to lead him closer to Jesus. In pragmatic areas of life, Jesus' teaching was so attractive to him, and his practice of that teaching was so comprehensive, that he already considered himself "Christian" in one sense. He was not yet ready to accept Jesus as Son of God. But he was ready to accept Jesus' teaching on how to live this life on earth. In our evangelistic preaching, this may thus be the best starting point.

CHAPTER ELEVEN

Preaching to Those Who Value Experience

Selling an Experience

Over a year ago, a Bass Pro shop opened near my home in Memphis, Tennessee. My father-in-law, an enthusiastic fisherman and boat lover, visited the store with me during one of his trips to Memphis. The owners of the store had purchased an abandoned warehouse-sized room in an old and abandoned strip mall.

When we walked in, the ordinariness of the store was overwhelming. The walls were void of anything except an unexciting new coat of beige paint. Boats were neatly placed next to one another in two long rows that ran the length of the store. Fishing and boating equipment was displayed nearby on unadorned Peg-Board.

The store was as plain and basic as could be—one large room with rows and rows of boats and equipment.

Recently, however, the owners adopted a different sales philosophy. The store closed for several weeks and then re-opened. When I walked in for the first time again, I did not recognize the store. The plain banner-like store sign on the outside had been replaced by a huge hunting-lodge motif that made the outside look like a larger-than-life cabin plucked from the shores of the finest Montana lake.

Inside, the store had also been transformed. Instead of being greeted by plain beige walls, cold grey floor tile, and undecorated sales displays, now there were aquariums filled with the kind of fresh water fish which makes fishermen drool, stuffed animals surrounded by their "natural" habitat which were teasing the hunter-shoppers to take aim, and brand-new carpet.

Interested in bow hunting? You could flex the latest bows in their indoor archery range.

Want the latest in fishing lures? You could watch them at work in the two hundred gallon aquarium.

Duck decoys were strung from the ceiling. The latest outdoor wear was fashionably displayed. Walking through the store was now an experience, an assault on all the senses. Even if you had no interest in fishing or boats, it was worth coming just to see the stuffed animals and to try on the latest hiking boots.

The difference between the two stores is, in some ways, the difference between modernism and postmodernism.

Modernism majored on the rational, the factual, and the informational. Just throw up four walls; toss the merchandise inside in some organized fashion, and people will buy it. What really matters is the product. Moderns could be persuaded to purchase the product with a simple list of facts and figures.

Postmodernism, however, majors on the emotional, the intuitive, and the experiential. What really matters is the experience. Postmoderns are persuaded to purchase the product not just by facts and figures, but by an experience that produces a positive emotional response to the produce. Thus stores like the Bass Pro Shop strive not to just sell a product, but to sell an experience.

In their book *The Experience Economy: Work Is Theater and Every Business a Stage*, Joe Pine and Jim Gilmore write that we live in an "experience economy" in which cost or quality alone doesn't sell a product. Today, people demand an experience.[1] This is the kind of person we are trying to reach today with the gospel. Concerning their willingness to "buy into" a specific faith system, they are "sold" not simply by facts and figures about the "product." Rather, they are sold by experiences that create a positive emotional response to the product. Often, experience is more important to them than straight and factual information. How do we preach evangelistically to such postmoderns?

Preaching an Experience

The evangelistic lesson today will seek to create an experience for postmoderns—a positive emotional reaction concerning

Christianity. In broad terms, "Churches in postmodern communities will be built not around great preachers, but around great experiences. Preaching must cease to be the...presentation of points of view or the representation of arguments that can be verbalized; rather it must become a rushing mighty wind that blows through the congregation . . ."[2]

Evangelistic preaching which is effective in the postmodern era will not seek to persuade solely through argument and logic, but also through experience. It will not convince postmoderns of the truth of the gospel simply by building watertight cases for truth. It will also enable postmoderns to experience that truth itself. Evangelistic preaching will seek to allow the word of God to be "living and active" and "sharper than any two-edged sword, piercing until it divides soul from spirit" (Heb. 4:12).

Experience, however, can be overemphasized so that it eclipses substance. Even in the ecstatic worship of the Corinthian church, Paul called for reason and sensibility. It does little good for the spirit to be engaged while the mind is unfruitful (1 Cor. 14:14). It is possible for the pursuit of an *experience* of God to replace the pursuit of *truth* about God.[3] One may leave with warm and fuzzy feelings but with no greater insight into or knowledge of God (at least true knowledge of God).

What are some ways in which we can make preaching "experiential" while at the same time retaining its substantive focus on the truth of God? Here are four strategies that may help: attention to the GREs of worship, evocative language in the lesson, inductive structures in the lesson, and testimonies within the lesson.

Strategy One: The GREs of Worship

The Graduate Record Exam, or GRE, proved that I was fit to enter graduate school several years ago. In a similar way, the GREs of worship create worship that is "fit" to connect with postmoderns. In previous chapters, I've discussed the *G* and *R* in GRE: God-encountering worship and Relational worship. The *E* in GRE stands for *Experiential*—worship that creates an emotional, intellectual, and physical experience for the worshiper. Experiential worship connects with postmoderns in a saving way.

In his study of Generation X, Tom Beaudoin found that many members of this generation value experience. They come to know and be persuaded of truth through experience. Thus, Beaudoin urges churches to use three things in worship:

symbols
silence
darkness

These three elements are experiential in nature.[4]

Leonard Sweet suggests that music is the key to connecting with the postmodern bias for experience. He urges churches to cultivate a worship that is summarized by the word EPIC (Experiential, Participatory, Interactive, and Communal). It is significant that he places a high priority on the importance of an experiential worship. Sweet contrasts Pentecostal, Eastern Orthodox, and Episcopalian churches that use physical movement (kneeling, hand raising, etc.), symbols, and icons in their worship versus evangelical churches that ultimately create what he calls "pew-potatoes."

Sweet argues that postmodern people come to worship to encounter God, not just to understand God, and that the worship style of the former churches, therefore, is better suited to reaching postmoderns than the latter. Postmoderns want experience, not simply explanation. As a result, Sweet states, Eastern Orthodox churches are growing in today's postmodern culture. But one particular element of worship is especially important, according to Sweet: music. Music is critical in helping create an experience and an encounter.[5] Sally Morgenthaler, in her book *Worship Evangelism*, discusses the role of worship music in evangelism.[6]

In general, we are trying to create a worship that not only engages the mind, but the heart, the eyes, and the body. We are striving for a worship that affects as many senses as possible. What follows are suggestions for creating this kind of experiential worship.

Lighting—As noted above, lighting is an important element in creating a worship that engages all the senses. Often, a darker setting can create a feeling of intimacy. Candles could be lit instead of flooding the room with electric light. On the other side of the spectrum, bright light can create a feeling of excitement. Someone on the worship team could coordinate lighting to match the mood of the songs and other elements in worship, changing lighting throughout the service as the mood dictates.

Prayer—Rather than having everyone close their eyes, bow their heads, and remain seated while praying, it could be helpful to have them engage their bodies in prayer. For instance, everyone could be asked to write down their requests and then bring their requests to the front. While up front, they would then pick up a slip of paper left by someone else, return to their seat, and pray for the need mentioned on the slip. In addition, simply asking people to stand while praying, or even kneel while praying, can help engage them physically in worship.

Drama—When people can see and hear a spiritual truth, rather than simply hear it, that truth can more greatly impact them. Drama has become almost a norm in churches that are reaching postmoderns today. The drama can simply introduce a spiritual issue that will be resolved by the sermon. Or the drama can illustrate the central point of the sermon. Or, drama could be used to simply enact biblical events and "bring them to life" during worship. This might be especially appropriate on special days like Palm Sunday. Imagine the impact on worshipers of watching an actor actually riding a donkey into the worship area while throngs of people shout and lay down palm branches! Christmas and Easter provide opportunities for this kind of biblical reenactment.

Video/Images—Image-driven worship is experiential worship. While singing, images or videos could be shown which illustrate the point of the songs. For instance, while singing about creation, images of mountains, flowers, and rivers could be shown. While people are walking into the worship area, videos or images can be projected which relate to the point of the lesson or to the theme of the worship songs. In addition, videos can be used in the same way drama can be:to introduce an issue that will be addressed in the sermon. Churches can create their own "man on the street" videos by going to a local mall or university and asking people to comment on the topic that will be addressed in the sermon. Professional videos are also available in this regard. Highway Video produces 3–5 minute topical videos for use in worship (www.highwayvideo.com).

Communion—Communion is, by nature, one of the most experiential elements of worship. We not only see and hear. We taste and touch. It may be the only time in worship when we get to utilize the sense of taste. Both biblically and evangelistically, communion should play an important part in every worship service. It provides an enormous opportunity to create a visceral experience for worshipers. Many things can be done to capitalize on this opportunity.

For instance, in one gathering recently, men brought in an actual cross and hammers during communion. People were asked to go to the front, write down a struggle, and nail that struggle onto the cross. Then they went back and ate and drank the supper.

A video of Jesus on the cross can be shown during communion.

Music videos such as "Watch the Lamb" can be integrated into communion.

A small group could simply carry a cross through the audience during communion.

Worshipers could be encouraged to share a prayer with the person or persons seated next to them during communion.

Testimonies from Christians could be given during communion concerning ways in which they've experienced forgiveness in Christ.

Baptism—While being baptized is certainly an experience, so is witnessing one. There are few things more powerful than watching someone commit his or her life to Christ in baptism. Sadly, many churches do not integrate baptisms into their worship services. They thus rob non-Christian postmoderns of this potentially life-changing experience of witnessing a baptism. Every effort should be made to make baptisms a part of the worship service. When they cannot, due to circumstances of the one being baptized or due to the lack of a baptistry in the worship area, baptisms can be videotaped and shown during next week's worship service.

Handouts—Putting something meaningful into the hands of worshipers helps create even more of an experience. For instance, if preaching on love, the elders of the church might stand at the doors and hand out flowers to each person entering or exiting the worship area. This touch and smell adds to the worship experience.

Special music—Choruses or solos can be a powerful way to use music to create an experience for worshipers. While congregational singing should be the norm (because it is biblical and experiential), this type of special music, when well done, makes an impact on those listening.

As much thought should be given to these issues as is given to the preparation of the sermon itself. The physical setting in which the sermon is delivered (i.e., the worship center, sanctuary, etc.) should be utilized to its greatest extent to create a "mood," an "atmosphere," an experience, for the worshiper. Evangelistic preaching will need to be accompanied by a worship that uses as many tools as possible to be experiential.

The importance of this is seen in a 1999 survey of college students from fourteen countries. While these students were Christian (representing forty-one denominations), the attitudes about worship they represent are thoroughly postmodern. When asked what kind of worship they desired, they stated that they did not want "contemporary" or "traditional." Instead, they were seeking worship with these characteristics:

- provides a genuine encounter with God
- provides depth and substance
- involves more frequent observance of the Lord's Supper
- is more participatory than passive
- is contemplative rather than noisy
- involves more creative use of the senses.[7]

These students were looking for a worship that provided experience and encounter.

A recent study asked members of my own movement, Churches of Christ, who had left one church for another, why they left. Selecting from thirty-two possible reasons, the top two reasons given were these:

- Seventy-seven percent said they were drawn to a church with a more *heartfelt/expressive* style of *worship*
- Seventy-three percent said the *worship* service at their previous church was *uninspiring*.

These items far surpassed others such as a desire for more gender inclusion and conflict over doctrinal issues.[8] As in the previous study, this study reflects attitudes about worship present in Christians. These attitudes, however, represent typical postmodern attitudes—a desire for a greater experience in worship. Of those leaving churches within Churches of Christ, experience in worship is one of the primary factors leading them out. It may be one of the primary factors keeping non-Christian postmoderns out. They, too, desire worship which offers an experience and an encounter.

Strategy Two: Language

In order to connect with the postmodern value for experience, evangelistic preaching can not only utilize a certain kind of worship, but a certain kind of language. It can preach the gospel in language that not only seeks to persuade the head of the truth of the gospel, but the heart as well. *Preaching needs language that not only convinces the mind but inflames the soul.*

There are, in general, two kinds of language. One kind is propositional and informational. It seeks to spell out everything, leaving no questions unanswered. It consists primarily of factual statements.[9] Using this kind of language, Psalm 42:1 might read, "In the same way that four-legged animals seek liquid refreshment from a naturally occurring stream, so I sense within me a spiritual desire to know more about you God, the God of Scripture."

A second kind of language is imaginative in nature. It is the kind used in novels and poems. It evokes emotions and creates experiences for the listener. Psalm 42:1 is originally written in this kind of language: "As a deer longs for flowing streams, so my soul longs for you, O God."

This is the kind of language, for instance, used by Eugene Peterson in his translation called *The Message.* Read his take on Psalm 63:1–5: "God—you're my God! I can't get enough of you! I've worked up such hunger and thirst for God, traveling across dry and weary deserts. So here I am in the place of worship, eyes open, drinking in your strength and glory. In your generous love I am really living at last! My lips brim praises like fountains. I bless you every time I take a breath; My arms wave like banners of praise to you. I eat my fill of prime rib and gravy; I smack my lips. It's time to shout praises!"

Properly used, language can help create an experience for the listener during evangelistic preaching. It can evoke feelings from the heart and soul.

It does this when it is image-driven. In the modern world, the *word* was the primary unit of cultural currency. In the postmodern world, however, the *image* is the primary unit. The modern preacher exegeted *words* to make a point. The postmodern preacher exegetes *images.*[10]

This is the kind of language in which Jesus often preached. He described God's rule as a mustard seed, a sower sowing seed, a pearl of great price, and a shepherd searching for a lost sheep. He didn't just use language to tell things; He used language to show things. Listeners could "see" what Jesus was talking about. Consider the Sermon on the Mount. By one count, Jesus used 142 comparisons and 348 images, pictures, examples, and illustrations in the course of a sermon that is easily spoken out loud in about twenty minutes.[11]

The point here is simple: in order to work together with the Holy Spirit in moving the hearts of the postmodern listener, in order to help create a listening experience, we can use language in our preaching which is creative and image-driven.

Strategy Three: Inductive Preaching

A third way evangelistic preaching can aim to be experiential is through the use of inductive structures. Until recently, most preaching (including evangelistic preaching) assumed that the listener believed in the authority of the Bible, the preacher and the church. Preachers therefore used a deductive form in their sermons.[12]

Generally speaking, deductive reasoning moves from a general statement of truth to particular statements of truth. The preacher announces the general point of the sermon at the beginning (e.g., we are sinners in need of atonement) and then develops that main point in particular ways (drawing out the implications of that main point, giving examples of it, providing a rationale for believing it, or applying it to different spheres of life). The strength of the deductive sermon is its clarity. The listener has every opportunity to "get the point." *The deductive sermon assumes that the listener believes in the preacher's authority and thus will believe the preacher's main point ("It must be true, the preacher said it.").* The preacher doesn't have to prove his point. He can merely state it and then illustrate it.

Inductive speaking, however, moves from the particular to a general conclusion. In the inductive sermon, the preacher moves from particular observations, questions, examples, or experiences (e.g., particular instances of people who act sinful and appear to be in need of atonement) to a major conclusion, which makes sense of those particulars (we are all sinners in need of atonement).

The strength of the inductive sermon is that it invites the listener to participate in the sermon and maintains a certain suspense, which sustains the listener's attention. "The point" is withheld until the end of the lesson. In addition, the listener is not asked to "take the preacher's word for it" from the very beginning. Instead, the listener is drawn by the particulars to convince himself of the truth of the general conclusion.

Inductive preaching therefore both creates an experience (by withholding the general [and most important] conclusion until the end) and utilizes the authority of experience (by starting with particular experiences familiar to the listener rather than starting with the general conclusion stated by the preacher).

Deductive preaching has been the form of choice for much evangelistic preaching in the past and present. The five evangelistic sermons by older Restoration Movement preachers and the six by contemporary preachers in the Restoration Movement in Gresham and Keeran's *Evangelistic Preaching* depend heavily upon deductive forms.[13] In an analysis of the persuasion techniques of seven preachers in the Churches of Christ, Eddie Cloer found that out of their thirty-nine evangelistic lessons, twenty-four were deductive.[14]

Deductive preaching depends upon the listener already accepting the truth of the opening claim, or at least being willing to be convinced of its truth through logic and empirical evidence. Such an approach fits the context of pre-modernism or modernism. *With postmodernism's pluralism, anti-institutionalism, and experiential bent, however, strict deduction may not be the best approach.* If the listener does not agree with the proposition set forth, or is hostile to the topic or to authority, the deductive approach can create more problems than it solves. The postmodern listener is more likely to say to the preacher, "Well, that's just your opinion."

Strict deductive preaching serves "only to add more information to that which already lay listless and useless on the minds of the hearers." Deduction can lead a person to agree with the statement, "I am a sinner." What is needed, however, is a manner of communication that leads the listener to "experience in every corner of mind and heart" that "I am undone!" Obviously, this ultimately takes place only through the work of the Holy Spirit in the heart of the listener. Preachers, however, can assist or hinder this work of the Spirit by the way they preach. Preachers best assist the convicting work of the Spirit by using inductive communication in the same way that Jesus did in his parables.[15]

A sermon that allows the listener to walk with the preacher through particulars that finally lead up to a conclusion, rather than stating a conclusion up front, creates its own kind of authority—an authority independent of the preacher, Bible, or church. It creates an authority of experience.[16]

Nathan's sermon to David after David's sin with Bathsheba illustrates the ability of the inductive form to overcome negative listener bias.[17] The sermon needed to persuade David of his personal sinfulness. David, however, was in a state of rebellion against God. Had Nathan deductively started with a general conclusion like "David, you are a sinner," and then proceeded to particular examples of sinfulness, the lesson would have failed. Starting inductively, however, with a particular (and seemingly unrelated) story of someone else's sin, Nathan was able ultimately to move to the general conclusion of David's sinfulness.

There are many different forms of induction and ways in which induction can work within a sermon. Summaries of the various models of inductive preaching can be found in David Buttrick's *Homiletic: Moves and Structures*,[18] Richard Eslinger's *A New Hearing: Living Options in Homiletic Method*,[19] and Eugene L. Lowry's *The Sermon: Dancing on the Edge of Mystery*.[20] But while each of these inductive models is distinct, they share certain similarities. *The defining characteristic of most of them is this: a plot that moves in a "strategic delay" in getting to the point.*[21]

It is this plot and strategic delay that seem crucial to creating an experience and thus connecting with postmoderns. Where deductive sermons have little plot and no delay in getting to the point (they actually start at the point), inductive sermons, ideally, develop a plot, similar to a story, withholding crucial information and resolution to the plot as long as possible. The point of the lesson comes as close to the end as possible.

Not every evangelistic lesson needs to be inductive. Inductive forms can be abused to the point that the sermon's message gets buried in the particulars, lacks an adequate and authoritative conclusion, and remains unnecessarily obscure.[22] In addition, due to the biblical ignorance of postmoderns, deductive teaching sermons will be needed as part of evangelistic preaching. Pure induction, in fact, may be counter- productive in a postmodern era. A purely inductive lesson rarely deals in a direct way with an actual biblical text and its specific words, doctrines, interpretation, and literary and historical contexts. In its effort to maintain a narrative plot that builds to a climax of suspense, the purely inductive sermon cannot afford to stop and deal with such deductive issues. As a result, the listener walks away with many questions about the text, its meaning, and its application unanswered.

Certain types of induction, however, can help the lesson be more experiential in nature. At least some evangelistic lessons should be inductive in nature. *In general, postmoderns will respond more favorably to an inductive homiletic method because they are skeptical, subjective, and non-sequential in their thinking and crave stories.*[23]

Evangelistic preaching can thus use induction to varying degrees. One can even use inductive/deductive forms in which the lesson begins inductively and arrives at the general conclusion (the point), perhaps midway or two-thirds of the way through. That general conclusion is then fleshed out deductively, spelling out implications and applications.[24]

This is similar to what Jesus often did with parables. Jesus would tell a purely inductive parable which imaginatively captured people's attention and communicated godly truth in story-like fashion. Then the disciples would ask questions about the parable and its meaning and Jesus would deductively explain the parable to them.

Whatever their form, however, it seems clear that inductive elements are critical in creating an experience in sermons. When, for example, was the last time you got caught up reading the owner's manual to your car (strict deduction)? When was the last time you got caught up in reading a good novel or watching a powerful movie (pure induction)? Postmoderns crave the experience of the latter. Inductive structures in our preaching can provide this.

Strategy Four: Personal Testimonies

A final tool for connecting with the experiential bias of postmoderns in a redemptive way is personal testimonies. *Personal testimonies help establish the truth of the gospel through personal experience.*

Since postmoderns tend to make judgments based upon what is experienced rather than just upon what is logically or rationally true, they may be more likely to believe the gospel when they see that it has been proven true in the experience of one of their peers. In fact, one author suggests "the apologetic for this age is the reality of Christ in the life of the believer."[25]

For postmoderns, truth claims which have been experientially proven by those they admire have much greater authority than truth claims whose sole authority is "the Bible tells me so," or "this objective evidence tells me so." Ronald Allen argues that in the postmodern era, "The congregation is most persuaded of the truth of a claim when it is confirmed in the life story of a person or community with whom they can identify."[26]   Evangelism today works best through testimony/narrative evangelism that shows the plausibility and authenticity of the gospel through the story of an individual. This connects better with postmoderns because it is personal and not authoritarian.[27]

This is not to suggest that we cannot be authoritarian in our evangelistic preaching. Nor is it to suggest that we cannot use rational arguments and objective evidence to persuade postmoderns of the truth of the gospel. Apologetics and authoritative preaching still have a role to play, even in postmodernity. But the personal testimony can be used alongside these in a powerful way that connects with the postmodern bias towards experience. Apologetics and authoritative preaching provide something which personal testimonies cannot (an in-depth treatment of an issue and an explicit call for faith and repentance). Personal testimonies provide something that apologetics and authoritative preaching cannot (a lived experience of the gospel and an inductive and implicit call for faith and repentance). It is not either/or, but both/and. In the postmodern world, personal testimonies are a vital part of the evangelistic preaching toolbox.

Kelly Monroe has edited a book entitled *Finding God at Harvard*.[28] Its purpose is to address postmodern skepticism of Christianity through the use of personal stories of outstanding Harvard students and faculty who have found a relationship with God and Jesus to be essential to their lives. The book is meant to be used as an outreach tool for Christians to pass on to their non-Christian friends. It is an example of the reliance upon testimony as an evangelistic strategy for reaching postmoderns.

Such testimonies, in fact, revive an old and biblical method of evangelism:

In Mark 5:19 Jesus sends the now healed Gerasene demoniac to his people to *"tell them how much the Lord has done for you, and what mercy he has shown you."* Jesus anticipated that the man's testimony would make an impression on the non-Christians to whom he spoke.

Similarly, in John 4:29, the woman at the well testifies to her townspeople, "Come and see a man who told me everything I have ever done. He cannot be the Messiah, can he?" We are told later in John 4:39 that "Many Samaritans from that city believed in him because of the woman's testimony."

It was their testimony that the shepherds shared in Luke 2:17: "When they saw this, they made known what had been told them about this child."

Peter summarizes preaching as testimony when he says in Acts 4:20, *"For we cannot keep from speaking about what we have seen and heard."*

The simple description of the apostles as "witnesses" in Acts 1:8 implies that, at some level, their ministry was one of sharing their testimony, what they had personally witnessed.

This is not only a theoretical model for postmodern evangelism it has been proven experientially. Vickie, one of our teens, tells of a time when a Highland member came to speak at her school's chapel. Usually, she says, most of her friends play cards while the songs are sung and the speaker speaks. This day, however, her friends' eyes were fixated on the speaker the entire chapel. The speaker was a twenty-something former drug user. He told of how drugs had wrecked his life and of how God had saved his life. Vickie says, "It was weird to see everyone listening in chapel." Most of the teens in chapel that day were Christians. But the story illustrates the power that testimonies can have on a postmodern audience. Vickie says that through the rest of the day, friends came and wanted to talk to her about what the speaker had said.

Preachers can take advantage of this by using one or more of the following within the context of their lesson, or as a complement to their lesson at another point in the worship service:

- Their own personal conversion stories or testimonies of ways in which Christ has helped them
- Similar stories of members of their churches (best done in person by the individual him/herself)
- Or historic/biographical testimonies of significant figures in past and present (e.g., Leo Tolstoy; the apostle Paul; Franklin Graham, etc.)

Harold and I strive to use testimonies within our lessons as well as during the worship service. For instance, in recent lessons Harold and I used the stories of our own conversions. In a lesson once that explored Christianity in contrast to other world faiths, I told the story of the conversion from Buddhism and atheism of one of our Asian members (he was not yet proficient enough in English to give the testimony in person). I also had a young Christian physician get up after the lesson and tell her journey of searching through different religions and finally settling on Christianity.

A non-Christian acquaintance of mine named Lou was moved by this physician's testimony. He said that hearing how someone so educated in certain fields of science could still come to faith in Christ was inspiring and gave him courage to continue his investigation of Christianity. Lou said, "I'm probably right now where she was at one point. I'm on the same journey." He felt like her experience was his, that she was speaking for and to him, and that her experience was thus authoritative.

Missions or Manipulation?

None of this is an attempt to manipulate non-Christians through "wise and persuasive words" or to rely on fleshly strategies rather than the Spirit's work in the hearts of the listeners. It is simply an attempt to approach postmoderns from a missionary's perspective.

A missionary is forced to consider the specific language in which he is going to preach. The language which best reaches postmoderns is rich in images and metaphors.

A missionary will strive to understand what the natives hold as authoritative and strive to utilize that, when possible, to his advantage. Experiential worship, induction, and testimonies provide the opportunity to connect with something widely held as authoritative today.

In addition, a missionary will even critique things within the culture that stand at odds with the gospel. We too may critique the way that postmoderns often rely solely on an experience to make important decisions. For instance, my brother called recently. He had just met with church leaders from all over Texas in order to train them in evangelistic outreach to the international populations in their communities.

One of the leaders told of a couple from Jordan who moved into the Houston area. He and his church reached out to them, served them, and shared the gospel with them. Both husband and wife abandoned their Islamic faith and came to faith in Jesus. The wife's parents, however, learned of this and flew immediately from Jordan to Houston, Texas. They persuaded the wife to divorce her husband, to renounce Christ and return to Islam, and to move back to Jordan. The husband, however, remained loyal to Christ in spite of horrible cost. Today he cannot return to Jordan for fear of his life. He cannot ever see his wife or children again.

On the one hand, such an experience might be the very thing that would lead postmoderns to reject the gospel. In this sense, Christianity certainly doesn't "feel good." It's not a "good" experience. Postmoderns, because they often rely too much on experience, might thus be tempted to reject Christianity. "If that's the kind of experience Christianity brings, count me out," they might say. We need to help postmoderns understand that the lack of a positive experience alone is no reason to reject Christianity.

On the other hand, such an experience, told by the husband himself to a crowd of spiritually interested postmoderns, might be the very thing that opens their hearts to Christ. To hear from someone who has found in Christ something so precious that he would not exchange it for his wife, children, and even his life, would powerfully impact non-Christian listeners and likely move them to serious reflection upon their own values and spirituality.

These four tools are simply a way of opening ourselves up to the work of the Spirit. They make us more available to the Spirit and its convicting power. My hope is, that by means of them, the Spirit will make possible in our preaching what it did in Paul's: "For we know, brothers and sisters, be loved by God, that he has chosen you, because our message of the gospel came to you not in word only, but also in power and in the Holy Spirit and with full conviction" (1 Thess. 1:4–5).

CHAPTER TWELVE

The Sermon on the Postmodern Mount: A Test Case

Over the years, three images have been influential in my understanding of preaching.

First, Karl Barth, a prominent German theologian, once said that the church should preach with a Bible in one hand and a *newspaper* in the other.

Second, I once heard Billy Graham, the famous evangelist, update that advice by saying that the church ought to preach with a Bible in one hand and a *television* in the other.

Third, those who taught me preaching in graduate school used the image of a *desk* at which I might be preparing my Sunday morning sermon. On one side of the desk would be the biblical text along with the writers and thinkers of the ages giving commentary on the text. On the other side of the desk would be a representation of those who would be listening to the lesson that Sunday morning; a Bible in one hand and a *newspaper*, or a *television*, or the *world* in the other hand.

The point of these three images is the same: preaching is informed both by the Word we seek to share with others and by the World to whom we speak. Sole attention to *Word* without any recognition of the World results in the kind of sermon that an acquaintance of mine told me about over lunch recently. He reported that his preacher's last sermon took as its text Matthew 26:30, which reports that after the Last Supper, Jesus and the disciples sang a hymn and went out to the Mount of Olives. The preacher spent thirty minutes that Sunday morning explaining what hymn Jesus and the disciples might have sung. He gave reasons why he felt that it was hymn X and not hymn Y. To the teen anxious about school, to the mother needing help raising her child, to the accountant struggling at work, to the retiree wondering if anyone still cares, this is what the preacher preached. As a result, the Christians went home dry as a bone. And the non-Christians, if any were present, left no closer to God and to the gospel than when they arrived. All Word and no World results in preaching that misses the mark, that speaks to questions no one is asking.

Complete attention to *World*, however, without any recognition of the Word results in the kind of preaching I once heard at my brother-in-law's former church in Phoenix, Arizona. The preacher stood and talked about self-esteem but never once referred to God's word. I don't mean he didn't read four or five texts. I mean not once did he even read one biblical text, make an allusion to a biblical text, or cited a phrase from a biblical text. In fact, as best as I can remember, he never even mentioned God. Some may have left feeling warm and fuzzy, hearing the preacher's call to be the best we can be. But I, and others, left feeling rootless. All World and no Word results in preaching that may speak to questions people are asking, but it never roots us in God's answers to those questions. In addition, it may miss the most important questions of all.

Thus the church is at its best when it balances both Word and World.

We observe this delicate balance in the Incarnation. John tells us that "in the beginning was the Word...and the Word was God." But the Word "became flesh and lived among us" (Jn. 1:1, 14). Jesus, John also tells us, was "full of grace and truth" (Jn. 1:14). Jesus was all Word. Jesus was complete truth. But he was also all World. The first century Palestinian world influenced how the Word was presented in the Incarnation. Can you imagine if Jesus landed in Palestine as a white-skinned German-speaking man? He would have still been full of truth and Word, but no one would have listened, no one would have understood the Word. Instead, Jesus came as a brown-skinned Palestinian man speaking Aramaic and Greek. Because the Incarnation took the World into account, the Word found its way into people's hearts.

Often, it's a lack of attention to either Word or World that causes preachers to become ineffective in their ministries. And there's a great deal of ineffectiveness going on in churches today, as I noted in Chapter One. Some might suggest that the problem lies in our imperfect understanding of the Word. But I would suggest that part of the problem lies in our imperfect understanding of the World. Put simply, the World has become postmodern, and much of the preaching in our churches has not.

The word *postmodern* immediately causes confusion for many of us. Someone in our church, upon hearing that word recently, said, "Postmodern?! What in the world is that!?" That's exactly how many of us feel. What in the world is postmodernism? And what does it have to do with church and ministry and effectively sharing the Gospel? At its most basic, postmodernism is a confession that the people described in that newspaper which is in one hand, or the television which is in one hand, or who sit at my desk when I'm preparing a sermon are very different than the people who might have been in that newspaper or on the television or at my desk fifty years ago. Postmodernism is simply an acknowledgement that the World has undergone a radical change.

Perhaps the easiest way to explain postmodernism is to do a case study. Let's imagine that we are preparing to preach from the Sermon on the Mount to a group of postmoderns. And let's use that image of a desk with which I began. On one side of the desk let's place the Sermon on the Mount, the Word we'd like to share. And on the other side of the desk, let's place some postmoderns. They will attempt to coach us so that we can leave our study equipped to preach the Sermon on the Mount with postmoderns in an effective and fruitful way. While we study the Sermon, we'll hear each postmodern sitting at the desk make a particular request. Each request represents a characteristic of postmoderns. Each request has a way of influencing how we might eventually preach the Sermon on the Mount to postmoderns.

Include Some of the Basics

As we begin prepping our sermon from the Sermon on the Mount, we hear from one of the postmoderns at our desk. "*Include some of the basics*," she says. "As you prepare to share the Sermon on the Mount with my peers, would you please cover some of the basics, some of the ground level stuff?" Postmoderns are uninformed about basic Christianity. As a result, when it comes to the Word, they don't even know the fundamentals.

Thus, as we contemplate preaching the Sermon on the Mount to postmoderns, this first request will likely influence what we share and how we share it. For instance, here are some of the concepts in the Sermon that we'll likely need to define for our postmodern listeners:

- Kingdom of heaven
- The Law and the Prophets
- Righteousness
- The Pharisees and teachers of the law
- Sanhedrin
- Tax collectors
- Synagogues
- Fasting
- Solomon
- Prophesy

You and I may know what all these things are. The Sermon assumes we do. It's unlikely, however, that most postmoderns do. Preaching without at least briefly defining these terms in the course of the sermon will result in listeners who have no idea what Jesus is talking about.

In addition, this characteristic of postmoderns will likely cause us to trim down our preaching. We might be tempted to try to preach a whole chapter of the Sermon to a postmodern in one sermon, but with so much material that is so unfamiliar to postmoderns, a better strategy will be to choose a much smaller portion of the Sermon for each sermon, thus minimizing the amount of unfamiliar material.

"Include some of the basics," this postmodern says. It's a request we can grant. A request which, if granted, will increase the effectiveness of our preaching.

Make It Practical

As we continue studying the Sermon at our desk, a second postmodern speaks up. "*Make it practical*," he says. "Don't give me something that's all pie-in-the-sky. I need something that's going to make a real difference on Monday morning." Postmoderns are less interested in theology for its own sake than in how theology can resolve daily problems. They want a spirituality which makes a difference in their daily lives and which helps them make a difference in the lives of others.

Such a pragmatic perspective will influence how we present the Sermon on the Mount to postmoderns. In a postmodern context, we will want to especially present Jesus' teaching from the Sermon that deals with daily life. Here are some of the texts from the Sermon that might appeal a great deal to our pragmatic postmoderns:

- Dealing with anger (Matt. 5:21–22)
- Advice on broken relationships (Matt. 5:23–26)
- Words about building a strong marriage (Matt. 5:27–32)
- The importance of honesty (Matt. 5:33–37)
- How to deal with demanding people (Matt. 5:38–42)
- What to do about people who dislike you (Matt. 5:43–48)
- Gaining a healthy perspective on money and possessions (Matt. 6:19–34)

This does not mean that we ignore the rest of the Sermon on the Mount. It does mean, however, that we give this practical material high priority. By granting this request of postmoderns, they may be even more likely to give the rest of the Sermon on the Mount a hearing.

Guide Me to Deeper Spirituality

Still sitting at our desk, a third postmodern speaks up. *"Guide me to deeper spirituality,"* she says. "When you get ready to preach to me, give me something that's going to help me get in touch with God. Provide me something that's going to feed my soul." It turns out that while postmoderns are generally ignorant of basic Christianity, they are very interested in spiritual issues.

Knowing this will obviously influence our approach to preaching the Sermon on the Mount. For instance, we may want to give special attention to Matthew 6:1–18 that covers three "acts of righteousness": giving to the poor, praying, and fasting. All three are classic disciplines that have led seekers to deeper levels of intimacy with God. In our preaching to postmoderns, we might spend a significant amount of time here discussing Jesus' words, especially his words on prayer.

In addition, we may want to draw the attention of our postmodern friend to some specific beatitudes. One promises to enable us to "see God" (Matt. 5:8). Another promises to make us "sons of God" (Matt. 5:9). A third promises to fill us with God's righteousness (Matt. 5:6). These are appealing promises in a spiritually minded postmodern world. We may want to camp out on these beatitudes for a while in our preaching.

Finally, this characteristic of postmoderns may influence our broader approach to preaching the Sermon on the Mount. Rather than simply helping our friend understand a specific text in the

Sermon (bibliocentric), or gain practical knowledge that affects daily living (anthropocentric and factocentric), we will want to ultimately help this postmodern encounter God in the Sermon (theocentric). We will want to explore with him what the Sermon says about God. We will want to search it for how it points to the Father, not simply the Father's will for our lives.

For instance, there are at least ten images of God in the Sermon:

- One who blesses (5:3–10)
- Father (5:16, 45, 48; 6:1, 4, 6, 8, 9, 14, 15, 18, 26, 32; 7:11)
- One who is perfect (5:48)
- One who rewards us (6:4, 6, 18)
- King of a kingdom (6:10)
- Forgiver (6:12)
- One who delivers us from the evil one (6:13)
- Provider of the necessities of life (6:25–34)
- Parent who gives good gifts (7:11)
- Judge (7:1–2)

Since postmoderns are spiritually interested, we may want to spend some time with them exploring these images of God in the Sermon. We might have easily overlooked these images if it weren't for this postmodern at our desk making this request: "Guide me to deeper spirituality."

Lead Me to Warmer Community

Soon a fourth postmodern at our desk speaks: "*Lead me to warmer community.* As you preach, help me see how Christianity will make it possible for me to form intimate relationships. And, don't just preach about relationships. Do something that will connect me meaningfully with others." Postmoderns are seeking a spirituality that is relational in nature. They value and seek community.

Knowing how much they value community will impact our approach to preaching the Sermon on the Mount. For instance, much of the material in Matthew 5:21–48 deals with relationship issues. Jesus discusses the following relationships:

- Relationship with friends and family (5:22–24)
- Relationship with spouse (5:27–32)
- Relationship with others in general (5:33–37)
- Relationship with those who treat us badly (5:38–42)
- Relationship with those who are our critics (5:43–48)

Thus, we may want to focus on these texts, showing our postmodern friend how Jesus' teaching enables rich and healthy relationships.

In addition, this characteristic of postmoderns reveals the weakness of just preaching. We must also provide a way for postmoderns to experience community, not simply hear about community. That's why ministries such as the teen Huddles or adult Reach Groups and Sunday school classes at my church are so critical. Postmoderns are desperately seeking authentic relationships. These ministries provide this very thing.

Show Me Tolerance

Still reading through the Sermon at our desk, a fifth postmodern speaks. Here's what he says: "*Show me tolerance. Whatever you preach to me, I want to hear something about acceptance and tolerance. I want a spirituality which has room for all colors, all genders, all ages, and all beliefs.*"

This particular postmodern characteristic presents both opportunities and challenges. It creates an opportunity for us to highlight the inclusivism and tolerance of Jesus revealed in the Sermon on the Mount. For instance, in Matthew 5:46–47 Jesus urges us to not simply love those who love us, and to not just greet those who are our brothers. The underlying principle is one of tolerance. We are to love all people and to greet even those who are not like us. This text presents a very powerful message in a postmodern culture which values tolerance.

In addition, the picture of God in what is called the Lord's Prayer (Matt. 6:9–13) is one of a God who is very inclusive. We address him not as "*my* God in heaven." He is not the God of only one race or one nationality. He is "*our* Father in heaven." Further, he gives "*us*" "*our* daily bread." He does not simply provide the needs of a particular group of people. He is the provider for us all. We may want to spend some time on this image of God when preaching to postmoderns.

Finally, the text in Matthew 7:1–5 on judging others is perhaps the most appealing text in the Sermon to postmoderns. While Jesus' words here are often misinterpreted, the general concept of not judging and of removing the plank from our eye before we try to remove the speck from someone else's eye is highly valued by postmoderns.

The pluralism of postmoderns however creates some challenges as well. The Sermon ends in 7:13–27 with words certain to rub postmoderns the wrong way. Jesus concludes with four statements of exclusivism.

First, there is only one gate and one road that lead to life—Jesus' gate and Jesus' road (7:13–14).

Second, there is only one tree that bears good fruit—Jesus' tree (7:15–20).

Third, there's only one kind of person who enters the kingdom—those who obey Jesus' words (7:21–23).

Fourth, there is only one house that stands against the storm—Jesus' house (7:24–27).

Knowing that postmoderns will object to such there-is-only-one-way-kind of statements doesn't mean we skip this part of the Sermon. It does mean, however, that we approach it with great sensitivity. One way of doing this is to help our postmodern friend understand the basis for Jesus' exclusivist statements. What gives Jesus the right to say his way is the only way? When preaching the Sermon to postmoderns, we must be prepared to answer that question. As a result, when we come to these concluding texts, we will likely need to go outside the Sermon to establish Jesus' right to make such claims. In particular, we will need to visit the manger, the cross, and the empty tomb. Jesus' statement that his way is the only way only makes sense in light of his birth, death, and resurrection.

Don't Give Me Religion

Nearing the end of our study of the Sermon, a sixth postmodern speaks. She says, "*Don't give me religion*. Whatever you're going to say to me, I don't want to hear about why I should be in church. I've had it with organized religion."

As the previous characteristic did, this characteristic presents certain challenges. One of the primary ways of addressing this obstacle is to help postmoderns see the concrete benefits that come from being part of an organized spiritual community. Through our preaching we can help them realize that church makes possible many of the things they already desire. For instance, they desire help in daily living, they hunger for deep spirituality, they long for community, and they want help in understanding the basics of faith. Our preaching can make it clear that these things, and more, can be found in an organized body of Christians.

Specifically, we might address the texts in the Sermon on the Mount that deal with relationships (5:21–48). While speaking on these texts, we could illustrate their truths with stories from our

Sunday school classes, small groups, or informal friendship networks at church. The more they can see that what Jesus talks about in the Sermon on the Mount is being lived out in our church, the more likely they will be to give church a chance.

In addition, we might address the texts in the Sermon that discuss spirituality, such as Jesus' statements on giving, prayer, and fasting in Matthew 6:1–18. While speaking on these ideas, we could illustrate them with stories of how our involvement in church has helped us to better understand and practice these spiritual disciplines. When postmoderns come to see how church involvement has deepened our own spirituality, they may be willing to seek those benefits in church as well.

Finally, this characteristic of postmoderns may influence us to pay attention to places in the Sermon where Jesus joins postmoderns in critiquing organized religion. In Matthew 5:20, 33–37; 6:1–18; and 7:22–23 Jesus rebukes the leaders and followers of the major religious institution of the day for their superficiality, hypocrisy, self-centeredness, and lack of authentic spirituality. Postmoderns will find in Jesus one who joins them in seeing the ills of organized religion. By helping postmoderns see this side to Jesus, they may become more willing to give Jesus a chance.

Give Me an Experience

We're almost done studying the Sermon on the Mount in preparation for a sermon of our own. But as we reflect on it and how we might preach to postmoderns, a seventh and final person at our desk speaks: "*Give me an experience.* I don't want information about God. I want an encounter with God." A seventh and final characteristic of postmoderns is that they are seeking a spirituality that is experiential.

There are three ways in which this postmodern characteristic might impact how we communicate the Sermon on the Mount to postmoderns.

First, when it comes to a corporate worship format, this characteristic might prompt us to be multi-sensory in our communication to the postmodern. We might not just preach, which is caught by the ear, but we might also use visual aids or Power Point or lighting, which is caught by the eye, to help create a more experiential event. This is one of the reasons Harold and I use Power Point slides to illustrate points from our lessons. It also helps explain why we went to the expense and trouble of having two houses made and placed on stage for our Sunday morning series on the

Sermon on the Mount that we called "This Old House." By engaging the eyes as well as the ears, we are helping create a multi-sensory experience for the postmodern listener.

Second, this experiential characteristic of postmoderns might lead us toward a more narrative style of communication. Rather than preaching in a didactic, logical, and point-by-point way, we might instead choose a narrative fashion using multiple stories and withholding our main point until the end. Stories grab people's attention and, when well told, draw people into their world and create an experience.

Third, knowing how much postmoderns value experience, we may use personal testimonies when preaching the Sermon on the Mount. Postmoderns trust what someone they know or admire has experienced. We can use this to our advantage. For instance, if a particular postmodern knows us well or admires us, we might tell a personal story illustrating how we found a particular truth from the Sermon on the Mount to work in our life. Or, when speaking to a group of postmodern college students or teenagers, we might get a Christian peer of theirs to stand and tell how she has found Jesus' teaching in the Sermon on the Mount to be true in her own experience. These types of testimonies are very influential in a postmodern world.

This is just one example of the way in which the material in this book might impact our preaching in a particular area. Churches need to understand the questions held by and the issues revolving around the non-Christians around them. It's my hope that we'll more often hear the postmoderns sitting at this desk. It's my hope that their questions and requests will influence the way we do ministry. It's my hope that by hearing them and coming to understand them, we'll become more effective in reaching them.

CHAPTER THIRTEEN

Epilogue

Each year I pull out a legal-sized manila envelop and put it on my bookshelf in my office. I write the year on it. And when notes of encouragement arrive in the mail, or are slipped into my hand on a Sunday or Wednesday by a member or guest, I put them in that envelope. At the end of the year, I pull those notes back out and read them.

The notes are often reminders of high points in the year. When I'm feeling down, they pick me up. When I'm discouraged, they encourage me.

Rifling through this year's notes recently, I came across one that I'm especially thankful for. It's from a Highland member named Terri. She is a twenty-something professional in Memphis. She is very evangelistic. It's normal to see her in the hallway or foyer after Sunday morning services. "Chris," she says, "I'd like you to meet…" And she'll introduce a non-Christian friend from work or her neighborhood whom she's brought to church that morning. She recently served two years as a missionary in Italy. When I think of Highland members active in personal evangelism to postmoderns, I think of Terri.

Terri wrote me a card. It centered on my preaching. She wrote this: "Thank you so much for all your time and energy that goes into your ministry. The guests I bring invariably tell me how much they enjoy your sermons and how nice it is to hear the gospel preached in a manner they can understand."

Reading that note, I thought back to that Bring Your Neighbor Day ten years ago in New Mexico. Something was missing from

150

my preaching. Something was keeping me from connecting effectively with the lost.

I believe that I've found that something. It's what I've discussed in this book. I cannot say I've mastered these concepts. But I can say I've made progress. Significant progress. The more time I've spent shaping my preaching in the ways discussed in this book, the more impact I feel that I've made on the lost.

Terri's note was a nice progress report. I've not yet reached my destination. There are still some miles to go. But I've made progress. Her postmodern guests enjoy my sermons. And they tell her I'm preaching the gospel in a way they can understand. That is music to my ears.

I'm not sure if evangelistic preaching is something we ever truly arrive at. In some ways, it's always a journey. But I feel like I'm farther along that journey because of the concepts in this book. At least according to Terri.

My prayer is that God will use this book to help you move further along in your journey. My prayer is that because you've read this book, you'll soon be receiving a card from someone like Terri; someone in your church who has brought a postmodern friend. Someone who watches that friend come to faith in Jesus because of what and how you've preached.

Notes

Chapter 1: Something's Missing

[1]George Barna, *Evangelism That Works* (Ventura, Calif.: Regal Books, 1995), 11.

[2]Ibid., 17.

[3]Ibid.

[4]Barna Research Group, "Annual Study Reveals America Is Spiritually Stagnant," *Barna Research Online* (March 5, 2001) and Barna Research Group, "America's Faith *Is* Changing—But Beneath the Surface," *Barna Research Online* (March 18, 2003), www.barna.org.

[5]Ibid.

[6]George Hunter III, "The End of 'Home Field Advantage'," *Epworth Review* 19:2 (May 1992): 69–76.

[7]Don A. Pitman, Ruben L. F. Habito, and Terry C. Much, *Ministry and Theology in Global Perspective* (Grand Rapids, Mich.: Eerdmans, 1996), 371–79; The figures for 2000 were estimates based upon information available to the authors in 1996.

[8]Darrell Guder, *Missional Church* (Grand Rapids, Mich.: Eerdmans, 1998), 1.

[9]David F. Wells, *No Place for Truth* (Grand Rapids, Mich.: Eerdmans, 1993), 80.

[10]Leonard Sweet, *Soul Tsunami* (Grand Rapids, Mich.: Zondervan, 1999), 50.

[11]Craig Van Gelder, "A Great New Fact of Our Day: America as Mission Field," in *The Church Between Gospel & Culture: The Emerging Mission in North America*, ed. George R. Hunsberger and Craig Van Gelder (Grand Rapids, Mich.: Eerdmans, 1996), 57–68.

[12]Tom Clegg and Warren Bird, *Lost in America* (Loveland, Colo.: Group Publishing, 2001).

[13]Phil Sanders, "Light the Fire," *Gospel Advocate* (March 2001): 26–28.

[14]Thom Rainer, *Effective Evangelistic Churches* (Nashville, Tenn.: Broadman & Holman, 1996).

[15]Ronald Allen, "As the Worldview Turns: Six Key Issues for Preaching in a Postmodern Ethos," *Encounter* 57 (Winter 1996): 23–25.

[16]Marva J. Dawn, *Is It a Lost Cause?* (Grand Rapids, Mich.: Eerdmans, 1997), 23–27; I'm offering an interpretation of what Dawn actually says, which may be different than what she intended.

[17]Sweet, 17–18, 45, 47.

[18]Jimmy Long, *Generating Hope* (Downers Grove, Ill.: IVP, 1997), 11–14.

[19]William Barclay, *Turning to God: A Study of Conversion in the Book of Acts and Today* (Philadelphia, Pa.: Westminster Press, 1964); Jerry Vines, "Evangelistic Preaching and the Book of Acts," *Criswell Theological Review* 5 (Fall 1990): 83–92; Thom S. Rainer, "Church Growth and Evangelism in the Book of Acts," *Criswell Theological Review* 5 (Fall 1990): 57–58; David Larsen, *The Evangelism Mandate: Recovering the Centrality of Gospel Preaching* (Wheaton, Ill.: Crossway Books, 1992), 52; Rainer, *Effective Evangelistic Churches*, 11–64; David Gaylor, "A Study of Largest Number of Baptisms Among Churches of Christ," Guided Research, Harding University Graduate School of Religion, 1977, 30–32; Earl V. Comfort, "Is the Pulpit a Factor in Church Growth?" *Bibliotheca Sacra* 140:557 (January–March 1983): 64–70; The Barna Research Group, *Never on a Sunday: The Challenge of the Unchurched* (Glendale, Calif.: Barna Research Group, 1990), 25.

[20]For a history of evangelism and evangelistic preaching, see John Mark Terry, *Evangelism: A Concise History* (Nashville, Tenn.: Broadman & Holman, 1994); Darius Salter, *American Evangelism* (Grand Rapids, Mich.: Baker, 1996), 85–130; William Packard, *Evangelism in America: From Tents to TV* (New York: Paragon House, 1988), 22–200; Michael W. Casey, *Saddlebags, City Streets, & Cyberspace: A History of Preaching*

in the Churches of Christ (Abilene, Tex.: ACU Press, 1995); Charles Gresham and Keith Keeran, *Evangelistic Preaching* (Joplin, Mo.: College Press, 1991); Eddie Cloer, "Profiles in Evangelistic Persuasion: A Descriptive Analysis of the Persuasion Techniques of Seven Preachers of the Churches of Christ" (D.Min. thesis, Harding University Graduate School of Religion, 1991), 274.

[21]Ronald J. Allen, Barbara Blaisdell, and Scott Black Johnston, *Theology for Preaching: Authority, Truth and Knowledge of God in a Postmodern Ethos* (Nashville, Tenn.: Abingdon Press, 1997), 35–41; See also Fred B. Craddock, *As One Without Authority: Essays on InductivePreaching*, rev. and enlarged ed. (Enid, Okla.: Phillips University Press, 1974), 14; Ronald J. Allen, *The Teaching Sermon* (Nashville, Tenn.: Abingdon Press, 1995), 142–43.

[22]This specific analogy using these two television shows is not original with me. In the course of my research, I discovered the analogy in several places. Sadly, I did not record where I first discovered it and thus I cannot give credit to whom credit is due. To its original creator, I apologize.

Chapter 2: Postmoderns Are Uninformed and Spiritual

[1]The names and some details concerning individuals in this book have been altered to protect their privacy.

[2]George Hunter, *How to Reach Secular People* (Nashville, Tenn.: Abingdon Press, 1992), 43–54.

[3]D. Michael Linday, "Biblical Illiteracy," *Rev* 7:2 (Nov./Dec. 2003): 124.

[4]George Barna, *Evangelism That Works* (Ventura, Calif.: Regal Books, 1995), 35–37.

[5]Cited in Leonard Sweet, *Soul Tsunami* (Grand Rapids, Mich.: Zondervan, 1999), 60.

[6]Elmer Towns, "Reaching the Buster Generation" *Church Growth Journal* 2 (1992): 78.

[7]Margaret Miles, *Seeing and Believing: Religion and Value in the Movies* (Boston, Mass.: Beacon Press, 1996), 3.

[8]Barna Research Group, "America's Faith *Is* Changing—But Beneath the Surface," Barna Research Online, www.barna.org (March 18, 2003); See also, Barna Research Group, "America's Religious Activity Has Increased Since 1996, But Its Beliefs Remain Virtually Unchanged" June 17, 2002, www.barna.org

[9]Tom Beaudoin, *Virtual Faith: The Irreverent Spiritual Quest of Generation X* (San Francisco, Calif.: Jossey-Bass, 1998), xiii-xiv.

[10]Cited in David G. Myers, "Wanting More in an Age of Plenty," *Christianity Today* (April 24, 2000): 96.

[11]Marc Gunther, "God and Business," *Fortune* (July 9, 2001): 59–80.

[12]Barna Research Group, "America's Faith *Is* Changing—But Beneath the Surface"; see also, Barna Research Group, "America's Religious Activity Has Increased Since 1996."

[13]Charles Van Engen, "Evangelism in the North American Context," *Journal for the Academy for Evangelism* 4 (1988–1989): 51–54.

[14]Jacinthia Jones, "Reel-igion," *Commercial Appeal,* 29 June 2003, F1, F4.

[15]Http://movieweb.com/movie/alltime.html.

[16]Miles, ix.

[17]Sweet, 412–19.

[18]Mark I. Pinsky, *The Gospel According to The Simpsons* (Westminster John Knox Press, 2001), 2–3.

[19]Ronald J. Allen, Barbara Blaisdell, and Scott Black, *Theology for Preaching* (Nashville, Tenn.: Abingdon, 1997), 114.

[20]Darrell Guder, *Missional Church* (Grand Rapids, Mich.: Eerdmans, 1998), 1–18.

[21]Ibid., 44.

[22]Sweet, 49.

[23]James F. Engel and H. Wilbert Norton, *What's Gone Wrong with the Harvest?* (Grand Rapids, Mich.: Zondervan, 1975), 45; James F. Engel, *Contemporary Christian Communication* (Nashville, Tenn.: Thomas Nelson, 1979), 183; James F. Engel, *How Can I Get Them to Listen?* (Grand Rapids, Mich.: Zondervan, 1977), 32; The scale continues on from +1 to infinity describing the stages of growth in Christ of the new convert.

Chapter 3: Postmoderns Are Anti-institutional and Pluralistic

[1]Barna Research Group, "Annual Study Reveals America Is Spiritually Stagnant," *Barna Research Online* (March 5, 2001), www.barna.org.

[2]Barna Research Group, *The Barna Report* (April–June 1999).

[3]Barna Research Group, "America's Faith *Is* Changing—But Beneath the Surface," www.barna.org (March 18, 2003); See also Barna Research Group, "America's Religious Activity Has Increased Since 1996, But Its Beliefs Remain Virtually Unchanged" (June 17, 2002), www.barna.org.

[4]George R. Hunsberger, "The Newbigin Gauntlet: Developing A Domestic Missiology for North America," in *The Church Between Gospel & Culture: The Emerging Mission in North America*, ed. George R. Hunsberger and Craig Van Gelder (Grand Rapids, Mich.: Eerdmans, 1996), 17.

[5]Randall Parr, "Gimme That Old-Time Religion?" *Ministries Today* 12:3 (May/June 1994): 48–52; See also George Hunter, *How to Reach Secular People* (Nashville, Tenn.: Abingdon Press, 1992), 43–54.

[6]Ronald J. Allen, "As the Worldview Turns," *Encounter* 57 (Winter 1996), 28-35.

[7]Tom Beaudoin, *Virtual Faith* (San Francisco, Calif.: Jossey-Bass, 1998), 41–42.

[8]Thomas G. Bandy, "Transformational Journey," *Net Results* (October 1999): 16–19.

[9]Leonard Sweet, *Soul Tsunami* (Grand Rapids, Mich.: Zondervan, 1998), 47.

[10]Barna Research Group, "The Year's Most Intriguing Findings," *Barna Research Online* (December 17, 2001), www.barna.org.

[11]Barna Research Group, "Barna Identifies Seven Paradoxes Regarding America's Faith," *Barna Research Online* (December 17, 2002), www.barna.org.

[12]John C. LaRue, "What Do We Believe?" *Your Church* (July/August 2001), 72.

[13]Craig Van Gelder, "Defining the Center—Finding the Boundaries," in *The Church Between Gospel & Culture*, ed. Hunsberger and Van Gelder, 34–38; Darrell Guder, *Missional Church* (Grand Rapids, Mich.: Eerdmans, 1998), 40–44.

[14] "Divining the God Factor," *U.S. News Online* (October 23, 2000).

[15]Hunter, *How to Reach Secular People*, 26–29.

[16]Hunsberger, "The Newbigin Gauntlet," 16; Lesslie Newbigin, *Foolishness to the Greeks* (Grand Rapids, Mich.: Eerdmans, 1986), 15–19; Newbigin, *The Gospel in a Pluralist Society* (Grand Rapids, Mich.: Eerdmans, 1989), 14–16, 27; Charles Van Engen, "Evangelism in the North American Context," *Journal for the Academy for Evangelism* 4 (1988–1999): 45–48; James V. Brownson, *Speaking the Truth in Love* (Harrisburg, Pa.: Trinity Press International, 1998), 6.

[17]Gene Edward Veith, Jr., *Postmodern Times* (Wheaton, Ill.: Crossway Books, 1994), 176, 193–94, 199.

[18]Brownson, 7.

[19]Veith, *Postmodern Times*, 16.

[20]Beaudoin, 25.

[21]Cited by Tony Carnes in "Bush's Defining Moment," *Christianity Today* (November 12, 2001).

[22]Alson Hornstein, "The Question That We Should Be Asking," *Newsweek* (December 17, 2001): 14.

[23]Kenneth Woodward, *Newsweek* (December 31, 2001): 102.

[24]Veith, 19–20.

[25]Paul Braoudakis, "Why They Struggle to Believe," *Leadership* 18:1 (Winter 1997): 40–45.

[26]Donald McGavran, *The Clash Between Christianity and Culture* (Washington, D. C.: Canon Press, 1974), 5–6, 14.

Chapter 4: Postmoderns Are Pragmatic, Relational, and Experiential

[1]Darrell Guder, *Missional Church* (Grand Rapids, Mich.: Eerdmans, 1998), 25–31.

[2]William A. Dyrness, *How Does America Hear the Gospel?* (Grand Rapids, Mich.: Eerdmans, 1989), 48–57, 132–42.

[3]George Hunter, *How to Reach Secular People* (Nashville, Tenn.: Abingdon Press, 1992), 43–54.

[4]Steve Brown, "Preaching to Pagans," in *Communicate With Power*, ed. Michael Duduit (Grand Rapids, Mich.: Baker, 1996), 26–27.

[5]Bill Hybels, "Preaching to Seekers," in *Communicate With Power*, 74.

[6]Brian D. McLaren, "Emerging Values," *Leadership* (Summer 2003): 35–36.

[7]Barna Research Group, "Practical Outcomes Replace Biblical Principles As the Moral Standard," *Barna Research Online* (September 10, 2001), www.barna.org.

[8]Ronald J. Allen, Barbara Blaisdell, and Scott Black, *Theology for Preaching* (Nashville, Tenn.: Abingdon Press, 1997), 137–40; Ronald J. Allen, "As the Worldview Turns," *Encounter* 57 (Winter 1996): 28–35; Jimmy Long, *Generating Hope*, (Downers Grove, Ill.: IVP, 1997), 69.

[9]George Barna, "Boomers, Busters, and Preaching," in *Communicate With Power*, 13–16.

[10]Leonard Sweet, *Soul Tsunami* (Grand Rapids, Mich.: Zondervan, 1999), 195.

[11]Mark Driscoll and Chris Seay, "A Second Reformation Is At Hand: Why Youth Workers Must Lead the Way," *The Gospel and Our Culture* 12:1 (March 2000): 5–8.

[12]Gene Edward Veith, Jr., *Postmodern Times* (Wheaton, Ill.: Crossway Books, 1994), 211.

[13]Sweet, 199.

[14]J. I. Packer, *Knowing God* (Downers Grove, Ill.: IVP, 1973).

[15]Henry T. Blackaby and Claude V. King, *Experiencing God* (Nashville, Tenn.: Lifeway, 1990).

[16]Guder, 25–31.

[17]Allen, *Theology*, 35–41.

[18]Ibid., 65.

Chapter 5: A Theological Model for Postmodern Preaching

[1]The first two points of the following material are inspired by Dr. John Mark Hicks of Harding University Graduate School of Religion and Lipscomb University. In a private setting, Dr. Hicks briefly articulated some of his thoughts concerning the goal of creation and the role of evangelism in fulfilling that goal. I, however, take full responsibility for these ideas as they are spelled out.

[2]Jerry Vines, "Evangelistic Preaching and the Book of Acts," *Criswell Theological Review* 5 (Fall 1990): 83; Thom Rainer, "Church Growth and Evangelism in the Book of Acts," *Criswell Theological Review* 5 (Fall 1990): 57–58.

[3]David L. Larsen, *The Evangelism Mandate* (Wheaton, Ill.: Crossway Books, 1992), 52.

[4]Barna Research Group, *Never on a Sunday* (Glendale, Calif: Barna Research Group, 1990), 25.

[5]David Gaylor, "A Study of Largest Number of Baptisms Among Churches of Christ," Guided Research, Harding University Graduate School of Religion, 1977, 30–32.

[6]Thom Rainer, *Effective Evangelistic Churches* (Nashville, Tenn.: Broadman & Holman, 1996), 1–53.

[7]David Bosch, in *Transforming Missions* (Maryknoll, N.Y.: Orbis, 1991), 70, states that the word "contextualization" was first coined in the 1970s, in the circles of the Theological Education Fund.

[8]Charles Kraft, in *Christianity in Culture* (Maryknoll, N.Y.: Orbis, 1979), 279–81, calls this "transculturation"—the process by which one translates not just the words but the form of a message to be best understood by a different culture.

[9]Lesslie Newbigin, *Foolishness to the Greeks* (Grand Rapids, Mich.: Eerdmans, 1986), 1–6; Newbigin, *The Gospel in a Pluralist Society* (Grand Rapids, Mich.: Eerdmans, 1989), 235–38.

[10]George R. Hunsberger, "The Newbigin Gauntlet: Develping a Domestic Missiology for North America," in *The Church Between Gospel and Culture*, ed. George R. Hunsberger and Craig Van Gelder (Grand Rapids, Mich.: Eerdmans, 1996), 3–25; George R. Hunsberger, "Good News," *The Gospel and Our Culture* 10:4 (December 1998): 7–8; Kenneth Cragg, *The Secular Experience of God* (Harrisburg, Pa.: Trinity Press International, 1998); James V. Brownson, *Speaking the Truth in Love* (Harrisburg, Pa.: Trinity Press International, 1998); Darrell Guder, *Missional Church* (Grand Rapids, Mich.: Eerdmans, 1998).

[11]George Barna, *Evangelism That Works* (Ventura, Calif.: Regal Books, 1995), 19–46; William A. Dyrness, *How Does America Hear the Gospel?* (Grand Rapids, Mich.: Eerdmans, 1989), 143–53; Donald McGavran, *The Clash Between Christianity and Cultures* (Washington, D. C.: Canon Press, 1974), 16–17; Donald Posterski, *Reinventing Evangelism* (Downers Grove, Ill.: IVP, 1989); Charles Van Engen, "Evangelism in the North American Context," *Journal for the Academy for Evangelism* 4 (1988–1989): 45–55; George Hunter III, *How to Reach Secular People* (Nashville, Tenn.: Abingdon Press, 1992), 55–77; Gene Edward Veith, Jr., *Postmodern Times* (Wheaton, Ill.: Crossway Books, 1994); Stanley Hauerwas and William Willimon, *Resident Aliens* (Nashville, Tenn.: Abingdon Press, 1989), 15; David Lyon, *The Steeple's Shadow* (Grand Rapids, Mich.: Eerdmans, 1985); Jimmy Long, *Generating Hope* (Downers Grove, Ill.: IVP, 1997), 11–193.

[12]Don Bartel, "Evangelizing Postmoderns Using a Mission Outpost Strategy," in *Telling the Truth*, ed. D. A. Carson, (Grand Rapids, Mich.: Zondervan, 2000): 343–51.

[13]Newbigin, *Foolishness*, 1, 5–6.

[14]Bosch, 455.

[15]Guder, 18.

[16]Paul Scott Watson, *Imagination of the Heart* (Nashville, Tenn.: Abingdon Press, 1988), 177–97.

[17]Bosch, 426–27.

[18]Millard J. Erickson, *Christian Theology,* One Volume Edition (Grand Rapids, Mich.: Baker, 1985), 153–98.

[19]David J. Schlafer, *Your Way with God's Word* (Boston, Mass.: Cowley Publications, 1995), 1ff.

[20]Bosch, 297.

[21]William Barclay, *Turning to God* (Philadelphia, Pa.: Westminster Press, 1964), 32–33.

[22]Ibid., 34–36.

[23]Bosch, 447–48.

[24]Charles Kraft, *Christianity in Culture* (Maryknoll, N.Y.: Orbis, 1979), 175.

[25]Bosch, 122.

[26]Ibid., 420–21.

²⁷Paul G. Hiebert, *Anthropological Reflections on Missiological Issues* (Grand Rapids, Mich.: Baker, 1994), 66.

Chapter 6: Preaching Evangelistically to the Uninformed

¹Ronald Allen, *The Teaching Sermon* (Nashville, Tenn.: Abingdon Press, 1995), 20–21.

²Alan Walker, *Evangelistic Preaching* (Grand Rapids, Mich.: Francis Asbury Press, 1983), 57; V. L. Stanfield, *Effective Evangelistic Preaching* (Grand Rapids, Mich.: Baker Book House, 1965), 20–21; Robert C. Shannon, "Preparing Evangelistic Sermons," in *Evangelistic Preaching,* ed. Charles Gresham and Keith Keeran (Joplin, Mo.: College Press, 1991), 122–30; Lewis Drummond, "Charles G. Finney and His Impact on Evangelistic Preaching," *Preaching* 7:1 (July–August 1991): 42–43; Bernard Brunstin, "Evangelistic Preaching," *Christianity Today* 7:3 (November 9, 1962): 17; Bryan Chapell, *Christ-Centered Preaching* (Grand Rapids, Mich.: Baker, 1994), 348–49; David L. Larsen, *The Evangelism Mandate* (Wheaton, Ill.: Crossway Books, 1992), 79–82; Craig Loscalzo, *Evangelistic Preaching That Connects* (Downers Grove, Ill.: IVP, 1995), 68–73.

³This is the thesis of William Willimon's *Peculiar Speech: Preaching to the Baptized* (Grand Rapids, Mich.: Eerdmans, 1992).

⁴D. A. Carson, "Athens Revisited," in *Telling the Truth*, ed. D. A. Carson (Grand Rapids, Mich.: Zondervan, 2000), 386.

⁵Ibid.

⁶Ibid., 387–98.

⁷Keith A. Day, "The Gospel for a New Generation," in *Telling the Truth*, 352–68.

⁸Michael R. Weed and Jeffrey Peterson, eds. *Things That Matter*, Second Edition, (Austin, Tex.: Christian Studies Press, 1998).

⁹Rick Warren, *The Purpose Driven Church* (Grand Rapids, Mich.: Zondervan, 1995), 354.

Chapter 7: Preaching Evangelistically to the Spiritually Interested

¹Quoted by Toby Lester in "Oh, Gods!" *Atlantic Monthly* (February 2002).

²Ibid.

³"The Church of O," *Christianity Today* (April 1, 2002): 40.

⁴Ibid., 42–43.

⁵Ibid., 39.

⁶Ibid.

⁷Ibid., 43–44.

⁸Bonnie Thurston, *Spiritual Life in the Early Church* (Minneapolis, Minn.: Fortress Press, 1993), 3, italics mine.

⁹Stanley Saunders, " 'Learning Christ,' " *Interpretation* 56:2 (April 2002): 160–61.

¹⁰Ibid., 161.

¹¹Ibid.

¹²Ibid., 166.

¹³Paul Scott Wilson, *The Practice of Preaching* (Nashville, Tenn.: Abingdon Press, 1995).

¹⁴Ibid., 20.

¹⁵For a fuller description, see Marjorie Thompson, *Soul Feast* (Louisville, Ky.: Westminster John Knox Press, 1995), 17–30.

¹⁶Ibid., 24.

Chapter 8: Preaching Evangelistically to the Anti-institutional and Relational

[1]Jimmy Long, *Generating Hope* (Downers Grove, Ill.: IVP, 1997), 206.

[2]Jimmy Long, "Generating Hope," in *Telling the Truth*, ed. D. A. Carson (Grand Rapids, Mich.: Zondervan, 2000), 334.

[3]James Engel and H. Wilbert Norton, *What's Gone Wrong with the Harvest?* (Grand Rapids, Mich.: Zondervan, 1975), 75.

[4]Ronald J. Allen, *The Teaching Sermon* (Nashville, Tenn.: Abingdon, 1995), 69–70.

[5]Tom Beaudoin, *Virtual Faith* (San Francisco, Calif.: Jossey-Bass, 1998), 161–74.

[6]Rick Warren, *The Purpose Driven Church* (Grand Rapids, Mich.: Zondervan, 1995), 36–46.

[7]Ibid., 119.

[8]Leonard Sweet, *Soul Tsunami* (Grand Rapids, Mich.: Zondervan, 1998), 196.

[9]C. Peter Wagner, *Your Church Can Grow: Seven Vital Signs of a Healthy Church* (Glendale, Calif.: Regal Books, 1976), 97.

[10]The material in this section is directly indebted to material in John Mark Hicks, *Come to the Table* (Orange, Calif.: New Leaf Books, 2002).

[11]Ibid.

[12]Ibid., 125–26.

[13]Andrea Buczynski, "Examples of Effective Evangelism," in *Telling the Truth*, 316.

Chapter 9: Preaching Evangelistically to Pluralists

[1]Barna Research Group, "The Year's Most Intriguing Findings," *Barna Research Online* (December 17, 2001), 2.

[2]John C. LaRue, "What Do We Believe?" *Your Church* (July/August 2001): 72.

[3]Daniel B. Clendenin, "The Only Way," *Christianity Today* (January 12, 1998).

[4]Statistics cited by the Memphis Child Advocacy Center.

[5]Harold Shank, Anthony Wood, and Ron Bergeron, *Up Close and Personal: Embracing the Poor* (Joplin, Mo.: College Press, 2000); Harold Shank, *Children Mean the World to God* (Springfield, Mo.: 21st Century Press, 2001).

[6]Tim Keller, "Preaching Amid Pluralism," *Leadership* (Winter 2002): 34–36.

[7]Bill Hybels and Mark Mittelberg, *Becoming a Contagious Christian* (Grand Rapids, Mich.: Zondervan: 1994), 155.

[8]Keller.

[9]Ibid.

[10]Lee Strobel, *The Case for Christ* (Grand Rapids, Mich.: Zondervan, 1998).

[11]*Leadership* (Summer 1999): 28.

[12]Harold Netland, *Dissonant Voices: Religious Pluralism and the Question of Truth* (Grand Rapids, Mich.: W.B. Eerdmans, 1991), 36–111.

[13]Ibid., 261–62.

[14]Clendenin.

[15]Lee Strobel, Evangelism Conference, Willow Creek Community Church, October, 2000.

Chapter 10: Preaching Evangelistically to the Pragmatic

[1]Ronald Sider, *Good News and Good Works* (Grand Rapids, Mich.: Baker, 1999), 83–84.

[2]Barbara Brown Taylor, "Easter Preaching and the Lost Language of Salvation," *Journal for Preachers* (15:3) Easter 2002: 19.

[3]Ibid.

4Ibid., 20.

5Ibid, 21.

6Sider, 86.

7Ibid.

8Ibid., 87.

9Ibid., 89.

10Darius Salter, *American Evangelism* (Grand Rapids, Mich.: Baker, 1999), 157.

11David F. Wells, *No Place for Truth* (Grand Rapids, Mich.: Eerdmans, 1993), 77.

12David J. Bosch, *Transforming Mission* (Maryknoll, N.Y.: Orbis, 1991), 11.

13Paul G. Hiebert, *Anthropological Reflections on Missiological Issues* (Grand Rapids, Mich.: Baker, 1994), 66.

14Charles Engel and H. Wilbert Norton, *What's Gone Wrong with the Harvest?* (Grand Rapids, Mich.: Zondervan, 1975), 45; Charles Engel, *Contemporary Christian Communication* (Nashville, Tenn.: Thomas Nelson, 1979), 183; Idem., *How Can I Get Them to Listen?* (Grand Rapids, Mich.: Zondervan, 1977), 32.

15Engel, *Contemporary*, 77, 112, 117; Idem., *Getting Your Message Across* (Manila: OMF Literature Inc., 1989), 90.

16William Willimon, "Been There, Preached That: Today's Conservatives Sound Like Yesterday's Liberals," *Leadership* 16:4 (1995): 76.

17Idem., *The Intrusive Word: Preaching to the Unbaptized* (Grand Rapids, Mich.: Eerdmans, 1994), 39.

18Ibid., 24.

19Susan Hecht, "Faithfully Relating to Unbelievers in a Relational Age," in *Telling the Truth,* ed. D. A. Carson (Grand Rapids, Mich.: Zondervan, 2000), 247.

20Ronald Allen, Barbara Blaisdell, Scott Black Johnston, *Theology for Preaching* (Nashville, Tenn.: Abingdon Press, 1997), 140.

21William A. Dyrness, *How Does America Hear the Gospel?* (Grand Rapids, Mich.: Eerdmans, 1989), 82–102.

22George Hunsberger, "Good News," *The Gospel and Our Culture* 10:4 (December 1998): 7–8.

23Barna Research Group, "Most Americans Satisfied with Life Despite Having Quality of Life Issues, " *Barna Research Online* (March 26, 2002), www.barna.org.

24Opinion Research Corp. for Simply Sleep, cited in *Rev.* (May/June 2002): 92.

25Dr. Ed Gray, Presentation at Highland Street Church of Christ, Memphis Tenn., January 20, 2002.

Chapter 11: Preaching to Those Who Value Experience

1Joe Pine & Jim Gilmore, *The Experience Economy: Work Is Theater and Every Business a Stage* (Boston, Mass.: Harvard Business School Press, 1999).

2Leonard Sweet, *Soul Tsunami* (Grand Rapids, Mich.: Zondervan, 1999), 199.

3David Wells, *No Place for Truth,* (Grand Rapids, Mich.: Eerdmans, 1993), 174.

4Tom Beaudoin, *Virtual Faith* (San Francisco, Calif: Jossey-Bass, 1998), 161–74.

5Sweet, 208–25.

6Sally Morgenthaler, *Worship Evangelism* (Grand Rapids, Mich.: Zondervan, 1995).

7Robert Webber, "Authentic Worship in a Changing World," *Theological Digest & Outlook* 16:2 (September 2001): 4–9.

8Andy Wall, "A Study of Disaffiliation from Churches of Christ in Southern California," D. Min. thesis, Fuller Theological Seminary, 2001.

9Ronald Allen, Barbara Blaisdell, and Scott Black, *Theology for Preaching* (Nashville, Tenn.: Abingdon Press, 1997), 164–72.

10Sweet, 200–209.

11Ralph Lewis & Gregg Lewis, *Inductive Preaching* (Wheaton, Ill.: Crossway Books, 1989), 70.

[12]Ronald J. Allen, *Preaching the Topical Sermon* (Louisville, Ky.: Westminster/John Knox Press, 1992), 11–12; Fred Craddock, *As One Without Authority,* enlarged and revised ed. (Enid, Okla.: Phillips University Press, 1974), 54.

[13]Charles Gresham and Keith Keeran, *Evangelistic Preaching* (Joplin, Mo.: College Press, 1991), 179–349.

[14]Eddie Cloer, "Profiles in Evangelistic Persuasion: A Descriptive Analysis of the Persuasion Techniques of Seven Preachers of the Churches of Christ," D. Min. thesis, Harding University Graduate School of Religion, 1991: 258–59.

[15]Fred B. Craddock, *Overhearing the Gospel* (Nashville, Tenn: Abingdon Press, 1978), 83, 87.

[16]Kent D. Richmond, "Preaching in the Context of Pluralism," *Quarterly Review* 3:2 (Summer 1983): 82.

[17]Craig Loscalzo, *Evangelistic Preaching That Connects* (Downers Grove, Ill.: IVP, 1995), 62–68.

[18]David Buttrick, *Homiletic: Moves and Structures* (Philadelphia, Pa.: Fortress Press, 1987), 483–84.

[19]Richard Eslinger, *A New Hearing: Living Options in Homiletic Method* (Nashville, Tenn.: Abingdon Press, 1987).

[20]Eugene Lowry, *The Sermon: Dancing on the Edge of Mystery* (Nashville, Tenn.: Abingdon Press, 1997), 22–28.

[21]Ibid.

[22]William H. Shepherd, Jr. "A Second Look at Inductive Preaching," *Christian Century* 107:26 (September 19–26, 1990): 823.

[23]Craig A. Loscalzo, *Apologetic Preaching* (Downers Grove, Ill.: IVP, 2000).

[24]Ralph L. Lewis and Gregg Lewis, *Inductive Preaching: Helping People Listen* (Westchester, Ill.: Crossway Books, 1983), 83–102.

[25]Andrea Buczynski "Examples of Effective Evangelism," in *Telling the Truth,* ed. D. A. Carson, (Grand Rapids, Mich.: Zondervan, 2000), 316.

[26]Allen, *Theology,* 35–41, 65.

[27]Jimmy Long, *Generating Hope* (Downers Grove, Ill.: IVP, 1997), 188–93.

[28]Kelly Monroe, *Finding God at Harvard* (Grand Rapids, Mich.: Zondervan, 1997).